Whims of the Fates

Whims of
the Fates

Leslie Stone

WHIMS OF THE FATES

This is a work of fiction. All of the characters, names, incidents, organizations, and dialogue in this novel are either the products of the author's imagination or are used fictitiously.

iUniverse books may be ordered through booksellers or by contacting:

iUniverse LLC
1663 Liberty Drive
Bloomington, IN 47403
www.iuniverse.com
1-800-Authors (1-800-288-4677)

ISBN: 978-1-4917-3408-7 (sc)
ISBN: 978-1-4917-3410-0 (hc)
ISBN: 978-1-4917-3409-4 (e)

Library of Congress Control Number: 2014909499

Printed in the United States of America.

iUniverse rev. date: 06/03/2014

Contents

Istanbul—Three Days Before

He was sitting at a small table in the Golden Horn Lounge when he first saw her. She was with several women, listening to one of them carry on about something. He didn't want her to see him looking at her so he looked away quickly and continued glancing around the room before turning his attention back to his drink and his traveling companion, Mitch McConnell. This whole scheme had been hatched by Mitch, his idea from the gitgo, and Grant had been kicking himself for agreeing to it ever since he signed on.

"The thing is," Mitch said, "you have to move on, have to put it all behind you. It doesn't make you any kind of a hero to mope around, so you might as well get on with it. Now, let's go over the list again. It seems to me we are in the perfect place for it, freedom and privacy, and women everywhere. Hell, I've already seen three or four that look like pretty good ones to me."

"There are a lot of women here, aren't there? They all seem to be in groups, which complicates things. There are a lot of women in Palmer Plantation too, in case you haven't noticed, Mitch. We didn't have to go half way around the world to find women. You said yourself that the women there swarmed around you like bees."

"Well, maybe I exaggerated a little. But this is no time for you to pull that crap about honor and integrity, and all that other stuff you were feeding me on the plane. The last thing I need is to be with a guy who won't keep his end of the bargain. Did you even do one thing on the list today? I think we should meet every day for a review, just to keep us on track."

"Yeah, I did a few things. But once this Istanbul part is over it's going to be a hell of a lot harder staying out of the bulls-eye of the Palmer Plantation people. I didn't think there were going to be this many of them. Didn't you say there were just a few? I thought the whole idea was to be away from them, for the privacy thing."

"There's only about a dozen or so of them. I never got the final count, but it won't make much difference. They might even come in handy, you know, us sort of being with a group of folks from home. Kind of keeps us looking legitimate. After two or three days we can figure out how to avoid them and by then we'll both be pretty busy. There's one I'll point out to you from that singles club I told you about. She's pretty nice, but we can't afford to get too friendly with her. She's the membership chairman and she's been calling me since she found out that you and I were going to be on the same cruise. She calls me all the time about joining the group. She asks about you, too. She said she was glad there were going to be a few single guys along because usually only the women take their trips. That gal who is running things said the same thing. Well, they better not have their sights on us because we have bigger fish to fry."

"How did they find out we were going?" Grant asked. "Did you tell them?"

"Hell no. I didn't say anything to any of them. It must have been the trip lady. She's the one who always sends out the blurbs to everyone telling about a trip she has planned. It isn't just for the singles club. I think she gets a free trip if she books a certain number of people so she probably isn't too happy that we didn't book the trip through her. I'll schmooze her a little and see if I can get a list of who is in the group. I think her name is Betty."

"How did she know we were going? I thought we weren't going to tell anybody."

"I called her one day about some information on a cruise, right about the time you and I started talking about a trip. She asked me where I wanted to go and I said Istanbul, just off the top of my head. I thought that it wasn't a very popular place and might be a good place for us to start. The next thing I knew she started emailing me stuff and sending brochures. You saw all of that. Then one day she called and asked if we were ready to book a trip with her and I told her no thanks, we had already made our plans. She wanted the details and all, just being friendly, so I told her. But I didn't say anything at all about what we were planning to do. She sounded really nice and offered to get us more information if we needed it. She was real helpful. I was completely blindsided when that membership lady from the singles club called."

"It better not be a problem. I'm having second thoughts about this whole thing and I sure don't want it to get back to everyone at Palmer Plantation. You know how they talk. Vonnie knew everything about everyone and she was only involved for a few months. We hear plenty on the golf course, too. Do you know most of them or just the ones from the singles club?"

"I have only seen that one I recognized. I don't know many of them anyway."

"I thought you knew all of them. You're always talking about it, wanting me to go with you, telling me what a great group they are. Now you tell me you don't know them?"

"Well, maybe I exaggerated a little. I only went once. But I think you need to join, Grant. It would be good for you. You need to get out with some different people. You can't just hang out with me all the time. This trip is going to be good for you, too. You're going to really enjoy it."

"I plan to enjoy the trip. It's the list I'm dreading. I think this whole thing is a bad idea. You know I'm not the least bit interested in meeting women."

"You think that now, Grant, but once you get back into the swing of things, you'll be glad you did it. It will be fun. Just relax and think of it as a game. Or a business plan. We only have to do three things each day. Start at the top of the list and work your way down. You'll probably get to the bottom line before I do."

"Fat chance. You have some pretty slick moves, Mitch. I think I'm up against a pro when it comes to women. You can charm the snake right into the basket. Maybe we should lay a bet on that too, whoever gets laid first. Add that to the list, like bonus points. Spice up things a little while we're at it."

"Okay, I'll take that bet. We'll put another hundred on the guy who gets to the bottom line first. It's not as easy as it looks, Grant. I'll have to work at it. With your good looks it's going to be easy for you. You've been around a lot more than I have. You've been to fancier places, and you have fancier ideas. Women go for that stuff. This is going to be a piece of cake for you."

"I keep telling you I'm not that interested, Mitch. This whole list thing was your idea. I agreed to come, and I agreed to take the job, and I agreed to be sociable and friendly, but I never agreed to the bottom line."

"Don't you ever think about sex, Grant? Don't you miss it? I read once that the average guy thinks about sex every ten minutes or so. Sometimes more often than that."

"Sure I think about sex. I think about it a lot. I'm just not ready yet."

"You will be. You are just a little gun-shy, but once we get one under the belt, it will get easier."

"What! I thought you already crossed that bridge. You said you were getting plenty."

"Maybe I exaggerated a little bit. But the thing is, Grant, life is passing us by. I have just spent four miserable and bitter years because I refused to grasp any chance I might have had for happiness. I hate to see you go through that."

"I didn't know you were miserable and bitter. You go out all the time. Everybody in Palmer Plantation knows you. You play golf three or four times a week. How bad is that? If I handle things half as good as you have, I won't have any complaints."

"I haven't handled it, Grant. I have avoided it. I have avoided any and everything that reminds me of her. Sure, I'm out and about. But, each and every time, I come home to an empty house."

"Well, I avoid things too, especially women. The last thing in the world I want right now is any kind of involvement with a woman. You know how I feel about things. I don't see the point in any of this."

"Grant, I have almost nine years on you. It's probably too late for me. This might be my last shot at it. But you are only fifty-five.

You have good years in front of you. Don't waste them. Reach out for happiness, Grant. Get back into the game."

Grant shook his head in frustration, feeling more and more uncomfortable about the whole idea, but he wanted to keep Mitch enthusiastic. It was Mitch who needed to get his mojo back, get his life on track. Grant didn't care about himself. Life had kicked him in the gut, had ripped his heart out, and he had no intention of tempting the fates again. He would play the hand he was dealt, let the chips fall where they may, and take no more chances on happiness.

"Alright, I'll keep my end of the bargain, but I can't make any promises. You know where I stand on things, Mitch. Life is just a crapshoot. You roll the dice and you get what you get. There's not much point in trying to change my luck, but I'll give it another shot. We have enough money riding on it now to make it worth the effort, but you better get your game on, Mitch, because I intend to win, fair and square. I also intend to enjoy the sights along the way. What did you think of the tour today? There's a lot more here than I expected. Guess I never thought much about Istanbul at all. Did you read up on the places? I never heard of most of the stuff we saw."

"Naw, I didn't read anything. Like I said, I only suggested Istanbul off the top of my head, not because I wanted to come here. The guides tell you more than you want to know, anyway. Some of them are pretty long winded. Some of them just bore the hell out of you. I don't even listen to most of it. Things will get more interesting when we get started on the list."

"Things will get more interesting when we see the famous stuff tomorrow. Do you want to go out to dinner somewhere now? I can ask the concierge for some suggestions."

"We probably should go out somewhere to some popular place so we look like we know what we're doing, like we're real experienced. We want to be able to talk about being there or drop the name even if we only walk by and don't go in. And we should order the native food everywhere we go. They appreciate it and you get better service that way. And even if it tastes awful, we should say something about how good it is. That's usually what people do, at least the ones who are trying to impress someone."

The waiter was approaching their table just as Mitch made his comment. Both men stifled laughs, hoping the waiter hadn't heard or didn't understand English, which was wrong on both counts because Mitch had a loud voice that carried everywhere and most people in Istanbul who dealt with the tourists spoke pretty good English.

"Okay, Mitch. What will it be? Here or go out? You decide."

"I'm pretty bushed from that flight last night. Let's eat here now. We can wait until tomorrow to get the lay of the land."

The waiter had been listening politely and finally asked in perfect English if they would like to order. "Would you prefer to dine on Turkish cuisine tonight or would your preference be something more in the American style?" he asked. "And might I suggest that you select a table on the terrace. It is a lovely night to dine outside."

"That's a good idea," Grant replied. As they followed out to the terrace Grant turned and looked again at the blonde he had been eyeing. She appeared younger than the women she was with, classier, and she was very pretty. He found himself intrigued, wondering what would bring a lovely girl like her to Istanbul.

He and Mitch were seated at a table near the railing and began to examine the menu. Grant ordered first. "I think I would like to try something Turkish, tonight. You know, when in Rome, as they say. Do you have any recommendations?"

"Yes sir. May I suggest the Hunkar Begendi. It is one of our specialties. It was devised centuries ago in the Ottoman palace kitchen."

"That would be great, something really traditional and authentic. What's in it?"

"It is a delectable combination of succulent lamb in a tomato and butter sauce served over pureed patlican. Its name actually means 'his majesty liked it.'"

"Great. And I'll have Turkish coffee and Turkish Delight for dessert," Grant added, trying his best to sound nonchalant and worldly for Mitch, who seemed to think it was necessary to put on some airs to impress people with how sophisticated they were. It came easy for Grant because he actually was a rather nonchalant and worldly guy. He had been very successful and had lived in the right part of town, belonged to the right clubs, and associated with the movers and shakers. And he was pretty damned comfortable in most situations.

Mitch had a rather sheepish look on his face and didn't want to sound like a wimp, so he said in his usual loud voice, "I'll have a hamburger and frites." He thought that sounded a little more sophisticated than saying fries. Mitch was no slouch when it came to social situations, either. He had been a hugely successful businessman, but he was intimidated by what he called "foreign stuff" when he ordered from menus, so he usually played it safe. He liked to know what he was eating.

"Very good, Sir," the waiter said. "And would you like catsup with your fries? And coffee? We have Starbucks coffee, decaf, if you prefer."

"Yeah, yeah. That would be fine. And cream for my coffee too. And I'll have vanilla ice cream for dessert."

"Way to go, Mitch. That is bound to impress the pants right off of some poor unsuspecting gal you meet. You can probably get miles of impressive conversation out of this dinner, right here in the hotel, dining alfresco on the terrace, overlooking the Bosphorus. You better hope to hell I like what I get or I'll tell everyone what a chicken you were, afraid to order Turkish food after talking me into it."

"Well, I didn't know what any of that stuff was. How do you know what that was you ordered, besides that it has lamb in it? I thought you didn't like lamb. What was it he called that stuff, pureed pelican?"

"Yeah, something like that. Just so it's not eggplant. I hate eggplant."

"Alright," Mitch said. "Let's go over the list again. So what did you do today?"

Grant stretched the truth a little and said, "Well, I introduced myself to a guy on the elevator this morning. He was with a good looking woman so I thought I might get an introduction."

"So what happened?"

"Nothing. Neither of them spoke English and they got off at the next floor."

"So what did you do? You've got to be a little aggressive if you want to get anywhere with this."

"Like I said, I did nothing. I went down to the breakfast buffet and ended up sitting with a guy from Palmer Plantation. He lives near the marina. His wife was upstairs exhausted from the flight and I haven't seen him since. The rest of the time I was on the bus riding all over this place while you slept next to the window."

Grant signaled for the waiter and ordered another martini for himself and Mitch ordered another beer and then excused himself and headed for the restroom. Grant leaned back in his chair, relaxing, taking it all in. He had a good view into the lounge and admired the beautiful tiles on the walls and floors and the copper sconces that lighted everything with flickering flames. The hotel was quite a showplace. The rooms had beautiful furnishings and exquisite tile work on the floors and in the bathrooms. It was a great place to start the trip. If everything along the way was as nice as this, as nice as the cruise line brochure showed, it was going to be really special. Now, sitting here on the terrace as the lights began to glow across the Bosphorus on the Asian side of Istanbul, watching boats skittering across the water, about to enjoy a fabulous Turkish dinner, for one brief moment, he began to feel at peace with himself and with life. Maybe Mitch was right. Maybe this trip was just what he needed. He might even indulge in a Turkish cigar after dinner. He took one more glance around the lounge, but the blonde was gone.

Mitch returned to the table as the waiter appeared with a huge dinner tray on his shoulder. The plates were covered with fancy silver domes and the waiter paid meticulous attention to placing everything just so. He finished with a flourish, smiling brightly as he removed the domes, revealing their dinners.

"That," Grant said, "is the biggest tadoo any hamburger has ever been accorded." He took his phone out of his pocket and took Mitch's picture with his hamburger. "I'll get a print made for you and you can use it on your Christmas card with the caption, 'Mitch enjoying a fabulous dinner in exotic Istanbul.'"

"I wouldn't laugh. That mess on your plate doesn't look so appealing to me. You'll be sorry you didn't order a hamburger, too."

"We'll see about that," Grant laughed, as he took a forkful. "Wow! This is really good. Surprisingly so. I guess I get the last laugh." They continued eating and joking about the food and Grant rubbed it in about how delicious his dinner was. The waiter returned to the table with the coffee and asked if everything was to their satisfaction and Grant told him how much he enjoyed it and thanked him again for the fine recommendation.

"What did you say was in that puree? That was especially good."

"Patlican," the waiter replied. "It is a favorite in Turkey. We serve it many, many ways, sir."

"What is patlican?" Grant asked. "I have never heard of it."

"Aubergine, sir. It is aubergine."

Grant waited until the waiter was out of earshot and then turned to Mitch with a disgusted look on his face. "I can't believe I ate that. I hate aubergine."

"What the hell is aubergine?" Mitch asked.

"Eggplant, damn it. I just ate pureed eggplant!"

Mitch laughed so hard he could barely talk. "Who gets the last laugh now? Next time just order a hamburger."

"Yeah, with *frites*." Grant said, imitating Mitch.

The waiter returned with dessert, Turkish Delight for Grant and vanilla ice cream for Mitch.

"So what is Turkish Delight?" Mitch asked. "It sounds like the name of a stripper I saw once in Chicago."

"It's some kind of sugared fruit. Sort of like candy. Here, try a piece."

Mitch popped the whole thing into his mouth. "This is pretty good stuff."

"Yeah. It's the only piece you'll be getting tonight," Grant joked.

"Ain't that the sorry ass truth."

"Let's have a cigar and enjoy the view for a while. Turkish cigars are supposed to be really great. There was a big humidor off the lobby. Did you go in and look? Let's ask the waiter for a suggestion. He'll be happy to get us one."

The waiter brought out a silver box with about twenty cigars in it, explaining which ones were mild and which were the stronger, more popular traditional Turkish ones. Mitch selected a mild one and Grant decided on the traditional Turkish one. The waiter proceeded to offer them a light, and then placed the open flame lighter on their table, in case they needed to relight. He stood patiently waiting while they each took a puff. Mitch leaned back in his chair and blew out the smoke, a broad smile of satisfaction spreading across his face.

"Not bad. Not bad at all."

Grant took in the full bodied flavor of his cigar and then blew it out as fast as he could, coughing slightly and blinking back the tears that were burning in his eyes. "Wow," he said. "They could use these things as weapons of mass destruction. Just offer free cigars to the enemy."

The waiter could hardly hold back his laughter, but said politely, "Slowly, sir, smoke it very slowly. Then you will enjoy its richness."

The two sat smoking for another hour, soaking up the view, reviewing the day, and musing about what lay ahead of them in the coming weeks. They sat silently for a few minutes before calling it a night.

"Don't forget," Mitch said, "tomorrow everyone else will be arriving in Istanbul. We should be able to make some progress then. I don't want to waste any time."

"I know. But I want to take in as many of the sights as possible. We only have tomorrow to spend here. I'm really enjoying Istanbul. I want to see as much as I can. There's plenty of time once we get on board."

"It won't hurt to get an early start on things. We didn't come for the sightseeing."

They walked through the lobby toward the elevators and Grant took a last sweep of the ornate reception area, catching only a glimpse of a flowered dress as the elevator doors closed. He lingered, watching as the light stopped on the third floor.

Ahmet Hotel—Istanbul

Earlier, in room 312, Shay Porter had been neatly arranging her clothes for the next day, placing her flowered sundress and little white pique jacket neatly on the lounge chair and smoothing out the wrinkles, pondering her choice again. She really didn't know what the others were planning to wear, but judging from what she had seen today, she was worried that she had brought all the wrong things. She had gone on line to check on the climate in Istanbul and read the suggestions in the brochures that were sent along with her reservations. It was still hot in Istanbul in September, and it would be pretty hot in the other places on their itinerary. She had packed mostly summer clothes, pretty little dresses that would be flexible, appropriate for daytime wear and easily accessorized with a simple necklace or scarf for dinner or some other event. She had added a light weight summer jacket and a sweater to drape over her shoulders if it was cool somewhere. And she had put in several pairs of sandals she bought at the end of season sales to complete her look.

She had brought two pairs of Bermuda shorts in case she needed some on the ship, but she didn't plan to wear them often. She had only one pair of long pants for day trip activities, and several pretty linen pairs for on the ship. Mostly she had worried about the fancy or formal affairs. She had asked Chrissie if she knew what her mother wore on these trips and Chrissie said she thought everything was pretty casual except for the formal nights. She had bought one new cocktail dress, but kept it pretty simple because she had no place to wear anything like that in Charlotte, although she couldn't resist splurging on the beautiful deep blue lace creation that accented her perfect figure and exposed a bit of cleavage.

Chrissie was Shay's next door neighbor and it was she who had hooked her up for this trip, to go with Joan, Chrissie's mother. Shay had very little travel experience, just one trip to Paris years ago when she was a student at Queens College, and a trip to New York City with her sorority sisters her senior year. She had gone to California once, taking her parents to San Francisco for their fortieth anniversary. And she went to Disney World once. But that was it. Almost every other vacation had been spent in Myrtle Beach at the dilapidated beach house her grandmother had owned in Cherry Grove since forever.

She unpacked what she needed for the next two days and headed to the bathroom, ready for a hot shower to wash off the wear and tear of the long overnight flight and the bus tour today. She planned to order room service and spend the evening reading. As she was about to step into the shower the room phone rang and she answered it, wondering who in the world would be looking for her.

"Hi," Joan's cheery voice rang out. "We've all decided to go down to the Golden Horn Lounge for a few drinks and a light supper. I'll knock on your door in about ten minutes." Before Shay could protest, Joan was gone.

"Good grief, this woman is a live wire, just the opposite of me," Shay thought, and all of her fears and doubts about the trip seemed to be coming true. She had met Joan for the first time last night at the airport and was surprised to discover that two other ladies would be traveling with them. The three ladies sat together on the plane. Shay was in the middle between two business men who talked across her for most of the night. She had read about Istanbul most of the way. Today she had sat on the bus with Joan and the woman had talked nonstop, all about her life, her trips, her daughters, her this and her that, and Shay could see that she was needed just as somebody to sit next to Joan. The three women also talked back and forth across the bus aisle, leaving Shay out of the conversation while they talked about some mutual acquaintance. She could see already that this trip was one big mistake, a very expensive mistake.

She quickly jumped into the shower for a quick rinse off, put on the flowered sundress she planned to wear tomorrow, and pulled her blonde hair back in a loose ponytail gathered together at the nape of her neck. There was only time to add a smidgeon of lipstick when the knock came on the door.

The three ladies that she would be with were all friends at Palmer Plantation and had needed a fourth so they could each have a roommate and save the single supplement on the cruise. They were part of a larger group from there but Shay didn't know that when she agreed to the trip. She didn't know any of them. It was Chrissie's idea that she go and be her mother's roommate. She said it would do Shay good to get away from everything for a while. "Meet some new people, see something different, enjoy your new freedom," Chrissie had said. "My Mom is a great traveler. You will enjoy her, hit it right off. Go on, Shay, kick up your heels for once. You will have built in friends and won't have to be by yourself all the time. This is just perfect."

Chrissie and Shay hadn't been close friends very long, but ever since Shay's mother had passed away, Chrissie had become obsessed with her. She was always coming over with cookies or some other treat, making it impossible not to invite her in. And she was always making suggestions about how Shay should live her life, bringing brochures about places, and constantly talking about Palmer Plantation, where her mother, Joan, lived. It made Shay uncomfortable, like she was thought of as a poor, pitiful, lonely old maid, desperately in need of a life. She resented it. She thought the whole trip thing had more to do with helping out with the need for a roommate than it did about Shay's use of her new freedom. Of course, Shay didn't express these thoughts to Chrissie for fear it would hurt her feelings. Chrissie had things rough enough as it was. Besides, the trip did sound wonderful. Maybe it was a good idea, a perfect interlude before she started on her own plans.

Well, she had made her decision, had plunked down a tidy sum, and here she was in Istanbul. Who would have thought it? Here she was, Shay Porter, school teacher extraordinaire, caretaker superb, daughter wonderful, homebody personified, a proper, middle aged, (fifty-two was middle aged, wasn't it?) very nervous lady with a bunch of total strangers, in Istanbul, Turkey, no less. "My God, Shay, what were you thinking?" she asked for the zillioneth time. But she sucked it up and greeted the three new friends with a bright smile and headed to the Golden Horn Lounge.

The other two ladies, Maureen and Wanda, seemed really nice. They were warm and friendly, very talkative, and laughed a lot. Shay tried to contribute to the conversation, but her life dulled in comparison to all of their activities. Several couples from Palmer Plantation stopped by the table for introductions before heading out for dinner and they all seemed nice too, but Shay worried that she would never remember all the names and who went with whom. They were all older than Shay. Somehow, at fifty-two, she didn't seem to fit in anywhere. Most of the women in her neighborhood were younger and had little kids. The others were the leftovers from when Shay's folks had first moved there, all in that age group. Most of her friends were married and busy with family and careers of their own. Was she destined to always be a misfit? She vowed to make the effort to fit in with this group even though she wasn't much of a joiner and usually avoided group activities. This gang appeared to be ready to party, raring to go, so maybe she wouldn't be missed if she slipped away early.

The Golden Horn Lounge was beautiful, the epitome of Turkish elegance. There were gorgeous tiles everywhere in a burst of color and patterns, and blue and white ones very much like the ones she had read about, the famous blue and white Iznik tiles. There were gorgeous copper sconces with live flames flickering through the ornate filigree work in the metal. The ambiance was pure Turkish and she was anxious to explore more of the place tomorrow. There weren't many people in the lounge, just two more couples and two men sitting by themselves, laughing about something. They looked like Americans and she wondered if they were part of the Palmer Plantation group, though one of them looked a little young for that. The Palmer Plantation group appeared to be all retirees, several years older. She looked away and began to peruse the menu. When she looked back, the two men were gone.

There was a beautiful terrace beyond the huge double doors and she wanted to go have a look before the waiter served their food, but there didn't seem to be a break in the conversation for her to politely excuse herself, so she kept seated. She had ordered börek, a famous Turkish menu item she had read about. The others asked what they were and she explained that they were little pastry triangles filled with cheese and herbs and then deep fried until they puffed. "Sort of like an hors d'oeuvre," she explained. "I think I would like some Turkish Delight, too," she added.

"That sounds perfect," Joan said. "Just like a school teacher to read up on everything. We will depend on you now to help us with all the menus, Shay. Wasn't that Turkish Delight they were making in the Spice Bazaar? I couldn't hear everything they were telling us, but I think they said it was fruit, didn't they?"

Shay hoped they weren't put off by her knowing something about the food, but she went on to explain that she thought it was sugared dried fruit and that it was exported around the world. It had become a real favorite in England, especially during the holidays. "I have seen it in some catalogs and have wondered about it. It will be a real treat having it right here in Istanbul," she added. "It might be a nice little something to give as a souvenir. Tomorrow at the Grand Bazaar I'll look for a shop that has small, easy to pack boxes, and take some home.

"That's a great idea, Shay. I might do that too. And if you can think of anything else that is special, tell us about it too," Maureen said. "I never know what the heck to take back for my grandkids. I always try to buy stuff I can pack and take home with me in the suitcase, so just look for little things."

"Well, there are a million places in that Grand Bazaar," Wanda said. "We ought to see plenty of junk there. You are supposed to bargain for everything, you know, try and get them to come down on the price. I've never enjoyed a place where that was expected. I think I'll just look and then shop on the boat. Cruise ships always have pretty good stuff in their gift shops. That's where I usually shop. And they'll ship it wherever you want. You never know what you're getting in these foreign places. Howard, my late husband, always said never trust those foreigners. We never bought anything in the local shops. Howard said they were just tourist traps, out to get your money. And Howard wouldn't use his credit card in these foreign places either. He didn't trust them. He would go to the money exchange and get a little foreign money at each country, just enough for a cab or lunch or something because you don't want any of their money left after you leave a place because it is worthless. You all better follow my advice or you will get taken to the cleaners," she chided. "Howard and I traveled extensively, you know. I have a great deal of experience in foreign countries."

The other two listened politely, maybe even a little impressed, but Shay wondered if maybe some of the fun, some of the experience of travel might be participating in the local customs at least a little. She kept her thoughts to herself. Wanda was probably trying to be helpful and Shay didn't want to say anything that might be taken as disagreeable. She didn't want to sound too confident, either, since she had such limited travel experience herself.

Shay was relieved when the conversation turned back to the happenings at Palmer Plantation. The three women were laughing and talking about people there and filling Shay in on all the latest gossip, and pointing out some folks to her when they walked past the lounge. She found herself enjoying it all and the time passed quickly before Wanda reminded them of the late hour.

"Time to call it a night, girls," Wanda said. They immediately started to gather their things and follow along. It was becoming rather obvious that Wanda seemed to be the leader of their little troop, either self-appointed or by default, it was hard to tell, but nonetheless, it was apparent to Shay that the other two were quite content with the arrangement. It wasn't real clear if the others expected the four of them to hang together all the time or if Shay was expected to do her own thing. Since she was always a little awkward in social situations, Shay wanted to be very careful not to offend them by appearing to be a little too independent.

"Please, go on without me," Shay said, rather timidly. "I think I'll have a look out on the terrace before going up to my room."

"Well," Wanda said. "Don't stay too long. The buses leave at 8:30 and the breakfast buffet starts at 6:30."

"I'll knock on your door at 7:15, Shay," Joan said. "I think that gives us plenty of time, don't you?"

"That sounds perfect, Joan. I'll be ready."

Shay glanced around the beautiful lounge one more time, reluctant to leave the ambiance of the lovely place and wanting to soak up as much as she could. She walked out to the terrace where she could see the sparkling lights shining from small boats on the water and lights twinkling on the other side, which she thought was the Asian side of Istanbul. She wasn't sure exactly what direction she was looking in and didn't know what body of water it was, but the view was spellbinding. She drew in a deep breath of the night air, the smell of water, and spices, and cigar smoke. Two men were sitting by the railing smoking cigars, laughing and enjoying themselves, the same two she had seen in the lounge earlier. She stepped back into the shadows where she wouldn't be seen if they turned in her direction. She wasn't interested in meeting men and she knew from experience that a woman alone in a place like this appeared available. She glanced at the younger, handsome one just as he stood and she quickly turned and darted toward the elevators.

Palm Springs—The Day Before

She carefully placed her sequined gown on top of everything she had squeezed into her suitcase and closed the lid. Then she hauled it into the bathroom and placed it on the scale. She was limited to forty pounds or she would have to pay extra and her budget was stretched pretty thin as it was. The bag was too big for the scale and she couldn't get a reading, so she moved the scale to the center of the bathroom, but still no luck. With a sigh, she kicked off her shoes and then weighed herself, dreading the reading, but she couldn't think of any other way to do it. She stood up straight and sucked in her tummy, as if that would make a difference, resigned to the results, but that damned voice that spoke out the number like some skinny bitch mocking her had more bad news. "Your weight is 140 lbs," it mocked. "Jesus," she muttered, picking up the bag and stepping back on the scale. The skinny bitch inside the scale announced the results again. "Your weight is 188 lbs." "Dammit!" She returned the suitcase to her bed and started to think about what she could do without. Maybe she could cram more into her carry-on. Or she could eliminate some shoes, but shoes were really important to her, so she continued digging through the stuff, finally taking out her sweats and yoga clothes and athletic shoes.

"Screw it," she said. "Rosemary Clooney made her comeback heavier than this and she did alright. If I get anywhere with this maybe I can become one of those celebrity fatties who sign on with some diet company." She hauled the suitcase back to the scale. "Your weight is 182 lbs," the skinny bitch taunted.

"If the airline wants to charge me I'll just go in the ladies room and put several more layers of clothes on. It's not fair, anyway. Some people need to take more stuff than others."

She had been planning for this day for six weeks, (that was all the time she was given), saving what little she could, frantically putting a wardrobe together, and desperately trying to lose weight. She had had a terrible year, eating her way through the whole mess and gaining fifteen pounds, which weighed more heavily on her self-esteem than on the scales. She hated how she looked, blind to her own beauty, her gorgeous eyes and hair, and an hourglass figure that attracted the eyes of every guy she passed. At fifty-four, she could hold her own in the beauty department with any gal out there, rather flashy, with a million dollar smile and an infectious throaty laugh. But to her, those fifteen pounds symbolized all the failures in her life, defining her, mocking her, refusing to go. She really hated her rear end.

She had to check in three hours before her 5:00 p.m. flight. She looked at her watch, took inventory of the contents of her pocketbook one more time, double checking that the letter and contract were safely there, and hauled her suitcase to the foyer. As usual, the temperature in Palm Springs was above 100° and she could feel beads of perspiration popping out on her forehead and she patted herself dry as she waited for the cab driver to put her bag in the trunk. Her carry-on was bulging with cosmetics and CDs, and old photos. She had wanted to transfer the CDs to an iPod but could never figure out how to do it, so she had stuffed them in her bag, all she had left to show for her lifetime of work, all on just a few disks. She took one last look at the building and climbed into the back seat.

The air conditioner was blowing cold air right in her face and she started looking for the vent so she could divert the air, but nothing seemed to work. She turned away from it as best she could and decided not to complain. Determined to face the future with optimism, she choked back the tears and fears that had been dogging her for days, drew in the cold air, and began to practice her slow breathing exercises.

If there were no delays, she would arrive in Istanbul late tomorrow. That is, if she had calculated all the time changes correctly. The ticket gave a 6:30 p.m. arrival time, but she didn't know how much Istanbul was ahead of Palm Springs. All she knew was that it was going to be one heck of a long trip. Well, she was on her way, no turning back now, and she was filled with excitement, almost like on an opening night. Only this was going to open more than a night. This was going to open doors, open up opportunities, and give her another chance for a life that she had lost all hope for.

She took out her wallet and retrieved a twenty dollar bill. That was all she could spare for this part of the trip. There would be no tip money if the guy charged more than the fifteen dollars that the dispatcher said it would cost. She tucked another five in her pocket, ready to pay the guy who took her bag at the sidewalk. Jeez, what a racket. The list of expenses she had prepared was right in the side pocket of her pocketbook, right where she could look at it and record every cent she spent. Thank heavens the sale of her condo went through yesterday, although it meant that she was now officially homeless. She had taken out a second mortgage on it and was nearing foreclosure. What a relief that was to have it behind her, to finally be out from under it.

After the closing there was just enough money left to pay her expenses on this trip. The ten thousand she had put away, her life's savings, was still safely in the bank. Her friend Sherry had offered to supervise the moving people, two guys and a truck, and would make sure that her stuff ended up in the storage unit she had rented. She had spent the last few days removing her personal things, hauling the boxes herself. Most of her furniture stayed with the condo except some pieces left over from her Dad and from husband number two. She had bet the whole enchilada on this deal and was filled with excitement, enthusiasm, and terror. Sherry had talked her into going to some new age guru who taught relaxation and meditation, and a whole lot of other crap, but she hadn't found any of it very helpful. The guru said it was because she didn't release herself from her fears, but what the hell did he know about her fears. She was freak'n terrified.

The first of her three flights, the one that would take her to JFK, was running thirty minutes late, but that shouldn't cause a problem because she had a three hour layover at JFK before her flight to Paris. Then she had a six hour layover in Paris before the flight to Istanbul. There were easier ways to do it, but this combination saved her over three hundred dollars, a huge sum to spend just to arrive earlier, in her estimation. If she didn't eat anything expensive and didn't shop in any of the duty free shops, she could use that money to buy something for Leighanna, something for a peace offering.

Leighanna was her thirty-two year old daughter, mother of her only grandchild, and her biggest headache. She could handle her own busted career, her own failed marriages, her own horrible financial situation, but how she had hoped it would all be easier for Leighanna. She worried herself sick about her. And now it was Leighanna who was angry about this trip, this idea, this plan that could save them both. Foolish, she had called it, beyond foolish, stupid, inconsiderate, selfish, thoughtless, mean. All those words had been hurled at her during their last phone conversation.

"How can you do that to your own daughter?" Leighanna wailed. "How can you do that to your only child just when she needs you?"

It wasn't that Leighanna was just having a hard time. She was really a good person and a hard worker, but unfortunately, she seemed to have inherited her mother's penchant for making bad decisions. Each time there was a crisis in her life she depended on her mother to help fix things. Only this time her mother was going to be far away. Not only could she not be there, but she couldn't write a check to help out, either. "Just try to keep calm," she had told her daughter. "Try not to make things worse. I'll help you when I get back. We'll figure it all out then. It's only a few weeks, Leighanna. I'll be back in a few weeks." Actually, if things went well, she would be gone longer, but she would give her that information later.

She drew in another deep breath of the frigid air and tried to put Leighanna out of her mind. "I'm on the way back, all the way, this time," she said softly. That was one of the affirmations the guru had suggested, and she repeated it often. "I'm on the way back," she said again. "I'm on the way back. The world has not seen the last of Jodee Jordan. I'm on the way back." If only she could believe it.

Istanbul—Day 2

Three buses were parked in front of the hotel and quite a few people were beginning to gather for the grand tour of Istanbul. Grant and Mitch had decided to go by themselves, to get in a cab and tell the driver what they wanted to see. Grant had picked up lots of folders and brochures and was looking at a map to figure out what instructions to give the driver so they didn't get taken on a joyride around town with the meter running. Mitch was busy talking to some people already in line, charming all the women, laughing, having a good old time and letting Grant take care of the arrangements. According to the map, the Sultanahmet district, in the heart of the old city, which was on the European side of Istanbul, looked like the best place to start. Once you are in this district most of the major sights are within walking distance. Their hotel was right on the edge of that district, so Grant would suggest that they set out on foot.

As he was folding the map, Mitch came up beside him. "Man, I think we are making a big mistake going by ourselves. The women were telling me that the bus deal is better because they tell you everything, like they did yesterday. They said the traffic is terrible. We could be stuck in traffic all day. Lots of the folks from Palmer are already in line by the first bus. Have you figured out where we should be going? They might be right, it probably is better on the bus."

"Well, OK," Grant replied. "But it looks like we could walk from here. If you think the bus would be better, it's alright with me. I like hearing what they have to say about the places anyway. Let's see if they can take two more." They went over to the excursion desk to inquire, and before they knew it they were seated on Bus #3 with a whole gaggle of people from Minnesota. Mitch greeted everyone as he went down the aisle, and then stopped to let Grant in first.

"Your turn to get the window," he laughed. "We better remember that we are on Bus #3 because all the buses are going to the same places."

He just made that comment when the local guide, Ari, took the mic and welcomed everyone to exotic Istanbul. "And remember, please, that you are on Bus #3. Very important," he said again. "Very important that you should remember Bus #3. See the sign in the front window. Bus number #3!"

"I hope he doesn't keep that up all day," Grant commented. "Does he think we are all idiots? How many times do we need to be told, Bus #3?" Just then another guide came on board, and after a short discussion with their driver, an announcement was made.

"Are the Jacksons from Louisville on this bus? Mr. and Mrs. Jackson from Louisville, KY? Your party is waiting for you." Two people from half way back raised their hands. "Here," said the Mr. "We're right here," said the Mrs. The other guide said, "Yes, yes, come quickly. They are waiting for you on Bus #1. Your ticket says Bus #1. Everyone waits for you! You are on the wrong bus." The Jacksons from Louisville looked a little sheepish but gathered up their stuff and headed for the door. The tour guide, Ari, said one more time. "Bus #3, ladies and gentlemen. You are on Bus #3!"

Grant looked out the window to see if he could see down to Bus #1, but instead he caught a glimpse of a flowered skirt just boarding Bus #2. He craned his neck to get a better look, but she was gone.

"Now, again, welcome ladies and gentlemen," Ari started in an enthusiastic, almost dramatic manner. "Welcome to beautiful Istanbul. Istanbul, the only major city in the world that straddles two continents. It is defined by its rich and complex culture and influenced by its extensive history over the past 2500 years. Very old place, you see. It was once capital of three empires, the Roman, the Byzantine, and the Ottoman," emphasizing the importance of that fact. "And now Ari give you a short history lesson. But no tests today. For you I make it easy and no tests," he continued, pleased with his little joke and receiving an appreciative round of applause from his audience.

"Istanbul remains today a melting pot for an exotic mix of people, cultures, and customs. It's strategic location between the continents and connection between the Black Sea and the Bosphorus, and its natural harbor, the Golden Horn, made it a perfect place for trade. In the year 330 AD, Emperor Constantine officially declared Istanbul the capital of the Roman Empire, and it became known as Constantinople. It was under his influence that the city took on many of the characteristics of Rome."

He stopped to talk to the bus driver, apparently conferring about some traffic disturbance, and then continued to tell them what they would be seeing on the tour. "There is evidence of the Romans everywhere in Istanbul, monuments, aqueducts, baths, and a Hippodrome. Emperor Constantine built the first Hagia Sophia here, for the Christians." Ari thought that this was very important information since he was aware of the fact that the majority of the people he ushered around each day were Christians and did not share his Muslim faith. In fact, his experience as a guide had shown him that most Christian visitors in Istanbul were not even aware of the Christian impact on the city, so he took it upon himself to give a little more information on the subject.

He continued, "In the sixth century, Emperor Justinian ordered the building of the Hagia Sophia you will see today, the most imposing place of Christian worship for over one thousand years, you know. So now you have learned all about Istanbul. Two thousand twenty five hundred years in just ten minutes. Like time travelers, yes?" He obviously had recited his spiel many times and he had it down pat. Mitch had already started to doze off and Grant had noticed several other heads bobbing around him, but this stuff was right up Grant's alley and he had been listening carefully.

The bus maneuvered easily through the streets and Ari continued telling them more about how all of the water had to be delivered via the huge aqueducts and stored in the great cistern under the city.

"Isn't that the one in the James Bond movie, *From Russia with Love?*" Grant wondered aloud. "Remember, with Sean Connery. It started out in Istanbul. Remember the scene where he and this guy go down into the cistern, all the pillars, and stuff?"

"Yeah, I remember that one. Too bad we don't get to go down there."

"Maybe we can go tomorrow morning before we leave. I'll ask Ari if you need tickets or if anyone can just go."

"Now, ladies and gentlemen, our first stop will be at the Hippodrome. Please, you may leave your things on the bus. It will be quite safe, locked up tight. But I ask you to please stay close, to not be wandering off. See here, this yellow umbrella. Be always looking for it. I will be under it. And remember, Bus #3. Now you all say it together. Bus #3!"

Grant couldn't help but smile. This Ari guy was alright, seemed to know his stuff, and enjoy his job. He and Mitch stayed near the group and listened intently as Ari told them about the Serpent Tower and the Egyptian Tower, and the Hippodrome itself, explaining that chariot racing was the biggest event for the people of Constantinople.

Ari continued. "What is so exciting, so big, like your super bowl, only everyday they are racing here. Nine times around the track they are racing, and as many as twenty two races in one day. The Emperor and his family are coming here too. Everyone has a favorite team. It is like a political party, almost like a religion. Thousands of people assembled here for these races, many times even fighting among themselves. And the charioteers are the heroes of everybody. Just like Super Bowl, yes? Today there is a large park in this hippodrome. It is where all of Istanbul celebrates Ramadan, the high holy days of Islam."

Mitch had wandered off to the side, probably not listening at all since he seemed much more interested in the woman he was talking to. Grant moved in a little closer to Ari, listening intently, enjoying it all. He was especially interested in the part about the spoils of victories, and that much of what they were looking at was brought from Greece or Egypt. But some things had been taken from the Hippodrome too. The Venetians had seized four bronze horses and had taken them back to Venice, where they stand today in St. Mark's

Basilica. Grant was sorry he hadn't known that when he and Vonnie were in Venice.

"Now we go to the bus, ladies and gentlemen. Bus #3 waits for us. Follow me. There are many buses today. We must go to Bus #3." He took off at a pretty good clip. Grant started to follow, just assuming that Mitch was coming up behind, but when he turned to look, Mitch was nowhere in sight. Grant hesitated for a few seconds, and then turned to see where Ari and the group were, deciding he better keep up with them, quickening his pace. At the bus, Grant stepped to the side to let the others board while Ari stood with the yellow umbrella urging folks to watch their step and looking at Grant with a questioning expression, wondering why he wasn't boarding with the others. Grant didn't want to create a scene or sound like an alarmist, but Mitch still wasn't in sight so he said, "My friend will be here in a minute or two," sounding nonchalant, but hoping that Mitch hadn't wandered off in the crowd somewhere. Grant boarded the bus and took his seat.

Ari began walking down the aisle, counting bodies once, then twice. "We are missing one more, one more is still coming here. So we are waiting one minute, maybe two minutes, for one more." By now the others were turning in their seats to see where the vacant seat of the missing person was, and Grant was anxiously looking out the window for the missing Mitch, trying to decide whether he should get off the bus and wait for him or to leave him behind. He stood up and went forward to ask Ari what the procedure was if someone didn't return.

"Come," Ari said. "We wait outside the bus. We are waiting a little while longer, but outside the bus. Perhaps your friend has decided to explore on his own, but we give him some more time." He opened the yellow umbrella and held it high in the air. There were several other buses loading in the vicinity and Ari strolled over to talk with another tour guide, a woman standing with a huge sunflower on top of a yardstick. Ari walked the length of several other buses, holding the umbrella up high so it was seen through the windows, and then turned back to his own bus.

Grant was pretty sure that Mitch was OK, that he would make it back to the hotel on his own, so he said. "Let's go. He will be alright. Where are we headed next in case he calls me?" Just as the door closed and the driver began to ease the bus from its parking space there came a loud pounding on the back of the bus and a voice hollering, "Wait! Wait!" The driver immediately stopped and opened the door and there was Mitch, red faced, out of breath, dripping with sweat, frantically climbing up the stairs and heading down the aisle to his seat. He was welcomed with a loud round of applause and a few snide remarks, the gist of which was that they had almost left him and next time stay with the group.

"Where the hell were you?" Grant asked. "We've been waiting for you quite a while. Didn't you see us walking to the bus? I saw you talking to some woman."

"Yeah, I was talking to this gal from another group and didn't notice when you left and when I looked you were gone. So I went back to her bus with her. She is staying at our same hotel so I figured it wouldn't make any difference. She saw Ari's umbrella out the window and told me I better get off and go on the right bus because they were probably looking for me. But when I got off, the bus was leaving so I had to run like hell to catch it. Man, I'm wiped out. I must really be in bad shape." He began wiping the sweat that was running down his face.

"From now on you better pay attention to the group instead of chasing women, Mitch. You're apt to spend the day chasing the bus instead," Grant laughed.

"Hey, it was worth it. I've already done the three things on my list today. She was a real nice lady, got her name and even found out what level of cabin she has on the boat. I'm already way ahead of you. I'm going to look for her when we get to the next place. Her name is Joan."

"What bus was she on? We may not always be at the same places at the same time."

"She is on Bus #2. Look for Bus #2. She is with that blonde you were eyeing last night. They are with the lady with the sunflower."

Bus #2

Several people from Palmer Plantation had been assigned to bus #2 and the tour guide, Jasmeen, had admonished them to tend to the #2 bus with the same sense of urgency that Ari had emphasized on Bus #3, obviously both very experienced with the foibles and failings of the people they so happily guided day after day. She had also made sure that they knew to always be looking for her bright sunflower that she would be holding high above her head so they could always identify their group. This business of holding some unique item or color above the heads of the guides is not just a little gimmick or cutsie trick. It is a widely used technique around famous travel destinations all over the world. Travelers have welcomed this little sign of identification, and this group of enthusiastic, mostly American tourists was no different. They would all keep a close eye on the bright sunflower for the entire day as they visited the fabulous attractions of Istanbul. Of course, unbeknownst to Jasmeen, two others would also be keeping an eye out for the bright sunflower, but for an entirely different reason.

Joan and Shay had chosen seats about midway toward the back of the bus, and according to Jasmeen's instructions, they returned to those same seats. When Mitch McConnell boarded the bus, having lost track of his own group, choosing to follow Joan to bus #2 instead, he had headed to the back of the bus to a vacant seat and planned to just tag along with the Sunflower group. After all, what difference did it make? They were all going to the same places. But when Joan saw the yellow umbrella pass her window she left her seat and went back to Mitch and suggested that he was being looked for and he should probably leave Bus #2 and return to Bus #3, where he belonged. Overhearing this little conversation as she was counting the bodies, not yet aware that she had added someone, Jasmeen said, "Yes, yes. Hurry now. They are looking for you. Come. I will show you Bus #3. You must always be on Bus #3," she scolded. Mitch, who didn't embarrass easily, felt a little foolish, but did as she said, and was almost happy to see Bus #3 pulling away from its parking spot, hoping to continue on Bus #2, but Jasmeen said, "Run. Run fast. You must ride Bus #3. You cannot ride Bus #2!"

Joan returned to her own seat next to Shay and listened politely while Jasmeen again emphasized the importance of always being on Bus #2, reminding them not to be getting on any other bus. Shay couldn't help but laugh. "Who was that? Is he someone you know from Palmer Plantation?"

"No, I never met him before. Just some guy who started talking to me at the monuments. I thought he belonged in our group, but he said he couldn't find his group so he would go with us until he caught up with them. His name is Mitch. Seems like a real nice guy. Maybe we'll see him again at one of the next stops."

The next stop was at the Blue Mosque and Shay began to sort through her brochures so she would have the information handy when they arrived there. She had brought along her scarf and a light weight cardigan so she would have appropriate head and arm covering, and had worn sandals that were easy to remove. Seeing her prepare, Joan said, "Oh, do we have to cover our heads? I don't have anything but this baseball cap that says *Palmer Plantation* on it. Do you think they will let me in?"

"I would think they probably see a lot of caps with writing on them, but I am not sure of all the customs. I believe I read that head coverings are available at the mosque for women who are unprepared, but I don't know what exactly they have. Your arms are to be covered, too, and you will have to remove your shoes."

Shay had noticed that the other three women were wearing pretty heavy duty sneakers and white athletic socks, but she hadn't packed any because she thought they would look awful with her dresses. As a matter of fact, most of the woman were wearing similar sneakers or heavy duty walking sandals, even with socks. She cringed at the sight, but worried that she was a little overdressed. She had expected that the women would be wearing rather smart casual clothes for sightseeing and was surprised that so many of them were in rather plain, mostly khaki or black, Bermuda shorts and only a few had bothered to tuck in their shirts. The men were dressed exactly the same way.

"I'm going to have to ask you what is expected at all the places we go to," Joan said. "Did you read all of this? I didn't read anything. Do I have to take off my socks, too? There better be a place to sit down. I tied knots in my shoelaces so they wouldn't keep coming untied. You were smart to wear sandals, Shay." Joan leaned across the aisle and told Wanda and Maureen what was expected, sounding like she was the originator of the information. They immediately began to rifle through their bags for the appropriate attire, but Wanda just shook her head.

"I don't see why these foreigners expect us to follow their rules. After all, we're not Muslims."

"Shush," Maureen cautioned. "We are guests here. They are only asking that we respect their customs. Do you have a scarf? I have an extra one. And I have a jacket in my backpack. Just do as you are told."

"Well, Howard, my late husband, always said that all these foreigners want is our money, so what do they care what we wear?" But she took the scarf and jacket anyway and hoped she could get her shoes off without falling over.

The Sultan Ahmed Mosque, known as The Blue Mosque, is the most famous mosque in Istanbul. It is also one of the most recognized structures in the world. Its great size and extraordinary beauty hold it in high esteem and it is visited by millions of people each year.

The group followed Jasmeen as she led them to the entrance through the outer court. Upon entering, they were given a plastic bag in which to place their shoes and the women adjusted their head and arm coverings, and then gathered around the guide who would tell them about the beautiful place. The mosque is magnificent, huge, almost overwhelming. They listened intently as the guide explained that the interior of the mosque was covered with over twenty thousand handmade tiles from Iznik, many decorated with tulips representing more than fifty different tulip designs. The upper levels are painted blue and the overall impression from the tiles and paint gives off a blue hue, from whence the name is derived. It is built in the traditional style of a mosque with rounded domes and four huge pillars that support the structure. There is no blue on the exterior.

Two hundred and sixty windows bathe the space in a soft light that enhances the blueness of the tiles, an effect that changes with the movement of the sun throughout the day. Wanda had gotten over her snit about the shoes and head covering and became extremely interested in the place. She was a flower lover and avid gardener and wanted to ask about the tulip designs in the famous Iznik tiles. She was astounded to hear that the tulip was native to Turkey and was beloved in the country.

"Why, I never knew that," Wanda gasped. "I always thought the tulip was native to Holland."

The guide went on to explain that many people thought that, since Holland has pretty much taken the tulip as its own, but the fact was that the tulip was native to Turkey and had been discovered there by early Dutch traders who took bulbs back to Holland. It has been growing in Turkey for centuries and it is artistically represented in fabric and ceramic designs throughout the country. Wanda couldn't wait to get back to her garden club in Palmer Plantation with that information.

They learned that the women were separated from the men in the mosque, and that prayers and other services were held there regularly. The Muslim tenets require prayer five times a day but the prayer call is made six times. The times are not set by the clock but are traditionally set by the movement of the sun, although many mosques call to prayer by a set time, which is generally associated with two hours before dawn, dawn, midday, afternoon, sunset, and right before last light of the day.

The call to prayer can be heard everywhere in Istanbul. It is broadcast loudly from the multitude of speakers located at mosques throughout the city, since Islam is the majority religion. Most visitors find the sound rather beautiful, a lovely haunting sound that enhances the exotic feel of the city.

And no visit to the Blue Mosque is complete without hearing about the six minarets. Traditionally mosques have four, two, or just one, but apparently, when the young Sultan directed his architect to design gold minarets he had been misunderstood. The word for gold is very similar to the word for six and six minarets were constructed. This was quite scandalous since the Haram Mosque in Mecca, the holiest in the world, had six minarets, and this new mosque must not be equal to that. The story has it that the young sultan solved the problem by sending his architect to Mecca to construct a seventh minaret at the Haram Mosque.

Bus #3 had arrived at the Mosque and the group was together near the other side of the building. Grant was taking it all in and listening to every word, admiring the awesome beauty and construction of the place and thinking about the fact that they had just come from the ancient hippodrome to this place from the early seventeenth century, which made it seem almost young. He was always amazed when he traveled in Europe at how old stuff was compared to the stuff in America, just the huge difference in years, yet so much lovely evidence remains. The great cathedrals of Europe always impressed him this same way. And the ruins in Rome had fascinated him. He had been there with Vonnie on the same trip they went to Venice, their last trip together.

Mitch immediately began to look for the sunflower group, but the sunflower could not be held high inside the mosque, so he craned his neck to look over the crowds. Mitch whispered to Grant that he would meet him outside and began to ease his way through the groups, heading to the door and courtyard beyond, where he thought he would have a good chance to see the sunflower lady. Instead, he ran into the lady from Palmer Plantation, the one who had organized the trip. He decided it might be a good time to schmooze her a little and smiled brightly as she made a beeline for him.

"Oh, Mitch, how nice to run into you. I have been looking for you, and here you are right at the Blue Mosque. I have made a list of the members in my group and have one for you. I hope you don't mind, but I put you and your friend on the list too, even though you aren't officially with me. And I included your addresses and phone numbers too, but I will have to get your stateroom number when we get on board. I know all the others will want it. It is right here in my tote bag."

Mitch, caught by surprise, began to sputter as he took the list from her. "That was nice of you to include us. We were afraid you wouldn't want us hanging around all the time since we didn't book the trip with you."

"Don't be silly. Of course I want you in my group. I will see to it that you are included in everything. I think you already know some of the people. Didn't you go to the singles group a few times? I don't remember seeing you there but one of the ladies said she thought you had gone a few times. And where is your friend Grant? We are all anxious to meet him. Have you been hiding him? It is just going to be so much fun, all of us together."

Mitch began to sputter again, knowing that Grant would really be mad if all the Palmer people clustered around them. He didn't want to encourage her. "What bus are you on? I'll keep an eye out for you."

"Most of us are on Bus #1, but some are on #2. I already know what bus you are on," she said coyly.

Anxious to get away, he said, "Well, good to see you, Betty."

"Barbara," she corrected. "But you can call me Babs. And I have put a star by my name on the list. Call me anytime, Mitch. I'll get in touch with you just as soon as we board the ship tomorrow so you can give me your stateroom number. We're going to have a little welcome aboard cocktail party and I want you to promise to come. Grant, too."

"Well, we might be a little busy, you know, but I'll see if we can be there."

All the while he had been talking, groups of people had been entering and exiting the mosque, but he had not seen the sunflower lady. He excused himself and began to search the crowd when he caught sight of Ari's yellow umbrella and headed right for it. Better not push his luck. Grant was boarding the bus when he caught up. With one last look around for the sunflower, Mitch boarded and took his seat.

"That was interesting, wasn't it? Did you listen to much of it? I'm really glad we decided to take the bus. We would have missed a lot. Who were you talking to? I walked right by you, but you didn't see me."

"That was Betty. She heads up the trip. She seems real nice. Gave me the list of the group."

"Let me have a look and see if I know any of them. Do you think it's going to be hard to avoid them? They seem to be everywhere. Oh my God! Look! She put our names on the list. And our phone numbers! Shit, we'll never be able to keep away from them. How the hell did she get away with this? We're not part of her group. They better not start pestering us. Did you know she was going to do this?"

"No, I didn't have any idea. She saw me out there and came right up. Said she had the list and told me we're on it. What could I say?"

"This could just screw up the whole plan, Mitch. It isn't that there is anything wrong with that group, it's just that we want some privacy. And if we do get on to something we sure don't want it blabbed all over. This could really get to be embarrassing."

"I know. She wants our stateroom number too. And we're invited to a welcome aboard party tomorrow."

"Shit. That's all we need. Did you see the sunflower lady?"

"No. Maybe we'll see them at the next stop."

Ari had finished his head count and started telling them about their next stop, Hagia Sophia, considered the greatest structure in the city. It is a masterpiece of architecture and one of the largest structures in the world to have withstood the ravages of time. It stands today as a museum, a tribute to those who conceived her and those who built her, as well as a treasure of two of the world's great faiths. It has served as an Eastern Orthodox Church, a Roman Catholic Church, and as an Imperial Mosque.

Built in a mere five years, between 532 AD and 537 AD, it has commanded the awe and respect of people around the world for fifteen hundred years. For over one thousand years it was the largest Christian church in the world. To see Hagia Sophia, to stand in the mammoth place and gaze at the huge dome suspended almost two hundred feet above and bathed in light from the embedded windows, feels almost like you are seeing the sky, or even heaven. The place itself is nearly as long as a football field and it is almost as wide as it is long. It is opulently decorated with mosaics containing thousands upon thousands of colorful stones, individually cut and set by hand. Richly painted icons add to the overall magnificence of the place and its Muslim heritage is seen in the elaborate calligraphy and geometric shapes that were added during the Ottoman years, since icons and renditions of people are not found in mosques. The exterior is of traditional Byzantine style and the huge flat shaped dome distinguishes it from the familiar style of the later period European Cathedrals with their towering spires.

Grant could have spent hours there just absorbing the place, but the group was already being urged along as the tour concluded. Mitch was again hanging around outside trying to see the sunflower, but joined his own group and headed to the bus.

"Wow. That was really something. I could spend a week in Istanbul. I never knew there was so much to see here. Maybe can we can get another gig and come back here, Mitch. What's next?"

"Lunch. I'm starved."

"They are taking us to some restaurant that overlooks the Bosphorus. I'm hungry too. I wonder if all three buses are going to the same place."

The restaurant turned out to be a lovely place with a huge terraced dining room overlooking the Bosphorus. The other two buses were already unloading when they arrived. They would be seated at large tables and Ari was directing his group to their spot and pointing out the location of the restrooms. Grant was relieved that they would be seated with their own bus group and wouldn't be with the Palmer group, but his relief was short lived. They had no more than sat when Babs appeared, excitedly telling them that she had arranged for her group to all be seated together.

"Come," she said. "We have saved two seats for you. We are so excited that you will be a part of our group. The ladies are asking about you, Mitch, and we all want to meet Grant." She turned toward him with her outstretched hand. "It is so nice to meet you, Grant. Everyone is asking who the mystery man is with Mitch. This is going to be so much fun."

"Nice to meet you, too, Betty."

"Barbara," she corrected. "But just call me Babs. I have put a star by my name on the list."

Mitch didn't dare look at Grant. He got right up without offering any excuses, hoping he would see Joan from the sunflower group. Grant got up too and followed the exuberant Babs to her table.

"Look, everybody. Look who I have found. Mitch, you are right here next to me. And, Grant, I have put you at the other end. This table is all on Bus #1 and Bus #2 is right behind us. We know what bus you two are on, don't we," she said with a giggle.

Grant's eyes immediately turned to the other table, searching for the blonde. He saw only the back of her head and his eyes lingered on her hair, admiring the pretty twist in what he would have called a loose ponytail, and he felt a surge of disappointment that she was with the Palmer group. No way was he going to mess with someone from Palmer Plantation. He took his seat and joined the conversation. They were all friendly, and rather experienced travelers, so after the usual questions about where you live and about golf, the talk was mostly about Istanbul. Thankfully, no one brought up Vonnie, which was the one subject Grant didn't want to talk about, something that still made every casual conversation he had anywhere a tense situation for him. So many people knew about her even though they had only been in Palmer Plantation a little while, but even well intentioned comments about his situation were awkward and sometimes hurtful.

Mitch was trapped between Babs and some woman who just adored traveling in groups and just adored every place she had ever been, and just adored the fabulous Turkish food, and just adored everyone in Palmer Plantation, and just adored this opportunity to meet Mitch, because she had heard so much about him. The waiter appeared with the news that there was a choice between three meals, and rattled off the choices, which all sounded like so much gibberish to Mitch. He didn't want to sound ignorant, so he said, "I'll have the first one," hoping to hell it was something he would at least recognize.

Well, it was music to the ears of the lady seated next to him, because she just adored moussaka and was ordering it too. "Oh, we are going to hit it right off. We have so much in common. Don't you just adore it when you meet someone and right away you just know that you will be great friends? I just adore that feeling. Just adore it!"

Overhearing this conversation and feeling a little left out, Babs chimed right in. "Now tell us all about what you are going to be doing, Mitch. Have you booked any of the shore excursions yet? I would love to add you to our shore groups so we can all be together. Wouldn't that be fun? And I will make dinner arrangements for you, too. Most of our group is eating early so we can go to the shows, but there are some eating later, too."

Mitch glanced down the table where Grant was laughing and enjoying himself, and answered Babs with some vague excuse about needing to spend his time with Grant since this was such a difficult time for him.

"Oh, I know. Poor thing. The ladies were telling me all about it last night." She didn't add that the general consensus was that he wouldn't last too long, with his good looks, and, seeing the handsome Grant for the first time today, she could see what all the buzz was about. He was one great looking guy.

The waiters were bringing the food, moving pretty fast, apparently experienced with large groups, and Mitch was pleasantly surprised that his looked pretty good and tasted great too. "I wonder what is in this," he said, making conversation. The woman who adored everything started right up again. "I just adore moussaka. I adore anything with eggplant. Just adore it!" And Babs added that it had lamb in it too, and chevre. Mitch didn't let on that he didn't know what chevre was and said, with slight airs, "Yes. Aubergine is a favorite in Turkey. They serve it many ways. And the spices are blended perfectly in this moussaka. They complement the lamb, bringing out the full flavor." The two women were duly impressed, reinforcing Babs' opinion that Mitch was probably one of the most sophisticated men she had ever met. And the lady on the other side of him just adored refined men, just adored them. Mitch was pretty pleased with himself too. Too bad Grant didn't hear that. He glanced Grant's way and saw that Grant had ordered the same thing and he couldn't wait to ask him how he liked his eggplant.

At the other table, Shay Porter was rather uncomfortable seated with so many strangers, but she was pleased to be so cordially welcomed into their group and cheerfully answered all their many questions, revealing as little personal information as possible. "No, she didn't live at the Plantation, but, yes, she was traveling with the group, and, no, she and Joan were not longtime friends, and no, she was not planning to move there even though it certainly sounded wonderful, and, yes, she hoped to visit their little corner of paradise soon."

Seated two seats away and overhearing the word 'move', was a fellow named Ralph Carrawat, who immediately produced his calling card. "Well, little lady, you come right on down and visit anytime you want. I will be happy to show you around." Shay glanced at his card, a little embarrassed, and saw that it said, *Ralph Carrawat, Real Estate.* Under his name it said "I know what you want and I can fulfill your needs. Satisfaction Guaranteed" She almost laughed out loud, but stifled the urge. "Thanks. I'll keep you in mind." She had no idea what she wanted, let alone what she needed, but she was darned sure he was not the one to provide it.

Shay's back was to the other tables so she didn't get a good look at the rest of the group, but Joan had a bird's eye view and was barely listening to the conversation because she was intent on watching the proceedings at Babs' table. She could see Mitch animatedly talking to the women he was seated with. While she was happy to see that he was with Babs' group, she didn't recall ever seeing him at Palmer, so she reached in her handbag and retrieved the list of members in the group, scanning the names until she found "Mitchell McConnell."

She ran over the street names in her head, trying to remember where Saltflower Dr. was. He was really nice looking, probably in his sixties, still had his hair, and was pretty trim, and she was a little disappointed that he seemed to know these other women. For all she knew, maybe one of them was his wife. Joan wasn't much of a social butterfly, hadn't joined a lot of things at Palmer and didn't know all that many people. Her good friends, Maureen and Wanda, were in her bunco group and, since they were the only widows in the group, they had become close and she was content just being with them. And she had her book club, but that was all.

Maureen was the social butterfly in the group. She had joined a long list of things, flitting off to this and that and keeping Wanda and Joan informed about everything happening to everyone. Maureen also went to the singles club and she tried to encourage the other two to attend. "We have the best time. We go out together and have little parties, and meet new people. It's not about men, for Pete's sake," she would say, but her conversation also included tidbits about who was there, and who was there with you know who, and who was out to catch a man, any man, it didn't matter who, and who was a womanizer, and who was the latest widow or widower.

Wanda's late husband, Howard, had warned her to avoid men after he was gone because all they wanted was her money, and she had plenty of that. She avoided men like the plague and defiantly said she would never, ever, attend any of those singles functions, and she certainly wasn't even the slightest bit interested in men, for heaven's sake.

Joan was maybe interested in men a little, but the whole singles scene scared the crap out of her, so she just stayed home, even though her daughters frequently reminded her that "Daddy would want you to be happy." Well, she wanted to be happy too, and for the most part she was. Maybe a little lonely, but pretty happy, and a man in her life seemed like something that was probably not going to happen. It wasn't that she was opposed to it, it just didn't seem likely. She listened to all the stories about the singles club from Maureen and even read the newsletter and the announcements of their coming events and who was hosting some little get together.

She even thought it sounded nice, but she couldn't make herself go. She didn't recall Maureen ever mentioning a guy named Mitch.

Wanda and Maureen were chatting with a couple that Wanda had met at one of the progressive dinners that she and her late husband, Howard, had attended eleven years ago, shortly after moving to Palmer Plantation. Wanda's social life pretty much consisted of reliving times that she and the late Howard had enjoyed together and she constantly mentioned him, frequently quoting something or other that he had said, or recalling advice or words of wisdom he had imparted, including him in conversations in a way that was rather off-putting. It was hard to tell if she couldn't let go or if she didn't want to, but Howard was obviously going to take this cruise whether he wanted to or not, and most folks began to wonder if there was a little problem there since poor Howard had departed almost ten years ago.

But Wanda was happily recounting the details of that dinner almost like it had taken place last week, reminding the couple of who else was present, and reminiscing about how much Howard had enjoyed the evening. "It was the beginning, you know. He got diarrhea just when we got home. His cancer just got worse and worse right after that. Oh, how the poor man suffered. Could hardly eat a thing. Just went right downhill after that. I knew something was wrong. We took a trip to Mexico and he got such bad diarrhea, just awful. The worst diarrhea I ever saw. He just couldn't stop going. We had traveled quite a bit during our marriage, you know, and he got diarrhea just about everywhere, but that Mexican diarrhea was the worst. I don't think this Turkish food would have agreed with him either. All these spices cause diarrhea, you know." The waiter was just placing their plates in front of them, but no one seemed very enthusiastic about eating.

"OK. Enough of the sick talk," Maureen said emphatically, desperately wanting to change the subject. "So, folks, are you going all the way or are you leaving at Rome?" Much to their relief, the conversation was changed and they attempted to enjoy their food before it got cold. Maureen continued to tell them that she and Wanda were leaving in Rome, but how glad she was to have met

41

them. "Perhaps we can have dinner together one night," she said, but she was pretty sure the couple would not be looking forward to dinner with Wanda and the late Howard.

Maureen and Joan had talked about the long departed, ever present Howard, and tried to think of ways to help Wanda let him rest in peace, but had finally decided that it was just Wanda's way of handling her grief. As good friends they needed to be supportive, but, good grief, how much longer was it going to go on. Maureen's Bill was peacefully resting in his hometown in New Jersey and Joan's Ted was back home in Indiana. Both men were dearly loved and greatly missed, but rarely interrupted conversations. That happened mostly when they were alone, or with their kids, or during the holidays, when memories wreaked havoc with the realities of their lives, disturbed their sleep, and even brought occasional tears.

Lost

The afternoon was to be spent visiting Topkapi, the palace of the Sultans. It is the oldest and largest palace remaining in the world, but it is rather unpretentious compared to the more familiar ones found throughout Europe because it is constructed in the Ottoman style of lower buildings surrounding courtyards, spreading over one hundred and seventy five acres. The buildings served specific functions since the palace was more than a residence and served as the seat of the government as well. Each courtyard is entered through the courtyard before it. Originally there were between seven hundred and eight hundred residents in the palace buildings, but that number eventually grew to five thousand and the palace was the largest in the world, a city within a city. It was turned into a museum in 1924. Guides lead groups through the many popular buildings displaying a wide variety of porcelains, weapons, and artifacts of all kinds collected from around the world, many decorated with huge precious stones. Thousands of other items are housed in the museum of fine arts, outside of the palace. The huge kitchens are of special interest to most people. Turkish cuisine is respected everywhere in the culinary world and many dishes originated right in these kitchens, since the sultan was to be served only the finest food. Meals for the entire palace population were prepared in the same kitchens.

Many visitors find the Harem the most fascinating building in the Palace; the word means forbidden in Arabic. Consisting of over four hundred rooms, it housed the Sultan and his family, including all those concubines, although the guides emphasize that all the stories told might be exaggerated. Black eunuchs guarded the wives, children, and concubines. The sultan himself was guarded by white eunuchs. And there was even a circumcision room used exclusively for the sons of the sultan.

"Mitch, did you ever see that old movie, *Topkapi*? Remember it? It's the one about a caper to steal the sultan's dagger, the one with the huge emerald in it? They dangled a guy down, sort of like a *Mission Impossible* episode. It probably wasn't as hard as it looked in the movie, now that I see how low these buildings are, but I'm going to get it on Netflix when I get home. I can't believe I'm actually right here in the place."

"No, I never saw that one. Who was in it?"

"I don't remember. I'll get it and have you over and we can watch it together. I'll get *From Russia With Love*, too. And I'll get that one with Jack Lemon and, what's that guy's name, Walter Matthau? The funny one about the two old guys who get a job on a cruise ship. We'll have a guy's night."

"Maybe we can invite some of the others, or at least some women. Might as well get some extra mileage out of it."

"Is that all you think about, women?"

"Yep! Pretty much!"

Bus #3 was the last to leave the palace. They would visit the famous Bazaar 54, the leading establishment in the Grand Bazaar, for a demonstration of fine Turkish rugs and then they would be turned loose for shopping. The bus could stay there for only one hour.

Grant didn't intend to spend any time shopping, maybe just look around a bit, but shopping wasn't his idea of fun. Their hosts in the rug shop, who were also powerful sales people, served them each a cup of hot apple tea. They had been advised by Ari that this was expected in rug shops and it would be considered rude not to accept. So there they all sat around the perimeter of the room, sipping from their little cups, as the men rolled out rug after rug after rug, explaining the intricacies of knot tying, dyeing, and design. Some of the rugs were incredible, one more beautiful than the other, and Grant got pretty interested, even thinking that he might buy one. Just a small one, he thought, just for a little memento of his trip, but they were pretty expensive and he would have liked a little more time.

Mitch wasn't interested in the rugs at all and slipped out of the room, roaming the other showroom areas, looking for the sunflower lady. Apparently that group was in a different gallery because he didn't see them anywhere. He was heading back to find Grant when he saw his lunch companion, the lady who just adored everything. He did some quick thinking and squeezed behind one of the rugs hanging from fasteners on the wall, peeking out from behind to see if the coast was clear. Not seeing her anywhere, he decided to ease his way behind the rug and exit at the other side. But he had not gone undetected. Seeing the bulge moving behind the rug and suspecting that someone was up to no good, a security guard was waiting for Mitch and demanded to know what he was doing.

"Just admiring the knots, sir. So many knots, sir. Thank you so much. So many knots," Mitch said in his most charming manner, but the security guard kept a tight grip on his arm. Two salesmen appeared, admonishing him in loud voices not to touch the rug.

"See here," one said, pointing to a sign on the rug. "Do not touch! This is a very rare rug. It is priceless, sir. You must not touch this rug."

Grant had just passed the door when he heard the commotion and immediately went to Mitch's side. "What's going on here?" he asked.

Mitch just rolled his eyes. "I touched the damned rug," not telling the whole story.

Grant stuck out his hand to shake hands with the salesmen and security guard, pointing to his head in that universally understood gesture of insanity, and muttered, "So sorry, so sorry," and guided Mitch from the room and right out of the shop on to one of the busiest corridors in the Grand Bazaar. "Good God, Mitch. What was that about? I was afraid I was going to have to get you out of the hoosegow. What the hell did you do?"

"I told you. I touched the damned rug."

"Well, you're lucky they didn't make you buy it. I wonder how much it was."

"It was priceless, Grant! They said it was priceless."

"In that case, I admire your exquisite taste. The ladies will be impressed. How about a few laps around this place and then we head back to the hotel."

"OK by me. I've already seen enough."

The Grand Bazaar is a vast warren of passages, a giant labyrinth of narrow pedestrian streets lined with over three thousand shops. It is the largest and oldest covered market place in the world. Just about everything can be found there, but mostly the shops carry things for tourists, gold everything, prayer rugs, jewelry everywhere, scarves, and intricately carved trinkets of all manner. Istanbul is now a modern city and the locals shop at modern malls and buy modern things, just like people everywhere, but wandering in this cavernous place is like stepping back in time, perhaps the way it was centuries ago, and most tourists soon find themselves caught up in the exotic charm of noise, and scents, and very persistent shopkeepers. "Just say no," Ari had instructed them. "Just say no, but kindly, please. They are just working, just selling. It is the way it is done."

Grant and Mitch strolled down a few passage ways, stopping occasionally to examine or admire something and Grant found himself thinking about his kids and grandkids and decided to pick up a few things. There would never be a better place to choose gifts, so he bought some scarves for his daughters and some pretty little bracelets for the little girls, but the bracelets would probably be too big and would have to be saved. He hadn't seen the little girls since June. "How old were they now, two maybe? No, just one." He bought toy daggers for his two grandsons, replicas of the sultan's dagger. And he bought his son and sons-in-law each a nice tiled knife box. Vonnie had always taken care of this job, buying things for the kids, and he had never paid too much attention to what she bought, so he bought some tiles with "Istanbul" written in Arabic, or maybe just calligraphy, he wasn't sure, and for good measure he bought everybody a tee shirt with "Istanbul" on it, buying a variety of sizes and hoping for the best.

"Maybe I should pick up a few things too," Mitch said.

"How many grandkids do you have, Mitch?"

"I think there are about twenty now, but I lost count. Some of them are in college and some of them are still little. I can't even remember all their names. The Mrs. always did all of that, kept up with everyone. Now I just send a check to each family for Christmas and let them divvy it up. It sure beats shopping."

"Well, maybe we can find something that would work for everybody," Grant suggested, and they strolled down to yet another shop displaying gold items.

"Look, Mitch. These little gold charm things are nice. The girls can put them on a chain or on a charm bracelet, and the boys can put one on a key ring or a chain. I wonder what it says or if that is just decoration."

Mitch had picked one up and was examining it and Grant asked the eager salesman what it said.

"Peace and love, sir. They all say peace and love. And these here say Istanbul. They are all made right here in the bazaar by finest goldsmiths. Twenty one karat gold. Very good gold, sir."

"These are great, Grant. Good idea. I'll buy a whole mess of them and figure it out at home," and he started to count them out. "Think I'll take thirty. That way if I forgot someone I'll have extra." He gave his credit card to the very excited salesman, who rang up the sale and began to wrap each one in thin tissue paper. A salesman from a nearby gold shop came right over to help with the wrapping, a brother, he said, and Grant saw that several other sales people from nearby shops had strolled over, watching the activity.

While the wrapping continued, Grant went up to a counter of gold jewelry that was under lock and key. Another salesman was on his heels and began to open the glass cabinet and Grant selected two lovely gold charms, miniature replicas of the Hagia Sophia and the Blue Mosque. He added them to his purchases and placed them safely in his pocket. Mitch's wrapped gifts were placed in a bigger than necessary flimsy box. Noticing the empty space in it, Grant suggested that they add the two tiles he had purchased and the two small knife boxes, consolidating things so they didn't have so many packages to keep up with.

"Good idea, Grant. We can sort them out when we get on the boat tomorrow." He put the flimsy box on his arm so he could support it. The two shopkeepers smiled broadly, thanked them profusely, and shook their hands, mighty pleased with the sale.

"How much were those, Mitch? Everyone seemed pretty excited about the sale."

"I don't know for sure. It was written in Turkish lira and I couldn't do the math in my head. Maybe a couple hundred dollars. It doesn't matter. Now I'm done for the whole trip. I hate to shop."

Grant took the sales slip out of Mitch's shirt pocket where he had seen him put it and did some quick math. "Well, it's a good thing that those kids have a rich Grandpa, because those little things were $125.00 each."

"How much is that all together. About a thousand dollars?"

Grant laughed, "No wonder you always beat me on the golf course. You can't add. It costs $3750.00, Mitch. Those kids have one cool Grandpa."

"Well, I can't take it with me, so might as well spend it here." But he knew he was in for some good natured ribbing about it anyway. At least he didn't have to do any more shopping.

The two headed to the exit and were surprised to see one of the buses still parked right in the same place as it was before, Bus #2. The lady with the sunflower was talking loudly to a small group of people and Mitch saw that his new friend, Joan, was involved in the conversation. He and Grant walked over to see what the fuss was about. Grant had recognized the flowered sundress, too, but neither of them saw anyone else from Palmer Plantation, not even Babs.

Mitch walked right up to the group and asked what the problem was and Joan, obviously relieved to see him, began telling him that two members of their group were missing, the two other ladies she was traveling with, and she was very worried about them. "Shay and I have been waiting for forty five minutes and we just don't know what to do." The lady with the sunflower interrupted with great drama, saying that she could not hold the bus there any longer.

Always the perfect gentleman and always eager to help a damsel in distress, Mitch took right over. "OK. I will find them. They can't be very far away. Let the bus go. We can take a cab to the hotel. Here," he said, and handed the box of gold trinkets to Grant. "Hold these. I won't be long."

"Mitch, it probably isn't a good idea for you to go wandering around in there. It is like finding a needle in a haystack. Maybe we should go in together. We can each start at a side and meet in the middle. I'll look for a security guard. They probably have lots of people get lost in there. Or we can call the authorities. They will help." He turned to Joan, who seemed to be doing the talking and asked, "Do you remember what they had on? Give me a description."

"Oh, my gosh," Joan said. "I can't even think, I'm so upset. Do you remember, Shay? Did Maureen have on her little backpack? Do you think they have some ID on them?"

Shay knew that Joan was beside herself so she tried to sound calm, in control, but she couldn't remember what they were wearing either, only that they were in Bermuda shorts and sneakers with socks. "They are two women in their sixties, one with rather reddish gray, fluffy hair, and one with very short white hair," pleased with herself that she had said something that was at least intelligent or helpful. "And I believe that the lady with the white hair was wearing a belly bag around her waist."

Grant had begun to write the information down. "What are their names? We will need to give that information to the authorities too."

Each time Joan heard the word "authorities" she became more distraught, scared that perhaps something terrible had happened. "I can't even think straight. It's Maureen Jackson and Wanda . . . ? Wanda . . . ? Oh, Shay, do you remember Wanda's last name? Her husband's name is Howard."

Shay wasn't sure that she had even heard Wanda's last name, and was feeling a little foolish. Here she was half way around the world and didn't even know her traveling companion's names.

Seeing that this wasn't getting anywhere, Grant took Babs' list out of his pocket and started to scan the names.

"I don't see a Wanda on the list. Maureen is here, but there is no Wanda."

Joan went next to him and started to scan his list and then she saw the problem. Wanda was listed as Mrs. Howard Watson. "That's it, right here. Watson, that's her last name."

"Oh," Grant said. "Is her husband with her? Then we are looking for three people, right?"

Shay looked at Joan and for a nanosecond almost made a wisecrack about the late Howard. "No," she said. "Just the two ladies."

The others had boarded the bus, and Jasmeen was on the stairs when Mitch had a great idea. "Give me the sunflower," he demanded. "I will leave it at the front desk in the hotel, but I need it now." The rather surprised Jasmeen did not protest and handed over the sunflower, and Mitch held it high, ready to begin the search. Grant started to go with him, a little reluctant to leave the two ladies standing there alone, especially if there was to be some bad news, but Joan solved that little dilemma.

"Mitch, why don't I go with you and Shay can stay here with Grant so she isn't alone? That way they will be here if the two find their way out."

"OK. Let's set a time for you to meet back here," Grant said, and he handed his notes to Mitch. "Let's say one hour. If we haven't found them by then I will contact the authorities."

Joan and Mitch headed into the Bazaar, Mitch waving the sunflower high above the crowd. They would attack the place in order, up one row and down another. "Now stay close to me," Mitch instructed. "I don't want to lose you too."

Grant stood with Shay, shifting the flimsy box to his other arm along with the bags of his other purchases and looked around for a better place to wait, instead of standing by the curb. "Over there," he said, "Let's go over there by that little wall. We can at least lean on it. This could be a long wait. We can see them if they come out." He also planned to watch for a security guard or a cop and get some information about their procedures, just in case.

Shay gathered the purchases that she and Joan had made and followed Grant to the little wall, relieved to not be waiting by herself or just with Joan, because neither of them knew what to do, and they were both a little upset with the situation. But Grant seemed confident, sure that the two women would show up pretty soon, so she began to relax a little.

"I guess we haven't been properly introduced, have we? Grant Albright," he said. "And I take it you are Shay."

"Yes, Shay Porter. I am pleased to meet you, and grateful for your company. I find this a little scary, standing here in this crowded place and not knowing my way around."

"I'm glad Mitch and I happened along. But just a little advice. Be sure you always have the name of your hotel or ship, and a telephone number on you when you take these day trips. That way you can always get back in a cab or the authorities can return you to the ship or hotel. And always write down the names of the people you are with. Always have that list that Babs gave you. Some women are careless about that sort of thing."

Shay thought it was a little demeaning that right away he started giving her advice, insinuating that she would do something so stupid. Did he think she was a ninny? Of course she had that information with her. But she would remember to always have Babs' list of names with her. She hadn't thought of that.

But he wasn't through yet. "You ladies should have a system too, like a buddy system, not just wondering off willy-nilly. Are you sure they are together, that they didn't separate? Never separate when you are in such a busy place. It is just stupid to make yourself an easy target. There is safety in numbers."

"We went off two by two, just like Noah's ark, because it was impossible to shop in that crowd and have four people together. And I'm pretty sure they would stay together too. You couldn't shake Wanda if you tried. She is probably hanging on to Maureen, complaining about how they do things in these foreign places and how this wouldn't happen if her late husband, Howard, was with her."

"Well, that part is probably true, about the husband. A husband is a good thing to have around on a trip."

"Yes, I suppose so. One would come in handy for carrying the luggage," she laughed.

Grant realized that the lady had just one upped him, but she was pretty darned attractive and he didn't know one damned thing about her except that she was from Palmer Plantation so he decided to tamp it down a notch.

"Here, give me your packages. They must be getting heavy. I'll put yours and ours together in these two bags. We can sort them out later." He casually took the packages from her before she could protest, and set them on the ground by his feet. "There," he continued. "No need to be any more uncomfortable than we already are.

Shay wasn't sure if he meant they were uncomfortable standing there or uncomfortable standing there together, but she was happy to be relieved of the packages. She and Joan had had a ball shopping but hadn't thought too much about carrying the stuff and her arms were beginning to feel the consequences.

They stood there in awkward silence, Shay thinking how silly it was that, here they were, two adults standing on a busy corner in Istanbul and she couldn't think of one single thing to say. But, wow, he was handsome and she was dying to know his story, curious to know what all the excitement was about. She would ask Maureen later. Maureen seemed to know everybody.

Grant broke the silence. "So, have you lived in Palmer Plantation long? Are you with that singles group?"

Mortified that he would just assume that she was with the singles group, super sensitive to the issue, even hurt a little, she said, "No."

Not to be cut off again, he said, "No what?"

"No to both," she said. "No, I haven't lived in Palmer Plantation very long and no, I am not with that singles group."

Obviously this wasn't going very well, but Grant's interest was piqued and his competitive nature, fueled by testosterone, no doubt, was taking over. At least she hadn't said she had a husband, late or otherwise, so that was a good sign. He didn't want to appear aggressive, but he didn't need to get cut off at the knees either. It had been a long time since he had attempted to make a move on a woman, but he didn't remember that it was all that difficult. Maybe he was just a little rusty. Or maybe he should have started with a less attractive one, one who would appreciate his attention. After all, it wasn't that he was interested in her, or in any of them, for that matter. He just wanted to practice, just to get started on the plan. Women in Palmer Plantation were off limits as far as he was concerned.

Adopting a more nonchalant approach, he said, "I've been there a few years. It's a nice place. I wonder how the search is going on in there," keeping the conversational ball in his court. "You are at the Ahmet Hotel with the group, aren't you? I think I saw you there last night."

"Yes, all of the Palmer Plantation people are there. It is a beautiful place. But seeing so many new faces at once makes it almost impossible to remember who you saw."

"I saw you," he said with a wink.

Inside the Bazaar Joan and Mitch were wending their way through the maze of passages and people, hoping for the almost impossible probability of just running into the missing ladies. Mitch held the sunflower high above the crowds and Joan had taken his arm, at his suggestion. "Just a precaution," he had said. "Hold on to me. Two missing ladies are enough." It had been quite a while since Joan had walked arm in arm with a man, feeling that protective strength that was so familiar to her and was so missing in her life now, that sense of belonging to someone, being half of a better, stronger whole, awakening a longing that she had buried as she struggled to find new strength deep inside herself. They continued their search for nearly an hour, going up one passageway and down another, but it was pretty obvious that this was probably an exercise in futility, when the loud familiar sound of call to prayers echoed through the place. "That's what we need," Mitch said. "Something to draw attention to the sunflower, some kind of noisemaker. I saw a shop that had a bunch of stuff in it like toys. Maybe I can find something to make noise with."

"Mitch, we will never find a specific shop, never find that place again. Maybe we should just ask someone for help." Mitch engaged the man in the next shop in conversation and the man just nonchalantly dialed his phone and within minutes two security guards were at their sides. One was carrying a megaphone type of contraption and the other was writing down the information that Joan was giving him. The one security guard handed the megaphone to Mitch.

"Sir, you can walk up and down the rows calling their names. Sometimes that helps to be heard. And we will give out the descriptions to guards all over the place. Also all exits will be watched. See here, the number, sir. Be looking for the shop numbers." Mitch had never noticed, but each shop had a rather large number prominently displayed. "That is how you know where you are. We will call you on this phone when we find them." He pointed to the megaphone, which turned out to be some sort of walkie-talkie with a loud speaker. "Please do not be leaving the Bazaar. Be waiting for our call."

"Thank goodness they will help. At least there is something positive we can be doing," Joan said, relief in her voice. Mitch took the megaphone in one hand, and still holding the sunflower in the other, said "testing, testing," checking out the operation, and then he put it to his mouth and let out the loudest Tarzan yell she had ever heard.

"Oh my Lord, Mitch. That is enough to wake the dead. Does it have to be that loud?"

"It has to be loud to be heard over all the other noise in here. The idea is that they will hear me and look to see where the noise is coming from and then they will see the sunflower. Let's walk slowly and I will keep making a racket," and he let loose with another Tarzan imitation. By now many people were looking at them, some even grinning with recognition of that familiar sound known worldwide. Joan felt a little foolish but Mitch was not to be dissuaded. They continued down another row, and another, Mitch yelling and holding the sunflower high, when faintly, almost imperceptibly, came, a distant response. Thinking it might just be an echo, Mitch let loose again, and this time the response came more clearly, sounding closer. He drew a deep breath and let loose a holler that Tarzan himself would have been proud of, and the response came again, clearly a woman's voice now, but a damned good Tarzan yell. Mitch and Joan rounded a corner and he was just about to holler again, when they heard them. The two women were headed right toward them, calling "Here we are! Here we are. Wait! Wait! Here we are!"

"Oh, thank goodness, thank goodness we have found you," Joan squealed through tears of relief. "Thank goodness you are alright."

"Of course we are alright. We were just running late because Wanda kept stopping to buy things and then we couldn't figure out how to get out of here," Maureen said, but relief was evident in her voice. Wanda had been leading the charge, spying them first, and had practically knocked Mitch down with a bear hug. "I told Maureen we turned the wrong way, but she wouldn't listen. She knows I have traveled more than she has, but, no, she wouldn't listen."

"Well, the important thing is that we have found you," Mitch said. "Did you hear the racket I was making or did you just see the sunflower?"

"It was the racket. We didn't even think to look for the sunflower, but when Wanda heard that Tarzan call she just went berserk, just went nuts. Freaked out! Said it was Howard. Said he had come to rescue her. And then she started doing it. Just kept hollering like Tarzan."

"Well, it was Howard," Wanda said. "Howard loved Tarzan and made that sound all the time. We would call to each other that way. He's the one who taught it to me. I can do it just like Carol Burnett. I knew right away that it was Howard. Either that or some crazy call to prayer. You never know in these foreign countries. But I knew it was Howard and I had to answer him. It worked too. We just followed the call. And here you were, Mitch. I think Howard wants me to stay close to you in case he needs to call me again."

The other three exchanged knowing glances and just let Howard take all the credit.

Ataturk Airport, Finally

J odee Jordan had survived worse things in her life, but there was something about this long flight that had just about done her in. "My God," she thought. "Where the hell is this place? I could have gone to the moon and back quicker." She knew about her long flights, and she knew about her layovers, and she knew that she would be arriving in Istanbul around 6:30, but what she didn't know, what she had forgotten about, was the time difference, that the clock would keep being set forward as she flew eastward. She had no idea what time it was. All she knew was that it was taking a damned long time to get to Istanbul. Scrunched into a coach seat with her large handbag at her feet, hungry, miserable, and tired, she half expected to see the Statue of Liberty greeting her when she arrived. They didn't get any more tired, poor, or huddled than she was on these flights.

At the announcement that they were finally there, she began to gather her things. She smoothed her platinum hair and added some lipstick, carefully examining her reflection. She had been a real beauty in her younger years but the ups and downs of her career and her personal life had taken their toll; her weight had crept up, only fifteen pounds, but she felt like a blimp. Her platinum hair was still thick and lush but she couldn't afford to have it done regularly because she opted instead to spend her money on her nails. She wore her hair short enough to be above her collar, but it was full and hung in a casual wave that complimented her high cheekbones. Her makeup came from the drugstore, but she was pretty handy applying it and the final result was striking, belying the self-conscious, insecure woman underneath. Her motto was, when in doubt, add some bling, and that was pretty much what she was about, bling, sometimes over-doing it but needing the boost to her sagging self-esteem.

She was stretching her foot under the seat in front of her, trying to retrieve her shoe, when the man in the aisle seat next to her, noticing her struggle, stood and politely asked the lady in front of him for assistance. He handed Jodee her shoe and said, with a twinkle in his eye, "Madam, if the shoe fits you get to marry the prince."

"He was so charming. So polite," she thought. "Really a charmer." He had sat next to her on this last lap, a kind speaking, older gentleman, and they had kept good company. She hated to complain about anything to him because he had come all the way to Istanbul from Las Vegas so she kept her discomforts to herself, even though he didn't seem nearly as tired as she was. He had bought her a drink, stood graciously each time she needed to get up, even helped put her bag in the bin, joking about how heavy it was. And he was interested, asking about her affairs, where she was going, where she was from, and she found herself sharing her plans, and sharing her fears, and her history, and her crappy financial situation. He had already suggested that they share a cab from the airport to the Ahmet hotel. They had only a short wait in the immigration line and she noticed that his passport looked different than hers, a lot thicker, but she didn't comment. When they arrived at the hotel, he reached for his wallet and insisted on paying for the cab. They were met at the door by a uniformed valet who spoke with the man briefly and escorted them to the reception desk. There the gentleman engaged in a brief conversation with the man behind the counter. Jodee presented her papers to the woman who had come to assist her, but there seemed to be some problem with the computer because the man who was assisting the gentleman came over and spoke to the lady on the computer, apparently trying to help solve the problem, and then returned to the gentleman and said something to him. Jodee was feeling a little anxious about the delay, when the gentleman turned toward her and said pleasantly, "Nice meeting you, lady from Palm Springs. I wish you much success with your new endeavor. Perhaps we shall see each other on the ship."

"Jodee Jordan," she said. "It was very nice to meet you, too. I hope you come to hear me one night."

"Yes, I will. I plan to do that."

It was the first that he had mentioned that he was taking a cruise, that he was going on the same ship, and she wondered why he hadn't mentioned it sooner. She probably wouldn't have told him so much if she had known. She thought he was just some stranger, just someone on the flight, someone she would never see again. "Me and my big mouth," she said to herself. She didn't even know his name. The woman who was checking her in came right over with papers in her hand, apologizing for the delay, and handed her the little envelope with the key card. "Please enjoy your visit to Istanbul. It is a pleasure to have you here, Ms. Jordan." A valet was already at her heels with her luggage, ready to escort her to the elevators that would take them to the grand mezzanine where the finest suites were located, where he would be opening the double doors with a flourish, and showing her around the beautiful suite, asking about her comfort and inquiring about her wishes.

She opened her pocketbook to get out some tip money for the valet and offered him a five dollar bill but he refused it. "No, no, lady. It has already been done," and he excused himself and left the suite. She wouldn't touch anything, wouldn't sit down, not even on the toilet. She would go back downstairs as soon as the coast was clear and straighten things out. There was no way she could afford to pay for this palace. How this happened she didn't know, but no way could she stay here. She glanced around the beautiful suite with its elegant furnishings, its opulent bathroom with a huge chandelier, over-sized fixtures and exquisite tile work.

"Wow, this place is beautiful. I can't imagine being able to live like this. Just imagine, a life with no problems, all beauty, your every whim provided. I feel like a queen, or a princess," and then she laughed at that thought. "Wasn't that what the gentleman had said? If the shoe fits I get to marry the prince. He should see me now!"

She took one last look around the suite and then headed downstairs to the reception desk. The lady came right over to help her and Jodee began. "I am so sorry to trouble you, but there is some mistake. I have been taken to the wrong room."

Puzzled, the lady went back to the computer to see what mistake had been made. "No Ma'am, everything is in order. You are in the Princess Suite, Ma'am."

"But, I mean the mistake is I am not supposed to be in the Princess Suite. I am supposed to be in a regular room, just a plain average room."

"No, Ma'am" the lady insisted. "There is no mistake. Are you unhappy with the Princess Suite? Is there something you need? We will be happy to assist you."

Several women had approached the reception area, laughing, talking excitedly, asking about some dinner or something, and the lady behind the counter excused herself and retrieved a paper and handed it to the man who was trying to solve their problem.

Standing next to Jodee was a man holding a ridiculous sunflower on top of a yardstick, and another man, a really handsome one, was standing there holding a bunch of shopping bags, listening, and Jodee hoped that he hadn't overheard her problem. When the lady returned her attention to Jodee, she said, "Would you prefer a different suite, Madam? We would be happy to move you to another suite. It is no bother."

"No, I want you to move me to a regular room. Is that so hard? Just a plain regular room. Can't you do that?"

"No, ma'am. You see, we are all filled up. So many people here. You must stay in the Princess Suite."

"Look, miss, listen very closely. I cannot pay for the Princess Suite. I have no money!" Jodee was getting a little worked up and Grant was taking it all in, enjoying it. Jodee continued, louder, "Now get it through your cotton pickin' head. I cannot pay for the damned Princess Suite."

The lady picked up her phone and called someone. Jodee couldn't understand a word of it, but within seconds a man approached, probably a manager or something, but he was grinning. "Madam," he said. "Please not to be so worried. The Princess Suite has been provided for your pleasure. We are all wanting you to be enjoying our hotel. You will not be paying anything. It has been provided for you. You are not to be paying for anything. It has already been paid."

Jodee was flabbergasted. "Who?" she asked. "Who paid for this? Nobody here even knows me. Are you sure, absolutely sure? It is a wonderful surprise and I don't want to appear to be ungrateful, but who would do this? Are you sure there is no mistake?"

"Quite sure, Madam, but we are not to be telling. We are not to be telling, Ms. Jordan. Shall I escort you to your suite now?"

"No. No thank you. I think I need a drink first."

Grant watched her head for the Golden Horn Lounge. Mitch had handed over the sunflower and returned to the ladies who were excitedly telling him that there was still time, he could still go with them to the planned traditional Turkish dinner and belly dancing show. "Hurry," Maureen said. "The van is coming now. We bought a ticket for you. Are you sure you don't want to come, Grant?"

About the last thing in the world Grant felt like doing right now was going to some hyped up tourist dinner show with the Palmer Plantation gang, so he continued to beg off. "No, I think I'll just get ready for tomorrow. I have to go over a few things. But have a great time. And stay together. No more lost ladies for today."

Wanda spoke right up. "We'll be safe. Don't worry about us. We have Mitch to take care of us from now on."

Mitch exchanged a look with Grant and shrugged his shoulders as if to say, "What could I do?" But Grant wasn't buying it. Mitch was in hog heaven. Grant watched them climb into the van and waved them off and then turned toward the Golden Horn Lounge. He was going to buy a lady a drink.

He sauntered into the lounge, made a quick assessment of things, and then took a seat at the small table next to his target. He still had all the packages with him, his and Mitch's, and Shay's, and all the stuff from Maureen and Wanda that had been handed to him at the last minute. He crammed it all together in three bags and put them on the vacant chair next to him, catching her eye as he did so, commenting, "Beautiful day, isn't it? Perfect for sightseeing."

He was the most handsome guy she had ever seen, at least if you didn't count that guitar player with the Hot Balls Band she sang with thirty years ago. Of course, she was young then, but this guy was jaw dropping gorgeous and she straightened a little in her seat. "Yes, it is lovely. I've only just arrived and haven't done any sightseeing yet. I'll only be here a short time."

Warming up, he said, "Do you have business here or is this a pleasure trip? I hope you get to enjoy some of the city."

Jodee was the talkative type and had never met a stranger, so, eager to keep things moving along, she continued. "I'm leaving tomorrow. I doubt that I get out of this hotel. How about you? Are you going to be here awhile longer?"

"No, I'm leaving tomorrow too. He leaned back in his seat and turned slightly toward her and took a sip of his martini. She took a last swallow of her drink, holding her glass toward him. "Well, here's to you."

Seeing her empty glass, his opportunity, he said, "Let me order you a refill. What are you having? It's nice to have someone to share a cocktail with, isn't it?" She offered no resistance whatsoever, and the attentive waiter responded immediately, understanding perfectly well what the hand signals meant when Grant pointed to her glass. He returned with a vodka gimlet for her and another martini for Grant.

"Now, for a proper toast," Grant said. "Here's to a lovely lady and to Istanbul."

"And to you too and to Istanbul," she said.

"And where is the lovely lady headed off to so soon? Are you headed home?" he continued, starting to gain a little confidence.

"No, I'm on the road," she laughed. "I'm getting on a cruise ship tomorrow, the Atheneè."

"Really? I'm getting on the Atheneè tomorrow too. But it's more like going on the water, isn't it."

"Well, I suppose so, but in my business it's called going on the road or being on tour."

"Oh. What will you be doing on the road?"

"I'm a singer. I'll be appearing with two others, in a small trio. One is a keyboardist and the other is a guitar player."

"No kidding. Have you been doing it very long, performing on cruise ships?"

"No, this is my first time and I'm scared to death. I've never met the other two in the group. I'm a last minute substitute. They lost their chirp, so I'm it."

"Chirp? I never heard that expression."

"It's very common in the business. It means the girl singer with the group. Sometimes she's called a canary. They're real old terms from the big band era. That was the best time for a chirp, really good bands and terrific music. Today it's just a lot of crap."

"Yeah. I love that kind of music too, stuff from Dorsey and Goodman, and Glenn Miller. Kids today don't even know what good music is. I love the great musicals, and Sinatra and Cole Porter. Do you sing that stuff?"

"It's my favorite but it's hard to get booked for that sound today. It helps if you have your own pianist, but I don't, so I have to try and fit in with someone else's style. I sure hope I can make it work with this group. I'm trying to make a comeback."

Grant got caught up in the conversation, trying to get as much information as possible and mentally checking off items on his list. She was easy to talk to, funny, a great throaty laugh, a little bawdy, ribald, but Grant liked that in a woman. She was fun to be around and they continued to talk for about a half hour, laughing together like old friends.

She thought he was pretty knowledgeable about music, very interested in the business and very interested in her new gig and she soon was telling him the whole story, everything about her busted career, and her failed marriages, and her desperate financial situation, and about Leighanna. There was no other attraction between them, just the music stuff. She knew he wasn't trying to pick her up, wasn't interested. But, boy, was he good looking.

"Well, nice talking to you," she said. "I should probably be heading to my room and get some sleep. It's been a long day. Tomorrow is a workday for me." She stood to leave and then turned toward him and offered her hand. "I'm Jodee Jordan. I hope we see each other on the boat sometime."

"Grant Albright," he said. "Nice meeting you, Jodee. I'll look for you and catch a performance. Come on. I'll walk you to the elevator and we can ride up together. What floor are you on?"

"The mezzanine. You gotta hear this," she laughed. "There is some mix up somewhere and they've put me in the most fabulous room, a gorgeous suite. I tried to tell them but they wouldn't listen. You should see the place. Come on, I'll show it to you. They said it was all paid for and everything. It will just take a minute. It's really swanky."

Grant didn't hesitate a second. This was too good to be true. Wait till he told Mitch that he was invited to a woman's room. He wouldn't believe it. He was going to give Mitch a run for his money, just leave him hanging, not tell him for days that he just went to see the room. He would describe the suite and everything, make him think he got lucky. Then the pressure would be off.

The Atheneè

All new personnel were to board at the forward gangway at ten o'clock and be ready for an orientation meeting at ten thirty. Mitch and Grant met in the lobby, had a quick cup of coffee, and headed for the van that would take them to the ship. The ship had docked at 6:00 a.m. and would start disembarkation around 8:30. New passengers would start boarding around 1:00. And then it would begin.

"Post time," Grant commented. "The horses are nearing the post."

"Yep. Time to go to work. We should get a good start on things today."

"You know, Mitch. I got invited to a woman's room last night. Met her in the lounge while you were out with your harem watching the belly dancers. She's staying in a ritzy suite in the Ahmet. Boy, you should have seen it. It was huge with chandeliers all over the place, oversized fixtures in the bathroom, tile everywhere. Beautiful furniture, big king sized bed. It was really something."

"You shitt'n me? That really happen?"

"Yep, I'm way ahead of you, Mitch."

They boarded the ship and were given a packet of information and headed to their stateroom, surprised to see that it was a lovely standard room with a fairly large window, a bath with walk in shower, and pretty spacious.

"Well, which side do you want, Mitch? I don't care, so take your pick. It's been a long time since I've had a roommate, since college or maybe on a golf outing a few times. It seems funny."

"It feels strange to me too. But I got used to bunking with a lot of other guys in the army. Women travel together like this all the time and no one thinks anything of it, but when two guys do it, people talk. Well, I guess we are just like the women, just two widows traveling together."

"We're widowers, Mitch. They call men widowers."

"I know. I hate that word."

"Me too."

There was a pause, as if the word itself had silenced them with a blow, had made its painful appearance when they least expected it, sucker punched them, briefly knocking the wind out of them. Grant drew in a big gulp of air. "This really isn't a bad room. I thought we might end up way down below without a window. I'll just put my stuff on this side. We can unpack later. Let's go. It's time for the meeting."

When Mitch had first come up with the idea of a trip together, it was a hard sell to Grant. Mitch thought it would be a great way for Grant to get back on his feet and Mitch was wanting someone to go on a trip with, anywhere, just a trip. He wouldn't travel alone so he had been considering one of the Palmer Plantation trips, but he didn't want to go by himself. Grant didn't like the idea at all, had no interest in Turkey or Greece, or any of the other places in the brochure, but when Mitch hatched the idea of them actually working on a ship, Grant began to listen.

Mitch had come over to watch a movie with Grant one night, just keeping company, just being there for him, but he had arrived a little early. When the doorbell wasn't answered, he cracked the door open and then stopped dead. Beautiful piano music was coming from the study. He knew there was a piano in there so he walked on into the foyer and looked in to see who was playing. He had no idea that Grant played, it had never entered his mind, but even he could tell that this was special. Grant really could play. Not just sort of good, but really good. And then it hit him. They could get jobs on a boat. Grant could play the piano and Mitch would be one of the roving ambassadors he read about. So Grant made a deal with Mitch. "You get me a job as a piano player and I will go." So Mitch worked on it, arranged for a CD to be made, sent it in, went along to Miami for Grant's audition, negotiated for his ambassador job, did it all. This sort of thing was right up his alley. He had been a wheeler and dealer all his life, knew how to get things done, and loved a good challenge. His juices were flowing and by golly, he got them the perfect gigs on the beautiful Atheneè.

They were to attend different meetings. Mitch went to the hospitality staff meeting and Grant went to the entertainment meeting where he was introduced, given a folder full of requirements and expectations of a staff member, dress, rules and regs stuff, and his assignment. He would be playing in the Casablanca Lounge, nightly from 9:00—until. He was also expected to play for functions as assigned, such as a reception or church service, or private party. And he was expected to be available for day trips when needed, to ride along on a bus as a representative of the ship. When not actively assigned, he was to be a presence around the ship, always appropriately dressed, visiting with the passengers, joining them in the dining room, signing autographs and posing for pictures.

Mitch was hearing the same stuff, only he was assigned to a hospitality desk for four hours each day. He was to study the manual, familiarize himself with the ship and be a source of information for the many passengers. When not at the hospitality desk his job was pretty much the same as Grant's. They were going to be two very busy guys.

Next they were to report to photography for photo ID's which were to be attached to a lanyard and worn at all times. Grant also needed to sit for some publicity shots that would appear on poster sized tripods placed around the ship. Several sport coats and a tux were waiting for him to slip on for different shots. That was probably why they asked for his size on one of the many forms Mitch had filled out. As they left, the photographer said, "Nice pictures, Mr. Albright. Your performance wardrobe will be delivered to your state room today. If there are any problems or you need anything else just call wardrobe. They'll have whatever you want."

"I wasn't expecting to be treated like a star, Mitch. I guess they were afraid I wouldn't bring along the right clothes."

"Well, did you? Did you pack the right stuff? I think the stuff I have is mostly OK, but it says here that we can't wear shorts. I might need to buy some pants."

"I didn't bring a tux, but I did bring a few sport coats. I wonder if I'm supposed to wear a tie all the time. Jesus, Mitch, we may be in over our heads. This whole thing was supposed to be a lark, not something serious. What did you tell them on the application? Did you say something that sounded like we wanted a regular job? I thought the audition was to confirm the validity of the CD, just so they knew I could actually play, but now I think they are expecting a real pro. Didn't you tell them I have never played professionally? I don't want to make an ass out of myself."

"The application asked why you wanted to play on a cruise ship and I didn't know what to put so I said to further your career. Where it asked for professional experience, I put in 'extensive'. I didn't think it mattered what I put down. Once they heard you, they would be happy to have you. What difference does it make if you don't know what you're doing? Nobody ever listens to the piano player anyway, Grant."

"Yeah, you're right. They'll probably be talking and laughing and drinking and won't even hear me. Let's find the Casablanca Lounge. I want to get a look at the piano. I sure hope they didn't give me some piece of junk to play on."

There was no piece of junk anywhere on the beautiful Athenee. Standing in the back right corner of the lounge was a lovely ebony grand, 5'8", a perfect size for the room. Grant could feel his heart pounding in his chest and went right over and sat down, adjusting himself on the bench, and then gently touching the keyboard. "Speak to me, baby. Sing for Daddy," he murmured, and started to play.

No one had been more surprised to see Grant Albright at the orientation meeting than Jodee Jordan. Surprised probably isn't the best word to describe her feelings. She was dumbfounded, embarrassed, and furious. She and Grant had had a great time visiting in the lounge at the Ahmet Hotel. They had talked about everything and she had been impressed by his musical knowledge and flattered that he was so interested in her career. He had not mentioned one word about having this gig on the Atheneè, and here he was being introduced as the headliner in the Casablanca Lounge, appearing nightly. And she had told him everything. Everything! How hard up she was and how desperate she was, how terrified she was. She had even invited him to come see her perform. "Me and my big mouth!" she lamented. "When will I ever learn?" It wouldn't be so bad if he didn't already know everything, but it was too late now. She wanted to kill him. She hadn't even been introduced at the meeting. Her instructions said to report to rehearsal studio #4 at 3:00. The trio would be playing in the Fez Lounge at 5:00, their regular performance time. She headed for the Fez, planning to take a quick look before unpacking her music, but first she would find the Casablanca Lounge.

Soft piano music was wafting into the hallway. Jodee stood and listened briefly, and then slipped quietly in and took a seat, just looking at him. Another man was seated in a corner but it was dark in there and his back was toward her. The man she had seen with Grant yesterday at the Ahmet Hotel, the guy with the stupid sunflower on a stick, was sitting near the piano. Neither of them noticed her. Grant continued to play, oblivious to all of them, concentrating on the piano. It was obvious to her what he was doing. She had heard it for years, the sound of a musician getting acquainted with an instrument, trying different sounds, some louder, some softer, listening, listening to the room, listening for response, and adjusting his touch. It was the difference between good and very good and Jodee knew very good when she heard it, and she heard it now. He continued to play a few more lines from *Phantom*, and then stood up.

"Great. Just bright enough. I think I can make out OK with it. Sounds really good. We better go unpack while we have a chance, Mitch." He turned toward the door, heading right in Jodee's direction. Grant recognized her immediately.

"Jodee," he called. "Jodee, it's so nice to see you. Come over here and meet my friend. Jodee, this is my friend Mitch McConnell. Mitch, this is Jodee Jordan. She's the lady I told you about who had the swanky suite at the Ahmet."

She held out her hand to Mitch, who took it in his and held it while he said, "Nice to meet you, Miss Jordan. Grant told me all about you. Seems you two hit it right off."

Jodee nearly died, wondering what all he knew, but said, "Yes, we had a great time but Grant kept a big secret from me, didn't you Grant."

"I'm really sorry about that, Jodee. I wanted to tell you, I was going to tell you, but it was embarrassing. I didn't know what to say. You were so professional and so experienced about everything. It's the first time for me. I've never done anything like this before. Honest. I really appreciated some of the tips you gave me. I didn't want you to know how inexperienced I was. So now you know. I'm not all that great, either. I hope you weren't disappointed. I'm just doing it for the fun of it. I can't keep up with you and all of your experience, but let's get together again."

She guessed she wouldn't kill him after all. "I'll be in The Fez at five o'clock every day. Come by. I'll look for you. And you too, Mitch. I look forward to getting to know you better too."

Mitch couldn't believe the conversation he had just overheard. "What was that all about, all that stuff about you not having any experience and how embarrassed you were? And her being a pro! You made it with a hooker, didn't you? That doesn't count. Hookers don't count. That's not even fair. She's a hooker, isn't she?"

"She's not a hooker. She's a chirp. She counts."

* * *

In stateroom 602, Joan and Shay were unpacking and settling in. The room was lovely and spacious and they were delighted with everything, happy to finally be on board the beautiful Atheneè, and eagerly anticipating a great trip.

"I'm so happy that I decided to come, Shay. This is going to work out great. I was so nervous about meeting you. That first day on the bus, I'm sure I talked your ear off. Wanda and Maureen wanted me to take this trip and then Chrissie started in on me. I don't think I would have come if Chrissie hadn't mentioned you to me and asked me to be your roommate. She is so fond of you and I can tell she respects you, too. Sometimes it is hard for me to get information out of her but I know she is having a hard time. Do you think she is doing alright?"

"She gets a little lonely sometimes but I think she's alright. She seems to have her head screwed on right. I don't think you have to worry about her, Joan."

"Well, it's hard for a mother. She doesn't always want to hear what I have to say. She was always the one who could handle everything, but this is really hard on her. My other daughter would be a basket case if that happened to her, but Chrissie is tougher. I just don't know how to help her. I know from experience how hard it can be to wind up alone and I wish she could find someone nice. I'm so glad you are right next door to her so she has someone to talk to. You know what it was about, don't you?"

"I'm not sure I know all the details, but she has told some of it to me."

"Maybe you can give her some advice about a successful life as a single, Shay. I'm afraid she'll find some guy on the rebound. And this internet stuff really scares me. I know she goes on line to some of the dating sites. Can you imagine? She has even suggested that I try it. Me! Her Mother! She thinks I don't have enough social life, but she has no idea how hard it is at this age. She thinks that some perfectly wonderful man is just going to come walking into my life from out on the internet. She's such a romantic. It's going to get her in trouble. You have to be realistic about your situation, don't you think? You have to make plans for your life, not depend on some romantic notions about happily ever after. Like you did, Shay. Go on with things, make a life for yourself. And now here she is taking up real estate. What future is there in that, for heaven's sake? She was such a good student in school. She needs something steady and secure, like teaching. It was perfect for you, wasn't it? Security and good hours, and summers off. Maybe you can steer her toward that. And she needs to stop worrying about me. She is driving me nuts. I am just fine, perfectly fine."

"I know, Joan. She tells me things about you and how she wishes you would find someone, how you need to get out more. She does the same thing to me. She even feels sorry for me, although she doesn't come right out and say that. She keeps telling me I need to get out more, kick up my heels, whatever that means. And lately she's been trying to spruce me up some. 'Let's go shopping,' she'll say, and then she steers me to departments full of clothes meant for a much younger woman. I'm fifty-two, for crying out loud. And she has offered to show me how to go to those dating sites. She thinks I'm really desperate. She certainly is a romantic. She thinks men are the answer to all our problems. She is darling, though, Joan. She'll have someone else in no time."

"She says the same things about you, Shay. She thinks you are so pretty and she is sure that you have some deep dark secret, probably a broken heart from some lost love, and that is why you are afraid to love again. Is she right or did you just not want marriage or did it just never happen? Some women choose not to marry, but usually a girl as attractive as you gets grabbed by some guy, he just sweeps her off her feet. That's what happened to me. Ted just swept me off my feet. I wasn't even thinking about marriage, and there he was one day. I'm a nurse. Did Chrissie tell you? Well, her father was an intern at the hospital and he came into the nurse's station one night mad as a wet hen about something. Anyway, I went to his patient's room to assist him with something or other, and that was it. We were inseparable from then on, till the day he died. When it comes, it strikes you like lightening. I wonder if it's true that lightning never strikes twice. Lots of people in Palmer are on second marriages. You know, Maureen is real active in the singles group and is always pushing it. She says she's not interested in meeting anyone, but I think she is. She is more aggressive than I am and has even had some dates. I haven't had one single date in five years. Do you go on dates, Shay? Do men ask you out? I know it is none of my business, but I was just wondering if you wait for a man to call you or do you indicate to him that you would like him to? I wouldn't know how to begin dating. Everything is so different and men expect too much. I'm not sure I'm ready for that."

"No, Joan, no to all of that," Shay laughed. "I didn't choose to be single, and no, I don't date because I don't meet many men and no one asks me out. It's just that simple. I gave up all interest in that a long time ago. I'm not spending my time waiting for the phone to ring. And I am not dependent on a man for anything. I am quite content with my single state. It is not exactly *Sex in the City,* but it's the life I have. I am completely satisfied." Shay hated these conversations that forced her to talk about herself. God, how she hated being the poster child for spinsterhood. If you looked up old maid in the dictionary her picture surely would be there. Maybe she should write a book, one of those how to books, how to be happy alone, what it's really like to be single when all you ever wanted was to be somebody's wife, somebody's mother, somebody's lover. How to live your life after you have killed somebody.

"We're going to have a great time, Shay. This trip is perfect for us. We'll have a wonderful time together." Joan didn't believe one thing about Shay's satisfaction with her life. For some women it was perfect to be single. But Shay Porter wasn't one of them. Chrissie was right. Some man had broken Shay's heart. What Shay needed was to kick up her heels a little.

"When we finish with the unpacking let's go explore the ship. I've never been on a cruise ship before, Joan. What time is that welcome cocktail party for Babs' group? We have to find the room she has booked. It's near the library, I think. And then there is the sail-away party for everyone when we set sail at six o'clock. I'm not really much of a party person, Joan, so if you want to go on with the others, that's fine with me. I think I might spend the time taking in the sights, unless you think it would be rude of me not to attend."

"Of course you must go, Shay. For heaven's sake. It will be just the people from Palmer Plantation at Babs' party. You've already met most of them and I know they want to get to know you better. Everyone will be there. I'll call Maureen and see what time they want to go. Sail away parties are just everyone on the whole ship gathering for a drink and watching the shoreline disappear. You don't want to miss that. I overheard Mitch telling Maureen to be on the starboard side for the view of Istanbul. That's the right side, I think."

"I can never remember which is right and which is left, either. It will probably take us a few days to find our way around. It isn't one of those mega ships with four thousand passengers, but it is plenty big. We have sixteen hundred I think I read. They are serving lunch on the Lido deck until three today. We can find where it is and get a bite too. We don't have dinner until seven thirty."

"That's only for tonight because of the sail away party. Maureen already signed us up for early dinner the rest of the trip. She usually takes care of signing us up for everything. Did Grant bring our packages to you last night?"

"No, didn't he give them to you?"

"I haven't seen him today. Mitch was carrying all the stuff that Maureen and Wanda bought. Can you believe it? Wanda actually bought all that stuff after her big speech about never buying anything in a foreign country. Maureen said she just whipped out that credit card and bought everything she saw with a tulip on it. She bought about ten scarves and some tiles and several canvases with paintings of tulips. I saw Mitch hand those bags to Grant when he decided to come to dinner with us."

"He put our packages together while we were waiting for you and Mitch. He said we could sort them all out later. It was much easier to carry them in fewer bags, but we were in such a hurry to leave for the dinner show he just held on to them. I haven't seen him today either. He must have it all in his stateroom. They left so early this morning he probably decided to give them to us on board. We can get them when we find out his stateroom number."

"How did that go?"

"How did what go?"

"You know. Standing there with him, waiting for us. Did he tell you anything? He seems nice enough. All the women are atwitter about him, but no one knows much about him, only that he is Mitch's friend. All we know is what happened."

"He was perfectly polite. We talked mostly about Istanbul. He really likes Istanbul. That was it, just small talk. I don't think he was very happy being stuck there with me. What did happen?"

"His wife died. It was so sad. They just got to Palmer Plantation, built a big beautiful house in the new section. It was pretty quick. So young, just so young. Only fifty one, I think. He's only in his fifties, too. You certainly don't expect anything like that when you are so young. Being young should make it easier for him, but men usually prefer younger ones too. There sure aren't very many younger ones in their fifties at Palmer. He'll probably sell."

"How long ago was it?"

"Over a year now, I think. At least he waited that long. Some of the men don't wait long at all. In just a few months they are right back out on the market. Maureen keeps me filled in on all of that. But no one knows much about Grant. He is a mystery man. Everyone knows Mitch, though. He seems so nice and friendly and kind."

"Did you know his wife?"

"Whose, Mitch's? No. I never met him before either. Maureen said she's been gone awhile now, maybe a few years."

I meant Grant's wife. Did you know her? Did you ever see her?"

"No, I never met her. She was a very good golfer, I hear. Played a lot of golf and was in several other things too. But she got sick pretty soon after they moved there so nobody knew her very well. I heard she was cute, the outdoorsy type, jogged and worked out at the fitness center, stuff like that. All he did was play golf, I think. He sure is handsome. He won't last long."

"Yes, handsome he is. I suppose the handsome ones do go pretty fast."

They continued unpacking and making small talk. Maureen and Wanda arrived at their door and Joan welcomed them with a hug and they all oohed and aahed about the room, making comparisons, planning what they would wear tonight. Dressy slacks and tops was the consensus, with much ado paid to whether Maureen would have time to wash her hair before. It sounded more like they were going on the prowl rather than to a little cocktail party with friends. Shay just listened.

"I wonder if Mitch will be there. Isn't he just the nicest guy?"

"And did you see Babs sidling up to him last night?"

74

"Well, I think there is such a thing as being too aggressive, don't you?"

"I'm going to get him to join the singles group if it's the last thing I do. I am on a mission."

"Do you think he is interested in her?" Joan asked.

"Interested in who?"

"In Babs. He sat by her again last night. And at lunch, too. Maybe they are seeing each other."

"I doubt that. I would have heard about it if he was," Maureen insisted. "I think Babs is just out to land a big fish. Mitch is quite wealthy, you know. Owned BMW dealerships all over New Jersey. Or was it Lexus? Maybe it was Lexus."

"He drives a Lexus," Wanda said. "My late husband, Howard, said you can tell a lot about a man by the car he drives. And the house is gorgeous. I heard he hasn't changed a thing. I did several arrangements for him."

"What! You never told us that, Wanda. You've been in?"

"I don't think it's appropriate to talk about the people I do arrangements for, but I did several for the memorial service. I get in a lot of houses that way."

"Where is Salt Flower Drive? I never heard you speak of him before," Joan asked.

"You know, right off of Palmer Drive. Everyone knows Mitch. He is a great guy. I'm surprised he has lasted this long."

"Did you get in Grant's? I hear it is a showplace too."

"I made several arrangements for her when she first moved in, silk flower pieces that were beautiful, if I say so myself. She spent a fortune decorating. She went so fast I don't think too many got in to see the place. I never met him until this trip. It's just so sad, him being all alone in that big gorgeous house."

"What did he do? Does anyone even know where they are from?"

"I never heard anyone say. Nobody knows much about him. All I know is that he is Mitch's good friend. They play a lot of golf together."

"He's going to be so lonely on this trip."

"Poor guy. So young for such a thing to happen."

"I wonder if he will be at the cocktail party."

The four headed out for the grand tour of the good ship Atheneè. Wanda was not only an excellent floral designer, but she could also read a map, which the others always found a little challenging, so she was always the navigator on all of their little excursions. She took the lead. The plan was to first locate the room for tonight's cocktail party, then find the Lido deck where lunch was being served. They were lost in five minutes.

"Well, let's just head this way until we find something we see on the map," suggested Maureen.

"I think it's by the library," Joan added.

"Here it is," Wanda said, pointing to it on the map. "That's starboard, isn't it? That's the left side. I'm pretty sure, or maybe it's the other side. It depends which way you are going, doesn't it? Are we headed toward the front or the back? Which way is the boat pointing?"

"Let's find some elevators," Shay suggested. "There is usually a directory posted by elevators."

They rounded a corner to a bank of elevators and stopped dead in their tracks.

"OH MY GOD! Look at that!"

"I can't believe it. WOW!"

"I didn't know anything about this. Did any of you?"

"Holy Cow."

"He is drop dead gorgeous!"

Several other women were clustered around making similar comments, admiring the rather large poster mounted on a tripod right at the entrance to the elevators. And there he was, in a dark jacket with a pale blue tie, seated at a piano, smiling right at them, the bold letters above the picture announcing the keyboard magic of Grant Albright. Under the picture it said, "Appearing nightly in the Casablanca Lounge. 9:00—Until."

Wanda was already looking at the map. "Where's the Casablanca Lounge?"

The Casablanca Lounge

Grant and Mitch had their maps out and made a quick once around the ship, noting where the dining rooms were and the various lounges, the pools, the spa, and the Theatre Atheneè, where the big shows were. They located the hospitality desk that Mitch was assigned to. It was around the corner from the entrance to the Grand Dining Room Atheneè, conveniently located for those coming and going to dinner. Mitch stopped by the excursions desk at the main reception center and talked to the excursion director who immediately retrieved a thick binder of all the daily excursions offered during the trip so that Mitch could familiarize himself with the information and be prepared to answer the many questions that he would receive.

"Good God, I'll be up all night reading this stuff. I hope a whole lot of people don't show up before I learn all of this."

"You'll probably get the same questions over and over anyway. If I know you, you'll be able to bullshit your way through it. It's just like selling cars, Mitch. We should make another bet since I already won the first one. Let's bet who gets fired first, you or me. Between your bullshit and my lousy music, neither one of us will last very long."

"Now wait a damned minute. I didn't concede the first bet. I think we should start over. Let's start counting now, on the boat. What you did in Istanbul doesn't count. Does screwing a chirp count?"

"Sure, a chirp counts. Actually, a chirp should be worth bonus points."

"That's still not fair. You already did a chirp. What is a chirp?"

"A chirp is a pro."

"Alright, I'll count the chirp. You win the first bet, but I think we need to bet on the total. And only count on the ship. Outside doesn't count."

"If I already won the first bet, I don't have to keep working on the bottom line. You're the one who has to catch up, Mitch. Now you are telling me I have to start over on the ship?"

"Sure. You need to keep in the game. It's a long way from over."

"Okay, but we probably need to make some rules, like, only different ones or just how many times. And we're going to have to decide about some rules about using our room, too. This could get complicated. Also, what about Palmer Plantation women? Are we going to include them? I don't think they should count. I don't think we should mess around with them. The whole idea was to be away from them. That's just trouble looking for a place to happen."

"Yeah, I know. But it's going to be harder than I thought. Maybe we could include them in some of the stuff on our list. Just not everything."

"OK. But I still don't think they should count. You already know most of them, so that's not fair anyway. Let's just say they are not off limits but they don't count in the total. I think we are going to be so busy we probably won't do half of that stuff anyway. You've got it made. I'm the one who has to work every night. Speaking of which, let's get some lunch. I need to check my email and then go over some music to get ready for tonight. I'll probably really blow it. I hope no one shows up."

"Don't worry about it. Like I said, Grant, nobody gives a shit about the piano player. They just want to drink and have a good time."

"Yeah, I'm really just a shill for the bar. The more I play the more they drink. I guess that's how they'll rate me, by how much liquor I sell. I still hope nobody shows up."

After lunch Mitch headed to the room to start reading the information he had just received. "Think I'll get started on some of this stuff. I have to be at the hospitality desk from 5:30 until 8:30

tonight. Then I'll come by the Casablanca Lounge and see how you are doing. If I don't show up you'll know it's because I'm still working."

"OK. I'll go check email and see you back in the room."

Grant found his way to the computer center and logged on. He had three emails, one from each kid, and began to read.

To: Dad
From: Matt
Hi Dad,

I have my big day in court tomorrow, so keep your fingers crossed for me. My lawyer says we have a slam dunk but you never know what some SOB judge is going to do. I'll let you know how it went.

Enjoy the cruise, Matt

Reply: Hang in there, Matt. Timing on this is lousy but we can always go back to court if you need to. Dad

---

To: Dad
From: Megan

Hi Dad. Just a reminder. Don't leave your valuables lying around the room. Use the little safe in the closet, just to be sure. A lost passport will ruin your trip. I am watching the weather report wherever you are with crossed fingers. Did you pack your windbreaker? Have a good time.

Love, Megan

Reply: I will be very careful. Have the windbreaker. Don't worry so much! Love, Dad

---

To: Daddy
From: Misty

Hi Daddy. I have tears in my eyes as I write this, just knowing how much you will miss Mommy on your first trip without her. It just breaks my heart. I won't sleep until you are home. Have fun.

Love and kisses, Misty

Reply: I miss your Mom, Misty. But she wouldn't want you to be so sad for me. Get some sleep, baby. Love, Daddy

---

Grant sat back in his chair and drew a deep breath, then released a long sigh. He loved his three kids with all his heart, and they surely loved him, but for the first time in all his years of parenting he was facing the reality that he hardly knew them. When did it all change? Where was he when it all happened? One minute they were little kids and then the next they were grown, living their own lives. He thought he had been a good father, was there for most of it, at least the important stuff. But now he felt like he had missed something along the way. All their roles had changed and none of them knew their parts. Had he left too much of it to Vonnie? Was that it? The kids missed their mother and he couldn't fill her place. He felt like the relief pitcher, the substitute, like the default option. Matt would have been talking to Vonnie about his awful situation. They had been really close. And Misty wouldn't be in constant tears and Megan wouldn't be his watchdog. They would just be the kids, like they always were. Only it wasn't like it was. Everything had changed and he didn't know what the hell to do about any of it. He hadn't told them about the piano gig.

He checked his watch and headed for the stateroom. Mitch had unpacked his stuff and was nodding on the little settee under the window, the thick binder open on his lap. Grant opened his suitcase to the jumble of shopping bags he had crammed in there, the packages from the Grand Bazaar. He placed them on the only other sitting place in the room, and picked up the list of Palmer Plantation people that Babs had given them, quickly scanning the names and noting stateroom numbers. There was no way he could sort out the stuff, only what he and Mitch had bought, so he decided that it would probably be easier to have the ladies come to his room and sort it out themselves. He took his pencil and looked for their names. Apparently Wanda and Maureen were roommates and he found Joan's name, but there was no Shay on the list. What was it she said her last name was, Porter? There was a S. M. Porter on the list. He ran his finger across the line to locate her room number, which was the same as Joan's, but something else caught his eye. In the column under address, it said Charlotte, NC. No address for Palmer Plantation, no phone number, no first name. So she was incognito, anonymous, and mysterious. She had been very guarded during their time together standing vigil for the lost ladies, even aloof, and he thought she was just a little stuck on herself or maybe a little cold, rejecting him, and it had pissed him off. She probably had guys hitting on her all the time. Well, whatever her game was, he intended to play.

He continued to unpack and turned toward the closet, surprised to see several sport coats and some other stuff hanging on the back of the door. A sheet of paper was pinned to the clothes. In large letters, it said, "Grant Albright (Property of Wardrobe Dept.)" He counted six sport coats, assorted slacks, six dress shirts, a white dinner jacket, and a tux, with all the trimmings attached. An assortment of ties was hung over one of the hangers. This was getting serious now. Who gave a damn what he was wearing. No one paid any attention to the piano player. There was a pair of patent dress shoes on the floor with a note attached. "Check wardrobe if you need shoes. No sandals or flip flops allowed by staff. Proper attire required at all times, both on board and ashore." This was more than he had bargained for. Way more. The phone rang and he picked it up.

"Hi," she said. "Is this Grant? Grant Albright?"

"Yes, this is Grant."

"Hi, Grant," she cooed. "I thought it must be you because I would recognize Mitch's voice. This is Babs. I am so glad I finally got your stateroom number. I had to show my list of members to the people at the reception desk before they would give me stateroom numbers. But your secret is safe with me. Only the people from Palmer Plantation will have it."

"Hi, Babs. Are you and your group all settled in?"

Mitch was wide awake now, pointing to himself and shaking his head no and mouthing "I'm not here!" trying to avoid talking to her.

"Yes, we're all in our little spots, just as snug as bugs in a rug. I just wanted to call and let you and Mitch know that I am available if you have any questions or anything. And to be sure that you are coming to my cocktail party at five o'clock. You are coming, aren't you? Everyone is just so excited that you are in our group."

"Thanks, Babs, but I have quite a bit of work to do before tonight so I will have to miss the cocktail party."

"Oh, I am soooo sorry," she cooed again. "But you aren't going to avoid us all evening, Grant Albright. We all plan to go to the Casablanca Lounge at nine o'clock to hear you play the piano. Isn't it just so exciting?"

"Yeah, very exciting. Would you like to speak to Mitch? He is right here."

Mitch gave Grant a look of helpless despair and then said sweetly, "Hi. What's up?"

"Hi, Mitch. We are all so looking forward to my cocktail party. You will be there, won't you?"

"Boy, I'm really sorry, but I have volunteered to help on the hospitality desk during that time. Give everyone my regards, though. They can stop by and see me there after the party."

"Don't you be avoiding me, Mitch. I have my eye on you," she teased. "I'll stop by your hospitality table right after the party. Bye now, Mitch."

"Bye, Betty."

He turned toward Grant, rolling his eyes. "Don't ever have me talk to her again. Say I'm working, say I'm gone, say I'm dead. Tell her anything but don't have me talk to her. I can't get rid of her. I can't get away from her."

"I think she has the hots for you. You could knock her off right away and then the score would be tied."

"Palmer Plantation women don't count, remember?"

"I'd make an exception for her. By the way, Mitch, her name isn't Betty."

"I know."

They were still laughing when a folded slip of paper slid in under the door. They had seen that this was a common practice on the ship and they had already received several notices, the day's schedule and the daily newsletter, delivered the same way. Grant reached down to pick it up and noticed that "Grant" was scrawled on the outside. He unfolded the paper and read, a huge grin spreading across his face. He handed it to Mitch.

It said, "Break a leg, Kiddo. Hugs, Jodee"

Grant took out his pen and scrawled on the bottom, "Knock 'em dead, Baby. Hugs, Grant." She had begged him not to come hear her tonight. She was just too nervous. He would give it to the room steward to deliver to the singer in the Fez Lounge.

Mitch jumped into the shower and dressed for his stint at the hospitality desk and Grant gathered his music. After a quick review of his notes, he selected a fake book and dressed for the evening. "Well, here goes nothing. No point in sweating it now." He wore his shirt open at the collar, put on a navy sports coat and headed to the deck. He wanted to find a good place to see the fabulous view of Istanbul as they sailed away.

The view of Istanbul from the Bosphorus and the Marmara is incredible, stunning. The Blue Mosque and Hagia Sophia stand majestically representing all the beauty and history and mystery of the fabulous city behind them, standing as witness to and protector of all its might, sacred sentinels of two of the world's great religions. They are surprisingly close to the water, above, on the promontory, and the sight is frequently mentioned by travelers as one of the greatest sail-in experiences anywhere. The beautiful Dolmabahce Palace stands right at the shoreline. It was built in the eighteen hundreds and replaced the Topaki Palace as the official residence of the Sultan. The Sultans had many palaces that beautifully hug the shore, along with mansions of the rich from the Ottoman era. Many private residences, mansions called yali, decorate both the eastern and western shores of the Bosphorus. The Atheneè would allow for optimal viewing by circling twice.

Grant found the perfect spot, starboard, forward, and put his music book on a seat by a small table at the rail. The wait-staff was busy preparing drinks and bringing small trays of Turkish tidbits to serve for the sail-away party. People were beginning to come forward to join in the festivities and a small orchestra was assembling to provide live music for the affair. Sail-away parties are planned on most cruise ships and the Atheneè was pulling out all the stops for this one. Grant had been on several cruises and he could already see that this ship was to be a fabulous experience itself, almost as if it needed to present the same wow factor as the places it would visit.

Several people spoke to him and the staff all addressed him by name. Service personnel are encouraged to learn the names of the guests, but Grant was a little surprised that he seemed to be recognized by so many people. But the mystery was soon solved. A very large woman descended upon him, thrusting a flier and a pen in his hand. "May I please have your autograph?" she said excitedly. And then her friend held one out for him to sign, too. It was the first time Grant had seen one of the fliers with his picture announcing the "Keyboard Magic of Grant Albright" and he hadn't seen the posters either. And they continued to come, one after another as word spread that he was there, right over there, right by the railing. And a star was born. That's how it happened. He didn't have to play. It was enough just that his picture was on a poster, on a flier, signaling that he was somebody, somebody important, somebody who had his own posters and his own fliers. One woman told him she had been a fan for years and another asked if his CDs would be available on the ship, and another had seen him in Vegas at the Bellagio. He didn't bother to correct her, although he was pretty sure she had him confused with David Osborne. Well, they would know he was no David Osborne when he started to play, because nobody did it better than David Osborne.

The waiter brought him a plate of tidbits and he decided to order a martini to help him relax a little. He was beginning to feel the pressure of nobody giving a shit about the piano player now that he was recognized as that piano player on the flier, and he thought about Jodee and how nervous she said she was, and she was a real pro. She could probably give him some tips on handling the stress but he had promised her he wouldn't go see her tonight. She said she might come by the Casablanca Lounge after the late show. He would talk to her then. He leaned back in his chair and started to put his feet up on the other chair, on top of his music, when someone called his name.

"Grant! Grant! We have been looking for you. Mitch told us you were on deck. Are you going down for dinner? We asked Mitch to go but he has to work so he told us to ask you. We eat at 7:30 tonight. That will give you plenty of time before you start to play."

"Thanks, Maureen. But I think I'll skip dinner tonight and just fill up on these little things they are serving here. I'm planning on sitting right here to enjoy the last glimpse of Istanbul." Wanda and Joan were standing there and Joan spoke right up.

"Do you want us to come and get our stuff? Mitch said you had it all piled on the only chair. We'll be glad to come get it whenever you want us. It is probably really in your way."

Wanda chimed in, "We are going to the show right after dinner and then we plan to come hear you play. Shay isn't going. She is meeting us later. She wants to watch the land fade out of sight too. She is supposed to be up here somewhere."

"She didn't stay long at the cocktail party. Ralph in Real Estate was all over her. She was so cute trying to keep away from him. She's probably hiding out somewhere. If you see her, tell her we were looking for her."

"OK, ladies. Thanks for the dinner invitation. Enjoy your evening. I'll keep an eye out for Shay."

He turned back in his seat just as he heard Maureen call, "Shay! Shay! Over here."

He turned back to look and there she was, heading right for them. She was wearing slacks and a rather tight shirt with ruffly stuff around the neck and had her hair pinned up and he thought she looked really cute.

"We're so glad we found you," Joan said. "Grant is planning to sit right here and watch Istanbul drift by. He is skipping dinner too."

Grant immediately stood and removed his music book from the other chair. "Join me," he said. "This is the perfect spot."

"Oh my, no. I don't want to disturb your quiet enjoyment of this."

"Well, as I recall, you and I had no trouble at all being quiet together. As a matter of fact, sometimes the silence was so thick you could cut it with a knife."

She could feel herself start to blush. How dare he start right in on her, but he kept the ball in his court again. "Come on, take a seat. I'll get you a drink. What will it be, a Shirley Temple or should we be daring and try a big girl drink?" he teased

She was livid. She looked him right in the eye and said, "I'll have a vodka martini, straight up with a twist."

He winked and nodded in that infuriating way he had, and said, "One vodka martini, straight up with a twist, coming up," and he signaled to the waiter. The other three quickly excused themselves and could hardly contain their glee as they hurried away.

"Did you see the look on his face when he saw her? Do you think he was glad to see her? He is hard to read."

"This is just perfect, the perfect chance for them to get acquainted."

"I can't wait to see her and hear how it went."

"I hope she doesn't cut and run. She is such a scaredy-cat."

"I just know that some man broke her heart. She probably has a tragic past."

"Well, she is no pushover. He better mind his Ps and Qs. She has pretty high standards."

"Ralph, the Real Estate guy, seemed pretty interested in her. She is so attractive. She wouldn't have any trouble getting a man if she would just give them a chance."

"Ralph probably wants to sell her a house. My late husband, Howard, always said to never trust a real estate man. He is just trying to sell you something."

"Well, isn't that the point?"

"I heard Ralph does really well. I wouldn't rule him out. He is a pretty good catch."

Grant had turned his attention to Shay. "So, did you enjoy the cocktail party? I suppose the whole Palmer Plantation gang was there."

"Yes, it was lovely. I think Babs plans to keep us all very well entertained on this entire trip. She has lots of other things planned as well."

"Oh, really. What else has she planned for you?"

"Oh, just little parties and events. A birthday party night and an anniversary night. Things like that. I'm sure you wouldn't be interested in any of it."

"What makes you think I wouldn't be interested?"

She wanted to say because you are too stuck on yourself, intimidated by his confident, almost cocky attitude. "You will be busy with your job. Those type of activities probably seem pretty boring to someone in the entertainment business. Of course, you are included. I didn't mean to imply that you weren't welcome. I'm certain Babs would love for you to come. We just wouldn't want to bore you."

Feeling a little full of himself, he grinned. "Well, I might just show up sometime when I get a break from the entertainment business. Maybe you will see more of Ralph in Real Estate. I hear he has the hots for you."

She almost died of embarrassment. "Well, I don't see that that would be of any interest to you, but I can assure you that is not the case."

They turned in their chairs and watched silently for several minutes. The waiter brought her martini and Grant passed it to her.

"You don't have to drink this," he said with that wink and nod. "I'll order you something sweeter if you want. I'll drink the martini. That way I can be nervous, lousy, and drunk when I play tonight," he laughed.

She was surprised that he said something so disparaging about himself, but also embarrassed that he was on to her about ordering the martini just to impress him. He ordered her a gin and tonic and took the martini and they sat quietly, Grant occasionally pointing out something interesting and Shay responding with relevant comments, as interested in the sights as he was.

"It doesn't have to be this hard, Shay."

"What? What doesn't have to be so hard?"

"Being together like this. You make it hard."

"How do I make it hard? What am I doing to make it hard?"

"You know damned well what you're doing. You are defensive. You keep pushing me away. If we are going to get stuck together like this, we might at least be friends."

"Yes, I suppose you are right. One can't have too many friends," she laughed. Damn him, she thought. Did he think she was interested in him? Just because every other woman was gaga over him didn't mean that she was. Or was he trying to let her know that he certainly wasn't interested in her. That was perfectly clear. Of course they would only be friends.

They sat in silence until land disappeared and Grant stood. "Well, show time. Man the torpedoes. Time to go to work. Are you going to come with the ladies to hear me?"

"I haven't decided yet. Perhaps I'll drop by later."

"Just wanted you to know you were welcome, included, if you don't find that sort of thing too boring." He held out his hand to her. "Friends, right?"

"Friends, right."

The Casablanca Lounge was dimly lit with small candles in little hurricane lamps placed on each table. It was a casually elegant room with deep plush upholstered furniture arranged in little conversation groups, an ambiance that suited Grant's style. The room held about fifty, one of the more intimate lounges on the ship, and most of the tables were filled. He glanced around for familiar faces but didn't stop to greet the Palmer people. He headed right for the piano and was surprised when a round of applause greeted him. He patted the piano, a little quirk of his, and then adjusted himself on the bench. The room was absolutely silent. His fingers found their place and he started, slowly at first and then slightly increasing the tempo, expanding the melody, and finally embellishing with arpeggios as the beautiful strains of *Spanish Eyes* filled the room. He followed with a lively rendition of *Tico Tico* and then deftly slid into *Lara's Theme* from *Dr. Zhivago.* It was coming easier now, the music flowed and so did the liquor. Ethan, the cruise director, stopped by and took in the scene, exchanged a word with one of the servers, and then turned and gave Grant a high five.

He played for forty five minutes before taking a break, and then made a quick pass around the room, greeting the Palmer people and shaking hands along the way. Several people had requests and luckily he could oblige. Yes, he knew some of Sinatra's stuff, and yes, he could play many of their old favorites, and yes, damn it, he could really play, even if nobody did give a shit about the piano player. He played another set, leaning heavily tonight on old standards like *Stardust* and *Smoke Gets In Your Eyes*, relieved that he could remember them so easily and he could feel himself relax a little as the jitters were calmed. Several people were tapping their feet to the music and others were listening closely, and even those who were talking were doing it quietly. He acknowledged several rounds of applause and nodded in appreciation and mouthed thank yous.

One person was taking it all in with particular interest. Seated alone at a small table near the wall was a rather elegant looking gentleman. Itzach Schwartzman had come to check out the new pianist he had personally selected after reviewing the CDs of the five finalist for this position and he was eager to validate that choice. He had watched him at the orientation meeting and had gone undetected this morning as he listened to Grant check out the piano, and he was impressed. This guy seemed to have it all, the whole package, the looks, the presence, and the skill. Now he just wanted to see if he could carry a room, if he had that certain quality to connect with his audience. He wasn't looking for schmaltz and he wasn't looking for virtuosity. He wanted something far more important. He wanted perfection. She deserved that.

Grant checked his watch and had a fleeting thought that he should probably just put it on the piano where he could check it without people seeing that he was looking at it, and he wondered what time 'until' was. He really wanted to talk to Jodee so she could give him some more pointers since she was the only one on the ship who knew that he didn't have any professional experience, but she hadn't come in. Well, if he got fired it wouldn't matter because there were other pianists on this ship working with the show orchestra and in other venues. The only thing that mattered to him right now was not making an ass out of himself. He finished his last set just as the bartender came in and gave him the "cut" sign, that familiar gesture of cutting one's throat. Grant wrapped it up with *As Time Goes By* because he thought that was appropriate for a place called the Casablanca Lounge. He was gathering his music when the waiter called to him. "Mr. Albright, you better take this," and handed him a jar filled with money. Holy Cow! They had tipped him! Mitch had come in and joined the Palmer group. Babs was with him. The three gals, as he had started referring to Maureen, Wanda, and Joan, were seated with Ralph in Real Estate. They all left together. Shay hadn't come in.

Grant headed to his stateroom, ready to call it a night, nodding at folks as he went, shaking a few hands, and signing a few more autographs. It was nearly midnight when he entered his room. Mitch wasn't there but he noticed that some of the packages were spread out on his bed. Mitch must have had the ladies in to sort things out and he wondered if Shay had been with them. The red light on the phone was blinking. He picked it up to retrieve the message. It was Jodee.

"Grant, I really need to talk to you, Kiddo. Could you call me just as soon as you get in. Room 704. It's very important. I'll wait up. Hugs"

He called her room and she answered immediately. "What's up, Babe? You sounded upset. How did things go?"

"You wouldn't believe. Can you come up? Let's have a nightcap and I'll fill you in."

He scrawled a quick note for Mitch. "With Jodee," and left for Room 704.

Ephesus

The Atheneè would dock at the port of Kusadasi at 8:30 a.m. and passengers would begin departure for their shore excursions around 9:15. Neither Grant nor Mitch were officially assigned to a bus for the day, so they would be with the Palmer Plantation group. Babs had carefully gone over all the excursions in Mitch's binder and had marked all the ones that she had scheduled for her group. She had already made arrangements with the Excursion Director to assign her group to one bus. At first Grant was pissed off about her taking over the arrangements for them, but after the big fuss about autographs last night, he felt a little sense of relief that he wouldn't be hounded all day if he stayed with the Palmer people. Mitch was pretty content with the idea. Apparently Babs had pulled up a chair right next to him at his hospitality table last night and had acted like a co-hostess.

"I can't get away from her," Mitch complained. "The woman is everywhere. She's nice enough, and all that, but it makes it hard for me to work on my list. Several women traveling with some retirement group, AARPS or something, came up to our table and one of them was really attractive, but Babs jumped right in before I could even get her name."

"Well, I told you to just go ahead and do her and get it over with," Grant laughed. "Just a quick slam bam, thank you ma'am. Then maybe she'll leave you alone. Or maybe she is just testing you and if you go for it, she'll back off. Or perhaps she isn't interested in you at all. Did you think about that? She seems like a really nice lady. She probably thought she was being helpful. If she comes today think of some way to politely tell her she shouldn't be sitting there. Did she just show up after dinner?"

"Yeah, and I was swamped so it was good that she helped. She knows her stuff, knows it a whole lot better than I do, so I was glad to have her. I'm not complaining about that. How about you, are you making any progress on your list? You can't spend all your time with that chirp. Are we going to count doing the same one more than once or does it have to be a different one? I forget what we said. That doesn't sound fair to me. You didn't get back until four this morning. You could be racking up points that way."

"Yeah, I'm really racking 'em up. You'll never catch up. You might as well concede the bet right now. How much did we put on it, fifty dollars?"

"I ain't conceding nothing. Are you keeping the score? I'll lay you two to one I win."

"OK, you're on."

Mitch and Grant had met at a golf tournament the very first week Grant moved to Palmer Plantation. They were both low handicappers and they loved the trash talk of the game, that part where you put the verbal pressure on the other guy. And they loved all the bullshit, the jokes, and the camaraderie. They usually had a side bet or two going as well. They bet on everything. Mitch knew everybody and had pushed Grant into several groups and he kept Grant going, even when things were getting pretty bad at home. And when Grant had to spend more time at the hospital, Mitch would go and sit with him. And when Grant needed a quick round just to get away for a break, Mitch was there to play with him. He hung in there until the bitter end, long after most friends had despaired of the whole thing and had stopped calling. They had become best friends, with the type of friendship most people have only once or twice in a lifetime, and some never have, the kind based on respect, and acceptance, and loyalty, the kind where you didn't have to talk, or you could, and it didn't matter. Mitch talked more than Grant.

They boarded the bus and took seats midway back, on the right side. It was Mitch's turn for the window. A fellow named something like "Uumstasha" was their guide and no one could pronounce it, so they started calling him "Oomish." No one could pronounce Kusadasi either because it didn't sound anything like it was spelled, so most people referred to the whole place as Ephesus, since that was where they were heading. Kusadasi is primarily a resort town on Turkey's Aegean coast, a beautiful place. It is a playground for the wealthy and a popular stop for cruise ships that bring thousands of visitors to enjoy the shopping and the beautiful beaches and the incredible wonders of Ephesus, which lies about sixteen miles up the coast. They would spend the day there with "Oomish" as their guide.

The earliest information about Ephesus dates it back to about 2000 B.C. Greek and Roman influence are evidenced in the many archeological finds and in the ruins of the city itself. Since the city was completely covered by silt, these archeological wonders are rather well preserved and, while much of the city remains covered, what is now seen provides an incredible picture of life during the Augustan period, 63 B.C.-14 A.D. During this time Christianity spread through the region. Most Christians are aware of the fact that St. Paul preached to the Ephesians in the huge Grand Theatre of Ephesus and that St. John had brought Mary, Mother of Jesus, to live out her days in Ephesus. The house in which she is presumed to have lived has been preserved and is visited reverently by Christians from around the world. Although some doubt the authenticity of the place, it has been officially sanctioned by the Vatican as the place where the Virgin Mary spent the last years of her life.

The three gals immediately latched on to Mitch as they began to explore the fabulous ruins. They would start on Curetes Street, near the public baths. Several baths have been uncovered, well preserved evidence of the Roman period and the importance of these baths to the culture. Grant loved the history and the fabulous artifacts and followed along with the map as "Oomish" pointed out things. They paused at the Gates of Hercules, posing for pictures. Lore has it if you stand between the gates and touch both sides you will have the strength of Hercules. Mitch and Grant each took a turn posing as strong Herculean specimens while the gals snapped pictures, everyone laughing and joking. Shay stood to the side, watching. She couldn't help but notice how comfortable Grant appeared with them, compared with how awkward the two of them had been together. It embarrassed her to be reminded how he had mentioned being "stuck" with her. She had brought along her camera and snapped with the rest of them, but decided to walk ahead with Maureen and Wanda whenever possible, avoiding all chance of being left with him.

While the walking was not difficult, the marble streets had been worn to a slippery patina. Mitch had offered his arm to Joan. Wanda and Maureen were walking ahead, which left Shay bringing up the rear with Grant. She would maneuver herself next to them at the first stopping point. Shay was wearing another of her cute sundresses, the only one in their group in a dress, and she had on a cute pair of pink sandals, very flat, and pretty slippery on the bottom. She was paying close attention to where she stepped, aware that the shoes were going to be a problem. The group continued down Curetes Street, which is lined with pillars of various sizes that had been used as decoration and as support for the many commercial establishments that formerly occupied these ancient ruins. Shay stayed as far away from Grant as possible without being obvious, listening to Oomish and snapping more pictures. Grant was keeping tabs on her whereabouts too, but kept it from being obvious by taking his own pictures and absorbing as much of the place as he could.

Next they passed the public toilets, which fascinate all visitors. It is understood that only men used these communal facilities, long rows of side by side holes cut through slabs of marble, allowing for congenial visits while tending to business. Natural sponges from the sea were used, and with the usual Roman cleverness with water, the black water flowed to the sea where it was flushed away by the daily tides. Of course, Grant and Mitch had to have their pictures taken sitting side by side on the toilets, pretending, while everyone laughed and joked. Maureen threatened to print the pictures in the Singles Club newsletter. The brothel was next and again they all clowned around, even making some off-color jokes, which added to Shay's embarrassment because, while she was no prude, she had had very little opportunity to participate in such repartee in mixed company and she was pretty surprised at how easy it flowed from all of them, even Wanda, who could be a little priggish.

From the brothel they had a view of the beautiful Library of Celsus, the most recognized building in all Ephesus, and the most photographed, appearing on the covers of tour guidebooks, in textbooks, and on maps everywhere.

"Stand over there, girls, in front of those boulders. I'll get a picture of the three of you with the library in the background," Maureen instructed. "Get closer together. I can't see the library. See if you can get up on that rock."

The three obliged, going behind the rocks where they could get a foothold and step up, putting them about four feet off the ground.

"Good. Everybody look and wave. Smile now."

Shay was trying to hold her skirt close, aware that people could probably see up, and turned to wave, but just as Maureen hollered "good one!" Shay's sandal clad foot slid out from under her. She landed on her rear end and slid down the face of the boulder, splatting herself right at Grant's feet. He had attempted to catch her, but only succeeded in breaking her fall.

"Are you OK? Did you hurt anything?"

Joan scrambled down and rushed to Shay's side. "Oh Shay, I hope you aren't hurt. Does anything hurt?"

Stunned, Shay was mostly attempting to put her skirt back down where it belonged, aware of how unladylike she was sitting, and beginning to feel the sharp pain in her ankle. She made a game attempt to convince them that she was not injured but Grant had already bent down in front of her. "Let me have a look," he said. "Can you straighten your leg?"

Joan used her nurse's training to assess the situation and suggested that they might need to call for help. Mitch had come right over too. "Let's see if she can put any weight on it. Grant and I can hold her."

Grant took her shoulder bag from her and put it over his shoulder and the two men gently lifted her to her feet. "Just stand for a few minutes, don't rush things. Maybe you just have a minor sprain or a twist, but in case it's worse, let's start out real slow. What is it they say, Joan? RICE? Rest, Ice, Compression, Elevation?"

Ralph in Real Estate had come over and squatted in front of her, gently manipulating the ankle. "I have lots of experience with these things," he announced. "We get calls for it all the time. It doesn't appear to be swelling. We'll get ice as soon as we can. I have my stuff on the bus. I never leave home without it. We members of the Palmer Plantation First Responders handle this stuff all the time. We never know when we are going to need something. Let's try a little weight on it. Easy, just a little weight. That's a girl. Easy now." Grant and Mitch held her and Ralph continued to run his hand around her ankle, gently feeling around and poking. "I think you're going to be OK, Shay. Let's try a few steps. You guys keep a hold of her and let's see how it goes."

Joan had stepped aside when Ralph took over, and the three men continued to assist Shay, having her try a few steps. She was obviously in pain so Joan opened her bag and retrieved some pain pills she always carried, and Grant gave her a sip of his water, right out of his bottle. He could see that she was becoming more upset so he moved his hand from her arm and placed it around her waist, stroking with his thumb. "It'll be OK," he said gently. "We can handle this. I'll stay with you."

"I feel like such a fool." she said. "Don't let me ruin your day. I'll just make my way to the end of Marble Street and wait there."

"You'll do no such thing," he said firmly.

"OK," Ralph announced. "Once those pain killers kick in you should be able to hobble along. I'll walk right with you and we can get better acquainted."

"That won't be necessary, Ralph," Grant replied. "I'll call you if we need you. You might be needed to help someone else."

The others began to head down the street with Oomish and Mitch again offered his arm to Joan and she began to feel that same sensation she felt in the Bazaar, that sense of strength from a man, that which she so missed. Babs had come up to see if she could help and seeing Joan on Mitch's arm, immediately attached herself to the other.

Grant held Shay tightly around the waist as she gingerly took a few steps and they started slowly down Marble Street, pausing from time to time to admire one of the intricate Corinthian capitals that lined the way, placed there waiting to be perched on the proper column once it was unearthed and assembled. When they reached the Grand Theatre, Grant parked her on one of the capitals, insisting that the stairs would be too much for her to handle. He made a quick trip up to the theatre, an open air structure that resembles a modern amphitheater, somewhat awed to be in the actual place where St. Paul preached to the Ephesians. He quickly returned to Shay's side and sat on the capital next to her.

"Doing better?" he inquired. "We don't have to hurry."

"I'm so sorry, Grant. This is so embarrassing and now you are stuck with me again."

"Look, I apologize for saying that yesterday. It came out all wrong. It was a very bad word choice. Actually, I don't mind being stuck with you. I thought you didn't want to be with me. After all, you were stuck too and you didn't act very happy about it. And that crack about being bored. That was pretty bad too."

"It wasn't that I felt stuck. I was uncomfortable being alone with you. Everyone is interested in you and you have had so many more experiences than I have. And you were so critical. It was intimidating."

"Well, if it's any consolation, I was a little uncomfortable, too. I'm probably not the smoothest guy you ever met and I'm a little out of practice. But if you are going to get your hackles up every time I open my mouth, it will make things worse, so maybe you could cut me a little slack. I don't even know what I said that was so intimidating, so critical, but I promise to stop it," he laughed. "Why didn't you come last night? I looked for you."

"I felt so bad about our conversation and I knew I was rude. It seemed best if I stayed away. I heard you were wonderful."

"I wouldn't say that. I hit a couple of real clunkers and got lost in the middle of *Tico Tico* and had to repeat quite a bit before it came back. You didn't miss much. It's probably a good thing that nobody pays any attention to the piano player or I would be fired already. If you're up to it tonight, come on in. How is your ankle feeling now?"

"Quite a bit better."

"Good. I bet you skinned up your rear end too. Dresses probably aren't the best thing to wear rock climbing, although I did enjoy the view. And those sandals. For crying out loud, Shay. You should have better sense than to wear those around places like this. You're lucky you didn't break your neck. Didn't you bring any walking shoes? When we get back to the shopping area we should look for a shoe store." She could feel the color rushing to her face, anger and embarrassment bubbling up, cringing at the thought of what view he might have had, and incensed at the criticism. He had wrapped his arm tightly around her waist again and pulled her a little closer as they began walking so she kept her thoughts to herself. When they reached the bus he turned to her. "Friends, right?"

"Right, friends," she answered.

The bus ascended the steep and winding road to the preserved home of St. Mary. The group stood outside as Oomish gave his little talk and then they proceeded by foot up a rather steep incline to the sacred spot. Ralph had waited at the foot of the stairs to assist Shay off the bus. He had carefully attended to her ankle again and had placed an instant cold pack on the side of her foot. Grant had watched the proceedings, but stepped forward as they began to walk up the incline and wrapped his arm around her waist again.

There is an aura about the place, a sense of the sacred, and people approach the small stone cottage with hushed voices, many crossing themselves as they enter. It is a tiny place, humble and holy. An altar has been constructed in the corner of what has been identified as the kitchen, and after reverently taking in the awesome possibility of the prior presence of St. Mary herself, Grant and Shay approached the tiny altar and Shay lit a candle. Grant followed her lead and silently lit another candle and the two stood for a few minutes. Neither of them knelt. As they exited through the small door at the side Grant reached in his pocket and retrieved several folded bills and left a generous amount in the collection plate, offerings for the maintenance of the house.

At the foot of the incline, near the buses, there is the usual collection of small shops with souvenirs and assorted memorabilia of the place. "Do you want to have a look around?" Grant asked. "I'll stay with you." They entered the small shop and Grant purchased a package of lovely brocaded bookmarks and a beautiful gold charm, a replica of the Celsus library, and then headed for a wall full of pashminas of every color. They were extraordinarily soft and plush and he selected several for each of his daughters, choosing beautiful rich colors. Joan had come in and she purchased one for herself and one for Chrissie and one for her other daughter, Chloe. Shay was holding several and trying to make up her mind whether to buy one or not. Grant went to her side, observing that she was holding a black one and a bright pink one that went pretty well with the sundress she was wearing. Unsolicited, he offered his advice. "I like the pink one. It matches your dress." He reached up for a lovely lavender one and said, "This one is really pretty, too."

"I can only buy one. Which should it be? They are all lovely. I guess I'll take the pink one." Grant added the lavender one to his pile and they headed to the counter.

Back at the port of Kusadasi they would have lunch on their own and spend any remaining time shopping. It was an easy walk to the ship from the shopping area and Grant had read that there was an excellent rug dealer there and he wanted to spend some time looking, hoping to find a rug he liked. Most of the Palmer Plantation people were entering the courtyard that surrounded the shops where the rug dealer was so they all ended up sitting around the edge of the room for another rug demonstration. A lovely rug had caught Grant's eye as soon as he entered the courtyard. There was some sort of a contraption showing caterpillars making silk, and right behind it was displayed a beautiful shimmering silk rug. It was mostly in shades of turquoise that looked the color of the Aegean, but the part that most appealed to Grant was the unique design. The rug was divided into decorative framed sections, and each section had a little scene depicting animals or birds. Animals and birds decorated the entire border. Grant had never seen anything like it before and engaged the enthusiastic salesman in conversation. It was one hundred per cent silk, he was told, with four hundred knots per inch and the animals were incredibly true to life, highly detailed. While geometric patterns are most prevalent in Turkish carpets, animal and flower motifs are highly prized. The pictures in the rug represented stories told by Scheherazade in *A Thousand and One Nights,* and Grant was completely fascinated by it. He didn't know anything at all about Turkish carpets. Vonnie had talked him into a few oriental rugs for the house but they had been selected mostly for their decorative appeal and they had an Aubusson in the great room that he really liked, but this rug in front of him was intriguing, captivating. It wasn't a large rug, only about four feet by six feet, and he had the perfect spot for it, so he began to bargain the price. By now most of the others had heard that Grant was seriously looking, maybe going to buy, so they began to gather around. Grant glanced around for Shay. "Come here. Come give me your woman's opinion."

"Oh my, Grant. I know absolutely nothing about Turkish rugs. It is beautiful but I have no idea about them." She was grateful that he would never see the worn wall to wall carpet in her mother's house. He would surely never ask her opinion if he ever saw that.

"I know, but do you like it? What about you, Wanda. What do you think about it? You have a good eye for color. You did a great job with the floral arrangements."

Wanda was so flattered she could barely speak, but she put her glasses on and examined the rug closely. "Is it wool or silk?"

"It's silk."

"How many knots per inch?" she asked knowingly.

"Four hundred," he replied.

"Where will you put it? You have several beautiful Orientals already," aware that she was the only one who had been in his house and wanting that fact to be emphasized. Of course, Mitch had been in but he didn't count. "I don't think it should go in a high traffic area."

"I don't have any traffic, Wanda. But I'm thinking of putting it in my study. You can help me place it."

She was so flattered she almost fainted. "It is just gorgeous, Grant. I'd love to help you place it."

Grant was satisfied with the deal he had made and proceeded to give his credit card and shipping information to the salesman. By now most of the Palmer people were examining the magnificent rug, exclaiming and admiring, and wondering if it signaled that Grant intended to stay. Several wondered aloud what he had paid for it, and one woman actually turned the tag over and looked. The rug would be shipped to the Atlanta representative and personally delivered to his home in North Carolina, standard procedure for this prominent dealer.

He turned to Shay. "How are you doing? Should we look for a shoe store? I'll ask if there is one near and then we better get you back on board so Ralph can tend to your ankle." She purchased a pair of sensible walking shoes, which she knew would look awful with her dresses, and Ralph accompanied them back to the ship, taking over for Grant, and wrapping his arm around her and delivering her to her stateroom where he applied another cold pack.

When Grant returned to his room there was a message from Jodee. He looked at his watch, quickly calculating the time in California, and decided to go check his email before showering and changing for the evening. Jodee would be performing at five so he would drop in to hear her.

There was no email from Matt, so the waiting game would continue to worry Grant for the rest of the evening. There was nothing from Megan, but Misty had sent another one.

To: Daddy
From: Misty

I cried all night. I can't sleep. Pay me seepy, Daddy. Are you having a good time?"

Love and kisses, Misty

Reply: Good trip so far. Staying busy. Stop crying
and get some sleep, Baby

Love and kisses,
Daddy

Misty was the youngest of his three, his baby. "Pay me seepy, Daddy" was what Misty would say to him when she was a toddler. She had always been a terrible sleeper and had given them many a long wakeful night. He could see her now, padding down the hall in her sleepers. She would crawl right up on his lap and say "Pay me seepy, Daddy," which meant play until I fall asleep, and he would put her in her little swing right next to the piano and play until she slept. Even through her teen years she would ask him to play when she went to bed, and that baby talk would be repeated, like a family joke. She was a softy and had a harder time handling things than the others, probably because they had all babied her, even though she was the youngest by only two years. She couldn't handle her mother's illness and had not come to visit very often. She and her husband were both P.E. teachers, had no children, and stayed very busy coaching and playing every sport during every season. What she failed to do for her mother during her last year was atoned for with an avalanche of tears, and Grant knew much of it was driven by guilt about not being there at the end when he had called each of them to come. She and her husband came the next day, but it was too late. He wished there were some way he could comfort her, some way he could fix it for her, some way that he could help her understand that her mother was already gone, didn't even know that Misty wasn't there. He wanted her to understand that it was his fault for not calling sooner, for not doing it while Vonnie was still lucid instead of waiting until she slipped into that final coma. Somehow, when she was still lucid, he could deny the reality that death was so near, deny the inevitable, hold death at bay a little longer, and it was because of his own weakness that he had caused so much pain for his daughter. He hoped she would get pregnant so she would have something else to think about. The crying was killing him.

Mitch had dressed for the evening and headed to the hospitality desk. Babs was already seated there, organizing all of the papers and brochures for the next day's schedule. She had insisted on taking everything back to her stateroom yesterday after seeing how disorganized Mitch was, wanting to be helpful and enjoying the appearance of being his partner in all things trip related. Babs had only worked in the travel business for two years but had discovered that she had a passion for it, loved everything about it, and was planning to grow her business, customized stuff, high-end. She was beginning to think about taking a partner, someone with good people skills and some business smarts, because she wasn't as good at the business end of things and she was even thinking that Mitch might be able to give her some advice, might like to be involved. He was so affable, so likeable, and certainly attractive.

Mitch had planned to be a little firm with her tonight, take the reins, let her see who was in charge, but the first person to arrive with a question was the one who just adored everything, the one who he sat by at lunch in Istanbul, the dimpled darling of delight. She started right in on him.

"Oh, Mitch. Isn't it wonderful that you are seated right here where we can find you. Don't you just adore how wonderful everything is on this ship, how they have thought about everything. I just adore cruising, don't you? Now, tell me, Mitch, tomorrow we arrive in Rhodes, isn't that right? I was just wondering if you thought it would be a tiring day, because tomorrow night is formal, and I was just wondering if you thought we would be back in plenty of time to dress. I just adore the formal nights, don't you?"

Mitch started to say something, he didn't know what, but something like he didn't know what the schedule was, even though he was supposed to know it, and started leafing through his papers. Babs had overheard it all and immediately came to his rescue, sweetly telling the dimpled darling that they would be back on board early and she was sure there would be ample time to dress for the gala evening. "Just bring all your questions to me in the future, dear. That way we can let Mitch handle the more complicated questions."

"Well, I was just wondering about Rhodes, too. Isn't that where that big statue is? That one that stretches across the harbor? Do you think we sail right under it? Or is it worth going to see that? I was wondering whether if it's not worth it maybe I would just stay on the boat, you know. That is possible, isn't it. They will let you stay on, won't they?"

"Of course, dear. That big statue you mentioned is called the Colossus, one of the seven wonders of the ancient world. But it probably isn't worth going to see it because it collapsed in 226 B.C. only sixty six years after it was completed. A violent earthquake struck Rhodes and the statue collapsed. It was never reconstructed and science tells us that it never did stand across the harbor. That is just a myth. There are other interesting things to see there, other ancient ruins. But it will be just fine if you choose to stay on board."

"Oh, just more ancient ruins? Everything is just so old over here. Are all ruins so old? I mean, I adore old things, just adore them, but it's so depressing. I guess I won't go then. I just adore this boat."

Babs was always astounded at how little information some travelers had about the places they were visiting, how ridiculous some of the questions were, and even how annoying some of them were, but like most people in the travel business, she was patient and helpful, only telling the stories to her friends over a few glasses of wine. It would be nice to have a partner in the business, to have someone to share the funny stuff with, someone like Mitch who would appreciate the humor.

After the dimpled darling left, apparently satisfied with the information, Mitch turned to Babs. "Thanks. That one is a little more than I can handle. Doesn't she have a husband? She sure isn't burdened with intelligence, is she?"

"No, poor thing. He passed on last year. Let me deal with her. I encouraged her to come on this trip for a change of scenery but she might not be ready for it. She is driving everyone nuts."

Before Mitch could continue the conversation, about twenty people from a retirement place in Arizona approached the table asking a million questions about Athens. Babs calmly opened the large portfolio to the pages about Greece, so Mitch followed suit, surprised at how easy all this travel stuff was. Like Grant said, it's just a fact or two here and there and the rest is bullshit, just like selling cars, and God knows, he could sell cars. By the time they were ready to close up shop they had booked over one hundred day trips for Athens.

Grant had walked by the hospitality desk to see how Mitch was doing and stopped to chat for a minute or two, a little surprised to see Mitch and Babs working so comfortably side by side. Mitch had been talking to some woman, showing her a picture of something, schmoozing, looking perfectly at ease. He excused himself to talk to Grant. "How's it going, Buddy. Where you headed?"

"On my way to the Fez Lounge. Jodee left me a message, so I'll see what she wanted."

"Watch your step, Grant. I think she's getting to you. You're going to have to let her know you are playing the field."

"Yeah, I see that really worked for you. You and Babs make a pretty good team here."

"Babs only wants to help, Grant. Nothing else."

"OK, if you say so, but I'm willing to put fifty on it," Grant laughed.

"You're on. I'm betting on the chick too. Another fifty."

"It's chirp, Mitch. She's a chirp."

It was six o'clock. Jodee would be well into her set now. Grant planned to slip in and have a martini and stay until a break. Jodee and he had put in a long night last night. They had talked until he fell asleep on the chaise on her veranda. That must have been around 1:30 a.m. and it was four when he woke and slipped out of her room. She didn't wake him when she went to bed. She had covered him with a blanket and let him sleep there. She had already told him the bad news so he was anxious to hear how today had gone.

Jodee had been through some tough times, had been knocked around some, even knocked down, but she was still in the ring, still trying to land that knockout punch. Grant couldn't help but admire her drive, that light that still burned, that desire to succeed, to make it big. He didn't get it, but then he didn't have show business in his blood, didn't thrive on an audience, didn't need applause. He had never had to work very hard to get where he got. He was good at what he did and success had followed. He had had some luck along the way, too. Grant believed that life was one big crapshoot and he had had some lucky rolls. The cards hadn't been stacked against him. There was something about Jodee that touched him, an openness, an honesty, and a need that aroused some sense of desire in him. Mitch was right. She was getting to him, her vulnerability, her need for someone in her corner, someone to tend the wounds. Most of all, she needed an occasional long count. She needed a break and he wanted to help make it happen.

He entered the Fez Lounge to the twang of a guitar and monotonous chord repetitions on an electric keyboard, some cacophonous arrangement of *I Got You, Babe*, retro Sonny and Cher, but without Cher. He heard immediately what Jodee had been telling him. He had never heard Jodee sing, but this definitely was not right for Jodee. He looked around for her, but she wasn't in the room. He ordered a martini and sat and listened, thinking she was probably on a break, but when she didn't show up when the combo took a break he got concerned. He asked where she was. The guitar player shrugged and the keyboardist mumbled that she took the night off. Worried now, he headed for room 704. She let him right in.

"What's up? I went to the lounge and you weren't there?"

"Did you hear them? Rehearsal was more of the same, a total disaster. I was going to just suck it up, like you told me, but after the folks in the show production told me that Schwartzman was on board, I panicked. I am freaking out, Grant."

"Who the hell is Schwartzman?"

"Just one of the biggest names in show business, that's all. He is a critic and has been around for a long time. Can make or break someone with the snap of a finger. I couldn't risk him hearing me with those guys. They are trying, but they just don't get it. They don't need a chirp, they need a chick. If Schwartzman hears me in there, I'll never work again."

"Do you know him, this Schwartzman guy? If he is as big as you say, he must be able to judge talent on its own merits."

"I've never met him. They say he is retiring to Vegas so now he does critiques for this cruise line and some of the Vegas places. I don't know what to do."

"Alright, let's come up with a plan. First of all we probably need to sit down and talk to him, tell him the problem. Maybe even ask for his advice. Is he checking up on all the entertainers on board? He probably won't be very happy with me either."

"I heard you were spectacular last night, Grant, but he probably won't care about what you do. They don't pay a lot of attention to the piano bars, just to the drink count. It's mostly soloist and groups, plus he's really hard on the troupe performances, everything from dance routines to condition of the costumes. They are all nervous wrecks down there. He is already meeting with them and they say he is brutal. He will be at their big opening tonight, both shows. And you know what? They are all housed down with the crew. They have to double up and eat down there, too. We got lucky with our rooms. I can't figure out how I got a veranda and flowers and everything."

"Maybe the entertainment Gods are taking care of you, Jodee."

"Don't I wish. But I don't believe in good fairies anymore, Grant. Like you said the other night, life is just one big crapshoot."

"Well, here is an idea. If you don't want to perform with the disaster duo, come to the Casablanca Lounge tonight and sing with me. It might be better than nothing, better than refusing to sing altogether. We won't ask anyone. We'll just do it. There is no time for us to rehearse and I need to tell you I don't play accompaniment very well, so we will have to wing it. What do you want to sing? We'll do a few numbers to get the feel of it and then we'll practice tomorrow. I'll skip Rhodes and we'll work on your stuff. At least old man Schwartzman can see what you can do. Or he can fire us both, whatever. We'll deal with it."

"Are you sure, Grant? I don't want to screw you up. They were really bragging about the new piano man in the Casablanca when I was downstairs. I'm going to their rehearsals trying to see if they can use me in the chorus or as a stand in for someone."

"I'm positive, Jodee. What do you want to sing? We'll give it our best shot."

She was already getting her music, and they began to mentally rehearse. She would show up around ten o'clock. Grant headed to the dining room, signing a few autographs as he went and shaking a few hands. He spotted the Palmer Plantation group right away, seated together, all laughing, more acquainted now, and he scanned for Shay, planning to ask about her ankle. Mitch was seated between Babs and the woman who just adored everything, and Joan and Shay were across from them. Ralph in Real Estate was next to Shay with his arm casually draped around the back of her chair. Grant greeted everyone warmly as he passed by, only casually nodding at Shay, and took the last remaining seat at another table with two couples he hadn't met yet.

There were thirty two in the group, twelve couples, and the rest singles. Babs was looking over her little flock, making sure that everyone was having a good time. Babs spent a lot of time on the details for these trips and she was enjoying some success in her business as more and more people were hearing about how marvelous her trips were. The problem was that she wasn't making much money at it, but right now she was pleased with the compatibility of this group. She made note of where everyone was seated, who was with who, paying especial attention to where Grant ended up and wondering what was up with Ralph and Shay. She was a born matchmaker and had romantic notions about meeting the perfect man in some exotic place, probably because she had watched so many reruns of "Love Boat." Nonetheless, it wouldn't hurt business any if the love boat idea was floated around Palmer Plantation. She had become pretty good friends with Maureen, the singles group membership chairman, and sometimes the two of them giggled about such things, even floating the idea that they could plan trips just for singles, even though most of her customers were couples, most married, some not. She knew for a fact that two of the couples in this group were not married but nobody cared. Many had adopted this lifestyle as a matter of convenience or companionship, with or without privileges, as she put it, and she wondered about Mitch, what he would expect. One look at Grant and she knew what he was after.

Grant Albright had been the topic of the day. After last night's surprise in the Casablanca Lounge and today's attention to the injured Shay, and the purchase of the fantastic rug, his mystique grew and speculation was rampant. Where was he from, they wondered. Can you imagine, a musician, of all things! I never would have guessed that. He must have done well, that gorgeous house and all. I hear he has beautiful things. He's a great golfer, could be club champion if he worked at it. Does he have family nearby? He is pretty young. Do you think he'll stay? He's hard to read, nobody really knows him. He seems nice enough. I wonder why he moved to Palmer. He doesn't really fit in, does he, being a celebrity and all. He certainly was attentive to Shay. Do you think there is anything going on there? No, he was just trying to help.

Bob, who lived near the marina, offered his impression. "He just seemed like a regular guy to me. Talked about fishing. Asked about my boat, was real interested. I didn't get the impression at all that he felt out of place. Sharon and I are going to have him over for dinner on our boat when we get back."

But the speculation continued and they collectively began to claim ownership of him, announcing to others that they met along the way that they knew Grant Albright from home, that they all lived in Palmer Plantation, giving them an entreé to conversations with other passengers, enhancing their connection and encouraging others not to miss him in the Casablanca Lounge. One of the women in the group wrote little articles for the Palmer newsletter and was already composing one about this celebrity in their midst. Perhaps she could interview him and answer lots of questions about him, enhancing her own status not only as well traveled but well-connected too.

Grant finished his dinner and politely excused himself to go to work, as he put it. As he passed Shay's table he paused briefly, pointing his finger at her the way men do, in a gun like manner, taking dead aim. "How are you doing? Is Ralph taking good care of you for me?" he teased, taking aim at Ralph as well, thereby firing the first shot.

"She's in good hands," Ralph fired back. "The pleasure is all mine."

"Well, it's always comforting to have a medical man around when we need one. We all appreciate you, Ralph."

Grant headed directly to the Casablanca Lounge. He saw a group of folks standing at the entrance and several asked for his autograph and others extended their hand for a handshake. Ethan, the cruise director, was talking to them, explaining that the room was full. He suggested that the folks take in the second show in the Grand Theatre and come by the Casablanca Lounge after that performance. Seeing Grant, he said, "Well, well. Here is the man of the hour now." He led Grant past the line and into the lounge. "It seems you created quite a sensation last night. Hopefully the excitement will die down after tonight or we are going to have a riot on our hands," he joked.

"I'll try to do a little worse tonight, maybe hit a few more wrong notes."

"The magic will wear off, Grant. The first couple of nights they love everything. They'll all be getting tired after a few days and then you will end up playing to a few stragglers. Your drink sales were really up, though, so old man Schwartzman will let you get by with murder as long as the booze is moving. He's tough but he understands the business end of things too."

"Is this Schwartzman guy as important around here as I'm hearing? I don't think I've seen him."

"He's a real bastard. Has had whole troupes canned and we go through directors like crazy because no one can satisfy him. But top management listens to him and we do end up with the best entertainment in the cruise business. Like I said, he understands the business part. He doesn't just do the entertainment, he does everything, the wine lists, the food presentation, condition of everything, even off duty clothes."

"How often does he come? Do you get any warning?"

"A couple of times a year, we never know when. I guess the higher ups know when. He always gets a suite and everyone kowtows to him."

"I hope he doesn't come in to hear me. If he does you will probably be short a piano player."

"Don't worry about it, Grant. Nobody gives a shit about the piano player. Just keep on doing what you were doing last night and keep the liquor flowing. That's all that counts."

Grant couldn't help but laugh at the whole situation. Here he had been trying to put together a variety of sets, choosing groupings of songs, mixing it up some, trying to satisfy requests, all the while being told that nobody gives a shit about the piano player. Well, that was good to know. Now he didn't have to worry about giving some of his time to Jodee. He would play some light stuff until ten and then lay back and let her take over.

The Palmer group was all going to the opening show in the Grand Atheneè Theatre and planned to stop by the Casablanca Lounge for a nightcap. Joan was dying to hear about Shay's time alone with Grant last night at the sail-away but she and Shay hadn't had any time to talk about it because, when Shay returned to their room, Joan was so upset about the email she got from Chrissie that she could think of nothing else. Shay had tried her best to be supportive, trying to allay Joan's worry, but after hearing the story, Shay got a little worried too. Chrissie had written that she had met the most wonderful man on line and he was planning to come to Charlotte. Joan was beside herself.

"Can you imagine! Coming to Charlotte! From California! And she is so gullible to believe that he only wants to look at real estate! I know it is a trick. I can feel it. Mothers get a sense of these things, Shay. It just scares me to death. He is probably up to something sinister, something terrible. I think I better go home and go to Charlotte and find out for myself. I can't enjoy another day not knowing what's going on. I'll talk to Babs tomorrow and have her make arrangements for me to fly home from Athens."

"Let's try to calm down and talk this through. Did she say how she met him, on a dating site, or what? She does advertise real estate on the web. It could all be about that."

"You know her, Shay. Such a romantic. I knew she was having a hard time about what happened, and here I am half way around the world when she needs me."

"Joan, I think Chrissie is more level headed than you give her credit for. I understand the potential for danger, but maybe it won't happen. Maybe he won't even come, maybe she'll get cold feet and cancel. Did you reply yet?"

"No. Oh, Shay, what do you think I should say? She didn't ask for my blessing or anything and she doesn't take criticism very well."

"Let's go down to the computer center and compose a reply right now. If you would like, I'll write to her and casually mention what you told me. Maybe we'll get a different feel for the situation if she replies to me."

It had taken them two hours to compose four lines, but at least Joan felt a little better about it after asking Chrissie to please delay his visit until she got home. Shay's time alone with Grant wasn't even mentioned. Today had been so busy at Ephesus and then Shay getting hurt, there wasn't much time to talk or to worry about anything.

The grand opening musical production was spectacular. Several of the Palmer people sat together and others separated, choosing a seat in another area. The three gals and Shay were together. Wanda had chosen the seats because she had experience cruising and knew where the best seats were, but shortly after they were seated they decided to move because the air conditioner was blowing right on them. "It is cold in here," Joan complained. Maureen added that she was freezing. "Why didn't we think to bring our pashminas? Look how many women are wrapped in pashminas."

"That's probably why they sell them in Ephesus. They probably know how cold it is on these boats. Pretty smart of them. No wonder so many people were buying them. This room is the coldest one on the whole boat. Thank goodness we can control the temperature in our rooms. From now on we need to remember to bring our pashminas to this place."

They gathered their drinks and programs and headed to the upper level because Wanda said warm air rises so they would be warmer up there, which was only partially true, because there wasn't much warm air to rise, and they were only slightly warmer. Babs and the Dimpled Darling had come in with Mitch and Ralph and were seated right below them, where they could look down and see every move. Joan hated to stare but she kept glancing down, watching Mitch's every move, more disappointed than ever to see him seated next to Babs again. Babs was really getting her talons into him and he seemed to be enjoying her company and Joan felt like a fool for having such a strong attraction to him. She had loved holding his arm as they walked through the bazaar and again today at Ephesus.

Ralph was leaning back in his seat, pretty much ignoring the adoring one, scanning the crowd as he looked for Shay. Finally he stood up for a better look and spotted her in the balcony, seated with the three gals. A huge smile spread across his face and he waved, probably just waving to Shay, but they all waved back. After the show they all headed to the Casablanca Lounge.

Grant began to play promptly at nine, intending to do really light stuff, but there was a list propped up on the keyboard with the heading "Requests for Grant Albright."

He didn't know who it was from but he was intrigued by the list and decided to have a go at it. First was *Manhattan Serenade*. He hadn't played it in a long time but thought, "What the hell, nobody gives a shit about the piano player anyway," so he started, happy that it came back to him, relaxed with the pressure off, enjoying himself. Next was *Deep Purple*, one of his favorites, followed by *Malagueña*. It had been one of his recital pieces, eighth grade he remembered, a pretty big piece for him at the time. He drew in a breath and began to play, easing the slow tempo, gradually building, feeling the beauty and the tension rising, smiling at the memory of Ms. Eula Bartlette, his piano teacher, rapping with her baton. "Don't rush, Grant. Let it come naturally, building, building, building." He could hear her in his sleep. When he finished they stood and applauded, appreciative, wanting more. Jodee had come in, so he settled back down, playing a nice medley of *Beauty and The Beast* and *When You Wish Upon a Star*, ending with *A Dream Is A Wish That Your Heart Makes,* all beautiful music from Disney films. Then he started with Jodee's selections.

The plan was that he would start playing a few lines of her first number and she would come forward and start to sing. He glanced her way, nodded and winked and started softly with the familiar strains of *Begin the Beguine*. After a short introduction, Jodee slowly began to come forward, humming as she came, acknowledging the audience, looking radiant in a beautiful cerise cocktail dress cut to a pretty low décolletage and covered in crystal and lace embellishment. The skirt was just at her knees showing her beautiful legs and high heeled strappy matching sandals. Her platinum hair was cut to just below her ears, waving naturally. She looked like a million dollars. And then she started to sing, the words oozing like honey, rich and enticing. She swayed gently to the rhythm, occasionally glancing at Grant with a beguiling smile, flirtatious, and he responded, returning her smile, and getting her clues, sensing her breathing, and anticipating her phrasing. She occasionally gave him a little hand directive or began to snap her fingers to the tempo she wanted and he easily accommodated, gradually giving her more than simple melody, embellishing, stretching, and waiting when she needed it and filling in, giving that extra something to polish the performance. One thing was for sure, Jodee Jordan could sing. This was no amateur night. She was a pro. She held them in her hand, singing directly to them, connecting, loving the music, loving them, loving the applause. He started to play her second selection, something more recent, and she began the love song, *As Long As He Needs Me,* singing with such feeling that you could have heard a pin drop. She was pure sex. She had it all.

The Palmer Plantation group was entering the room as the song ended in another round of enthusiastic applause and he began to play *I Dreamed a Dream* from "*Les Miserables.*" Jodee was on a roll, feeding off the applause, and he could see that she was in her element, nursing each syllable, caressing each word. At one point she walked around behind him, stroking his shoulders, giving him a little pat of appreciation, and finishing to more applause, standing with her head slightly bowed, and blowing a few kisses. Grant rose and announced, "Ladies and Gentleman, Miss Jodee Jordan," leading another round of appreciation. She turned and wrapped her arms around his neck, kissing his cheek, and whispered, "Thanks Grant. Thanks for everything. Whatever happens, I will always be grateful." He returned Jodee's embrace and kiss. "You were great Jodee. Really great." She slipped out of the room.

Mitch was taking it all in, seeing for the first time the chemistry between Grant and Jodee and thinking that this whole trip was just one big mistake. Jodee Jordan was definitely not the right woman for Grant Albright.

Shay Porter was taking it all in too, her heart sinking at the ease and warmth that showed on Grant's face when he looked at Jodee. Grant took a little break, thanking folks and shaking a few hands, and headed right toward Shay. "Thanks for coming," he said. "Care if I join you for a few minutes?" He settled himself right next to her on the loveseat.

Shay felt like all eyes were on her, like his presence had somehow elevated her significance, her stature, that somehow his being near her was sending a silent message that she was his, that she mattered, that he cared, and she immediately began to shift her weight slightly away from him, surrounding herself in that protective shield she wore so well, afraid to appear receptive, afraid of sending the wrong message, afraid she was falling under his spell. After what she had just seen, that connection with Jodee, that kiss at the end, there was no way she could expose herself to the hurt and humiliation of being dumped by Grant Albright. Or worse, being used. There was no way she could compete with the sexy Jodee Jordan.

Mitch came over and shook Grant's hand. "Nice performance, Buddy. You did a great job. I see your friend Jodee was a hit too. Is this going to be a regular thing?" Mitch grabbed a chair and put it right next to Joan, sort of squeezing in between Joan and Wanda.

"I don't think so. We're just trying out a few things to see what works. She's pretty good, isn't she?"

Grant usually took only fifteen minutes for a break, but he seemed in no hurry to leave tonight, engaging them all in conversation, asking questions about tomorrow's plans, laughing and joking with Mitch and pretty much ignoring Shay until it was time to go. "So how's your ankle doing? Do you think you can handle Rhodes tomorrow?"

"I'm sure it will be fine, Grant, especially since you picked out the ugliest shoes I have ever seen to ensure my surefootedness," she laughed.

"What do you mean, I picked out? I distinctly remember picking out the black ones. You picked out the tan ones. I don't think they're that ugly. Now you will at least look sensible and I won't have to worry about you breaking your neck," again insinuating himself in her life in a way that suggested honest concern. "Mitch, you will have to take care of her for me tomorrow. I plan to skip Rhodes."

Shay hoped her disappointment at that news didn't show, but as he started to get up he said quietly to her, "I only have one more set, can you stay? We can get a nightcap or a cup of coffee afterward."

"That would be lovely. I would really enjoy hearing you play some more. I only heard that last song with Jodee, so this is the first time I get to hear you by yourself," surprising herself with her own response, almost as if someone else were speaking for her, and she was embarrassed that she sounded so eager to spend more time with him.

"Well, there's a first time for everything, Shay, so I'll play this set just for you. Come over here. Sit in this chair, right here where I can see you." He went to the piano grinning, and started to play a familiar tune, which at first Shay didn't recognize, and then she could feel herself turning red, embarrassed and thrilled at the same time as he played *I Only Have Eyes For You*.

There had been one other person observing the evening, listening to Grant, and then Jodee, and then watching Grant with his friends. Ethan, the cruise director, had been keeping a close eye on the events of the evening, not so much because he was checking up on Grant, but because he knew he would be called on the carpet if he didn't have a handle on things. He liked Grant a lot and the liquor sales were outstanding, but he wasn't sure what was going on with the Jordan gal and he had been asked to keep an eye on her. He didn't know for sure who had ordered that, but he had heard that things weren't going well in *The Fez* and he wondered what the connection was. He was usually notified of any changes and he hadn't heard anything, but whoever gave the green light on her appearance in the Casablanca Lounge was a mystery, one he needed to solve. And he needed to check out the *Fez* before old man Schwartzman got there. Apparently the Jordan gal was a no show there tonight, which was guaranteed to get her fired. And he would be in hot water for not being on top of the situation. He wasn't in charge of the performers, but he was the one who was to be the eyes and ears for those who were, hearing and reporting what problem areas there were. He planned to grab Grant as soon as he finished.

But Grant had other plans, still relieved to know that he would be cut some slack because nobody gave a crap about him anyway. He headed right for Shay. Ethan called to him. "Grant, wait a minute. Can I speak to you for a minute? I need to talk to you about something."

"Wait here, Shay. Give me a second to see what he wants."

Shay recognized Ethan. He was a very visible personality on the ship, so she figured it was some little matter, but watching Grant talk to him across the room, she could see that this appeared to be more than that. Ethan was waving his arms around and Grant appeared rigid, even defiant, finally just shrugging, but she couldn't hear what was being said.

"You can't do that, Grant. It's not any of your business what happens to her."

"Like hell it's not," Grant answered. "She at least deserves a fair shake. Did you hear her tonight? She's the best voice on the ship, and now you want to can her? I can't believe this."

"It's not me, Grant. It's policy. She's a no show. I know the rules. We have to follow the rules or everyone will pull that crap."

"Do me a favor. Keep it under your hat for another day, and keep Schwartzman out of the *Fez*. I'll talk to her tomorrow and meet with the guys too. We'll find a solution. Just don't make any report about her. If it comes up, say there was a mix-up, a misunderstanding. Blame me if you need to blame someone, but don't blame her."

"I'll sit on it as long as I can, Grant, but I can't make any promises. Schwartzman might have been told about it already.

Check in with me tomorrow. I have to stay on top of this." The two men shook hands and Grant returned to Shay.

"Ready? Let's take a stroll around the deck. Is your foot alright for that? I need some fresh air. Are you hungry? Do you want something to eat or a drink?"

"A walk would be fine, Grant. Is everything OK?"

"No, everything is fucked up, but I'll deal with it later."

Shay was a little surprised that he used that word, not offended, just surprised. Her own father had been a world class cusser until Parkinson's robbed him of the ability, and she was pretty familiar with the vocabulary in all of its applications. Grant sounded pretty upset about something. They strolled around the deck one time before he suggested that they sit in a quiet little spot they had just passed. He ordered them each a cappuccino and then turned to her.

"So, you are from Charlotte," he said.

"Yes, I've lived there all my life."

"You don't live in Palmer Plantation at all? How do you wind up with the group, just good friends with someone? Joan, I presume?"

"I've really just met her. Her daughter is a friend of mine and encouraged me to take this trip. It seems to be working out well for us both."

"Are you thinking about moving there, about leaving Charlotte?"

"I don't have any plans to do that, but it does sound lovely. I guess everyone there comes from somewhere else. Where are you from, Grant?"

"We moved from Raleigh."

She couldn't help but notice that he had said "we" and she felt awkward pursuing the topic knowing what had happened.

He continued, "We lived in Raleigh all our lives before that. I guess we are all Tar Heels, aren't we? Where did you go to high school?"

"Myers Park. Where did you go?"

"Broughton. But I know Myers Park. We played them every year. And I've played golf at the club there quite a few times. It's a nice area."

"We didn't actually live in the Myers Park neighborhood, just in the school district, but you are right, it is lovely. I went to a teacher's conference at Broughton several years ago. And I've taken some renewal courses at State. Raleigh is nice too."

"Really? What were you renewing?"

"I'm a teacher, Grant. Teachers need to be constantly renewing their licenses and getting certified in something or other. There is no end to it. I plan to renew just one more time and then that's it," she added laughing. "I don't suppose musicians have to do that, do they?"

"No, I don't suppose they do," he said. "But maybe I should consider it when this gig is over. Maybe I could find a real job if I just renewed something." He laughed, but decided not to tell her any more. "What do you teach, Shay? Maybe you can teach me something?"

"That is very unlikely. I taught first and second grades, mostly. Two years of third, but I really loved the little ones best."

"You said taught. Is that past tense? You aren't teaching now, obviously, since it is September, nearly October. Did you take a sabbatical?

"No, I took early retirement for personal reasons. It really hurts my pension not completing thirty years and it will make things a lot harder for me, but it was the right thing to do at the time. I think I can go back and add years later."

"Yeah, those personal reasons can really get in the way of the best laid plans, can't they?"

They sat in silence then, feeling somewhat uncomfortable with the topic of personal reasons, which always meant problems, code for trouble, and he wondered what kind of personal problems she had. He wasn't about to share his own. She thought she knew what his personal problem was, but she had no idea what was really eating at him. Grant checked his watch and said he better return her to her room before she turned into a pumpkin or something, and they strolled toward the elevators.

"Up or down?" he asked.

"Down," she said. "Six." He pressed the six and then stood close to her, almost touching, putting his arm lightly around her waist when the door opened, and then taking her arm as he walked her to her stateroom.

"Enjoy Rhodes, Shay. I want a full report. Thanks for tonight."

"Goodnight, Grant. And thank you, too."

She could feel her heart beat, not like it would if she had been running, and not how it did when Eddie died, but different, like excited, happy, in love. "Stop it," she said to herself. "Stop it right now. Grant Albright is out of bounds, off limits, untouchable and uninterested, a musician, for Pete's sake. Totally, just totally wrong," and the most handsome, wonderful guy she had ever met.

Grant headed for his own room, deciding not to check on his email until tomorrow morning. Matt would surely let him know something by then. Matt was his oldest, the perfect kid, and they had had such high hopes for him. For the most part, Matt had fulfilled every hope that every parent has for their kids, everything except the happily ever after part, and this mess he was in now was tearing Grant apart. If Matt had only opened up to him, let him know how bad things were, he wouldn't have taken this trip. He would have deadheaded to California, been there to offer his support, even testify, if that would help. But Matt had tried to solve everything on his own, had a naïve belief in the justice system and unswerving confidence in his lawyer and had convinced his Dad that everything was a "done deal", in that cocky manner of a thirty two year old who had never been reamed a new one. And now Grant was kicking himself for not going. Grant and his brothers had had plenty of experience in courts through the years, all business matters, but it was enough for Grant to know that there was no such thing as a slam dunk in court. Even when it was over, it wasn't over. And Matt's last email sounded full of uncertainty, sending that chilling message of danger that a parent recognizes, that which isn't always said, just felt, and Grant was feeling it now.

He entered the room quietly, expecting Mitch to be sound asleep, and planning to crash himself, but Mitch was waiting for him.

"What's up? I thought you would be asleep by now."

"Yeah, I would have been, but I have this teenaged roommate I have to wait up for," Mitch joked. "Grant, I think we need to talk."

"Yes, sir. Here I am. Talk."

"I know it's none of my business, Grant, but it seems to me that we have both gotten off our plan. Things have been pretty busy, I know, but I'll come right out and say it, that Jodee gal is putting a hit on you. You need to put the brakes on, Grant. She is going to ride your shirttails, if you know what I mean."

"I'm not sure I do know what you mean, Mitch. Ride my shirttails to where?"

"To wherever the hell you take her, that's where. She's slick, Grant. She's been around. She's a real looker, real sexy. Any guy would like to have her, you know what I mean, Grant, but you are playing with fire. She is hot and dangerous."

"What are you saying, that you don't think I can handle something hot and dangerous?"

"I know you can handle it, Grant. I just don't think you should. I don't think you are ready for the likes of her."

"Look, Mitch. You have it all wrong. Jodee is trying to get her career on track, that's all. That's all there is to it. She needs a piano player, nothing else. If I played the tuba she wouldn't give me the time of day. You can stop worrying. I'm not even keeping score anymore."

"How about last night? You spent the night with her. And I suppose you just came from her room again. She called a few minutes ago and left a message."

"What did she say?"

"She said to tell you thanks again for everything, that it was one of the best, Grant, right off the charts. It doesn't get any better."

"She was talking about the music, Mitch. You are jumping to conclusions. There is nothing cryptic about that message."

"Well, if she said that to me I would know what she meant. I saw her out there, Grant. It sure didn't look like it was just about the music. She's putting out so she can use you to get ahead and you are falling for it. Does she know much about you, what you have been through? You're thinking with the wrong brain, Grant."

"Yeah, that other brain buts in now and then, Mitch, but it was just show business. And for your information, I didn't just come from her room. Now go to sleep before I start asking you about Betty."

"It's Babs, Grant. She really knows her stuff."

"Maybe, but I'll lay you two to one it's you she wants to know."

"I'll take that and double you. Show business, my foot."

"Goodnight, Mitch

The Fez Lounge

There is a saying that a mother is only as happy as her unhappiest child, a sentiment that resonates with parents everywhere, regardless of age, crossing all financial or social status, spanning countries, even oceans, beyond caring, even beyond hope, resisting all rationale or reason. It exists deep inside, gnawing at the very psyche of parenthood in a way that no one can explain, only feel. For one passenger on the beautiful cruise ship Atheneè those words would be weighing heavily as the events of the day unfolded. Jodee Jordan had ended yesterday on such a high note, exhilarated, thrilled at how things had gone in the Casablanca Lounge. She was excited about working with Grant, and enthusiastic about their collaboration, and was eagerly anticipating meeting with him today. She would join him on the Lido deck for brunch. She had risen early and walked out on her private veranda ready to enjoy the coffee that had already been set out for her, enjoying the beauty of the Aegean and the early solitude of the day.

There had been a knock on her door at 8:00 and she almost waltzed her way to answer, surprised and thrilled to receive another beautiful bouquet, quickly glancing at the card, halfway expecting to see Grant's name. Instead, the note read, "I heard you were fabulous last night," that's all. Just brief words, like on the first arrangement that greeted her when she had arrived. "Now, who in the world could be doing this?" she wondered. "Perhaps Grant was right, the entertainment Gods are taking notice of me," she laughed. She selected a pretty pantsuit that had been delivered with the other clothes from the wardrobe department, another mystery but a welcome supplement to her rather sparse collection from home, and headed to the shower, singing. She paid meticulous attention to her hair and makeup, wanting to look her best for him. They were to meet at 10:30. She took one last look at herself in the full length mirror, pretty satisfied but still wishing she could shed some pounds, and turned toward the door, stooping to pick up several pieces of paper that had been slid under. The usual daily news and schedule were there, and a notice that there was a message waiting for her at Reception. There was also a sealed envelope, which she tore open. "See me at 4:00. Important. Ethan." She folded it and tucked it into the small imitation alligator bag she had packed for day excursions, and headed to the Lido deck.

Grant Albright had spent a restless night, tossing and turning, occasionally waking and thinking about Matt, debating whether to get up and check his email. He had gone to the computer center at 8:30 this morning, relieved to see that there was something from Matt. Megan had written too.

To: Daddy
From: Megan

Just wanted to say "hi" and mention something to you. We have never talked about this, Daddy, but you are a very attractive man for your age and there are women on cruise ships who are just out trolling for a man, and you are such an easy target, still so fragile from grief and all, and I just want to warn you about these women. Sometimes they are after money. I have read about scams where women will fake some crisis at home and get the man to send money, things like that. Sometimes they just want other things, you know. And, Daddy, there are diseases. Please, please be careful!! Of course, Misty and Matt and I want you to be happy, don't get me wrong, but a cruise ship can be very, very dangerous for an attractive single man.

There, now I've said it!! You know how I worry so, Daddy.

Love and hugs, Megan

Reply: No problem, no women on board. I got my flu shot. STOP WORRYING!

Love and hugs, Daddy

PS: What do you mean, for my age?

Megan was his middle child, a born caregiver. She was always playing dolls, always the mother, and looked after her brother and sister like a security guard, always doing for them. When her mother was sick she had been doting, caring, loving, taking care of them all. And she worried about everything. She had two little boys of her own that she doted on and hovered over, and now that her mother was gone she had transferred all of her caring and worrying to her Dad. It was driving him nuts. He didn't know how to handle it so he teased her a lot, making light of most of her advice, sometimes blowing her off and pissing her off, but realizing that it was a fact, if he ever needed help, it would be Megan he would turn to.

He opened Matt's email

To: Dad
From: Matt

No news. She nor her lawyer showed up so the

freak'n judge gave them three more days. It sucks! I'm still trying to slay that dragon, Dad. I miss Puff.

Love, Matt

Reply: You are right, that sucks. You'll get that dragon this time, Matt. I miss Puff too.

Love, Dad

"Shit!" he said out loud, loud enough for the woman at the computer next to him to hear, but she was good natured about it.

"That bad, huh? I heard from my kids too," she laughed. "Somehow we all survive parenthood, don't we? I saw you last night. That was a terrific singer you had. Will she be there tonight?"

"I hope so. If you see Ethan, mention it to him," he replied and headed to the Promenade deck for some fresh air and a quiet place to think. Matt didn't deserve this. What the hell did his lawyer say? Didn't he object? Christ. What a mess. He hurt for that little boy who loved to play with dragons. When Matt was about three or four he discovered dragons and when other boys were playing with dinosaurs or action toys Matt was playing with dragons, always pretending to be the hero, slaying one. He had a stuffed dragon that he carried around and slept with. They had named the dragon Puff and the song *Puff The Magic Dragon* was his favorite. Grant must have played it for Matt a million times. And they would sing it, usually in the car, and he and Vonnie had to kiss Puff goodnight when they tucked Matt in. Tears began to puddle in his eyes at the memory, a million emotions flooding him like a rising tide, washing over him, carrying him out to a dark sea of sadness, and he fought to stay afloat, desperately clinging to a reserve of inner strength that could sustain him, rescue him, grateful that the whole Palmer group would be ashore at Rhodes and he wouldn't have to deal with any of them.

He regained his composure and walked around the deck several times and then headed to the Lido deck where he was meeting Jodee. She was right on time, looked great, and planted a kiss on his forehead before taking her seat.

"Good morning, Sunshine," she said. "Have you had your coffee or do you want to go to the buffet?"

"Let's wait a few minutes, Jodee. "I'm not ready to eat."

"Just coffee," she said to the waiter and looked quizzically at Grant, sensing something, a pensiveness not present before and immediately jumped to the conclusion that he was having misgivings about last night, wanting to change things, wanting out. "Grant, you don't have to go through with this. If you want out, just say the word. No hard feelings, OK."

"What do you mean, if I want out? Of course I don't want out. I thought you were in agreement, that you were on board," he replied with a sharpness she hadn't heard before. "I'm trying to go to bat for you. Have you changed your mind?"

"Of course not, Grant. What you did last night was the nicest thing anyone ever did for me. You just seem a little less enthusiastic this morning, that's all, and I would feel terrible if any of this ended up getting you in trouble."

"Jodee, you were terrific last night. If I seem a little quiet it's because I've had an email from Matt and I'm really worried about him."

"Does he know anything yet, has he told you what happened?"

"No, everything has been delayed for three days. We're still waiting."

"From what you've told me it sounds like things should be in Matt's favor. A delay could be good news, Grant."

"Probably not, it's all just a crapshoot, Jodee. It's not about what's fair or what's right."

"Do you want to skip this stuff today? I can try to make the best of things."

"No, work will help me keep my mind off of it. We'll figure out a plan for you. We'll work all day if that's what it takes. Can you ask the duo to meet with us? I think you are going to have to work with them a little while longer. Ethan was asking about you last night."

"Ethan? That's funny. I had a message from him this morning. It's right here in my purse. He wants to see me about something."

Grant read the note, showing no emotion at all, covering the dread he felt. "Alright, we have until four o'clock to pull something together. We'll get something to eat now and then get started. And, Jodee, just so you know, I plan to meet with Ethan and you. You are not going in alone. Get a hold of the guys and set up a time as early as possible."

"I'll try to get them now, and then I have to go to the reception desk. They have a message for me."

"We'll go together, Jodee. I want you to stay right with me all day in case something unexpected comes up."

Jodee connected with Paul, the keyboardist, and he was very agreeable, eager to meet with her. "Have you seen old man Schwartzman?" he asked. "You really fucked us last night, Jodee, but he didn't come by that we know of. I'll see you at 12:30."

"I know, Paul, and I'm really, really sorry about that. I just freaked out. See you at 12:30."

With so many people off the ship enjoying Rhodes it was nearly deserted at the reception area so Jodee went right up and asked for her message. She was handed an envelope and together she and Grant walked over to a settee while she opened it. Grant watched her, carefully examining her expression as she read. The message had been sent to the ship as an email and the office had printed it for delivery. She read it carefully then looked up with a stricken expression, turning white in front of his eyes. He reached for her, taking her hand in his. "What is it, Jodee?"

"It's from Leighanna," she said, and handed it to him.

He read it and handed it back to her. She had confided in him, telling him a great deal about Leighanna and how much she worried about her. Grant had confided some things in her as well, had mentioned how worried he was about Matt and his situation.

"Let's get a drink. I think we both could use one. How about a Bloody Mary?"

"It's a little early for a drink, Grant, but I agree, a Bloody Mary would be great right now. We have a few minutes to sit and digest things before we meet with the boys. Let's go to that little bar across from the Fez."

They started toward the bar and then changed their minds and decided to have a drink around the pool instead. Grant guided Jodee to a small umbrella table away from the lounge chairs, but in full view of all who passed by. Several passengers acknowledged them, some complimented Jodee, others commented on Grant's playing. Ethan saw them from across the way and gave a little hand wave in acknowledgment but he didn't come over. The trombone player in the combo that played during cocktail hour in the Crow's Nest walked by and stopped to chat, and the lady who ran the jewelry store passed by and took a seat several chairs away, facing them. Grant and Jodee sipped their Bloody Marys and began to relax. They were not paying much attention to the comings and goings around them until Grant spotted a familiar face heading their way. Settling into adjoining lounge chairs, cuddling and snuggling, was none other than the Dimpled Darling from Palmer Plantation. She was with a rather pudgy, bald headed, sixtyish man. Grant turned his head away, hoping not to be seen, but it was too late.

"Grant, Grant Albright," she called, rising like a Phoenix from her lounge chair and making a beeline right for him, her camera at the ready. "Isn't it just wonderful that we are all here enjoying this beautiful day around the pool instead of dragging ourselves all over those awful ruins? I just adore this, don't you?"

Grant stood politely, thinking he should introduce her to Jodee, aware that he didn't even know her name, but before he could start, she was already pouncing on Jodee.

"It is so lovely to meet you, Miss Jordan. I heard you sing last night. I just adore meeting celebrities, and here you are with our very own Grant Albright. He is from Palmer Plantation, you know, in North Carolina. Grant, move over close so I can get a picture. Hold still for one more. Perfect! I'll send it to Maureen so she can put it in the singles club newsletter and I'll send one to Babs too. You two make the perfect couple, just perfect for her to use in her travel promotions. Just like the Love Boat. I just adore seeing pictures of celebrities, especially ones I know personally. Just adore it. I am going to come to the Casablanca Lounge to hear you tonight. I'm bringing my new friend, Joe, too. It's just been so lovely meeting you, Miss Jordan."

Jodee took the dimpled darling's hand in both of hers and said, "It has been my pleasure to meet you and to see that Grant lives in a place with such lovely people. What is your name, dear? I will dedicate a song to you and your new friend tonight."

"My name is Nannette, Nannette Guppie. I would just adore it if you did that. I've never had a song dedicated to me before. Grant, move over closer and put your arm around Jodee for one more picture. Perfect! I'll see you tonight." She happily returned to Joe, who was waiting to welcome her with a broad smile, thinking she was just the cutest thing he had seen in a long time, wondering what she saw in him. Maybe his luck was changing.

"My goodness, she is exhausting, all that adoring. Is she always like that?"

"From what I'm hearing, apparently she is. I had never met her before, but I hate the idea of her plastering our picture all over the place. That's embarrassing."

"That's show business, Grant. Consider it a compliment. It looks like she has found herself a sugar daddy. That guy she is with is some tycoon from Arizona. Worth millions, I heard. Some of the girls in the show chorus were talking about him last night. He takes these cruises all the time."

"Do you think there are really women just out to get a guy's money, that they don't care who or how?"

"Sure I do, Grant. A lot of that goes on. A guy just has to be careful, that's all."

"Well, if we aren't careful, we'll both be out of a job, so we better get to work. I think we should go get ready for the disaster duo. You and I can toss around a few ideas before they get there."

"That's a good idea, and maybe you can give me some ideas about how to deal with my problem, while you're at it. I don't know how to answer Leighanna, Grant."

"I know. We'll talk about that, too.

The disaster duo was right on time. Paul, the guitar player, and Tommy, the keyboardist, greeted Grant by name, calling him Mr. Albright, expectant and receptive of his ideas and letting him take the lead, both frantic for any help they could get.

"Look, guys. You are both really good in your own right, but this doesn't work as a group, and the Schwartzman thing is only making it worse. Let's try to keep him out of the picture, stop thinking about what he might like and think more about how we can best use your talents. It seems to me we have the ingredients, we just don't have the recipe. For starters, let's think in terms of sets, what things you can change in a certain time frame rather than trying to rebuild from scratch. As a duo you guys have a great sound, a synergy, and I suspect that your former female vocalist completed that, that you worked as a unit. But Jodee is a soloist. When she is singing you have to play accompaniment, backup, not compete with her, and that is where the adjustment has to be made. But Jodee is so good, if you just give her the rhythm she wants and some simple melody, she can carry you. She'll give you the tempo. Just watch her for the signals and really listen to the lyrics. You can fake the fills. I know that isn't what they teach in music schools, but it works. I would also suggest that you start by having Jodee sing in only one set. If you play three sets let her have the middle one. That way you can showcase your versatility without compromising yourselves. Let's come up with some light country for tonight. Jodee can do some stuff like *Don't It Make My Brown Eyes Blue* or some Dolly Parton or some Patsy Cline. Take your clues from the really great ones. Imitation is the best kind of flattery and it's also the best way to improve. I think you will be surprised with the results. Work on some of that for tonight. Just let Jodee carry you through it, then do your own stuff the rest of the time. Each day add some new things, like The Carpenters or Tammy Wynette, good stuff that people really like and that's easy to copy. Then, as you get used to each other, you'll discover your own sound, and who knows where you'll end up. You might even try some beach music. Remember, there is a dance floor here and people might want to dance some so don't play for them just to sit and listen to you."

"Gee, thanks, Mr. Albright. We were trying to make it work all at once, but you are right, we need to work around Jodee. We were beginning to think we were fucked, but we'll make Jodee look good and she can make us look good, and the hell with the rest of it. At least we will have something to show Schwartzman."

"That's the attitude, guys. Keep thinking that and relax. Jodee is a real pro. You'll do great. Practice for a while this afternoon, and good luck. Do you guys have cheat sheets? Just use some of the standard jazz riffs and the familiar embellishments that make it sound authentic. Or you can work from lead sheets if you want more melody. I get most of my stuff out of fake books. I have some in my room if you want to borrow them. That could be the perfect resource for you guys."

Jodee took his arm and gave it a little squeeze. "Thanks, Grant, I'll meet you at Ethan's office at four," reinforcing what the guys already suspected. Jodee Jordan was being looked after by someone and Grant Albright was not to be messed with.

The people who had visited Rhodes were beginning to return to the ship, happy and tired from their outing, but ready to dress in their gala best for tonight's formal affair. The Palmer group were all planning to dress to the nines. The men had decided to wear suits rather than tuxes, but the women would all be decked out in gowns. Babs had arranged for them to be together in the dining room and had planned a little cocktail party for them in the Crow's Nest at 5:00. A reminder had been slipped under Grant's door and he checked his watch, trying to decide if he would go or not, dreading the fallout from the meeting with Ethan and preparing for the worst. After meeting with Jodee's group he was encouraged that maybe they could actually pull this off, but if Ethan pulled the plug on her, he would have to be ready with Plan B. All entertainment staff were to appear in tuxes after five.

Mitch was lying on the bed when he entered the room.

"Hi. Didn't expect to find you here. How was Rhodes?"

"Interesting place, but, boy, I'm whipped. We saw some fantastic ruins but it was a steep walk and it was hot. I must really be out of shape, Grant. I didn't think I was going to make it."

"What do you mean, not make it? Didn't you feel good?"

"Joan looked at me and said my face was real red so she called Ralph over and he said I better just sit for a while. He's a pretty nice guy, Grant. He stayed with me and Joan did too. Ralph was with Shay most of the time, but he parked her with us too. Said that she shouldn't be walking on such a steep incline with that foot of hers. I felt a little better once we were back on the air conditioned bus."

"Good. Take it a little easy tonight, Mitch. Are you going to Babs' cocktail party or do you have to work?"

"Yeah, I'm going. Are you? She was asking about you. She offered to handle the hospitality desk for me again, but she is on a fast track keeping everyone organized. Real nice lady. I'm just going to blow off the job tonight. Nobody is paying attention to when we are there, so we are working around her schedule. I'm not much good without her anyway."

"I see that and it sounds like you enjoy her help. I'm going to win that bet for sure. I bet on her, remember?"

"Don't count your chicks before they're hatched, Grant. She is just helping out. What have you been doing all day? Bet you spent the day with that Chirp, didn't you? You better watch your step, Buddy. She's a hot one."

"Nothing to worry about, but I do have a meeting with her at four. I'll go to the cocktail party after that, but I have to put my tux on before I go. I've got about an hour free right now. Man, this little plan of yours is proving to be a full time job for me, Mitch. Next time you get a hair-brained scheme, we better check it out first."

"Yeah, no jobs. Just women. I can't handle both anymore."

Ethan was waiting for Jodee in his office and didn't seem surprised at all that Grant was with her, but he knew that Grant's presence wasn't just a social call.

"Thanks for coming," he started. "There are some things that have come to my attention, Jodee, and I think it is only fair that I have a frank discussion with you, inform you of the consequences of being a no show for a performance." He shot a quick glance at Grant, hoping that Grant wouldn't explode before hearing him out. "Jodee, if I could keep it quiet about last night, I would, but you know how the stories and gossip fly around here, so just about everyone knows that you were a no show, and you do know the consequences of that. It results in automatic dismissal unless you have a broken neck or something and have an excuse."

Grant stiffened in his seat but held his tongue, waiting to see Jodee's reaction. She was sitting there with no expression at all, just sort of a helpless acceptance of whatever came her way, accustomed to bad news, with expectation of disappointment. Her vulnerability was almost frightening, raising a determination in Grant to support her, to fight for her, to speak for her.

"So what exactly is it you are saying, Ethan? Has Schwartzman handed down a verdict or is this coming strictly from you? You've heard Jodee. She is really good. It's not her fault that she was put in the wrong place. She is knocking herself out trying to make it work. I think you are trying to cover your own ass, making her take the fall for someone else's mistake. Who the hell put her there? That's who should be taking the fall."

"It's alright, Grant," she said. "I really appreciate what you are trying to do for me, but Ethan is right. I should never have left the guys in the lurch the way I did."

"It's not alright, Jodee," he persisted. "Ethan, can I talk to Schwartzman and explain things? Just get her some more time, give her a pass. Work with us, Ethan. We met with the guys and they are willing to work on it. Can't you at least do that?"

"Schwartzman knows, Grant. Let me finish. He knows that it wasn't working and he knows that you met with them this afternoon, too. I don't know how he got wind of it, but I got a memo from him just a few minutes before you guys got here, and it's a good thing I got it because I was going to prepare Jodee for the worst. I don't have the authority to fire her but apparently no one else does either. I'll read the memo to you. 'It has been called to my attention that certain difficulties have arisen in the Fez Lounge. Please be advised that Miss Jordan is to be accommodated if she desires to change venues. Allow Mr. Albright to assist in any way he chooses. This information shall remain confidential. Signed: I. Schwartzman.'"

"So you see, Grant, I'm not trying to save my own ass. I am telling you what the SOB said and trusting that you will keep it to yourself. If he finds out I told you, my ass will be had. But don't get over-confident. This guy is a real tyrant. He's probably got his hands full upstairs and just doesn't want to be bothered with you yet. But look out. The other shoe will drop soon enough. Jodee, you have been getting pretty special treatment as it is. No one can figure out why you are not housed down with the rest of the staff and why you are getting wardrobe provisions. You're receiving the same treatment as special guest performers instead of regulars and he is probably pissed about that anyway. Trust me, he never cuts anyone any slack and he knows that everyone will be waiting to see how he handles your no show."

Jodee just sat there with a blank look on her face so Grant responded for her. "That note is a surprise, isn't it? I appreciate the chance you are taking for her, Ethan, and I apologize for accusing you of selling her out. I'll tell you what. We will continue to work with the guys and try to salvage them at the same time and Jodee can continue doing a set with me whenever she wants to. We will keep you posted so you will always be on top of everything. How does that sound to you, Jodee? Can you work with that?"

"Yes, of course. I'll do whatever you think is best. You guys are just the greatest. I can't thank you enough. Just point me in the right direction and I'll work my tail off," and she started to cry, big wet tears staining her cheeks, tears of relief and tears of gratitude, tears stored from years of disappointment and failures. "Just look at me, slobbering all over myself. This means more to me than you'll ever know. I'll go powder my nose and get ready. The boys are expecting me."

Grant reached over and took her hand, giving it a little squeeze. "Good luck, Jodee. I'll see you around ten."

Grant arrived in the Crow's Nest around 5:45, dressed in his tux and feeling pretty good about things, ready for a martini, and sweeping the room for the Palmer gang. He hoped to catch Shay before dinner. She was seated with the three gals and they were listening to something Ralph in real estate was telling them, sharing something they were looking at. He caught Mitch's eye. He was seated with Babs on a loveseat and they were in serious conversation about something, but when Babs noticed Mitch nod to someone, she turned to see. The minute she saw Grant she sprang to her feet, exclaiming to the group, "Here is our celebrity now," and all eyes were upon him.

"Wow," Joan whispered to Shay. "He is something! Get a load of that tux." Of course Shay was taking him in too but was determined not to join in the admiration of the very handsome, very talented Grant Albright.

"Come right over here, Grant," Babs continued. "What would you like, a martini? We have all been looking at Nannette's pictures of you, the ones she took with you and your friend around the pool today. And here we were all so sorry that you had to work and miss Rhodes and all the while you were enjoying yourself," she said in that little pouty, half serious, half mocking voice she assumed in some failed attempt at cuteness, a voice that Grant couldn't stomach and he wondered how Mitch found her so charming.

"Well, believe it or not we did work pretty hard. Those pictures were taken while we were on break," explaining and escaping to a seat with several other couples who were discussing the events of the day. He didn't have a good view of Shay's group and got caught up in the conversation. They all left for dinner soon afterward, leaving him alone with his martini, grappling with his busted plan to invite Shay to have dinner with him. Instead he grabbed a sandwich in one of the cafes and went to the computer room. There was one email from Misty.

To: Daddy
From: Misty

Hi Daddy. Heard from Matt yesterday and cried for him all night. Megan called and she and I are catching a 5:30 flight to L.A. so we can be in court with him. He needs us, even though he didn't ask."

Love and Hugs, Misty
PS: Hope you are having fun.

He sat back for a minute, reflecting on the situation, afraid for Matt, proud of his daughters, and guilty for not being there himself, regretting so many times of missed opportunity, words that were never spoken, support that wasn't offered, feelings that were never expressed, yet loving them with all his heart. He didn't respond to the email. Words failed him, words of comfort, words of wisdom, the words a Dad was supposed to know, the words of love that sounded corny when you spoke them, words that would probably spook his kids, cause them to worry that he was losing it, was wallowing in grief, despondent.

He arrived at the Casablanca promptly at nine and was greeted by a full room of people who applauded when he took his seat at the piano. He played some old favorites, acknowledged applause, and responded to a few requests that had been handed to him by a waiter. The Palmer folks were there and he looked for Shay, nodding at her when their eyes met. Jodee had slipped in, listening, waiting for her time. He paused, took a deep breath, and then stood and stepped forward and spoke.

"I don't usually dedicate songs, but I hope you will indulge me tonight as I play a song for a very special little boy I used to know. His name is Matt." He sat down at the piano and started playing, lost in the moment, as the strains of *Puff the Magic Dragon* filled the room. And they began to hum along, then singing, joining in the chorus, verse after verse, louder, carrying him along. Jodee stood and began to sing along with them, working the room, smiling, hurting for him, and stood behind him as he finished, stroking his shoulders, tears in her eyes for the second time that day. Although Matt or the girls couldn't hear the music, Grant had been touched by it somewhere deep inside, filling with a sense of understanding, a relief, remembering endless repetitions of *Puff the Magic Dragon* and the hours of playing lullabies to cranky babies and sleepless toddlers, and *Happy Birthday* to little girls at birthday parties, and hundreds of rounds of *Itsy Bitsy Spider* and *Old McDonald Had A Farm*, playing countless other songs, marches for Matt when he led his sisters around the house in a make believe parade, and little fairy dances he made up for little princesses to dance around to in their finery, and teaching them Christmas carols as they stood around the piano on Christmas Eve, hours and hours of playing, knowing that the words of his love for them had been spoken through his wonderful gift of music.

When he finished the set with Jodee, he took a very short break and headed straight for Shay's group. After a brief visit he turned back to the piano, then stopped and turned back to her. "Wait for me, OK?" he said, pointing his finger the way men do, winking and nodding, and she heard that strange voice from somewhere inside her answer. "Yes, I'll wait for you, Grant."

Mykonos

Mitch was an early riser and had already left for breakfast on the Lido deck when Grant began to stir, groggy from his deep sleep. He stretched lazily and checked his watch, contemplating whether to call her this early and willing himself to put Matt out of mind. He showered and shaved and dressed in his usual khakis and golf shirt, sockless in loafers, planning to enjoy the day in Mykonos, and grinning about yesterday. He was satisfied with the results of the meeting with Ethan, even though forewarned of looming disaster, and he was very pleased with the conclusion of the day. Mitch had left him a note. "Meet me on the Lido. Bring your list. Need to talk."

"Good old Mitch. He is probably going to give me another lecture about staying on track. You would think I was sixteen." Grant was still putting Mitch on about Jodee, still letting him think that she was a done deal, never letting on that nothing had happened in Istanbul. He had confided in Mitch about Matt's situation. He would join him now and make the phone call to Shay later.

In room 604, Joan was prodding Shay, wanting a complete report on how Shay and Grant had gotten along last night. The three gals, Joan, Maureen, and Wanda, had hashed it over after Shay stayed to wait for Grant, and they were all dying to know.

"Well, what did you talk about? Did he tell you anything about himself? He is still such a mystery man, nobody knows anything, Shay."

"We just talked about regular stuff, you know, like where we are from, and how nice this trip is, and how sorry he was about missing

140

Rhodes. I think he really enjoys seeing things, the sightseeing stuff, that's all."

"Did he ask you any questions about yourself, give any indication that he might be interested in you? That was the second time he has asked you to wait until he was finished playing, and you didn't come in until one this morning. You must have talked about something all that time. I know it's none of my business, Shay, but we all saw Nannette what's her name's pictures of him with that singer. What's her name, Jodee?"

"Honestly, Joan, it was no big deal. He is polite and funny, sometimes very funny, and I think he just likes being with someone from North Carolina. I told you he was from Raleigh, didn't I? You already know that he is a widower and he did tell me that he has three grown children. And he talked some about Jodee, too. He knew Nannette had shown those pictures to everyone and he made a point of letting me know that the pictures were posed at her request, that he and Jodee were just having a drink while waiting for their meeting. Between you and me, I don't think he was very happy about it, either."

"Well, she draped herself all over him last night while he was playing. Everyone saw that. Do you think you will keep seeing him, maybe a regular thing? I know I am sounding like a mother hen but he is pretty sophisticated, Shay, being a musician and all. He's probably been around a lot more than you have. He is charming, but I wouldn't trust him. A man like that can just snap his fingers and get what he wants, you know. I'm not saying that there is anything wrong with him, or anything like that. I just think you need to be very, very cautious."

"I know, Joan, but Grant and I are just friends. He even tells me that. 'Friends, right?' he says, making sure that I don't read too much into anything. But, you know, in spite of his good looks and his talent and his sophistication, he comes across as sincere. Sometimes I think he is just lonely, just wants to keep company. I probably seem pretty safe to him, just someone from home that he doesn't need to impress."

Grant Albright had told her quite a bit more than she shared with Joan. He had talked some about his wife, nothing real personal, but that it had been so hard on his whole family, and he told her about how Mitch had helped him through it. And he told her about his grandchildren, and how he loved to play golf. She had asked him about Palmer Plantation, even daring to ask if he planned to stay because she had heard some of the others wondering about that. And he had asked her lots of questions, and she had told him a lot, probably way more than she should have because now he knew her weak spots because she had let him crack that protective shield she wore. Joan was probably right, he shouldn't be trusted, and here she had already told him too much, not everything, but too much.

The phone rang and Joan picked it up. It was Maureen telling them to be ready to take the tender to the dock at Mykonos around 11:00. They had not signed up for a tour but it was one of those places where you could roam around by yourselves, see the sights, and have lunch at one of the many charming cafes. Shay had put on one of her sundresses and decided to wear sandals because there wouldn't be much walking, unable to bear the thought of the ugly walking shoes with a dress. The other three wore Bermuda shorts and Henley knit shirts.

Grant was on the Lido deck enjoying a big breakfast and trying to convince Mitch that he was working the plan just fine. "I'm still way ahead of you, Mitch. Show me what you have checked off. There's a lot of easy stuff on the list, like introduce yourself to three new women each day. That's got to be easy for you. They line up at the hospitality desk just to talk to you. Go ahead, check that one off. And number four, offer to help a woman with something. You do that every day, helping them plan excursions. Mark that one off too. You're not giving yourself enough credit."

"Yeah, well you skipped all that stuff and went right to the bottom line. You didn't even bother with the easy stuff."

"There's always Betty, Mitch. You can catch up in a hurry that way."

"It's Babs, Grant, and she's only interested in her travel stuff. You know, a guy could do worse than her, attractive enough and smart, but there isn't any chemistry there. Maybe I'm expecting fireworks, but this idea of just trying to score doesn't come as easy to me as it does to you."

"I thought that was the whole idea, just to get ourselves back in the game, get our mojo back. The fireworks come later, or maybe not at all, it doesn't matter. This is all just for practice so when we do meet one we want we're ready. I can't believe you're getting cold feet. This was all your idea. I thought you had already hit the bottom line, that you just wanted to expand a little. Do you want to scrap the whole thing? It's alright with me, but I'll lay fifty bucks that you get laid this week. You're just not trying hard enough.

"Maybe that's the problem, Grant."

Silence rained down on them like thunder, deafening, foreboding, chilling the conversation with an awkwardness, exposing a weakness, a fear and dread that wasn't easy to talk about.

"Are you sure or is it just something you are afraid might happen. It could just be a one-time thing, just temporary. That happens sometimes."

"It's why I wanted to try this away from the Palmer folks. God forbid if it got around that old Mitch couldn't perform. When we were just laughing and joking about the plan, I thought it might work, but now I feel different about it, like maybe I could actually fall for a woman again, actually love one, and I don't want to have been doing all this messing around in the meantime. I thought all it would take was opportunity, something new and exciting, but I think now that all it will take is just being with the right woman. I know it sounds stupid, but the Mrs. and I were good together, Grant, and I miss that."

"That's not stupid, Mitch. That's how it's supposed to be. So I'll tell you what. Let's scratch off the bottom line. That doesn't count anymore. But I've got to hand it to you, that was a pretty lousy way to win a bet. Now I'm way behind in the score. You racked up points doing the easy stuff I didn't bother with."

"Don't count me out yet. I might get back into the game. We have so much on the table now it makes it worth the effort. I'll let you keep your points with the Chirp."

"I thought you wanted to discourage that."

"I do. I can afford to lose the hundred, Grant. I just don't want you to lose your head. I better get ready to get on the tender now. Babs is planning on meeting me. Are you going?"

"I hope so, but I have to meet Jodee in the computer center. She has to use my email address to answer her daughter. I'll catch you later." On the way there he checked for messages in his room and placed a call. There was no answer. He didn't leave a message.

Jodee was waiting for him, looking great in white slacks and a lime green gauzy tunic cut pretty low. She had on a large medallion hanging from white beads, and a matching bracelet dangling from her wrist, and matching earrings, all set with enough shiny stuff to qualify as bling. She was wearing rather high wedgie sandals.

"Wow, you look great. Where you expecting someone important, or is this just for me?" he teased.

"All for you, Shug," she laughed. "Have to look the part, you know. Apparently we have raised a few eyebrows around here. Miss Nannette Guppie's pictures have gone viral. Even the wait staff has seen them. Apparently she shared them with the girl who did her hair. That was all it took, and from there they flew all over the place."

"That really ticks me off. It will start all kinds of rumors about us. What do you suggest we do?"

"I suggest we play it for all its worth, Grant. It's good free publicity. Maybe we can survive this whole thing if people start paying attention to us, not that you need it. You're doing pretty good on your own, but it sure could help me. You are the catch of the day, from what I'm hearing. Now if I can just figure out this Leighanna mess maybe I can concentrate on my music. What do you think I should tell her?"

She had told Grant all about Leighanna and about how she made such bad decisions and how she was really a lovely girl and it was really Jodee's fault because she hadn't been the greatest mother, always chasing rainbows, always trying to make it, and now Leighanna needed help again. Grant had offered the use of his email address because Jodee no longer had service since she had moved from her condo. He entered his password and opened his mail.

Jodee unfolded the email and read it again.

To: Mom
From: Leighanna

Hi, Mom. Well, guess what, you were right again.
Bill has left me. Went back to her again. This time I
think he means it and I am devastated. Thought I had it
right this time, but turns out I am just like you, Mom, no
money, no house, no job, no husband—only worse. I'm
pregnant, Mommy. When I told him, he just stormed
out. So now what do I do? Should I keep calling him?
Sorry for more problems, Mom.

Love and kisses, Leighanna and Josh

"Do you want me to help you put something together, or do you
want some privacy, Jodee? I can wait over there while you write."

"Grant, I don't know what to say. She has no money so there is
no point in telling her to go to school or do something useful, and
we have to think about Joshua."

"Who is Joshua?"

"He's her little boy, four years old. He's my only grandchild. It
just isn't fair to him that all of this is happening. He gets hurt too. I
should probably ask her if this Bill guy who just left her will let her
stay in the condo or if he is throwing her out. It sounds like he is the
father of the new baby. Surely he can't be that cold hearted. I have
a little money left over from my condo sale but I need that to get a
place when I get back. If she can just make it until then I can take
care of things. Or maybe I could send her enough to get through
this. What do you think I should do, Grant?"

"Do you have access to your money?"

"I don't know, I guess so. It is in my savings account but I don't
know how you go about wiring money."

"That can be done from the ship but you would need bank account numbers."

"I don't have that with me. Maybe I'll have to cut this gig short and go there."

"Where is there? Where does she live?"

"In Reno. I told her to leave the last time he left, but she wouldn't listen. He's married, Grant. He keeps promising to leave his wife and I told her, I warned her, but just like me, she wouldn't listen."

Grant drew in a deep breath, suspicion sloshing around in his head and that gut voice of caution rising in his throat, but, tempted by denial and ignoring the dire warnings of his own reasoning, he decided to take a chance, bait the hook a little, up the ante, raise the stakes enough to make it interesting. "Maybe I can help, Jodee. How much do you think it would take? How much would it take to make her independent of this guy, this Bill? A thousand? Five thousand? More?"

"I don't have that kind of money, Grant. I only have ten thousand to my name. I can't give her anything like that."

"I know, Jodee, but I have that kind of money. Maybe I could loan her something until she gets on her feet. That way you can continue singing and help her when you get back."

Jodee sat in silence, speechless perhaps, or for affect, he wasn't sure which, but he waited. Then she turned to him, looked him right in the eye and said, "Grant Albright, that is the second time that you have just floored me, shocked me with your kindness and I thank you from the bottom of my heart, not only for the kindness but for trusting me. You are just the greatest, Grant. But there is no way in hell that you are sending her one cent. There are three reasons for that. In the first place, if you loan her the money, she will not pay it back. I've been down that road before. She means well, but you will not get paid back. In the second place, if you send her money she will spend it foolishly. She has no money sense at all. The only way I have any success with that approach is to handle the money myself. Do you follow this, Grant? Am I making myself clear?"

"Crystal clear," he said. "And what is the third reason, Jodee?"

"The third reason is this. It is high time that the Jordan women, that would be me and Leighanna, stopped depending on men to bail us out of every jam, especially these jams we create ourselves. First it was my Dad, then it was husband number one, and then it was husband number two, and then there were a few in between that at least I had the good sense not to marry, and then there was husband number three. And there were a few band leaders that helped out too. You get the picture. At least Leighanna hasn't married her mistakes, but she ends up just as helpless as her mother. But being with you, Grant, a class act like you, a guy who has put it all together, gives me courage, some motivation to be my best, not just as a performer, but as a person. Now move over and let me write. You can watch."

To: Leighanna
From: Mommy
Hi Toots,

Things sound pretty bad right now but I have confidence that you will find a way to manage on your own, a way that will make you feel good about things, and that you will come through this proud of your achievement. I will be home in several weeks, darling. Then we can sort things out and plan for the new baby. What exciting baby news! Keep me posted.

Love to you and my precious Joshua.

Mommy

Grant was reading along. "Tell her she can respond to this address. It can be private for you that way."

PS: You can respond to this email address. It belongs to a very good friend.

She hit "send"

"There. It is done. At least for today, but she is made of good stuff, Grant. I think she can handle it."

"Yes, Jodee, she is made of good stuff. Let's go catch the tender. You deserve a few hours in Mykonos." He took her hand as they headed to the gangway, smiling as they went, satisfied with how he had played his cards, silently congratulating himself. He had confirmed his suspicion. Jodee Jordan was a pro. But he didn't understand why she was pretending to con him. He knew it wasn't a con, that the problem was real. Did she think he wouldn't help her if she asked? Was she afraid of offending him, afraid he would abandon her like the others? His heart went out to her.

Mykonos is one of the most visited of all the Greek Islands. A mere ninety some nautical miles from Piraeus, the main port of Greece, it is the quintessential Greek Island. It offers a unique beauty of contrasts from the beautiful Aegean hugging it shores to the barren rocky interior. There are beaches, water sports, hotels, and dining for every taste. It attracts the wealthy and the backpackers, the day trippers and island hoppers, and the repeaters, those who spend yearly vacations there. Its charming white-washed buildings are the stuff of postcards and the warm clear turquoise Aegean embraces yachts and small fishing boats, and all sizes in between. Some of the passengers from the Atheneè would be taking escorted tours and others would day trip to Delos to see the wondrous ruins there.

The Palmer group had all opted to hang out around the little harbor where they could venture up some of the little streets lined with charming houses adorned with flower boxes. Shay and Joan decided to visit several of the little shops and sit at one of the sidewalk cafes sipping coffee, enjoying the sights and people watching. Wanda and Maureen had wandered around checking out some flower boxes, and then joined Shay and Joan. Mitch and Ralph had decided to walk up the steep path to the thatched roofed windmills that are perched on top, but it proved too steep for Mitch, fearful that he might turn red again and become the object of everyone's attention. The two men joined the four ladies and pulled up chairs between them, putting Mitch comfortably close to Joan. He seized the opportunity to have a rather quiet conversation with her. Ralph was next to Shay, casually placing his arm around the back of her chair, asking about her foot, which he had determined was the location of her injury, and not her ankle, as everyone had suspected.

"It's a good thing you decided not to go up that steep walk to the top, Shay. You need to keep wearing those walking shoes. They offer the kind of support your foot needs. Tomorrow you better wear them in Athens because there will be some real walking when we get to the Acropolis. It's pretty steep in places," the voice of wisdom since he had been to Athens twice before.

Shay had grown quite fond of Ralph, sensing the sincerity of his concern, offered without criticism or judgment of her choices, even rather enjoying his attention, but for some reason the arm around her chair made her uncomfortable, awakening that feeling she had had with dates that she didn't care for, with men she wasn't interested in, evenings she had spent anxious to end. She liked Ralph, enjoyed being with him, was comfortable with him, but didn't want to do anything that might encourage him, might make him think she was interested in more of a relationship. They needed to get to know each other, become friends first, before she could jump to any conclusions about anything. At her age, friendship was what mattered, compatibility, trust, character, and it took time. She didn't expect fireworks or even much of a physical attraction, any of that sort of thing, yet it would be nice to have a man in her life for companionship and stability, even willing to settle for just a nice guy, someone she could respect and who would respect her. After all, those were really the important qualities, the things that really counted. She was only half listening to Ralph telling her something about Palmer Plantation, nodding occasionally, but mostly musing about a life there, perhaps with him, when her thoughts were interrupted by Mitch's rather loud voice.

"Well look who is here. Come on, pull up a chair, Grant. Jodee, good to see you too."

Shay looked up and there he was, all six feet something of himself, with his arm around Jodee Jordan. He pulled out a chair for Jodee at the end of the table, putting her right between Mitch and Ralph. He then grabbed another chair and put himself at the other end, right next to Shay.

Jodee looked lovely and was beaming, acknowledging each one with a smile and a pleasant greeting. She was delightful, thrilled to be there, couldn't have been nicer, and Grant leaned back in his chair, watching her closely, admiring her ability to mix right in, totally comfortable with the group, a chameleon, he thought.

Shay was enthralled with the rest of them, enchanted by Jodee's great looks and personality, and a little intimidated by her charisma and flashy appearance. She only casually nodded to Grant as he sat down next to her, trying not to show much interest in him at all.

Always looking for a lead and sniffing a possibility in this new arrival, Ralph took his arm off Shay's chair and turned his attention to Jodee and began telling her all about the amenities in Palmer Plantation. "You'll have to have Grant bring you down sometime so you can see for yourself what we keep bragging about, Jodee. He won't want to keep you a secret," half teasing and half capitalizing on the situation and the gossip that the pictures of Jodee and Grant had generated.

Mitch was furious about the pictures and all the gossip that linked Grant to Jodee and wanted to do his best to discourage the whole affair, so he tried to cut Ralph off at the pass, interjecting his own comments. "Now, Ralph, you know Jodee is very involved in her career and Grant needs to get home to his family. Jodee probably would find life in Palmer pretty limiting when it came to her career, even though she would be an attractive addition. That's right, isn't it Jodee? You want to focus on your career, don't you?"

"Well, Mitch, to tell you the truth, Palmer Plantation sounds pretty appealing right now. What do you think, ladies, would I like Palmer Plantation?"

"Why, yes, Jodee. You would fit right in," Maureen replied. "We are trying to convince Shay to move there too, aren't we Shay? You are thinking about it, aren't you, Shay?"

Shay nearly died. What was she expected to say, "Hell no, Jodee, you wouldn't fit in anywhere near Grant Albright," contradicting Maureen. Or, "Hell no, I wouldn't be caught dead in a place like

Palmer Plantation." Or perhaps she should say she was seriously thinking about moving there, risking encouraging Ralph in real estate. They were waiting for her to say something, hoping she would come up with some clever response, aware that there was considerable awkwardness created by the question. Shay squirmed slightly, embarrassed that at age fifty-two she still could be trapped in social situations, uncomfortable and unsure of her place, when she felt the unexpected comforting presence of Grant's hand as he wrapped his arm around her shoulder.

"Maybe we shouldn't put Shay on the spot. She hasn't had a chance to see the place yet, but I'm hoping she'll do that soon. I'm planning on showing her all around myself, aren't I, Shay?" effectively insinuating himself into her life, grinning as he met Mitch's eyes, and giving notice to Ralph that his services wouldn't be needed. His meaning hadn't been missed by Jodee either, and she winked at him when he looked her way.

Babs had just approached the table, enthusiastically announcing that she had made reservations for the whole group for lunch at the Mykonos cafe right around the corner, and when she saw Jodee in the group she invited her to join them. "How wonderful. We will have two celebrities with us. We will meet there at 1:00."

Mitch looked at Grant. "OK, Buddy. Let's order some ouzo and put it in our coffee."

They all decided to do that, but Grant turned to Shay and said quietly, "I don't think you'll like ouzo in your coffee."

When the waiter came to Shay and asked, "Ouzo?" she said, "Yes, please. I want to see for myself what ouzo tastes like, even though I have been duly warned," she laughed. Grant spoke right up. "Just give her a little bit," shaping his thumb and forefinger to show just a small amount. "That stuff is dynamite, Shay. I don't want you to get a headache and spoil your day."

Lunch was a fabulous spread of authentic Greek food, which stirred Mitch to announce to everyone how much Grant hated eggplant when moussaka was mentioned as the luncheon special, creating jovial conversation and much teasing directed at Grant, since eggplant enjoys the same popularity in Greece as it did in Turkey.

Jodee fit right in, could have passed for one of the wives, albeit the most flashy. She laughed and joked and listened, impressing them all with her congeniality and sincerity, making friends, gaining their confidence that she was a regular person, not just some show biz fluff, and accepting Babs' offer to join the group on the bus tour in Athens tomorrow. She found herself thinking about life at Palmer Plantation, envying these folks who had planned their lives in such a way to allow them to enjoy their wonderful retirement, observing the married couples, their lives secure with one another, hearing about all the wonderful amenities and activities, and picturing herself in such an idyllic setting. She avoided any reference to her own life of failure.

Grant sat next to Jodee at lunch, joining in on all the conversation, laughing, joking around with Mitch, but keeping close tabs on Shay, who was next to Ralph again. After dessert, Jodee turned to Grant and spoke quietly with him a minute. They stood, explaining that Jodee had to catch the tender back to the ship for an afternoon rehearsal and Grant would walk her to the pier, but before he left he made a point of addressing Mitch. "I'll be back in ten minutes. Wait for me."

Shay had taken it all in. Ralph again had his arm draped around her chair, never touching her, just draping the chair, but it made her uncomfortable, still feeling the warmth of Grant's touch and trying to ignore the sensation that it gave her. When Grant returned, he went right over to Shay. "Come on," he said. "Let's walk around the harbor. We have a little time." It was obvious that the invitation didn't include Ralph, and Shay felt a little awkward about that, even though she was pleased to be free of his arm.

Mitch was already at Joan's side, ushering her toward the door.

The four of them spent the rest of the afternoon browsing. Grant and Mitch each bought a Greek fisherman's hat and clowned around, saying "Opa, opa," to the delight of the two women, who were plenty pleased with the arrangement, exchanging occasional looks, especially when Grant clasped Shay's arm.

"Here," he said. "Let me hold on to you," and he continued to hold her arm until they returned to the ship. "See you tonight?"

he asked. And Shay heard that strange voice answer, "Yes, Grant. I'll see you tonight," not sure if he meant just see you later or if he meant wait for me.

Grant planned to catch up with Jodee and see her performance in the Fez Lounge and then have dinner with her, pretty sure that there would have been a reply from Leighanna by then. He headed straight for the computer center.

He didn't even hesitate when he saw the message from Leighanna. He opened it and read.

To: Mom
From: Leighanna
Hi Mom,

Thanks for such great advice—just when my whole life is in the toilet you decide to bail on me. Things couldn't be worse. Bill hasn't returned my calls and I have a car payment due next week. Josh is sick again, another sore throat and the doctor thinks he needs his tonsils out, not that I can afford that!!

So you have a new friend who lets you use his email—I say his because heaven forbid that we ever do anything without a man to help us out. Is he a good prospect? I am sworn off men forever!!!! At least until Bill comes back.

What should I do, Mommy?

Hugs, Leighanna

PS: I got a job, sort of. My neighbor got a job and I am going to keep her little boy while she works, but she can't afford to pay me because she won't make much, so I am just helping her out.

Grant pressed print and got a copy for Jodee, shaking his head in wonder at this latest development. They were a real team, mother and daughter, playing him for all that it was worth, and he wasn't buying it for a minute.

In room 602 Joan and Shay were dressing for dinner, both still on a little high from the lovely day they had spent on Mykonos.

"Shay, tell me, do you think Mitch is interested in Babs as much as we thought at first? He didn't seem to spend much time with her today, did he?"

"He didn't spend much time with her, Joan, because he spent his time with you. I saw how attentive he was, especially after lunch. He headed right for you."

"Grant seemed to be enjoying his time too, Shay. He sure is hard to read. What do you think about Jodee? When he is with her they act like a couple, but then he acts like he expects to be with you."

"I know, but we are just friends, remember. I guess he assumes I won't have any other plans so he feels free to be with me whenever he chooses. There really isn't anything wrong with that, I guess, but it probably is a little insulting, his just expecting me to be available. It's easier with you and Mitch because you have so many mutual friends, it is just a group thing. It probably doesn't matter who you are with. Everything is just so casual. You are lucky to be in a place like that, Joan, where everyone is so friendly, where it is so easy to be a part of things. You have no idea how hard it is to be single, living alone, out in the world by yourself. Girlfriends can be wonderful and that is enough for some women but it is really nice to be part of a group where there are some men, too, especially men who aren't other women's husbands, not because you are looking for a man, but because it is nice, natural. If I were you, if I were in Palmer Plantation, and my best friend was membership chairman of the singles group, I would join. Do you know if Ralph belongs?"

"I have never gone to one of their meetings but I'm beginning to seriously consider it, especially if Maureen talks Mitch into it. At least I would know one man there. Let's ask her tonight if Ralph goes."

"We don't have to ask her on my behalf because I won't be going to the meetings. I was just thinking about him. He is another one you would know, Joan, and he is really very nice. And he is very involved in the community, too. That could open up a lot of other doors. It would be a way to meet lots of people."

"Shay, I wish you would give some serious thought to moving down. Chrissie was right, you would be a perfect fit. You would love it. And think how many people you would already know. Let's plan for you to come down and stay with me. I'll show you all around. And speaking of Chrissie, let's go by the computer center before dinner and see if I have anything."

"Great, and then let's stop in the Fez Lounge and hear Jodee."

Athens

There had been one brief email from Chrissie.

To: Mom
From: Chrissie

Hi, all well here. My mystery man from California has temporarily disappeared. Nothing since last time, just that he is tied up with some family business and will get back to me. Bummer, because he sounded pretty serious about looking at houses. I told you he wouldn't be here before you got back. No, he absolutely did not come from a dating site, Mom. It really is just about real estate. And I sure could use a sale about now. Things are still pretty slow.

Hope you are having fun. Hi to Shay. I hope she isn't lonely. Tell her I said she needs to kick up her heels. Are there any interesting men?

Hugs, Chrissie

Reply: Glad mystery man is not there. Shay says "hi". Absolutely no men around! Love, Mom.

Maureen and Wanda had agreed to meet them in the Fez Lounge for cocktails and to hear Jodee sing there, and Wanda was almost giddy to share her big news. They took a seat near the front and each ordered a Cosmo and Wanda started right in as they listened to her news, but right in the middle of her story she stopped.

"Oh My God," she gasped. "Look over there!"

The other three turned in their seats to see what she was looking at. There stood Grant Albright with his arm around Jodee Jordan, whispering in her ear and giving her a little kiss on the temple. Jodee had wrapped her arm around his back, stroking him ever so gently, and then giving him a rather sound kiss on the cheek, before turning and heading to the front just as the keyboardist announced, "Ladies and Gentleman, Miss Jodee Jordan."

Grant took a seat near the back, anxious for her, hopeful, and apprehensive about the rumored visit of Schwartzman for tonight's performance. The guys had heard the rumor right before they were to appear and had warned Jodee, and she was beside herself when Grant arrived. He had been whispering encouraging words to her, holding her close before giving her a little good luck kiss, and she had returned the kiss and thanked him for all the help he had given the group. He had given a little pep talk to the guys too, ending with the universal middle finger salute, admonishing them to "Fuck Schwartzman, just go for it, guys."

The four gals turned to watch the lovely Jodee Jordan perform, and perform she did. Jodee was a natural, her beautiful voice oozed honey and sex as she sang *Crazy* and from time to time she appeared to be singing to one specific person in the back, even mouthing a kiss in his direction between songs. The combo playing softly in the background looked relaxed, professional, totally at ease, grinning from ear to ear as their new vocalist carried the room.

Unnoticed, an elderly gentleman had slipped in the side door and stood listening from behind a potted palm, his arms crossed in front of his chest, a slight frown on his brow, accented by an expression of total arrogance. He gave the impression of being elderly, dressed in a finely tailored business suit and tie, formal for daytime wear on a cruise ship, but, in truth, he had just turned sixty five, was rounding out a hugely successful career as an impresario, putting together performances and shows in worldwide venues, and establishing himself as one of the best judges of performance, talent, and potential in the business. Proud of his achievements and buoyed by his reputation as a ballbuster, he had spent the last two years in the highly lucrative position of consultant to luxury cruise lines and select high end casinos around the world. He had amassed a sizable fortune and was planning to indulge his own personal dream in Las Vegas, plans that were already underway, plans that only needed one last piece to be completed while on this cruise. He stood watching, listening closely, expressionless except for the arrogance, glancing briefly at Grant, observing, looking around the room, and then slipping out with the same stealthiness with which he had entered, accustomed to observing the unsuspecting, reserving his visual presence for times when he wanted to inflict pain or just scare the bejesus out of someone. Itzach Schwartzman had come to do what he had to do.

The only person in the room more interested in Jodee's performance than Grant Albright or the dreaded Schwartzman was Shay Porter. Seeing Grant holding and kissing Jodee had just about undone her, had shocked her that he had so publicly displayed his affection for Jodee, demonstrated the very thing that he had denied the night before when they had talked until 1:00 a.m. It was bad enough that he had arrived in Mykonos with Jodee today, but he had paid considerable attention to Shay, too. But this latest scene was more than she could bear. She felt exposed, used, disposable, embarrassed in front of her friends as he telegraphed his message of disregard for her feelings, his preference for Jodee, and total disinterest in her except as a convenient companion when Jodee wasn't available. Shay watched Jodee, beautiful in another rather sexy dress, and she wondered if Grant complimented Jodee's dress the way he had complimented her formal gown, telling her how becoming it was, and how he liked the sun dresses she wore, and her hair. He had actually touched her hair, just barely, but had touched it nonetheless. The prick!

The four women had ordered another Cosmo as soon as Jodee finished, and Wanda resumed telling her exciting news, each listening and oohing and aahing appropriately, and avoiding even looking at Shay, not mentioning you know who, aware of how the little Grant Albright show had probably upset her. The prick!

Wanda's news was pretty exciting. First of all, she had attended the floral department tour on the ship and was so thrilled to see the huge selection of flowers available for the floral artists to work with, that's what they called them, floral artists. "I had a lovely visit with the head floral artist and showed him some pictures of my work, and he said such nice things. He suggested that I apply for a job with a cruise line and then I could have the same dream job he had, playing with flowers all day. He even offered to let me come down and work with them for the experience and the fun of it and he would give me a recommendation. Isn't that exciting? I can't believe it. I think I will skip Athens tomorrow and spend the day with the flowers."

Wanda was ecstatic about it all. She did do beautiful arrangements and this recognition of her talent thrilled her.

"Lord, Wanda, don't do that, don't miss Athens." Maureen exclaimed. "Skip a day somewhere else, not the day in Athens, for Pete's sake."

"You will regret missing Athens, Wanda. It is one of the highlights, really important," Joan added.

"Oh, Athens, smathens. My late husband, Howard, and I have been to Athens twice before. We don't need to go again. Howard always said that the second time you went to a place was always a disappointment and the third time was just a waste of money. You three go on without me. Oh, I almost forgot. I have more news. Wait till you hear this. You remember I told you about my niece, Adrian. She is my sister's daughter. Well, she and her husband have just bought some old hotel or inn or something, in Vermont, and they have invited me to come see it and work with them remodeling and decorating the old thing. She is going to send pictures for me to show you. How do you do that, send pictures? I don't know, but if I get pictures I will show them to you."

"She will send the pictures with your email, Wanda."

"Oh, well when I get them you will have to come up to the computer to look at them."

"That is exciting, Wanda. When will you go?"

Before she could answer Grant and Jodee approached their table as they were leaving the Fez.

"Thank you so much for coming," Jodee cooed, smiling sincerely. "You are all so kind to me."

"You were wonderful," they enthused, rudely ignoring Grant, except for Wanda, who was staring daggers at him.

Noticing the snub, puzzled, Grant said, "Enjoy the evening, Ladies," and turned directly toward Shay, adding with a wink and a little nod, "See you later, Shay?"

And that stupid little voice from somewhere deep inside her said, "Yes, later." The prick!

Jodee and Grant headed for dinner in one of the small bistros on board. She had been so upset earlier about the Schwartzman thing that he hadn't given her the email from Leighanna. They ordered some French item on the menu, neither one of them knew what it was, but Grant didn't bother to ask about eggplant, just assuming that it probably wasn't a French thing.

"Did he come? Did you see him, Grant? I kept looking around but I don't think I saw him. I don't have any idea what Schwartzman looks like. Do you?"

"No, I haven't met him. Why don't you get some of your friends from the show to point him out to you? At least we would know who we're looking for. You were really good, Jodee, so I don't think you have anything to worry about. I hope he doesn't show up in the Casablanca while I'm playing. Did you pick out what you want to sing tonight? We are getting pretty confident, not even practicing anymore."

"Let's do some more Cole Porter. How about *What Is This Thing Called Love* and *Night and Day*, and *You Do Something To Me*. That's a good start, and then maybe switch to *Body and Soul* and then some blues. How 'bout *Blues in The Night* and *Birth of The Blues*. That's probably enough."

"Yeah, there might even be some requests, so we'll just wing it. By the way, you got an email from Leighanna." He handed it to her and she unfolded it and read.

"Did you read it?" she asked, handing it to him. "I don't know what to do. What would you do, Grant, if she were your daughter, pregnant, left like garbage? With a child, your grandchild. What would you do?"

Good shot, he thought. She led with her ace, daring him to trump it, but he wasn't ready to cash in, deciding to keep playing, put something else on the table. "I don't know, Jodee. I hate to tell you what to do, but if it were my daughter, pregnant, left like garbage, with a child, my grandchild, I would send the money. And I would go be there for support, to help her, move her out, whatever it took. And then I would go kill the son of a bitch, or maybe I would kill the son of a bitch first, I'm not sure. Which do you think I should do first, Jodee, kill him first or after?"

"Okay, that's what I'll do Grant." She folded the email and put it in her bag.

Surprised, he said, "Do what? Kill him?"

"No, of course not. I have already talked to the guy in the travel office. I can get a flight out of Athens the day after tomorrow, that's no problem. I'll fly from Athens to NY and from NY to Vegas, and on to Reno. I can be there in forty eight hours. I was just waiting to hear from her before I booked. We better say good night, Grant. I have to book the flight and then start packing. Will you say my good byes to the guys for me? I'm just too upset to talk to them, embarrassed to show my face. And tell Babs thank you, but I won't take the tour of Athens with your group tomorrow. I'll just stay in the room and pack and return all those clothes from wardrobe, and try to figure out what to do next. When Schwartzman hears about this I'll never work again so I better figure out plan B, whatever the hell that is." She got up and turned toward him, adding, "Grant, I can't thank you enough for all you have done for me. I will always be so grateful for your help, grateful that you were a part of my life, even if it was such a short time" She turned and walked toward the elevators.

"Damn," he thought. "I must be getting sloppy. I didn't see that coming. I thought she was out of aces." He called after her. "Are you going to sing tonight, Jodee? We make pretty good music together, don't we? At least come in and say goodbye to me."

"I'll be there at ten," she said, turning away as she choked back the tears.

She didn't show up. Neither did Shay.

They would dock in Piraeus early tomorrow for a grand tour of Athens. The Atheneè would remain docked at Piraeus overnight, allowing for night tours of the city and an extra day of excursions, browsing, and shopping. Several bus groups would head to Delphi on the second day in port and Grant had been looking forward to that, but these new developments with Jodee might put a real damper on it if he didn't do something fast.

Mitch and Babs had spent the evening together going over the plans for the tour of Athens. She had already had the excursion department make lunch reservations for her group at a special restaurant where they would have a beautiful view of the Acropolis. The morning would be a city tour and the afternoon would be spent touring the Acropolis with a Greek guide. "Mitch," Babs had said, "it is just so wonderful to have you working with me like this. I hadn't realized how hard and lonely it was doing this job all by myself. And I hope I have been of some help to you at the hospitality desk, too. I was thinking about the next trip I am planning to offer and wondered if you would consider helping me with the plans and going along as sort of a co-leader, my partner. Would you consider that?"

"Gee, Babs, I don't know what to say. You already know that I don't know much about the travel business. I'm not much help at all. Maybe you should look for a partner who knows a little more than I do. This is fun but I'm not sure I want to work this hard anymore."

"Well, of course, I wouldn't really expect you to work so much. Mostly I would just want your companionship and support. And if I book enough people you could go for free. Are you going to join the singles group when we get back? If we could plan some trips for them, even short ones like to a resort or Bermuda, or somewhere in the Caribbean, we could have a good little business and some great vacations too. I bet you could get lots of the women to travel with us. Would you consider it, Mitch?"

"Like I said, Babs, I'm not so sure about it. I'll talk to Grant tonight, see what he wants to do. I wouldn't do it without him."

His answer had floored Babs, not just because he was hesitant to work with her but that he wouldn't do it without Grant, that he had used Grant as an excuse. She knew they were close friends but it had never occurred to her that the über ladies' man, Grant, might be available as well. "Will Grant be joining the singles group? Maureen would be thrilled if the two of you would join. I'll tell her about our plans. She might want to work with us too. Wouldn't that be wonderful, the four of us on trips together! We'll sit together on the bus tomorrow, Mitch, and start making our plans. Let's go hear Grant tonight and maybe you can ask him when he takes a break."

They had arrived at the Casablanca Lounge just before ten and were surprised that Grant didn't take a break as he usually did. Maureen, Wanda, and Joan were already there, without Shay, but when Mitch showed up with Babs attached to his arm, they had a sudden impulse to head to the casino and play the slots. Mitch and Babs ordered a drink and sat listening quietly as ten o'clock became ten fifteen, and then ten thirty, and no Jodee. At ten forty five Grant abruptly stood up, closed the piano, and headed to Mitch without even acknowledging Babs. "I'm closing up shop early, Mitch. See you back in the room later," and strode out of the lounge. "Where the hell was she? The whole thing had gotten out of control, had gone too far. What game was she playing now? What the hell did she think she was doing?" he thought, and headed toward the elevator.

Shay had spent the evening in her room, ordering room service, begging off with the excuse of a headache, not fooling her friends for a minute. She was angry and hurt, beating up on herself for being so stupid, so gullible for letting him get to her despite being on to him from the beginning, him with his good looks and his talent, with his charming ways that were insulting and flattering at the same time, his compliments followed by criticism, his winking and nodding, flirting, that vulnerability that made her want to rescue him, wanting him to rescue her. She went over his every word a thousand times, his words of kindness, open, sincere, humble, breathing life in her, and hope. The prick.

Grant crossed the huge Grand Lounge and rounded the corner to the elevator alcove and then turned abruptly and retraced his steps to the small bar across from the Fez Lounge, walked behind the bar like he belonged there, and picked up the house phone and dialed. She answered on the first ring. "Where the hell were you?" he asked, anger in his voice. "You know better than to be a no show, Jodee." Waiters were walking behind him so he turned toward the wall and talked in a lower voice. "I'll cover for you, say I gave you the night off if it comes up. That message Ethan shared with us sounds like Schwartzman doesn't care what you do, but I don't like the sound of that either. Did you book your flight? I'm thinking maybe you shouldn't go. We need to talk this through, Jodee."

"No, I couldn't book it yet. The agent said they would enter the request in the computer tonight and let me know in the morning. Grant, I'm scared. I don't know what to do, but I can't just abandon her."

He could hear her voice quivering, tension verging on fear, thinking only of her daughter. It was the sound of a mother, and he knew it was no act. And he heard that vulnerability that was so frightening, that total surrender to her circumstances that touched him and stirred his desire to help. He had let things go too far.

"Jodee, don't go. Don't just blow it all off. Let me help. Give it another couple of days. Wait until Venice, at least. We will figure something out by then, some plan of action that will work for both of you. We'll send her another email and ask her what she thinks would be most helpful. I should hear something from Matt by then, too. I might even be heading to California if he needs me. God knows that is a mess. We can fly out together. Meet me for breakfast tomorrow morning and then you can go along on Babs' bus for the tour of Athens. It will do you good to get your mind off of things. We'll spend the day together. Okay?"

"Whatever you think is best, Grant. I don't know what to do."

"Okay. Meet me on the Lido deck at seven o'clock."

He hung up and headed back to the elevators, got on, and got off at six, walked to her door and knocked. Startled by the knock, Shay opened the door just a crack. "Who is it?" she asked.

"Me. Can I come in?"

And she heard that strange little voice answer, "Yes, Grant. Come in."

The Antiquities

It was already hot when the Palmer Plantation group boarded their bus at 8:30, excited about their tour of the city and their visit to the Acropolis. Several had been there before and were eagerly sharing their prior experiences while others were eagerly taking note of the seating arrangements. Babs had cornered Mitch right away, directing him to the seat next to her so they could co-host the trip, sort of a practice round, she explained. Babs had already caught Maureen, excitedly telling her about the plans for Mitch to help her with her business, adding that Grant might be involved too. "Think about it, Maureen. You could help too and we can plan all kinds of things for the singles group. We four could travel together. Wouldn't that be fun?" Maureen had been a little surprised at this latest development, a little suspect of the part about Grant Albright possibly being involved, but intrigued enough to suggest that they have a little meeting about it because, she assured Babs, "that does sound interesting."

Maureen took the window seat across from Babs, and Wanda, who had decided to come after all, sat next to her on the aisle, still grousing about deciding to spend the day in Athens instead of in the floral department. Shay and Joan went to the middle of the bus, and Ralph sat right behind them. Everyone was surprised when none other than the male half of one of the unmarried couples traveling together took the seat next to Ralph. His female counterpart boarded with one of the married couples, and she could be heard to say, "Let's not sit anywhere near the bastard." The adorable Nannette Guppie had brought her new friend Joe along and introduced him to everyone along the way as she headed toward the back, planning to snuggle and cozy up once they were on their way.

Grant and Jodee boarded last, not by choice, but having been delayed by Ethan when he hand delivered a message to Grant. "This is serious, Grant. I hear he is really hot about something. I don't know what this note says but you better read it before you go." It was stapled together with "Grant Albright, Urgent!" scrawled on the outside. Grant had torn it open and read, then folded it and put it in his pocket.

"Okay, Ethan. You can tell him I'll be there." He turned to Jodee, "Come on. They are probably waiting for us on the bus."

Grant and Jodee went toward the back of the bus and several heads turned to see where they sat, obviously interested in the significance of Jodee's presence in their group. There had already been considerable gossip about the two and some buzzing to one another about a possible affair, some even wondering if Jodee could be headed to Palmer. Grant had stopped and spoken briefly to Mitch as he passed his seat and when he passed Joan and Shay he nodded and pointed, acknowledging Shay's presence. She smiled gamely and gave a little wave, embarrassed by the awkwardness of the situation and the appearance of having been dropped for the more appealing Jodee.

This was not going to be a dull day.

The city of Athens is the very essence of all that is Greece, modern and bustling, ancient and historical, the birthplace of western civilization, the beginning of democracy, and philosophy, and medicine, art, literature, and science. The city possesses and protects some of the most astonishing antiquities in the world, maintained and prized as ruins and housed as priceless collections in grand museums. The morning's tour would include the usual sites, Syntagma Square, passing government buildings with imposing neoclassical architecture, the modern Olympic venues, The National Archaeological Museum, and the Agora, which was the market place and center of community activities in ancient Athens. They would also visit the Plaka, the oldest quarter in the city, defined by the picturesque winding maze of streets which have been inhabited for over three thousand years. At one point in history the Plaka had been the Turkish quarter, which was especially interesting to this group since they had just been to Istanbul and had learned of the entwined history of the Turks, Greeks, and Romans. The group would stop at a fine restaurant for lunch, one personally selected by Babs, one that enjoyed a reputation for serving outstanding Greek cuisine.

Because the restaurant was not very large, Babs had requested outdoor seating and, because their group was large for this small place, they would be limited to two entree selections. The happy, hungry flock swarmed into the restrooms and then seated themselves on the patio. Some sat with old friends and others staked out places with the best view for people watching and gawking. Wanda and Maureen found the perfect spot and saved seats for Joan and Shay. Ralph was hot on their heels and immediately seized two more chairs, one for himself and one for the now partnerless traveler in their midst, who was only too happy to join the ladies, asserting his sudden new found single status with aplomb, and eyeing the very attractive Shay Porter.

Grant and Jodee sat with Mitch and Babs. Grant had politely assigned the seats in such a way as to provide himself a clear shot of Shay, a fact that had not gone unnoticed by any of them. Mitch grinned and teasingly said, "Perfect, Grant. The view is perfect." Jodee turned to have a look, and was a little disappointed to see that the only other blonde in the group was seated directly in Grant's line of view. She felt a twinge of envy, reminding herself again of the fact that Grant hadn't shown any interest in her romantically, only in her music career. She valued his friendship above all and tried to convince herself that friendship was all it would ever be. He had never given any indication of romantic intentions, only affection. He would have made a move by now if he had sex on his mind, that was for sure. It had been pretty obvious to her that Grant sought Shay out whenever he had a chance and she wondered if he had had sex with her. The thought broke her heart.

As luck would have it, the adoring one was already making her rounds, snapping pictures of everyone. When she came to Grant and Jodee, she made the biggest, loudest fuss, asking them to "get closer,

Grant. Give her a kiss, Grant." Jodee laughed right out loud and turned and planted a big smooch right on Grant's forehead, leaving a bright red lipstick mark. Then she licked her finger and attempted to remove the evidence of their charade, wishing for all the world that things were different.

Mitch was furious about the whole episode and didn't care who knew it. He spoke right up, in his usual loud voice. "Better make sure she doesn't send those pictures all over the world, Grant. I think I'm going to talk to her about that before it gets to your kids. She should be more careful with that stuff before someone gets hurt."

Jodee was mortified at Mitch's response, hurt by his obvious disapproval of her, aimed more at her personally than at their little publicity stunt, making her feel cheap or unfit for the Golden Boy of Palmer Plantation. "Yes," she said. "We wouldn't want anyone to get hurt, would we? I didn't think about the possibility of hurting Grant's kids. Grant, the next time the little dear approaches us let's just stick our tongues out and stick our thumbs in our ears," doing exactly that and making the most outrageous face she could.

Relieved by her antics, Grant joined right in with the face making, mugging at Mitch and Babs, who had burst into loud laughter, also relieved that the tension had been lifted from her little group and wanting to project hilarious fun to the whole Palmer gang. She joined in the face making herself. When things settled down, Grant reached under the table and gave Jodee's hand a little squeeze. She returned the squeeze and moved her hand away from his.

The waiter had appeared while they were making silly faces at one another and stood politely, attempting to retain his poise before announcing that they had a choice of two entrees, moussaka or lamb kabobs. About the only thing in the world that Grant hated more than eggplant was lamb, or maybe squid, and he had had it with these limited choices.

Mitch was laughing at his predicament and finally spoke up to the waiter. "Can't you fix him something else? Make him a hamburger. As a matter of fact, make me one too." The poor waiter didn't know what to say, having had implicit instructions to make no substitutions, and turned on his heels to see what he should do. Mitch wasn't through yet and he turned to Babs. "For crying out loud, Babs. If we are going to work together you are going to have to do a better job of picking out menus. A little bit of this foreign crap goes a long way."

Now it was Babs' turn to be mortified and she immediately got up and followed the waiter, triumphantly returning to the group with the announcement that she had just arranged for two additional menu offerings, a hamburger with frites or a Greek salad, which was mostly zucchini, tomatoes, marinated olives and feta cheese served with Greek yogurt dressing. Maybe this idea of working with Mitch wasn't such a good one after all if he was going to expect to have some input.

After lunch the full and happy group would visit the most famous attraction in all of Greece. There is probably no more recognized place on the planet than the Acropolis, crowned by the magnificent Parthenon, epitomizing the grandeur of ancient Greece. Visible from almost everywhere in Athens, it remains today one of the most significant monumental treasures in the world.

Babs' group waited in a cluster while she went to the ticket window to retrieve the tickets she had ordered on line and to collect the local guide who would be their escort for the tour. The temperature was hovering around ninety five degrees but there was a rather brisk breeze offering some slight relief. There are accommodations for those needing assistance but for those in this group only the final ascent to the top was rather challenging. Shay was glad she had worn a pair of slacks today, even though shorts would have been cooler, and she had on her ugly, awful walking shoes. Ralph had made a point of commenting on her choice, especially noting that it was "good for her foot" that she had followed his advice and she was thinking that the breeze would have been way too much for a sundress to handle. At that memory of her embarrassing episode in Ephesus, she looked around for Grant. He was holding on to Jodee's arm, paying way more attention to her than what was necessary, and she wondered if he had dared chew Jodee out about her choice of shoes, the same rather high wedgies she had worn in Mykonos.

Jodee also had on pretty tight white slacks and a yellow knit top that left little to the imagination, revealing ample endowment, raising a question in Shay's mind if they were "hers." Probably implants, she concluded. All show business women had them.

Ralph had stayed by Shay's side all the way up, taking her arm occasionally, and the newly single Charley had taken over attending to Maureen and Wanda, making it very awkward for all of them because of the way that his former partner kept making loud comments about the jerk, the creep, the prick, the SOB, whenever she was within ten feet of him. Since the group was to be huddled together at each monument, listening to their guide, it was almost impossible to avoid this verbal assault, but the lady was obviously really pissed off and didn't give a damn what any of them thought. Several of the other ladies had surrounded her, offering comforting little pats and handing her tissues, because the rage was turning to tears, adding to the discomfort of the situation. The women were protective of the lady, who was a Palmer Plantation resident, one of them. She had met the revolting Charley, the outsider, on a cruise the prior year and this cruise was to have been a fabulous, romantic reuniting of the two. She had shared her excitement and anticipation of the event ad nauseam.

Most of the group was attempting to ignore the unfolding drama and listened intently as the guide told them about the various structures. The Parthenon is a masterpiece of Greek architecture and surprises most people by its sheer size. It is two hundred and twenty eight feet by one hundred and one feet, and forty five feet tall and outlined by huge Doric columns. Although it was originally built as a temple dedicated to the Goddess Athena, there is little historical evidence to support the use of the structure as a temple. The evidence more clearly indicates that it was a place for commerce, similar to banking. The guide was very knowledgeable, imparting historic facts, mentioning that in ancient times the temple had been painted brightly and richly decorated in vivid colors. He spent considerable time on the actions of the Earl of Elgin, who had ransacked the place and had taken an entire museum's worth of marble artifacts from the Parthenon to London, where they reside in the British Museum.

Known as the Elgin Marbles, these spoils remain in dispute today, the Greeks insisting that they should be returned to their prominent place on the Acropolis.

On the northern side of the Acropolis is another recognizable structure, the Erechtheion, distinguished by the six pillars carved as maidens. The guide carefully pointed out that the columns standing today are replicas of the originals, which now reside in the Acropolis Museum. There are several other structures that were described as well but Mitch didn't keep standing there in the heat to listen. His face was bright red and he was mopping the perspiration that was running down his face. Maureen had taken her little travel umbrella from her small backpack and was holding it over him to provide some shade. Wanda was fanning him with a brochure she had been fanning herself with, and Babs had opened her last bottle of water for him. Grant took one look at the little scene and decided that his friend needed some additional assistance and called to Ralph, who ran right over with Joan fast behind him. She began to take Mitch's pulse and Ralph poured some of the water from his bottle onto his handkerchief and placed it on Mitch's neck and then opened his little medical bag, snapped open a cold pack, and placed it on Mitch's forehead.

As Grant stood by Mitch, waiting for some assessment from Ralph, Jodee found herself standing alone. She casually walked over to join Shay and the outsider, Charley. Not knowing anything about his situation, Jodee smiled brightly and introduced herself, cheerfully asking, "Do you live near Grant at Palmer? I think Shay and I are the only outsiders with the group and I'm so envious of all of you living there together in that lovely place. They have all made us feel so welcome, just like one of them. Don't you feel that way, too, Shay?"

Delighted to be found standing with the two youngest and most attractive women in the group, Charley decided to capitalize on the situation. "It is so nice to meet you at last, Miss Jordan. I try to catch your performance whenever I can, and you are even lovelier in person than I imagined. Unfortunately, I too am an outsider but I have not been quite so warmly welcomed by everyone in the group. Perhaps you ladies can give me some pointers since my charms seem to have been lost on a certain resident there and it appears that I am now a persona non grata."

Aware of Charley's situation, Shay interjected, hoping to alert Jodee to the difficult circumstances Charley had found himself in. "Charley is traveling with the lady over there, the one in the bright pink shirt, but they are having a slight disagreement today so Charley has politely stepped away, as she has suggested, and is spending the day with Ralph. Just taking a little breather, you might say."

"Oh, well it happens to all of us, doesn't it?" Jodee replied. "Things don't always work the way we planned. Grant always says life is just one big crapshoot. It's just like lightning, you never know when it's going to strike. You will probably patch things up by this evening. Grant says it is really hard to stay mad for very long, especially if you respect each other or want the friendship to last. I'm sure everything will work out just fine. Grant's advice is just don't say anything you will regret."

Shay was stunned. Hearing Jodee so glibly quoting Grant, implying that they were so close, handing out his advice, was infuriating. Shay hadn't even told Joan about Grant's surprise visit to her room last night, hadn't mentioned one thing to anyone. Now she was hearing some of his very words coming right out of Jodee's mouth, the part about life being a crapshoot, about not staying mad. These were the very words he had spoken to her, words that were meant to explain his relationship with Jodee, words used to appease her, to persuade her to be patient with him, words that were pretty hard to swallow now.

Charley had just noticed the dimpled darling with her camera and motioned to her to come over. "How about a picture of me with these two lovely ladies. They are a whole lot more interesting than any picture of the Acropolis," he laughed. "Come on, ladies. Get right up close, one in each arm," standing between them with his arms around their shoulders. They were each obliging when his angry, tearful, former partner walked by with her friends. Looking at him with disdain, she said, "Ass Hole."

"Good God, Charley! What did you do?" Jodee exclaimed. "You must have been a very bad boy."

"Yeah, I guess I was. Seems we weren't expecting quite the same thing on this trip, Jodee. But she really is a pretty nice lady even though she is making a very bad impression on everyone right now. I think I'll take Grant's advice and try not to stay mad for very long. He's right about one other thing, too. Life really is just one big crapshoot, one big roll of the dice."

Ralph was heading toward them. Apparently his diagnosis of Mitch's condition was just too much heat after a big meal, but Mitch was to take it easy the rest of the day and evening. Joan was planning to stay with him just in case he felt dizzy again. The tour had concluded and they were told to meet at the bus in forty five minutes, allowing some time to meander around the monuments a while longer or to visit the nearby collection of small shops. Grant came over to the group.

"Well, our patient is on the mend. Are you ready to go down, Jodee? I would like to visit that little gold shop I saw. How about you guys, are you ready to go down too?" And turning to Shay, he said, "If we see a little shop with hats I think we should buy you one. It's too hot to be out in this sun all day without a hat. Mitch should have worn one today," clearly signaling to them all that he expected Shay to go with him. He hadn't mentioned anything to Jodee about wearing a hat.

Mitch found a nice shady spot to sit with Joan while the others browsed around the gold shop. Grant knew exactly what he was looking for and approached the salesman behind the counter filled with beautiful charms, selecting lovely, intricately cut charms of the Parthenon and one of the Erechtheion depicting the six maidens. The first two he bought were major pieces, quite heavy and expensive. Then, almost as an afterthought, he selected two more slightly smaller versions, just in case. He noticed Jodee browsing the counters filled with bracelets and necklaces and went to her side. "What do you like? Did you pick something out?"

"Everything is so beautiful, just such lovely gold work. Maybe I'll get something the next time I'm in Athens," she joked. "I had no idea they did so much gold jewelry here." The saleswoman at that counter had started taking things out for Jodee to admire and Grant watched closely as she selected a few pieces to examine, interested in her preference and speaking right up. "I like this one, Jodee. This looks like you." It was a beautiful thick cut necklace in the Greek key design, accented with pave diamonds, a solid, showy piece, just perfect.

"No, I think not, Grant. That is way more than I can spend. But I would like to pick up something for Leighanna, some little souvenir from Athens. Maybe I can find some earrings." They continued their browsing, selecting a pair of dangling gold earrings, not too big or heavy, just pretty, and Jodee made her purchase.

Grant noticed Shay at another counter, admiring a gold bangle bracelet with Greek letters on it and he went to her side. "Go ahead, buy it Shay. That is really pretty. Treat yourself."

"I think I'll call Joan to come in and give me her opinion," she said, leaving Grant to stand alone with the expensive bracelet while she went to the door and called to Joan, who left Mitch's side and followed Shay to the bracelet counter to render her opinion.

"What do you think, Joan? I have never had a piece of jewelry this expensive before. Do you think it is worth this kind of money?" she asked, turning the price tag over so Joan could see it. The proprietor had quite cleverly written the price in both Euros and dollars because experience had shown that the mere need to convert to dollars was off putting to some Americans, perhaps even a little intimidating, and sometimes resulted in lost sales. At these prices they might as well know what it costs right away.

"Wow! It is pretty expensive but it's the most beautiful one I've ever seen, Shay. It will go with everything. You will wear it forever. Go ahead and splurge."

And she did. She bought the heavy, beautifully decorated solid gold bangle bracelet for herself.

While they were holding their private discussion about the beautiful bracelet, Grant went to the front and made another purchase, requesting gift wrap, and then went outside to wait with Mitch.

Most of the Palmer group had planned to return to the city to see the beautifully lighted Parthenon and to enjoy some Athenian night life. Jodee and Grant both had to work so they would stay on board. Grant took the message from Ethan out of his pocket and reread it, planning to shower and dress for the evening first. He had not shared the note with Jodee and he was relieved that she had not asked about it. He was anxious to get to the computers too, to see if there was anything else from Leighanna and any news at all from his own kids. He had left Jodee off in the lobby and caught up with Shay and Joan as they were getting on the elevator. He got on with them.

"Are you going back to town tonight, Shay? I was hoping to see you later. If you get back in time, plan to wait for me in the Casablanca, okay?"

"Yes," she said firmly. "I would like to finish our conversation from last night," still upset by Jodee's comments indicating a closer relationship with Grant than he had admitted to. She wanted an opportunity to hear more if he brought up the subject again. He was a hard one to figure out. "I'll wait for you. I think we will return to the ship around ten thirty."

"Good, I'll plan on it," he said, detecting the new firmness in her voice and suspecting that she wasn't as comfortable with their agreement as he thought. He was determined to occupy her time after seeing the newly available and rather aggressive Charley following her around like a puppy dog and he was afraid she might have made plans with Charley, or even Ralph, for tomorrow, so he decided to go ahead and gamble, right there in front of Joan, risking rejection and embarrassment if Shay said she had already made plans.

"By the way, Mitch is staying on the boat tomorrow so I was hoping you would go to Delphi with me. There is a bus going at 9:30. If it is okay with you I will get you added to the list when I go to the computer center."

And she heard that silly little voice from somewhere deep inside her say, "I'd love to Grant. Put my name down and we can talk about the particulars when we meet later tonight," putting aside all resentment of his assumption that she would be available at his beck and call whenever he found himself needing a companion. Joan looked at her with raised eyebrows, questioning Shay's immediate acceptance of his invitation, and making a sudden change of plans for herself as well. She would stay on the boat to keep tabs on Mitch.

Grant arrived at Ethan's office promptly at 6:00. Itzach Schwartzman opened the door himself, offering his hand and introducing himself. Ethan wasn't present.

"Come right in, Grant. I'm glad we have this time together. I have a few things to talk to you about and I like to handle this kind of business personally, one on one. Do you want me to start with the good news or the bad news?"

Grant took a seat in the chair he had been directed to, right across from Schwartzman's desk. "Whatever works for you is fine with me. Have at it," sounding just a little cocky.

"You know, Grant. I like you. You and I are a lot alike."

"How is that?"

"Your attitude, for one. You are cocky or perhaps just self-confident, but either way, I think you are cocky. You know that I don't give a shit about the piano player and I know that you don't give a shit what I think. I like that. You know I have a reputation as a real ballbuster and you have the balls to totally disregard that, to actually tell people to 'Fuck Schwartzman.'"

"Look, Mr. Schwartzman. If you're pissed about Jodee, or about my playing, or whatever else might have pissed you off, go ahead and say so. At this point I don't know if this is the good news or the bad news. Just get to the point. But don't start attacking Jodee. I won't sit still for that."

"I know that, Grant. That's what I want to talk to you about. By the way, you can call me Izzy. Jodee thinks she got this job as the stand in chirp for the trio, but that isn't how it happened at all. That was the only legitimate opening we had, that's all. I knew she wasn't right for that group but I had to get her on this ship. You see, Grant, neither Jodee nor you are working these gigs for the cruise line. You are working for me, at my personal request. Believe it or not, I happen to have some clout around here. But now I have created a little situation for myself that I need your help with."

"Okay. Shoot."

"I listen to many, many auditions and performances throughout the year and I have been looking for the perfect female voice for a very, very special venue, and when Jodee's CD was forwarded to me and I heard that voice, I just had to see her perform, had to check her out. The cruise line did have a vacancy for a piano player in the Casablanca Lounge and five CDs were sent for me to make a selection. You were one of the five finalists. But I didn't give a shit about the Casablanca Lounge. I picked you because of how you played and I wanted to try you and Jodee out together. Of course, you jumped ahead of the game plan and invited her to sing with you before I got a chance. I do have my regular job to do here too, so I couldn't spend much time on you two at first.

"So what is the problem then? I think she is great."

"She's better than great. She has it all, but the problem is this. It was easy for my people to get background checks on you guys, all the information I needed, and it was easy to find out what flight she was on to Istanbul because the cruise line had booked it for her. I was already in Paris so I got on the same plane, only I was in first class and the plane was sold out. I asked the flight attendant to offer an upgrade to the guy sitting next to Jodee and I just switched seats. She had no idea who I was and she was just delightful. Just perfect. She talked and talked so I decided not to tell her who I was because it might scare her off. We rode to the Ahmet Hotel together and when I checked in I told the manager to give her my suite and I took her room. She never knew it was from me. And I arranged for her stateroom with the veranda, the flowers, wardrobe, everything. She still doesn't know. So now she thinks I'm some kind of bastard from hell because of what all she has heard, plus you telling her to 'fuck Schwartzman' every chance you get, so I need you to help me out. I think she is going to be really upset when she discovers that I am the same guy from the plane, because she told me lots of stuff and she will be embarrassed about that and won't trust me."

"So what are you suggesting, that I start talking nice about you? Look, I only want what is best for her. She has lots of personal problems right now but I'll be glad to help you out if you have something good in mind for her. I just want her to have a real chance to make something good happen with her career, a fair shot at it."

"Grant, I am involved in a personal project, one that is perfect for her. I recently purchased a penthouse in City Center in Vegas and I am opening a fine private dining club on the first floor, intimate, elite, exclusive. I will have a large library, a very elegant look, for the main dining room and I want to feature Jodee there. It will be her room, her signature. She is not a big name and not some has been making a comeback, so she will be synonymous with Izzy's, that's what I'm calling the place, Izzy's. She is just perfect, the perfect chanteuse, and I can groom her into the image I have in mind. I'm already providing clothes for her so I can see her in different looks, in different settings, see how she handles herself. I can just see her there, working the room, just sexy enough for the men but not too threatening for the wives. On the other side there will be a piano lounge, but the piano player will also play for her when she is performing in the library."

"And?"

"I would like to say I want you, Grant, but it just won't work. Let me tell you why. You have the perfect touch for her, a synergy, too much synergy. She is falling for you, Grant, and I don't want a husband and wife thing like Toni and Tennille, a duo. That always creates problems if they don't work out. She needs an accompanist dedicated to showcasing her. It isn't that you wouldn't do that, but you can carry a room all by yourself. You don't need Jodee. It's true, nobody gives a shit about the piano player, only about the liquor sales, but Grant, when you are out there, they care about you, you connect, you reach them. There is something else too. You don't want it, you don't need the applause, you don't need any of it."

"Well, you are right about that. Frankly I'm glad that you made that choice not to use me, not to use me in order for Jodee to have the job, because, Izzy, I would have turned you down."

"I know you would have, Grant. I've already booked another piano man for the Casablanca Lounge. He's coming aboard in Venice. I'll let Jodee work with the new guy and see how that goes. It's not going to be easy to replace you."

"So, I'm through then? This is my exit interview?"

"Hell no. I'm just moving you."

"Why is that? I like the Casablanca Lounge. I want to stay there."

"Because we can't have the corridors blocked every night with people lined up waiting to hear you. You will go to the Adventure Lounge upstairs, the same time slot. It is a much bigger room and wide open so you will catch all the traffic coming and going to the dining rooms. You'll really increase liquor sales up there. It's a business decision, Grant. You know how business works. You ran a large business yourself. It's not about you, it's about profits. It's a business. That's why it's called show business and not show fun or show games. You have to sell tickets. Sure we want our passengers to enjoy the music, to love the ship, go home happy and tell their friends, book another trip with us. But in today's competitive environment, we have to make some money off of the booze and the gambling or we might not make it at all. That's how it works. It's not even about your piano playing, it's about what works. By the way, did you get my errand done?"

"Yeah, it's right here." Grant got the wrapped gift out of his pocket and handed it to Izzy. "It's a great piece, a solid gold Greek key necklace, diamond accented. She doesn't know I bought it. They were expecting me and they charged it to your account without hesitation. Are you going to give it to her tonight?"

"Thanks. I knew I could count on you to pick out something classy. I try to stop in there whenever I'm in Athens. They are terrific goldsmiths but I couldn't get away today to do it myself. I'm thinking of inviting her for dinner and then telling her about the job. Did you know she tried to book a flight to New York? The guys in the purser's office alerted me to it, so I have to act fast. Do you know what that is about? It isn't another man, is it? You are already giving me a problem in that department. I'd appreciate it if you would back off, Grant."

"No, it's not another man, Izzy. Like I said, she has personal problems, a situation with her daughter."

"That shouldn't be so hard then. I can probably help with that. Those kinds of problems usually go away with a little money. Grant, do what you can to help me with the Jodee deal, but don't say anything until I tell you. And keep her off that damned airplane. She has got to stay on this ship. I just hope she isn't too upset to listen to me when she finds out who I am. I want to get this deal done."

"She won't be upset, Izzy. She will be thrilled. I'll do what I can to help it along. I think I have already convinced her to wait until Venice. You have a little time."

The two men shook hands as Grant headed to the door. Izzy called after him. "Thank you, Grant. And, by the way, you are one hell of a good piano player."

Grant headed for the computer center. "Jesus," he muttered. "That guy is a piece of work. Does he think he can play craps with people's lives, arrange everything just for the sake of his business? Jodee can't handle a guy like him, a slick insider, sneaky, with a personal agenda. Even though Jodee is pretty tough, she is no match for this guy. This is the big time and this deal for her sounds too good to be true. Any fool could see right through it. Schwartzman didn't say anything at all about what was good for Jodee or what he intended to offer her, any protection for her. He'll just use her to get started and then dump her for a big name. Or maybe he just wants someone kind of naive like her for some scheme he is up too. She needs to be forewarned before she gets sucked into something illegal or shady and she takes the fall. Las Vegas, for God's sake. No way."

The Con

There was an email from Megan and one from Leighanna.

To: Daddy
From: Megan
Hi, Daddy,

We should know something tomorrow. Glad we are here for Matt, he is a mess. The girls are just darling. It is heartbreaking.

Keep your fingers crossed. We three are going out drinking tonight. Therapy!! We're going to the piano bar in our hotel. Wish it was you playing. We all need you! Hope you are having fun.

Hugs, Megan

Reply:
To: Megan, Misty, and Matt
From: Dad

My fingers are crossed!! Let me know right away. I will come on the run as soon as I hear from you. No matter what happens, I plan to head to CA. Cruise is a real bummer anyway.

Love, Dad

To: Mom
From: Leighanna

Hi, didn't hear from you, Mom, but wanted you to know how things are going. (not!) Did finally get a call from Bill and I think he is coming over tonight around 8:00. I got another kid to baby sit with too so if he comes over he will have to contend with three little boys. If I get more than four I need a license as a daycare place, but at least the new one will pay me when she can. They count your own kid. I looked into it. How is your luck these days? Mine sucks. I think we have run out of men to rescue us, Mom.

Love and kisses, Leighanna

Grant printed it and headed to the Fez. Jodee was singing when he arrived and he was amazed at how good the group sounded, far better than he had expected. The guys had really taken his advice to heart and were giving Jodee a great backup, doing some things he hadn't thought of, and Jodee was working her charms on the room, loving it, soaking it up. Why the hell Izzy would want to change anything about her was beyond him. He thought she was perfect just like she was. She had seen him come in so she sashayed over and started singing right to him, running her hands across the back of his neck and meeting his eyes with an expression that left no doubt about her desire and he felt himself responding, locking eyes with her, sending a signal of recognition. Izzy Schwartzman was going to get a run for his money.

When she finished her set they left the Fez together. "There is an email from Leighanna," he said. "Would you like to go to the computer center and answer it? And we can have dinner together too, if you want."

Her heart skipped a beat, swelling with feelings for him that she dare not have, wanting something she had thought he would not give, thrilled at his response, and terrified that she had blown everything. "That would be wonderful, Grant. The more I am seen in public with you the more they recognize me. Our sales in the Fez have really improved, too," she said, trying to sound like she was still playing the publicity game for all it was worth, masking the fact that her feelings for him were for real.

Jodee read the email and then started to type.

To: Leighanna
From: Mommy
Hi, Toots,

I am proud of you for starting the baby sitting jobs. Who knows where it might lead. Honey, I HAVE GIVEN UP MEN FOREVER!! You and I can start over as soon as I get back. Be careful if Bill comes over. You already know what a prick he is and you can do better than that. Ask him how long you can stay in the condo. Does his wife know about you? Maybe you can use that for some leverage. You only need about two more months there. By then we will have made our plans.

How are you feeling? Any morning sickness? Don't be lifting those little boys all day. Did Josh get over his sore throat? We will find a doctor just as soon as I get there. My gig isn't going so hot and I am planning on coming home sooner than expected. Will head right for Reno. I think I am through with show business too!! I am already thinking about other jobs I could do, but God knows, I have no skills. We are quite a pair, aren't we? Will let you know when I am coming. I have to pay my own way for the flight. Hope it fits on my credit card.

I think I am maxed out. I'll see if they will give me my paycheck when I leave instead of sending it.

Love you Honey, Mommy

She hit send.

Grant had been reading as she typed but made no comment until she was finished, aware that parts of her reply were intended for him, part of the game. "So, you are still planning on leaving. I had hoped that now that things are going well in the Fez you would decide to stay on."

"I can't, Grant. She needs me. There is no one else to help her. I'm still leaving from Venice but I haven't booked the flight yet. I wonder who I talk to about my paycheck. Is Ethan the one I need to see or someone in the purser's office? I'll have to use my credit card for the plane fare, which is going to be a problem too. It might have some kind of overdraft or something, where they will let me charge. Do you think that is possible?"

"I doubt it. Let's go to that little place on the Lido and grab some dinner. I'm getting hungry." He took her hand in his and held it all the way to the restaurant. "I think we need to have a little talk, Jodee."

They were nearly finished eating before he broached the subject. "The more I think about your situation, the more I think you should stay and finish your gig. If Leighanna can talk this Bill guy into a couple of months, mention his wife to persuade him, you will be back in plenty of time to help her. There really is no hurry. Something might change in the meantime, Jodee. Why not just wait a little longer?"

"I can't believe you are saying this, Grant. You are the one who thought I should go in the first place. You said that you would go if it were your daughter, abandoned, broke, pregnant, cast out like garbage. Remember? There is no point in dragging this out."

"Yes, I did say that, if it was my daughter who was abandoned, broke, pregnant, cast out like garbage, I would go. I even said I would kill the SOB. Remember?"

"I knew you didn't mean that part, but I think you were serious when you said you would go and help her. And that is what I am going to do. Nothing else really matters."

"Look, Jodee. Life is just one big crapshoot, one big roll of the dice. We never know how anything is going to work out. We all just keep planning and plotting, even praying, but in the end none of that matters. You just roll the dice and see what you get. I think the only real problem you and Leighanna have right now is money, and I have offered to help with that. All you have to do is say the word and I will transfer some money to her. I don't even know if you are telling me the truth. This could just be a con, just you and your daughter rolling the dice and seeing what comes up."

"Grant, how could you even think such a thing, even possibly think that I would con you?" Her heart was sinking, realizing that she had blown the whole thing.

"Why wouldn't I think that? Guys get conned like that all the time. You were playing right by the script, Jodee, and you were good at it. It was textbook perfect, the pitiful situation at home, the unspoken plea for money from some unsuspecting, sympathetic guy. And when you turned down the money the first time, that was part of the script too, meant to convince me that you were so honorable you would never take my money. But I was on to you."

"If you think it is a con, why are you offering again?"

"Because I was just seeing how far you would go. But now it has gone too far and it is time to stop the little game. You do not need to pretend it is a con in order for me to help you, Jodee."

"What gave it away, Grant? How were you on to me? When did you figure it out? Didn't I play it good enough?"

"I said you were good at it. But if you ever do try to con someone, Jodee, don't fold so soon. When I offered five, or more, you should have raised me or called. If you are going to bluff you have to have enough on the table to make it worthwhile, but you folded when you said you wouldn't take my money, giving me a chance to walk away scot free, which I did."

"So that is what made you think it was a con?"

"No. I knew it wasn't a con right from the beginning because I knew the truth. I knew there really was a serious problem. I just didn't know why you were playing it like a con instead of trusting me enough to ask for the money. When you read that first email from Leighanna you turned white right in front of my eyes. The color drained right out of your face. No con artist can fake that."

"Well, it was real. I got the idea to make it sound like a con when you asked me yesterday if there were women who faked problems back home to get money from men. If it worked I would just leave in Venice, be gone, and you would never hear from me again. I wanted you to think you had been conned because if you got conned out of the money, you could handle that. You would have been mad as hell about it, but you could have handled it. I was too proud to ask for money, ashamed, humiliated, and I didn't want your pity. And I didn't want you to feel sorry for me, feel like you had to help me. But when you offered the money I just couldn't take it from you. I just couldn't do it. But I did wonder why you fell for it. You were pretty easy, you know."

"Easy? Wait a minute," he laughed. "There was nothing easy about it. It was hard not letting on and even harder seeing you so worried about Leighanna. But now that we understand each other, it will be easy."

She reached across the table and took his hand in hers. "You are one of the best things that ever happened to me, Grant. But I am curious. How high would you have gone?"

"High enough to regret it. From now on just level with me. No more games. If you need money, ask me for it. There still is the issue of you leaving the ship in Venice. Are you serious about that, because if you are, I think it is a mistake. I think you should stick it out, try to finish the gig. Roll the dice one more time and see what happens."

"Maybe you are right. Since I don't have any money for the ticket anyway I might as well take a chance and hope lady luck will come through for me."

"You know damned well that I will pay for your flight if you need me too. We'll wait for Leighanna's reply and then decide what the next move should be. Now it's time for me to go to work. I'll see you at 10:00. We'll just wing it tonight."

"What if Schwartzman comes in?"

"Fuck Schwartzman."

Jodee was singing when Shay arrived in the Casablanca Lounge at 10:30. Several of the Palmer people had gone back to Athens for the night tour and had decided to have a nightcap in the Casablanca, but there had been no seats available so they went up to the Adventure Lounge where there was more room. Shay assessed the situation, seeing one possible space on a settee next to a rather flashy looking woman who appeared to be with the couple seated across from her. Shay had been alone her entire adult life, but she still shuddered at every situation that required her to enter a roomful of people by herself. She felt like all eyes were on her, eyes that questioned why she was alone, why she would come by herself, why she couldn't find anyone to come with her. She had girlfriends who went out to dinner or even to bars by themselves, went all kinds of places alone, traveled alone, had accepted, even welcomed their aloneness, the freedom to do as they pleased with a lighthearted approach to life, satisfied and fulfilled with their own pleasures. Shay Porter wasn't one of them.

She stood at the door, hesitant, trying to decide whether to go in or to come back later, but Jodee had meandered behind Grant and was rubbing his shoulders, and he had turned to look up at her, and she had kissed him on the top of his head, and Shay took it all in. With a huge surge of determination, she entered the Casablanca Lounge, walked all the way across the room, right past all those questioning, judgmental eyes, and took the seat next to the flashy lady. Grant saw her and smiled in recognition, winking and nodding, and she returned his smile and blew him a little kiss.

This time, Jodee took it all in. It was her last song for the evening and the little peck on the head she had given Grant was just her way of saying thanks as she ended her set, but after the thrill of thinking he had looked at her with desire earlier in the evening, seeing the flirtatious welcome he had sent Shay's way was a hurtful surprise. She acknowledged her applause, and graciously left the room.

Grant always took a little break when Jodee finished, so he headed right for Shay. Several folks stood to leave and he immediately ushered Shay to a vacant settee and sat beside her.

"Hi, glad you made it. How was Athens by night?"

"It was lovely. The Acropolis looks just like a postcard. I'm sorry you didn't see it."

"Who all went? Who were you with, the gals?"

"Not really. We pretty much just sat on the bus wherever. Only got off at one place to look at some excavation going on right at the side of the street. The town is really alive at night."

"So you weren't with Ralph or Charley? Did they go?"

"They were on the bus, tagging along as usual, but not really with us. What did you do all evening?"

"Not much. Just some email. Had dinner at that little place on the Lido, listened to Jodee in the Fez for a while. She really sounded good. The group seems to be making some real progress now."

"That's good. I know you were concerned about that. She seemed very grateful tonight."

"I told you last night that it was all just show business, Shay. I don't want it spread all over Palmer Plantation that there is something going on between Jodee and me."

"Grant, I haven't heard anyone mention a thing about it."

"Good, but remember, you promised to help squelch rumors when you hear them. It's hard enough for me down there as it is without a lot of gossip besides. Would you like a drink while I play my last set? When I'm done we can get a bite to eat or just sit on the deck and relax, enjoy some peace and quiet."

"Do they serve coffee in here? I think I would like a cup of coffee now and then I'll have a drink with you later, during our peace and quiet."

He played for another forty minutes, occasionally winking and nodding at her, especially during love songs, all a part of their little charade. Shay had been furious with him just a few hours ago on the Acropolis, upset about Jodee's comments that indicated a closeness he had denied, and still burning from his rather public show of affection for Jodee last night, that sure didn't look like show business. She was feeling used by her own availability, her willingness to answer to his beck and call. Yet there was something about him, something that touched her, not attraction, not desire, just a feeling she couldn't explain, like a spell had been cast upon her. Grant Albright was a paradox, filled with charm and confidence, the essence of masculinity and success, yet wounded, vulnerable, lost, filling her with a need to somehow please him, to simply be there for him, to rescue him. How could one man stir so many emotions in her at one time? And she knew at that very moment, right there in the Casablanca Lounge listening to him play, that despite her resolve not to fall in love with Grant Albright, she would follow him to the end of the earth if he asked. And she knew he never would.

She had been dumbfounded by his surprise visit to her room last night, which upon reflection appeared to have been nothing more than an opportunity to ask for her help and support. He had come in and sat in the only easy chair and she had sat on the small chair by the dressing table. And they sat, awkwardly silent for what seemed like forever, before he spoke and it had struck her that his cockiness was gone, his patronizing attitude replaced with a quiet reserve. He had measured his words, explaining how Jodee was having such a bad time of things and that he had been trying to help her out and that the photos had given her the idea to fuel rumors of an affair as a publicity stunt, and, really, there was no truth to any of that. And he wanted Shay to know that and he wanted the others from Palmer Plantation to know that too. And then he had become pensive, hesitating before adding that Jodee would be with him all day today in Athens, and he wanted Shay to know that too, embarrassing her with his assumption that she would even care about what he did. And that was it. He stood to leave, stopping at the door and apologizing for bothering her, but the frown, the expression on his handsome face was one of wanting, wanting to say more, wanting something from her, reassurance, understanding, more.

"You do understand my predicament, don't you? This Jodee thing is sending the wrong message. If you don't mind, it would help if you more or less spread that word, too."

"Yes, Grant. I understand your predicament. I will do my best to squelch any rumors I hear. I'll say something to Maureen. That should help spread things fast."

"I didn't mean that, Shay. I really just meant for you to know. Maybe you could act like you enjoy being with me, even when we just get stuck together sometimes. Just take the heat off of the Jodee thing. Could you do that?"

"You are asking me to put on an act like she is? That is a little insulting, isn't it? I'm sure I wouldn't be as good at it as she is, since I haven't had nearly as much experience as she has had, and I certainly am not willing to be used in such a duplicitous scheme."

"Damn it, Shay. You know that isn't what I meant. Why do you make things harder than they are? I'm not insulting you. I am taking you into my confidence, asking for a little help. Forget the whole thing. Forget I ever mentioned it, before you go off in some hissy fit and get all mad and spoil everything. I thought we were friends, but if you don't want to help me, just say so, and I'll leave you alone. I won't ask again."

The anger and frustration in his voice had warned her to back off, had cautioned her to soften the rhetoric a little. She put aside her indignant attitude and adopted a more conciliatory stance. "I suppose you are right, and it could be fun, putting on a little act of our own, fighting fire with fire. But I'm not sure exactly what you have in mind."

"Most of the time you give me the cold shoulder when Jodee is around and I thought you could act a little friendlier toward her, and I was hoping you and I could spend a little more time together. I know this Jodee thing makes it uncomfortable, Shay, but it wouldn't hurt if you at least tried to help me with this. What do you have to lose?"

Struck by the insensitivity of his remark, the assumption that she had nothing more important in her life than to accommodate him, tempted to set him straight, withdraw, she was surprised to hear her own answer. "I'll do my best, Grant. Like you said, what do I have to lose? It won't be easy, but I'll try to control my inner primal self and not embarrass you in front of your neighbors, just pretending to like you."

"That's a girl," he laughed. "Show some Southern spunk. Thanks for your help. I'll see you on the bus tomorrow. Good night, Shay."

"Good night, Grant."

He turned to go, and then turned back to her.

"Inner primal self? Now that sounds like something worth exploring," he said with a wink and nod.

She had closed the door, her heart pounding, flushed with embarrassment. "Why the hell did I say that? Now he probably thinks I am some sexually repressed, dried up old maid just waiting for a chance to release herself on him." She knew exactly why her heart was pounding. "Sheesh! He is the most exasperating man on the planet."

She had put in a restless night. So had he.

Her ruminations about his night visit ended with the sound of applause as Grant finished with the familiar strains of *As Time Goes By* and then he was beside her. "Shall we head upstairs now?"

They strolled quietly for several minutes, only exchanging a few pleasantries before he got right down to the heart of the matter.

"That was quite an entrance you made, Shay. And the kiss was a nice touch. Does that count as our first kiss, or do I have to participate before it counts?"

She could feel herself blush. "I don't know what came over me. It was totally unplanned. I suppose it looked pretty silly. Maybe no one noticed."

"I hope everyone noticed. It was perfect, but I'm looking forward to the one I get to participate in."

"Good Lord, Grant. Is this how it is going to be from now on, constant banter about how silly I am acting? If you are going to make a joke about everything, it will make it much harder. I am already feeling foolish."

"Why feel foolish? It's all in good fun between friends. I don't want you to be uncomfortable with it, so just do what comes naturally. But I probably will need to participate when you release your inner primal self."

"I rue the moment I ever uttered those words. You are embarrassing me now."

"Why? It sounds pretty good to me. But if it is embarrassing you, I will stop teasing you about it. Let's find a few lounge chairs on a deck somewhere."

He took her hand in his and held it all the way.

The Oracle

After checking for email, Grant met Mitch for breakfast on the Lido deck.

"So, how are you feeling, Buddy?" Grant asked.

"Pretty good now. Guess the heat over here is getting to me. As soon as I get back into air conditioning I start to feel better. I'll take it a little easy today. Ethan mentioned to me that I could man the hospitality desk this morning since lots of people haven't booked anything for Venice yet, so I guess I'll do that. Babs is going with her group back into Athens so I'll have to bullshit my way through it. I waited up for you until after midnight. I suppose you were with Jodee again, scoring more points."

"Nope, no scoring, but I did make some points. I held hands. I believe that is item number five on the list. And I got kissed. I think that is item number eight. How about you? Did you do anything on the list?"

"I was looking at that list last night while I was worrying about you. I suppose hand holding is pretty minor stuff with you, the way you've been carrying on with Jodee. I sure wish you would cool it with her. Everyone is beginning to talk now, Grant."

"What are they saying?"

"They're saying that Jodee is the next Mrs. Grant Albright, that's what they are saying. I'm telling you, Grant, she is not right for you. She is all show business and you are a family man. Even Babs said something. She asked me if you were serious about Jodee. Once she gets a hold of something it will be all over the place."

"Why would anyone even care what I'm doing? There's plenty to talk about with that silly Guppie woman carrying on with that bald guy. And what about Charley and the mess he is in? That should have their tongues wagging. Maybe I should wear a sign around my neck that says 'We are just friends!' And for your information, just for the record, I wasn't with Jodee last night."

"Who were you with, then? Anyone I know?"

"Nope, just a gal I picked up. It's not on the list to say who it is, is it? You need to get out there more and razzle and dazzle the ladies, Mitch. Turn on the charm. It's easier than I thought. Roll the dice and see what happens. And lay off the Palmer women. You are getting roped in by Babs and that business plan of hers. And all those other ones. Did you see how they flocked around you when you got dizzy? You had an entire harem fussing over you like a bunch of mother hens. The whole idea is to be away from them, not to make friends with them. You must be seeing plenty of available ladies when you are working the hospitality desk. There are a lot of things on the list you could be doing, stuff that could end up on the bottom line if you want it to, like ask one to have dinner with you, or buy a present for one, or have a drink with one. And by the way, you are wrong about Jodee. She isn't all show business, Mitch. She has a family just like we all do. And she is kind and fun, a really good woman. A guy could do worse. At least be nice to her. Get to know her before you rule her out."

"Are you telling me that you are falling for her? If that is the case, I will be quiet. You know how I feel about the situation, but I won't mention it again. I have said my piece. Just make sure you aren't thinking with the wrong brain, Grant. That kind of thinking can get a guy in a lot of trouble. And if you are still fooling around with other women, that isn't such a good idea either."

"It was your idea that I couldn't count Jodee or anything that happened in Istanbul, so I have to start over. I know you changed your mind and said I could count Istanbul now, but I'm going to win this bet fair and square. And we can still eliminate the bottom line if you want to. Maybe that shouldn't even be in there. I never wanted that in there in the first place. We'll just add up all the other items on the list and see who has the most points."

"Hell, no. I'm still going for the gold. I'm going to work on that list all day today. Don't count me out yet."

"I'll lay you five to one I still win. You have a lot of catching up to do."

"Maybe we should add one more item to the list," Mitch suggested.

"What's that?"

"Don't fall for anyone. If you do, you lose."

"OK, that sounds fair enough. All we're really doing here is getting our mojo back, getting back into the game. Besides, I don't intend to ever fall for anyone, ever again. Once was enough for me."

"I know what you mean, Buddy. I don't think we can ever have again what we had before. Did you hear from Matt yet?"

"No. There is a ten hour time difference between LA and Athens. It is only ten o'clock last night there. I have to wait all day to hear something. I should know something this evening. God, I wish I were there with him. If things don't turn out right I'm going to head to California. The girls have to get back to their own families and I don't want him out there alone."

"That is really a tough situation. I sure hope it goes his way. What are you doing all day?"

"I'm going to Delphi. Maybe the Oracle can give me some advice. I could use some. God knows my life is fucked up. I should be back around five. Have a good one, Mitch."

"Yeah, you too."

Shay was waiting for him by the gangway. "Good morning. Ready for a day in Delphi?" She was wearing the flowered sundress that he had seen her wear in Istanbul and she had on cute white sandals. On her head was a floppy straw hat.

"You look nice, Shay," he said. "I like the hat." He was wearing a baseball cap that she hadn't seen before and he looked even more handsome, boyish and athletic. "Shall we get in line? I think that is our bus over there. It will probably be hot in Delphi. It feels a lot hotter here than in North Carolina. It must be the humidity. It is really getting to Mitch."

"How is he today?"

"He seems okay. He plans to work at the hospitality desk. I told him to pick up women in his spare time."

"I don't think he will be alone much. Joan is staying on board to keep an eye on him. And Wanda is spending the day in the floral department playing with the flowers and said she planned to check on him too. And Maureen is going into town with Ralph for a half day tour and then meet with Mitch in the afternoon about joining the singles group. She is determined to get him."

"Really? Good. At least Babs won't be with him. I think she is trying to rope him in to that travel business of hers."

"Yes, I've heard that. But he doesn't act that interested in it. Does he date? He seems like a terrific guy. Joan told me he was a widower, too." The minute she said the word, she knew it was a mistake. A strange expression had crossed over his face, just for a second, hardly discernible, but there nonetheless.

The word always had the same effect on Grant, a cross between being hit by a sledgehammer and being hit by a truck, out of nowhere, out of left field, with no warning, opening huge gaping wounds, painful, and he could feel his throat tightening.

He took in a deep breath and released a long sigh. "Yeah," he said. "He is. We both are."

Shay was desperate for words to mitigate the damage from the blow her words had inflicted, casually spoken, innocent, proper, and unwittingly hurtful, and powerful enough to spoil the entire day. "I'm sorry, Grant. I know it must be painful to be reminded of that so unexpectedly. It was careless of me. It is hard enough for you as it is."

"Some days are better than others but I hate that word, that's all. It sounds like there is something wrong with me, like I am marked, broken, damaged goods. I feel like I am defined by it, Grant Albright, widower, judged somehow. If I am having a good time, then I am not sad enough, in denial, even disrespectful. If I am feeling blue, then I am not healing properly, not recovering, a failure."

"Joan told me that Maureen has suggested support groups to people who have lost a loved one. She thinks I should try a support group to help me get on with my life now that I have the freedom to do so. Did you find Maureen's suggestions helpful?"

"I never heard from Maureen, but Mitch and I got talked into going to one of those groups once and all they talked about was crying, like if we didn't cry we would become walking time bombs, human hand grenades. It just pissed us off. We never went back. I think it's harder for men. I feel foolish talking about it with strangers. I'm probably too touchy about it, but damn it, I just want to be normal again. But please don't feel bad about bringing it up, Shay. And don't pussyfoot around me, either, treating me like some poor bird with a broken wing. I lost my wife, my whole world came crashing down on me. I loved her very much. And I miss her every day. It's something I have to live with, accept, adjust to, but I can handle it. Mitch has handled it too. He has been alone about four years now. I think he is a little lonely, that's all."

"He is doing the right things, though," she said, "Getting out, enjoying himself, getting interested in things, keeping busy. That's probably good advice for all of us who have found ourselves in difficult situations. Maybe the job with Babs is just what he needs."

"He doesn't need a job, Shay. He needs a wife."

They boarded the bus and chose a seat half way back. There were no other Palmer people, Grant had made sure of that by checking at the excursion desk and looking at the lists. He had no intention of spending the day with folks who were more interested in his activities than they were in their own. He and Shay had stayed out pretty late last night talking, sometimes just sitting, not talking about anything at all, and he had enjoyed being in her company. She seemed more comfortable too and he had teased her about the little act they were putting on. He couldn't deny his enthusiasm for spending this day with her without the prying eyes of the Palmer gang.

"So, here we are with a whole day in front of us," he said, settling into the aisle seat. "I really appreciate your coming with me. We can enjoy ourselves just as friends, old friends from North Carolina. It is a coincidence that we both grew up there."

"Yes, it is. And here we are in Greece. It's funny how these things happen, meeting someone from home in some faraway place. And I still don't know much about you, Grant. Was life in Raleigh good?"

"Raleigh was a great place to grow up. I lived in the same house my entire growing up years. I knew all the kids in the neighborhood. We lived in the right part of town, inside the beltline, belonged to the country club, went to the beach a lot for weekends and vacations, a pretty perfect childhood. How about you? How was it growing up in Charlotte?"

"Very much the same, except it sounds like maybe your family was a little more prosperous than mine. We lived in a nice average neighborhood and life was good there. I still live in the same house. My grandmother owned an old beach house in Cherry Grove and we went there for our vacations. My brother and I spent most of our summers there. Do you know Cherry Grove?"

"Yeah. I've been there plenty of times. Now all of that area is just called North Myrtle Beach. My best friend's family owned a place in Windy Hill. The beach is really nice around there. Did your family eventually sell the place? It is full of condos now."

"No. I ended up inheriting it when my mother passed away. I haven't been down there since. The place could have fallen down by now. My folks had several offers to sell it, but they wanted to hang on to it so I am still paying taxes and insurance. I will have to figure out what to do with it when I get back. I still have a lot to do with settling their affairs."

"How long ago did your mother pass away?"

"Nearly six months ago. It was a pretty long ordeal. That's how I ended up living back in the old neighborhood. My Dad got sick four years ago and I was having to run back forth after school to help out and then my mother started with dementia and I couldn't leave her alone with him, so I sold my condo and moved back home. He passed away first. When my mom got so bad I finally had to stop teaching and just stay with her."

"Are you going to stay there?"

"I don't know what to do. The house needs a lot of work. They never updated it. Chrissie, Joan's daughter, is in real estate and says that I need to update it or it will never sell, but there is no money for that. And I have all of that stuff to get rid of. I did manage to get rid of clothes and clean out some of it, but there are still big decisions to make and I think I am just prolonging it all by taking this trip."

"Aren't you enjoying yourself? This trip should be a welcome break for you, give you a new perspective on things. I hope the trip works some magic on Mitch too. Part of why I agreed to come was to give him a chance to get away, travel a bit. He talks a good game, but he is really pretty lonely."

"How about you, Grant? Are you still undecided about Palmer Plantation? You seem so comfortable around the folks from there. I would think it would be hard to pick up and leave."

"I'm still trying to figure it all out. Everyone puts their two cents worth in, telling me not to make any rash decisions or not to do anything too soon, so here I am eighteen months later still in limbo, just adrift in my thinking. I don't have any compelling reason to leave, but I don't have any real reasons to stay either. I'll ask the Oracle what to do. I sure can't make any decisions for myself anymore. I thought I had it all figured out and now here I am, fifty-five years old, with no idea what I'm doing."

"Do you think you will continue in the entertainment business?"

He laughed right out loud. "It sounds so funny when you say that. I'm not in the entertainment business, Shay. This gig is just part of Mitch's scheme. It was all his idea to get us jobs on a cruise ship. He was trying to talk me into going with him so I went along with his plan."

"You mean you are not a professional piano player, that wasn't your career? You play beautifully. I just thought you were always in the entertainment business. Didn't you study for it, go to some prestigious music school? Wanda said she thought you probably went to Julliard or someplace like that."

"You can tell Wanda she is wrong, I did not go to some fancy music school. No way am I good enough for that. Music schools get the cream of the crop, really talented pianists. I took lessons from

Ms. Eula Bartlette from second grade through tenth. Then I was playing football and discovered girls and that was the end of the lessons. She was a great teacher. She had trained at Julliard. I have always loved to play, but I have never played professionally."

Shay was taken back by this revelation, surprised and relieved, and not sure why. He certainly acted the part, and he sure looked the part of the handsome entertainer, but she was relieved that he didn't live the vagabond life of a performer.

"Do you think you would like to play professionally?"

"You know, there is a part of me that is enjoying it. And Jodee has encouraged it. She has hinted a few times that she and I could perform together, even in Vegas. If she pursued it I'm not sure what I would say. She needs a piano player. You know, Vegas sounds good. I could play golf all day and then play the piano at night. I retired pretty young. It might be good to have a job again. I don't really need the money but it might be a good experience to try out something new for a year or two, just to help her out. She has a much better chance at success if she has her own piano player. It's a good thing we are visiting the oracle today. Maybe he can answer questions for both of us. God knows my life is screwed up," he laughed.

"I feel the same way, Grant. Nothing in my life went as I hoped it would. I'll ask the Oracle what I should do, too."

"Good. After we hear what he has to say maybe we'll be able to get a handle on things."

"Maybe so, but I hear that he is a she."

"What? The oracle is a she? We'll see about that. Did you read that? I never heard that the oracle was a woman."

The trip to Delphi would take about two hours. Shay's delight at hearing that he wasn't a vagabond performer had been shattered when he said he would consider working with Jodee. But last night he had held her hand when they walked on deck, even though it was just part of their little sham to put the skids on the talk about him and Jodee. And she had fallen for it. She had let herself believe. And at her door when they said goodnight, he had put his hand on the back of her head, just for a second, but he had done it, just stroking her hair. And he thanked her for waiting for him and told her that he looked forward to spending the day *alone* with her, and she wanted to tell him that she would spend the rest of her life *alone* with him, if he asked. And she knew he never would.

The bus labored along the steep and winding road through the rocky hills that opened upon magnificent vistas of the Gulf of Corinth, breathtaking in its beauty, finally arriving in Delphi around noon. They followed a jagged, rocky path to the famous spot and listened as the on-site guide explained the history of the place.

The mystery of the Oracle of Delphi has existed for as long as history of ancient Greece has been recorded, much of it appearing in myths and later explained as some geological phenomenon. Myth would tell us that the Oracle spoke for the God Apollo, but the stories of the Oracle even predated Apollo. The many versions of the story all conclude that the area induced frenzies and those who were afflicted could predict the future. As the story evolved, the oracle became a priestess who would channel Apollo for his wisdom and predictions. The oracle herself was merely the medium. She would enter a trance like frenzy to summon her powers. The place itself was considered the center of the earth, emitting these special powers only to the oracle. Later geologist discovered that there was indeed some gaseous emission from the chasm which could have caused these hallucinating frenzies, but that the chasm had sealed these vapors off centuries ago.

"See, I told you the oracle was a woman," she kidded. "It was her voice they heard."

"Just like a woman to do the talking. But she had to ask a man for the answers. Okay, ask her your questions, but remember your answer is coming from a man."

Shay covered her eyes and said in a rather solemn dramatic voice, "Oh wise Oracle of Delphi, predict my future. Will I find happiness?"

Grant covered his mouth and said in his best imitation of a woman's voice, "Yes, my dear. Great happiness awaits you."

"Alright, your turn, Grant. Go ahead and ask."

He cupped his hands around his mouth and said, "Hey, down there. That you, Apollo? Got a question for you," he clowned.

"Go ahead, ask," she urged. "Ask him something hard."

He cupped his hands around his mouth. "Yeo, Apollo. Am I going to get lucky tonight?"

She couldn't believe her ears. She cupped her hands around her mouth and in her best dramatic voice replied, "Signs are not clear. Ask again later."

Grant turned to her laughing. "Was that a yes or a no?"

"You'll just have to ask later, like she said."

"Well, at least I get another shot at it, but be careful where you step, Shay. Keep on the path here. I don't want you to get too close to those vapors and go into a frenzy, releasing your inner primal self before I get to ask again."

"Grant, you are insufferable. You know that embarrasses me. If you are not careful I really will throw a hissy fit. Then you'll be sorry you kept teasing me."

"No I won't. I know how to stop a hissy fit."

She didn't even ask.

The little town of Delphi was charming, filled with little shops and sidewalk cafes. After some browsing in the shops they stopped to watch one of the local artists painting a picture of Apollo's Temple and Grant purchased two of his paintings for himself. "I like to buy some of the local street art like this. I have quite a bit of it but I've never had any of it framed. Perhaps I should ask Wanda to go with me to pick out frames. She's good at stuff like that. Are you ready for some lunch?"

He picked out a lovely spot, a small cafe with cute tables in shady spots and held her chair for her. "Let's see," he said, perusing the menu. "What do you want? I'm pretty tired of eggplant and zucchini. And I don't want lamb, either."

"Several things sound good. I love spanakopita."

"Okay, we'll start with that. What else?"

"How about some pastitsio?" she suggested. "That is a pasta dish. Are you real hungry?"

"Yeah."

When the waiter came Grant ordered for both of them and selected a bottle of the local wine. Shay interjected with a question of her own for the waiter.

"Is the ground meat in the pastitsio lamb or beef? We would prefer something other than lamb."

"It is beef, Mrs."

"And, please, no eggplant or zucchini on the side. Just a small salad would be perfect."

"Yes, Mrs. Do you want feta cheese on the salad?"

She looked at Grant. "Feta?"

"Yeah, that's fine."

"Yes, feta please."

"Very good, Mrs."

"Well done, my dear," Grant teased. "You sounded just like a wife. You fooled him."

"Well, there is no sense in ordering something you don't like, Grant. You need to speak up."

"Why? That's what wives are for," he said, laughing and tipping his wine glass to her.

She could feel herself blushing.

When the tab came, he picked it up. They had such an enjoyable time eating and drinking the whole bottle of wine that the time got away from them, but their little tête a tête was interrupted by the excited bus driver. "Hurry. Hurry. We are running late."

Once they were seated on the bus Grant resumed their conversation, relaxed, enjoying the casualness of being with her, natural and easy, without expectations or assumptions, free, good.

"Well, now all we have to do is just sit back and see if the Oracle's predictions come true. You want happiness and I want to get lucky. That sounds like a good combination. It shouldn't be hard to arrange that," he joked.

"It's hard to imagine that people actually believed in that, isn't it?"

"I don't know. They were ignorant or naïve, I guess. When I was a kid I got one of those Magic Eight Balls for Christmas one year. I loved that thing. Every time something important was happening, like a little league baseball game, I would ask it things like 'Are we going to win?' Or was I going to hit a home run. It was fun. It would answer just like you did, 'It is not clear,' or 'ask me later.' You sounded just like it."

"That's a coincidence. My brother had one of those things too. We had fun with it. The best part was if you didn't like the answer you could keep asking until you got one you did like."

"Yeah. Mine always said things like 'outlook not good' and 'it is decidedly so.'"

"Yes, and 'As I see it, no,' or 'It is for certain.' They were lots of fun. I guess people have always wanted to know the future. It would be helpful to have some idea about it so we could make plans."

"Well, it probably is a good thing that we can't predict the future. We probably wouldn't want to know. It's hard enough thinking about the past and dealing with the present without knowing what's ahead. People believe in all kinds of things, gypsy fortunetellers, tea leaves, Ouija boards, horoscopes, the Wizard of Oz, even angels, but in the end none of that matters. You might as well just flip a coin or pick a card. Life is just one big crapshoot. You just play the hand you're dealt."

"Don't you believe in anything, Grant?"

"You mean, like some higher power, something watching over us? Sure, I believe. I want to, anyway, but it's pretty hard to believe when you have been crapped on. My wife believed. I'll tell you a cute story about that. I haven't told anyone. Want to hear it?"

"I'd love to hear a story, Grant. Go on."

"Now don't think I'm nuts, okay?"

"I promise. I won't think you are nuts."

"Well, she had a little angel that her college roommate had given her and she called it her guardian angel. We kept it all through the years. It was about ten inches tall, pretty thing, blonde, like you, and we even laughed that she was in the wrong family because we don't have any blondes on either side. Matt has dark hair like me and all the girls had brown hair. Anyway, she was made out of paper or cardboard or something and sat on a shelf in the den and we pretty much ignored her. Well, after Vonnie got sick, she wanted the angel in the bedroom so she put it on my chest of drawers because she couldn't see it on her dresser. And she talked to her, especially when things got bad. I would hear her in there talking and go in to see and ask who she was talking to and she would say, 'Ariel,' that was the angel's name. 'Ariel and I were just having some girl talk.' So after a while I just let her alone because I thought it was bringing her some comfort."

Shay was listening intently, her heart filling with a warmth she had never felt before, engulfed by waves of sympathy and need and longing, enthralled with the man, motionless for fear of breaking the magic of the moment.

"Anyway, have you ever seen one of those paintings where the eyes seem to follow you? That's how this angel is. Whenever I went into the bedroom she was looking at me, wherever I went. It was eerie, spooky, sleeping in a room with those eyes on me. So, afterward, after Vonnie died, I was cleaning up the bedroom and putting things away and I started to throw the angel away because she was a little dirty after all of those years and I couldn't wash that paper stuff, but she was looking at me with those eerie eyes. She had one of those sweet little beatic smiles, like she had had a vision or something, and I just couldn't throw her out, so I started to look for a place to put her in a different room."

"She was probably papier mache."

"Yeah, she was real light. So I'm carrying this little angel around the house trying to find a place to put her and I'm thinking she is as light as an angel, which was a weird thought, because she was an angel. Now, don't think I'm some kind of a pervert, but I turned her upside down and looked under her skirt, and there was nothing there, no body, no legs, nothing. She was just an empty dress with a head and arms, and wings. She just stood on her dress, which struck me as kind of funny."

"So, where did you put her?"

"I couldn't find a spot until I went into my study. My piano is in there and my computer. That's another story I'll tell you another time. So, anyway, here was a big empty spot right on a shelf in my study, so I put her there. That night when I went in to play the piano, like I do most nights, there she was looking at me. I kept trying to ignore her, but every time I looked up there, she was staring at me with those eerie eyes and that shitty, all knowing, beatic grin. So I got up and went over and turned her around so she was looking at the wall. But when I started playing again I kept making all these mistakes and losing my place and I kept looking over at her, feeling a little guilty. So I went over and turned her around again. And this is the part. You are not going to believe this part. She was still looking at me but something looked different about her. And then I realized what it was. She was smiling. I swear to God. She had a great big smile on her face, like she was glad to see me. She's still sitting there. That was the night Mitch came over and started talking about this trip."

"That's a precious story, Grant. Maybe she is your guardian angel now."

"I hope so because I sure wouldn't want her as an enemy. Maybe I can introduce you to her someday."

"I'd like that."

Grant snoozed the rest of the way back to Piraeus.

Matt

Grant had left Shay at the elevator when they returned from Delphi. He hadn't asked her to spend the evening with him, deciding to give her some breathing room, but he had pointed that gun like finger and said, "Tonight?" And she said she would come to the Casablanca sometime after ten because she had promised to go to the early show with the girls. Grant made a pass through the computer center, just in case there was something, but there was nothing, so he headed to the hospitality desk to check on Mitch. He was starting to worry about Mitch. He seemed a little discouraged, a little dejected, and Grant planned to fess up about the Jodee thing and spend a little more time with him, guy time, time not thinking about women. He rounded the corner to the hospitality desk, and there stood Mitch, surrounded by a bevy of women, laughing, joking, holding court. Babs and Maureen were seated at the table with brochures and maps spread all around them and there was quite a line waiting to talk to them. At one point Mitch put his arm around one of the ladies and Grant heard him say, "Step right over here in this line and we'll fix you right up. Just tell the ladies what you want to see in Venice and they will make all the arrangements." And then, just as Grant approached, Mitch turned to a very attractive lady and said, "I'll be at your door at 7:30. I wrote it down, room 609. You pick the place."

"That will be just wonderful, Mitch," she said, all dewy eyed.

"What was that all about, Mitch?"

"Got me a hot one, Grant. That's what that is about. Look out. I'm gaining on you. Really made some progress today. How about you? Did you enjoy Delphi? I hate it you had to go alone."

"It was great. I'll see you later and we'll add up our scores."

He showered and dressed for the evening and headed for the Fez Lounge, arriving just as Jodee was singing. She maneuvered herself right beside him, flirting, making eyes, teasing. She did that with some of the other men, too, nothing offensive, nothing threatening to the women they were with, just having some fun, just show business. She could certainly work a room and he began to picture her performing in the beautiful library that Izzy was planning. Given the opportunity, Jodee would make it her own room, put her signature on it. Izzy was right. She would be perfect. When she finished, the duo started playing *Are You Lonesome Tonight,* sounding extremely comfortable with their new repertoire, and several couples got up to dance. Grant noticed that most of the tables had liquor glasses on them and two waiters were servicing the room. Jodee came right up to him.

"Dance with me, Grant."

"Jeez, Jodee. I haven't danced in quite a while. I don't even remember how."

"Oh, come on. It's just like riding a bike. You don't forget." She led him to the dance floor and placed her arm on his shoulder.

He took her in his arms, casually, holding her loosely, but close enough to feel her body, her breasts against his chest, smelling the sweetness of her perfume, and welcoming the sensation of holding a woman again, wondering if she was expecting more of him than he was ready to give. Not that he wasn't attracted to her, because he was. She was hard to resist. And not because Mitch considered her hot, because he liked hot. He could handle hot. But, damn it, he just wasn't ready, not quite there yet, primed, close, but not there. He relaxed his hold, slightly moving away, and Jodee sensed his retreat, releasing him.

"Thanks, Grant. That was lovely."

"It was nice, Jodee," but just as he said the words he saw Izzy Schwartzman enter the room.

"Let's dance one more," he said, surprising her by taking her in his arms and holding her tight against him, nuzzling her cheek with his own. She put her hand on the back of his neck, returning his message, melting into his arms. Grant swayed slowly, holding her tightly, waiting. It was just a matter of seconds before a confident tap was felt on his shoulder, and there stood Izzy Schwartzman. "May I cut in?" he said. "I'd like to dance with this lovely lady." Grant stepped graciously aside, welcoming the interruption, relieved that Schwartzman was making his move, and turned on his heels and left the room.

Jodee greeted the gentleman with her usual charm, masking her disappointment at the interruption, but sincerely happy to see the gentleman from the Paris flight again.

"It's you," she exclaimed. "How nice to see you. I was wondering if you were going to come listen to me. Are you enjoying your cruise?"

Izzy was taken back. He was fully expecting that Grant would have prepared her for this, but was now awkwardly aware that she thought he was just the guy from the plane. She had no idea who he was.

"Yes, I am. And you? You seem to be enjoying your job."

"Well, I am now. But it started out just awful. We couldn't get this group to work at all. We were terrible together. Then Grant, the man I was just dancing with, came in and straightened everything out. Have you heard him play in the Casablanca Lounge? He is wonderful."

Izzy was holding her away from him, but gracefully guiding her around the dance floor, listening as she prattled on before he answered. "Yes, I did hear him one night. I'm glad he was of some help to you."

"Boy, so were we. There's this big shot critic on board and he is a holy terror, just criticizing everyone. Half of the girls in the dance company are in tears every night because of him. He hasn't been in here yet and we are all scared to death he will get us fired, and I really need this job. We are complete wrecks every night. Grant says we shouldn't worry about Schwartzman, that's the guy's name. But, you know, that's pretty hard to do, not worry."

"Grant is probably right, Jodee."

"I know, but Schwartzman can just snap his fingers and somebody's career is ruined, just like that. It just isn't fair. He is a real bastard."

"Well, if he is such a bastard you should listen to what he has to say and not let it bother you. Ignore him."

"Yeah, that's what Grant says. Grant says, 'Fuck Schwartzman.'"

Jodee caught the eye of the guys in the duo. They were playing softly but trying to get her attention, making ridiculous gestures, like cutting their throats, or being hanged, and she couldn't figure it out. The gentleman from the plane said, "Thank you for the dance, Jodee. It was a pleasure seeing you again," and excused himself, promptly leaving the room. Jodee walked over to the duo.

"What are you guys doing? What's wrong?"

"What's wrong?" they said in unison. "Don't you know who that guy was? That was Schwartzman, Jodee! And instead of singing like you were supposed to be doing, you were out there canoodling with Grant. We'll probably all get fired now. Grant too."

Jody could feel the blood draining out of her face.

It was a little after seven, still morning in California, and Grant's anxiety was growing by the minute. He would grab a bite and then sit on the deck and watch the coastline as the Atheneè made her way to the little island of Corfu. Shay had promised to come to the Casablanca after the early show.

Jodee arrived promptly at ten, not looking her best. She had on a pretty dress, flashy jewelry, plenty of makeup, but it had been impossible to cover her tear swollen eyes. Grant could see immediately that she was upset so he started playing some familiar tunes, nothing they had rehearsed, and she made her way next to him. Matching her mood, he played a soft introduction before starting the melody of *Blowin' in The Wind*. She poured her heart and soul into it, and he followed with *Bridge Over Troubled Water* and then *Let It Be*. When she finished, after the applause, he stood and took her arm and headed to the door with her, just as Shay was taking a seat with the gals. He caught her eye and pointed that finger at her, acknowledging her presence, wanting her to know that he would be right back, but he needed to hear what had happened to Jodee, first.

"What's wrong? What happened?"

"I think I just got us all fired, Grant. You know that guy who cut in on us? That was my friend from the plane, the one who was so nice. Well, it turns out that he is Schwartzman!"

"Did he introduce himself to you?"

"No, we just danced and then he left. He knew I didn't know who he was, the rat. He just let me carry on, running my big mouth, as usual."

"Then how do you know it was Schwartzman?"

"Because the boys knew. They were trying to get my attention all the while but I didn't know what they wanted."

"Then why be so upset? You were great in there tonight. You should be glad that he was there and flattered that he asked you to dance with him. How will that get you fired?"

"Because I told him that you told all of us to 'Fuck Schwartzman.'"

Grant laughed out loud. "Well, good for you, Jodee! I'm sure he has heard that before, but now he knows you won't take any junk off him. I'm proud of you. You don't have anything to worry about now. He knows he has a tiger by the tail," he laughed. "Let me go. I have to get back to work now, but mark my words, he won't be firing you."

On the way back to her room Jodee stopped at the travel desk and asked the agent on duty to please book her a flight from Venice to New York as early as he could.

When Grant returned to the piano, Ethan was standing there with a martini in one hand and a folded sheet of paper in the other.

"Here," he said, "I think you will need this." Grant took the folded note and opened it. It said in very large letters, "SEE ME, ASAP." It was signed, "I. Schwartzman." Grant swallowed the martini in one big gulp.

When he finished his last set he went right to Shay's side, barely nodding to the folks from Palmer, even ignoring Mitch. "Shall we go?" he asked. He took her by the elbow and moved swiftly out of the room.

"I hope you don't mind, but I have some business to attend to. Can you wait for me?"

"I can just go on, Grant, if something has come up. Why don't I just plan to see you sometime tomorrow?"

"Because I want you with me now, Shay."

He sat her in the lounge outside Ethan's office, where Schwartzman had set up camp, and walked in without even knocking.

"You wanted to see me?" he said, sounding more than a little cocky, probably more like pissed, but taking Izzy by surprise.

"Sit down, Grant. We need to settle a few things once and for all. Apparently I didn't make myself clear at our prior meeting."

Grant always thought a good offense was the best defense, so he said, "I think you made yourself perfectly clear, Izzy. What part of it are you having trouble with?"

Taken back by Grant's brazenness, Izzy started in again. "It seems that you didn't quite get the part where I asked you to back off, Grant. I specifically asked you to back off from Jodee because she was falling for you and it was complicating my plans for my new dining club."

"Well, it might come as a surprise to you, Mr. Schwartzman, but your plans are not the primary issue here. If you are so hell-bent on having Jodee in your new dining club, perhaps you better get into the game and score a few points of your own."

"I started to tonight," Izzy said, almost timidly, "but she didn't know who I was and I didn't know how to tell her, especially after she called me a bastard. I don't think anyone has ever said that before, at least not right to my face. Well, maybe my wife did a time or two, but that was a long time ago. I expected that you would have prepared her for it, that you would have told her."

"Hell no, Izzy. And you just let her yammer on, making things that much harder now. And you know what is worrying her the most, what she is most upset about? She doesn't even care if you fire her. She's scared she is getting the guys and me fired because she told you I said, 'Fuck Schwartzman.'"

"It was funny when she said that, too. She is so pretty and sweet, but those words just rolled right off her tongue. I could hardly keep from laughing. I wanted to dance with her some more but the guys were making faces behind my back so I thanked her and left. But I saw how she snuggled up to you, dancing close, her hand on the back of your neck, eyes closed, all dreamy," and he began to imitate her, turning in a circle with little dance like steps. "I can't compete with you in that department, Grant. Are you serious or will you back off?"

"It's show business, Izzy. Jodee thinks it's good publicity to be seen with me. Part of our image. We're pretty close, you know. I thought you were a show business expert. I thought you understood everything about show business."

"I do understand everything about show business, Grant. It's women I don't understand."

"Neither do I, Izzy, but it's every man for himself in that department. You are going to have to get in the game just like the rest of us."

The two men shook hands, neither one quite knowing why, and Grant headed to the door. Just as he was leaving they were interrupted by an agent from the purser's office, who handed a note to Izzy.

"Holy God," he muttered.

"What's wrong?" Grant asked.

"She just booked her plane ticket from Venice. You gotta stop her, Grant."

Shay was waiting patiently for him, feeling uncomfortable that she had allowed him to call the shots again, that she had not resisted or insisted more. She was afraid she might be making herself too available, too agreeable. He didn't hesitate to ask her to join him when it was convenient, or to wait when something else popped up. Each time she was feeling great, even wonderful, about her time with him, she would land with an excruciating thud of disappointment. Or was it realization that she was being used, that perhaps this little ploy of his, this sham, this using her as a decoy, was his way of taking the attention off of his true feelings for Jodee. She felt a surge of emotion similar to a mild electrical shock, that same feeling she got whenever she looked at her college yearbook. There she was in her gown and crown, May Queen, and it filled her with resentment.

It reminded her of her mother's hurtful words. One day her mother had been thumbing through her yearbook and had opened it to the page of Shay's picture as she was crowned May Queen. "Well, there you are, the May Queen. Always the May Queen, but never the June bride." The words still stung. And the truth hurt even more and she feared she might be headed for more of the same heartbreak. She had vowed to never put herself in that position again, not even to start, not even to hope. But here she was, cooling her heels waiting for a guy, playing second fiddle while he tended to business. It probably had something to do with Jodee. She always came first.

"OK, done," he said. "I need to go to the computer center now and check for something important. You don't mind waiting again, do you?"

"Really, Grant, I think I'll just call it a night. You go ahead and finish your business."

"There is a lot happening tonight but I was looking forward to spending some more time together. It shouldn't take long at all, just a few minutes. It's not late. When I'm done we can go to our favorite chairs up on the deck, just the two of us. I told you a story today and now it's your turn to tell me a story, a story about you."

"Not tonight, Grant. Some other time. I'm a little tired."

"Alright, we'll call it a night, then. I'll walk you to the elevators."

To her surprise he got on the elevator with her and got off on six, and walked her to her room. "Can I come in? You're not going to leave me out here in the cold, are you?"

And that damned little voice said, "Of course not. Come in. Joan is out with the girls so we can visit a while longer."

Joan returned to the room around twelve thirty. She had let herself in, not expecting anyone to be there, and was flabbergasted to be greeted by Grant. He was in his stocking feet and had loosened his tie. Shay was still in her dress but had her shoes off too and had removed the ruffled scrunchie from her hair, allowing it to flow around her shoulders. She was sitting on her bed with her legs tucked under her and it was obvious he had been sitting on the bed with her. *An Affair to Remember* was streaming on the TV. Joan didn't know whether to retreat or to chat, but Grant had started putting on his shoes, and pulled his tie off and stuck it his pocket, casually announcing that he guessed it was time for him to be on his way. At the door he turned to Shay with a grin. "Thank you, Shay. It's been great. I'll see you on the bus tomorrow."

"Good heavens, Shay. I hope I didn't interrupt anything. I never dreamed you had company. We need to get some kind of warning signal. Why, I just never imagined anything like this, not that I am criticizing, but I am a little surprised. When did this start? I had no idea things had gone this far."

"Things haven't gone far at all, Joan. He just wanted a quiet place to relax. He picked that movie because he thought it was about a cruise ship."

"Everyone knows that is one of the most beautiful love stories ever. Didn't you tell him it wasn't about a cruise ship?"

"I told him it was about the Empire State Building. He said it was his wife's favorite movie and he had never seen it. I don't think that had any romantic message for me."

"Wow, was he in for a surprise."

"We didn't get to the real sad part."

"Let's open a bottle of wine and watch the rest of it together, Shay. It is just so wonderful, so sad."

Joan took off her shoes and propped up on her own bed.

Grant glanced at his watch. Two forty five in California. He headed for the computer center and signed on. Pay dirt!!! One from each of his kids and one to Jodee from Leighanna. He opened Matt's first.

To: Dad
From: Matt

GREAT NEWS!!!! I won, Dad. It's a long story and I'll fill you in later, but the important part is this. They are mine, all mine, and I couldn't be happier. God, what a relief!! Megan will fill you in. My sisters are the greatest. <u>Please don't plan on coming to CA right now. Big changes in the wind!</u>

Sorry the cruise is such a bummer. Just use the time to relax. It will be over soon.

Love, Matt

Reply: Great news, Matt. I'll wait for details. Kiss the girls, all four of them. Love, Dad

---

To: Dad
From: Megan

Hallelujah!! We won, we won, we won!!! I thought I would have a nervous breakdown from the worry, but, Daddy, Matt was just wonderful. I am so proud of my big brother. Details later. Misty was so nervous she threw up – not in court, but before.

We hate it that the cruise is so awful. You must be bored to death. Isn't there anyone there that is friendly? You need to be more outgoing, Daddy. Meet some people. Mix a little, get involved. It will be over soon. DON'T GO TO CALIFORNIA RIGHT AWAY!! Matt is making plans. I don't know how he will ever manage without us here, but do not plan to go right now!! Just try to enjoy yourself, Daddy. We are all worried about you. You can't become a recluse.

Hugs and kisses, Megan

Reply: I am thrilled with the news. Don't worry about me. I like being a bored recluse. Keep me posted. Hugs and Kisses, Daddy

---

To: Daddy
From: Misty

Happy, Happy, Happy, is what we are. I was so nervous I threw up. Matt is wonderful!! DON'T COME TO CA RIGHT NOW!! He is fine. More later.

Please, please try to have a good time, Daddy. It breaks my heart that the trip is so awful and you are so bored and lonely and sad. Maybe after Venice you will feel better. We know how hard Venice will be for you. I will cry all day, happy for Matt, happy for us, and sad for you. Can't you play Bingo? Or go to a movie? Maybe you could find a piano somewhere that you can play, maybe off in a corner somewhere by yourself.

Kisses, Daddy. Love, Misty

Reply: I will try very hard to make the best of things here. Hate Bingo, no good movies, can't find a piano. Stop crying! What does Matt say about your throwing up?

Kisses, Daddy

To: Mommy
From: Leighanna

"Hi, Mom. Guess what. Bill came over and we had a good visit. Josh was so thrilled to see him and Bill actually got down on the floor and played with the Legos with all three little boys. But here is the thing. Now he says he wants to get back together, but I don't know what to do. He stayed pretty late, but I did not sleep with him. Was that the right thing to do? I wanted to, but I didn't and now I am afraid he will lose interest again. He is coming over tonight. I need advice. Hope you get this soon enough to answer in time.

Love, Leighanna

Reply: DO NOT SLEEP WITH HIM! ABSOLUTELY DO NOT DO IT!!

Love, Mommy

He hit send, signed off, and headed to his room. Mitch wasn't in yet. It was 1:15 am. He turned on the TV, propped up on the bed, and watched the rest of *An Affair to Remember.*

Corfu

The Atheneè had wound her way through a maze of islands, each as beautiful as the other, docking in Corfu midmorning. Corfu was not a regular port for the Atheneè. The ship usually spent the busy summer tourist season plying the waters of the Black Sea from Istanbul to as far north as Odessa, Ukraine, and cruising the coasts of Turkey, Romania, and Bulgaria, ending with visits to popular Greek Islands before settling into Athens and reversing the itinerary. Since this was a repositioning cruise, placing her in Barcelona for her winter itinerary, she would be making call at several ports not usually visited by her crew and many staff schedules had been adjusted to accommodate off shore visits for officers and crew whenever possible. Grant had planned to ride the bus with Babs' group, but at the last minute Ethan had advised him that he would be needed as part of the count for ship's personnel on board at all times. He had been given no specific assignment.

Shay had boarded the bus with Joan, both of them still a little queasy from the bottle of wine they had washed down their tears of enjoyment with as they watched their tearjerker until after 2:00 am. They were both wearing large dark glasses. Mitch had been Shanghaied by Babs the minute she saw him, so he took the seat next to her. The newly available Charley seized the opportunity to occupy the seat behind Shay, and Ralph sat next to him, assessing the situation and noting the absence of Grant. The displaced Charley had moved in with Ralph, since the icy situation in his former accommodations had turned titanic, his overwrought and overbearing travel companion having made the situation untenable.

Ralph was glad for the company, but didn't especially like the competition for the ladies, as he had come to enjoy his singular status of availability since Babs had latched on to Mitch, and Grant seemed to be otherwise occupied.

The island of Corfu has less of a Greek feeling, influenced by its long occupancy by Great Britain and its proximity to the southern Adriatic. It is a popular vacation spot for tourists along the Adriatic shores, offering easy access to Eastern Europe as well. It was on this island that Empress Elisabeth of Austria, affectionately known as Sisi, built her summer residence, Achillion. The mansion itself is open to the public and the gardens are beautifully maintained with much of the original statuary left intact, most prominent being the large statue of Achilles, after whom the place was named. The large terraces at the front and back afford beautiful views of the blue Ionic waters below. It was to this place that the Palmer group was headed.

A local guide described points of interest along the way, many of which related to historical events and mythology unfamiliar to and not of particular interest to the group. Instead, they were enjoying the opportunity to catch up on the news from home, not bothered by the winding road and rather uncomfortable maneuvering of the bus by a driver who accompanied each twist and turn with jolting moves.

Maureen had been online early in the morning and was happily passing along the latest news from Palmer Plantation. For Maureen, news from home usually was highlighted by the obituaries, the lifeblood of the singles group, and she got most of her leads from that source. She was as goodhearted as they come, but sometimes her actions were a little off-putting. Perhaps it was just her timing, but some people described her as an ambulance chaser, which was pretty close to the truth. But she was a darned good membership chairman even if she did have the phone number of the local mortuary in speed dial.

Today's news included the passing of one of the Palmer residents, which sparked much commentary among the group. "Oh, the poor thing," they said. "And her in such bad shape. What will become of her? He did everything, absolutely everything for her." And others chimed in. "That happens so often, the one who was the caregiver goes first."

Maureen felt bad that she wasn't there because she had placed the soon to be widow on her 'watch' list after she had heard that the husband had been diagnosed a few months ago. She would move the new widow to the 'ready' list now. She had meant to get over for a visit sooner, as she usually did when a situation was arising, just to offer some information, like it would be necessary for the widow to have her husband's DD214 in order to collect his military benefits. She assumed that most of the men had served time in the military, although it was not always wise to assume that now that so many of the baby boomers were moving in. Maureen had a wealth of helpful information, like stuff about hospice, and oxygen deliveries, and home health care providers, and she was a welcome visitor to many who were dealing with end of life issues. She didn't bail when it was over, either. She would continue to offer support and advice to the newly bereaved, making sure they availed themselves of the many services offered by churches and service organizations. She was a great recruiter for the singles group, helping many a lost soul return to a society that was unfamiliar territory, welcoming them into a group of others who were navigating the same rocky waters.

Shay had been listening to all of this, mostly with her head back applying every mind over body technique she had ever heard of, fighting the very imminent urge to throw up. She couldn't have been more miserable. Her head was splitting.

"Are you OK?" Joan asked, not wanting to sound too alarmed, but retrieving some tissues from her handbag, just in case. "I feel pretty rotten myself." She tapped Wanda on the shoulder and asked her if she had any mints or something, because Shay didn't feel well, and Wanda began rummaging through her handbag. Maureen joined in the search as well, and the message spread throughout the bus.

"Shay isn't feeling too well," they said, and soon several folks produced a variety of mints, and gum, and stomach soothers. Ralph sprang into high alert.

"Keep your eyes on the horizon," he said. "I'll have the bus driver pull over in the first place he can. If you get out and walk around for a few minutes you will feel better." He dashed to the front of the bus.

It was bad enough that she felt like crap but now everyone on the bus was aware of it, asking what was wrong and offering every home remedy for motion sickness they had ever heard. Wanda turned in her seat and shared one of her late Howard stories. "My late husband, Howard, used to feel like throwing up on the bus, too. Every time we got on one of these winding roads he would feel like throwing up. Once he didn't make it, just threw up all over everything."

Shay thought she would die, but, mercifully, the bus had come to a stop and Ralph was ushering her toward the door. Joan came along too, just in case. The others had begun to count on the fact that Ralph, the first responder, and Joan, the nurse, would provide whatever medical assistance was necessary, and resumed their conversations, carefully averting their eyes from the windows least they witness some unpleasantness.

Ralph had wrapped his arm around Shay and was walking her away from the bus, Joan following. "Sometimes it is better just to go ahead and get rid of it, Shay," he said. "You probably ate something that didn't agree with you. Go ahead, just throw it up."

"Oh, for Pete's sake, Ralph," Joan interjected. "She will be fine. Just give her a little air. She had too much wine last night. That's all that is wrong with her." After a few minutes Shay did feel a little better, so they got back on the bus to quizzical expressions, folks wanting to know if the offending culprit had been rendered rid, but politely not asking.

Shay felt sufficiently better to follow along with the group as they toured Achillian, listening to all the history of the place and relieved to have the tour finally over and stroll through the gardens. Wanda and Maureen had cornered Joan to ask for her prognosis, and Joan had told them with a little giggle how she and Shay had downed a bottle of wine while watching *An Affair to Remember* and that was what Shay's problem was. They all giggled when Joan added that she hadn't had such a good time in ages.

As they headed back to the bus, Shay felt another huge wave of nausea so she and Joan headed to the restrooms, which were accessed from the exterior of the building, and Shay relieved herself of the awful feeling, while Joan wet some paper towels to be applied to her forehead.

"I am so embarrassed, Joan. Please don't tell anyone about last night. I would die if everyone knew I had too much to drink."

"Of course I won't tell anyone what a good time we had last night. And let's not tell Chrissie either. It is our secret," Joan giggled.

Ralph and Mitch were waiting for them. Mitch had asked Ralph what he thought was wrong with Shay.

"Nothing, just a hell of a good hangover. She'll be fine."

Back on the Atheneè, Grant was spending the day making himself visible, available if he was needed for anything. He hadn't had a chance to see Shay but Mitch had promised to keep an eye on her. Mitch had had quite a night himself. When he finally returned to the room he found Grant propped on his bed watching a movie.

"What are you watching? I thought you were probably with Jodee again."

"Nope, just watching a chick flick. Nothing else very interesting on."

"What's it about, travel?"

"No, it's about the Empire State Building. What have you been up to? Have you been with that woman all this time?"

"Yep, spent the whole evening with her. We can add up our points in the morning, Buddy, but look over your shoulder. I am gaining on you."

They had breakfast together, planning to join Babs for the tour of Corfu, but Mitch was eager to tell about his evening, embellishing as he went, emphasizing how many points he had and how many things on the list he could cross off.

"It sounds like you had a good time. Are you going to tell me how the night ended?"

"Yeah. Things went really good right up to the end and I would have asked her or let nature take its course, but you know, it's funny. Here we are in a place with a couple thousand beds and there was no place to go. She has a roommate and so do I, so there was no place to go."

"So, did you come right out and talk about that problem? That's what's good about Jodee, she has a private room. Maybe you should think about that ahead of time, Mitch. Are you seeing her again tonight? If you are going to need the room just say so and I'll stay away."

"I think we are going to have dinner together. Then go to the musical show. She is one of those planner types, had her notebook out and was writing the schedule down. We never came right out and talked about it, but, you know, sometimes you can just tell, but I'm not sure what she was thinking. I have her room number right here. I'm supposed to check with her at 5:00 to see if she is available because she has to rearrange her schedule to fit me in."

"It sounds like she is one very organized lady. Maybe you should try to get a look at her notebook and see what she has penciled you in for, especially if you want to spend the night with her."

"Yeah, I probably need an appointment for that. Man, there is nothing spontaneous about her. That notebook is full. I might just blow her off, play a little hard to get. I think Babs' group is going to the show. I might go with them. What will you do if I need the room?"

"I don't know. Probably hang out with Jodee. By the way, I heard from Matt last night."

"Good or bad?"

"Good. He said he won but I don't know any details. All three of them emailed and said it went good, but none of them would give any details. I still think I should head out there. They keep telling me not to come, which gives me a bad feeling."

"Yeah, that usually means they don't want you to know something. At least it sounds like it went his way."

They had started to head to the buses when Ethan caught up with them with the news that Grant was to stay on board.

With time on his hands and no particular assignment, Grant decided to look for Jodee and see what she was up to. He found her at the rehearsal for the evening's musical production. It was to be the first performance of this new show, which was to be one of the major numbers on the next segment of this cruise. She was surrounded by several girls in the chorus, explaining something, showing one of them how to turn, smiling, encouraging, laughing, and he stood watching her, admiring her warmth, her ability to just fit in, just like a chameleon. A very pretty chameleon, at that. She caught his eye and came right over. Several of the chorus members greeted him by name. "Come over here, Grant. Sit at the piano. We are having a little trouble with this beat. Give us a few bars, a strippers beat. We need to add a little pizzazz to this number." Laughing, he obliged, and the girls formed a line and went into their routine. Jodee began to dance with them, doing a pretty good bump and grind herself, right in the middle of a rather ordinary dance routine, definitely adding some oomph to it. Several other members of the cast joined in the fun, vamping and wiggling to Grant's hoochie coochie rendition of familiar belly dance music, and pretty soon they were all in the swing of things, laughing, adding moves, encouraging one another.

"Schwartzman will shit a brick when he sees this," one said.

"He does anyway so we might as well give him something to shit about," another laughed.

One of the girls who had been wiping tears when he first saw her, got into the act, giving her best imitation of *Tits And Ass* and the others all clapped along with approval.

"Boy, I can't wait to see his expression when he sees that tonight."

"Me either. I wouldn't miss it for anything." And they continued to rehearse, looking forward to the performance, no longer dreading Schwartzman's appearance.

Afterward Grant and Jodee went to the main pool terrace and ordered Bloody Mary's before lunch. "Wow. That was quite a performance, Jodee. Do you think they will go ahead with it?"

"I sure hope so because Schwartzman needs a dose of his own medicine. I work with them every day because somebody is always upset, even brokenhearted by his mean remarks. Somebody needs to put the bastard in his place."

"Maybe he isn't aware of how much his remarks hurt their feelings. Why don't you just have a talk with him?"

"I'm not giving him the time of day, Grant. I just hope all of them band together when I'm gone. I tell them they outnumber him. They should pose a sit down right on the stage, right in front of him."

"Are you still planning to leave, Jodee? I think it would be better if you stuck it out. Give Schwartzman a chance to react to some changes. He probably isn't as bad as everyone thinks he is."

"I have to go, Grant. You know the situation with Leighanna. She is probably right back in bed with the guy. I just don't know how to talk to her, how to get her to see that you can't be too easy to get. That's what always got me in so much trouble, just being too easy. Have you heard anything from her?"

"No. I'll let you know when I do. I did hear from my kids, though. It sounds like things went the right way for Matt but they don't tell me everything."

"That's great news. I know you were worried about him. I wish just once I got some good news from Leighanna. Sometimes I go for weeks not hearing from her and then when I do it's because all hell broke loose. She is such a worry to me and I blame myself for most of her problems."

"Running to her side every time probably doesn't help her. She has to learn to solve her own problems. Stay and finish your gig. Get your own career back on track first, then go. There doesn't seem to be an emergency. Please don't go, Jodee. I don't want you to go."

Jodee hoped that her surprise at his words didn't show, words that telegraphed something she never thought she would hear from him. He wanted her to stay. "Please don't ask me to stay. It is hard enough without making it harder. I would love to stay here with you. We are good together, Grant. We could perform together somewhere, even in Vegas. We could make a go of it. Are you suggesting that, or is this more personal?"

He took a big swallow, realizing that he had set his own trap, cautious, torn between telling the truth or wishing he had, or not telling the truth and regretting it. "Give things a little more time, Jodee. How will we know how the story ends if you run out on me?"

She sat back in her chair, looking at him with a warmth and understanding that transcended the shortness of their time together, seeing the man, feeling his guarded emotions, moved by his honesty, his desire for her success, but protecting his distance. It must have killed him to ask her to stay.

"Shit, Grant. You know I don't have any money to buy a plane ticket. I couldn't go if I wanted to."

"Does that mean you will stay?"

"Yes, I'll stay unless I find a sugar daddy to buy me a ticket somewhere."

"Who knows, Jodee. Life is just a crapshoot. Maybe this will be your lucky roll."

The waiter took their order and handed Grant a message.

"You are needed to play for a surprise birthday party in the Ottoman Lounge at 4:30. Your regular repertoire." He looked at his watch. When they finished their drinks he turned to her. "Now, don't go changing your mind on me, Jodee. We have a deal, right? I'll try to catch the early performance tonight and see how the show goes. Then I'll see you later."

"A deals a deal, Grant. See you later." On the way to her room she stopped at the travel desk and picked up her flight confirmation.

He planned to take a nap. The bus should be returning from Corfu around four o'clock. Mitch entered the room just as Grant was leaving for the Ottoman Lounge. There was time for only a quick exchange.

"How was your day, Mitch? Did you enjoy Corfu?"

"Yeah, it was okay. Babs was filling me in on all the stuff she has planned."

"You better be careful. She is trying to rope you in. Was everyone else there?"

"If you are asking about Shay, Buddy, yes, she was there and Charley hung around her all day. But it was Ralph who took care of her."

"Took care of her? What happened, did she fall again?"

"No, she got sick."

"Sick how? What was wrong with her?"

"She got sick on the bus and Ralph had the bus driver stop and let her off for some fresh air. I think she felt better later."

"I hope she isn't coming down with something."

"She isn't. Ralph said it was a hangover."

"A hangover! Shay? She hardly drinks anything."

"That was the problem. She and Joan had a bottle of wine late last night, watching some sad movie. Guess she had too much."

"Who told you?"

"Ralph told me. Joan had told him. And Joan told Maureen, so the whole bus knows it. It must have been some movie."

"Yeah, it was."

"Joan told me not to tell you, so don't let on. OK?"

"I won't. Do you think she will come by the Casablanca Lounge tonight?

"Yeah. They're all going to dinner and then to the early show."

"And you, Mitch? Don't forget to call your new hottie at 5:00 and see if you are on her schedule. I have to go play at some birthday party now, but just send a note. Let me know if you need the room tonight. See you later."

"OK, have a good one. See you later." Mitch never placed the call.

Jodee arrived in the Casablanca lounge wearing a beautiful dress and a huge smile. "Grant, you should have seen the show. The kids were fabulous, did everything just like they rehearsed. It was hysterical. The audience loved it and even Schwartzman looked like he was enjoying it, but he didn't stay after and say anything to them. He was probably so shocked he had to recover somewhere."

"That's great. At least they overcame their fear of him. Is he going to the late show, too?"

"No one knows, but I am going to cut this short and head up there again. I want to see his expression again. You don't mind if I don't sing tonight, do you? I sang two sets with the boys earlier, so it's not like I'm not working. They are really doing great, too. Maybe you are right, Grant. Maybe something good will happen if I stick it out."

"No, I don't mind, Jodee. Go ahead and enjoy yourself. I might cut things a little short myself. I played a party for two hours already, so it's not like I'm not working, is it? I'll see you later."

He played his first set and part of the second before she came in with Charley. The three gals were with Ralph, but Shay and Charley sat by themselves. Grant sized up the situation, filling with an unexpected anger, disappointed, jealous. Charley? How the hell did that happen? After the set, he took a break, didn't even look her way, didn't nod or point his finger in recognition, just stepped outside the lounge. He was seriously considering not returning, but his decision had already been made by someone else. Standing outside the door was Izzy Schwartzman.

"Grant, I have to talk to you. Close up shop and come to my office."

After waiting several minutes, it became obvious to those in the lounge that Grant wasn't returning. Shay excused herself, leaving Charley sitting alone. He had latched on to her at the elevator and had ushered her to that seat, but she certainly wasn't under any obligation to spend the evening with him. She had used the excuse that she wasn't feeling well, which she wasn't, but she was beside herself that her little episode on the bus might have been told to Grant and he was upset with her. What if he thought that she had gone out drinking after he left her room last night, after the wonderful time they had had together, sitting side by side on the bed watching a love story? And now he had just walked out without even a nod to her presence. That sick feeling of loss began to fill her like some poison, some venom, some evil force once again coursing through her veins, her hopes shattered and her dreams replaced with reality. He probably wasn't thinking about her at all. He had never indicated any real depth of feeling for her, never had spoken any words of endearment, or shown any desire. All of his attention was merely interest, concern for her comfort, her convenience, but her heart was telling her something else. She headed to her room, intending to sit alone in the quiet, licking her wounds, but without realizing it, guided by some invisible force, she ended up on the upper promenade, sitting in one of the lounge chairs that he usually guided her to for their quiet times together.

Grant sat listening intently while Izzy ranted and raved about how Jodee had spoiled the entire performance tonight, how she had managed to make him look like a fool, had undercut his authority, how Grant and Jodee had conspired to turn the whole cast against him, had undone hours of planning and rehearsing with their demeaning plot, and, by God, he wasn't going to stand for it.

"Hold on a minute," Grant interrupted. "I don't intend to sit here and listen to this crap, Izzy. I have enough problems of my own. For your information, Jodee is a real positive influence on your cast. She has been working behind the scenes cleaning up your messes this whole cruise. She deserves credit for most of the good stuff that has happened, too. She has turned around the Fez and made the group work and increased the profits. And she has kept several cast members from quitting on you, and she probably is responsible for the fact that you haven't been forced to walk the plank by now."

"I know what you are saying is true, believe me. I saw the rehearsal, saw how good it was, but I can't be undermined like this. I am losing all credibility. But since you are the only one she seems to listen to, you are the one who is going to have to straighten her out. I can't work under these circumstances."

"Izzy, cut the crap. Why don't you change your approach? I know everyone respects your work, your history of success, but it's not necessary for you to hurt people like you do. There is no excuse for plowing over people like a bulldozer. Soften it up some, make suggestions instead of going for the jugular, cutting people down. You know there is a better way to do things to get the results you want."

"Grant, I have to disappoint people every day, fire some, shatter some dreams. It makes it so much easier on them if they can just call me a bastard, hate me, despise me, even blame me. Sometimes their rage has a positive result and they begin to see how they need to improve. Other times they realize that they weren't as good as they thought. It's part of show business, rejection and failure are just part of it. It's not easy on me either. I don't like to hurt people. But acting like a SOB makes it easier on everybody else."

"Well, here's an idea for you, Iz. If it is so hard for you to soften up a little, why don't you work with Jodee instead of against her? She has wonderful people skills, is kind and caring, and can smooth things over after your carnage. That new supper club of yours isn't going to work either if you think people are going to spend big bucks to support some bastard's operation."

"She confirmed her flight today, Grant. It's too late for me to work with her."

"Bullshit! She told me she was going to stay. But damn it, Izzy, you better start wooing her yourself. I am not going to do it for you. Just do it with integrity, Izzy. Level with her and ask for her help. Life is just one big crapshoot, but you have to roll your own dice. I'm done. I'm through with the whole thing. You are on your own."

Grant got up and walked out, no handshake, no nothing. He had had enough. He began to walk aimlessly around the ship, thinking about his kids, his life, his wife, his future, angry about Shay and denying why. He headed to the upper promenade deck, planning to sit quietly alone, making some plans. He rounded the corner to their usual spot, disappointed to see someone occupying one of the chaises, tempted to turn in his tracks and retreat, then shocked by the realization that it was Shay. He swallowed, recovering from his surprise, relieved, and then pointed that finger and winked. "So here you are. I was hoping you would be here."

And that little voice inside her said, "I was just getting some fresh air, Grant. It's been a long day. Join me."

He was already settling in the chaise next to her, signaling to the waiter who was approaching. "The lady will have some hot chocolate. I'll have a martini, straight up with a twist." He turned to her. "I hear hot chocolate is good for a hangover."

She thought she would die. "I'm so embarrassed by that. It wasn't what you think, Grant. It was all just so dumb. Joan and I decided to finish the movie that you and I had been watching."

"The one about the Empire State building," he interjected.

"Yes, that one. And Joan thought it would be nice to drink a glass of wine as we watched, that's all. I guess the wine didn't agree with me."

"No, I don't suppose finishing off the whole bottle would agree with you."

"For heaven's sake, who told you that?"

"Mitch told me. Everyone on the bus knew, Shay."

"It's the very first time that has ever happened to me. Did you ever have too much to drink, Grant?"

"Oh yeah. More than once, as a matter of fact. There is the first time for everyone, Shay. It's nothing to be embarrassed about, as long as you didn't make a fool out of yourself, or worse, release your inner primal self. I want to be with you when you do that. I'm sure it won't happen to you again. You aren't much of a drinker. You probably should always stop at two. Are you feeling better now?"

"Yes, but it was sure an awful feeling on the bus. I have learned my lesson. When did it happen to you, Grant? You seem to be able to drink whatever you want."

"No I can't. I've had some pretty bad hangovers in my day, not many, but a few. Once after a fraternity party and once on a golf outing with a bunch a guys from the club. And once in Vegas. Do you want to hear a funny story about that?"

"Yes, please. I could stand to hear something funny about now."

"Well, my brothers and I were in Vegas for a convention. We went every year. It was a big convention for people in the heavy equipment business."

"Is that the business you were in?"

"Yeah, my brothers and I owned a big equipment company and we had pretty good deals with most of the big players in the field. Anyway, it was during the time that Vonnie wasn't doing well, so her sister came over and stayed with her and I went with my brothers. We were drinking quite a bit and gambling, having a big time. I was at a poker table, pretty smashed, and this sexy gal comes up, draping her big boobs around my neck, really coming on to me, so I folded and left with her."

Shay was listening politely, even giggling. "You went with her?"

"Yeah, just over to the bar for a drink and a few laughs, nothing more. Look, I'm not bragging about what I did. I'm not proud of it, but it is kind of funny. When I woke up I didn't even know where I was. You know, like sometimes when you wake up in a motel and for a second you forget where you are. I was lying on the bed, fully dressed, even had my shoes on. At first I'm thinking, 'Oh, shit! She rolled me.' You know, put something in my drink, stole my wallet and money and credit cards. But my wallet was still in my pocket with all the money, everything. Then I remembered that I was staying there with my brothers. I didn't even remember going up to my room. Boy, was I pissed."

"Why were you pissed? She didn't steal anything. And apparently nothing happened."

"I was pissed about the $7000.00."

"$7000.00! You paid her $7000.00?"

"No, she didn't cost me anything. I lost the $7000.00 at the poker table when I folded to leave with her. That really pissed me off."

"I know you probably felt bad about the whole thing. You were probably very, very distraught about things at home and weren't thinking clearly."

"No, I was just very, very drunk. There are two things that a guy should never do when he is drunk, Shay. One is pick up women and the other is play poker, because one or the other is going to end up costing him plenty. Boy, Vonnie would have been mad."

"I suppose most wives would be pretty mad to hear that their husband had picked up a woman."

"She would have been really mad about the $7000.00. She hated to lose money. I never told her."

"Did you tell her about the woman?"

"Hell no. She would have killed me for that. But I was always faithful, Shay. She knew that."

Dubrovnik

Grant had walked Shay back to her room sometime around 1:30 a.m. They had talked and laughed and he had told her more about growing up in Raleigh, relating some stories about teenage antics, about the time he and his brothers had climbed a fence at a little swimming lake and someone had called the police and they got arrested and his dad had to come down to the police station and get them. And he told about swimming out too far in the ocean and being grounded by his mother for the entire week at the beach. And Shay told him about summers at her grandmother's place in Cherry Grove and about the time a big wave knocked her down and scared her to death and how she hadn't really enjoyed going into the ocean since then, only taking long walks along the shore and sitting gazing at the waves.

And he told her about school, about picking up girls on Hillsborough Street, embellishing quite a bit. "Once we picked up these two girls, my best friend and I, and we both wanted to get a little bit, so we took them to an old motel out near the airport. I don't know if it is still there or not, but we felt like big shots, like we were really doing something special going to a motel. It was the first time I ever had sex in a bed," he laughed.

"What! Where did you have it before then, pray tell? Or maybe I shouldn't ask," she laughed, acting a little shocked, but more than a little curious nonetheless.

"Anywhere I could," he laughed. "Mostly at the beach. Didn't you ever have sex on the beach, Shay?"

"Grant, for heaven's sake. Of course not."

"Well, there is a first time for everything," he teased. "Now you have something to look forward to."

"Well, with my luck I would probably just get arrested for indecent exposure, or something. I haven't been too lucky in that department," she laughed. "And after Eddie died I never really felt like going very often. I would take my parents to the beach house, but my mother just wallowed in her misery all the while she was there, asking over and over, 'Why did it happen?'"

"What did happen?"

"I shouldn't even have mentioned it, Grant. I'm sorry. All this talk about the beach reminded me of it."

"Go on, tell me about it. I'd like to know. Who was Eddie?"

"He was my brother. He died in a car wreck on the way home from the beach. He was twenty two, had just graduated from Carolina. I was eighteen, had just graduated from high school. His friend had spent the weekend with him. They were both killed. My parents never recovered from the tragedy. It pretty much changed my life too."

"How was that? I'm sure you loved your brother and it was hard, but how did it change your life?"

"I was in the car too, but I wasn't hurt that bad. Only a few broken ribs and cuts, and a pretty bad concussion. I was in the hospital for three weeks. My mother never even came to visit me. She was just destroyed by it, and she never came out and said it, but I think she blamed me, even though the other driver was charged."

"Why would she blame you?"

"Because I was driving."

"If she knew that it wasn't your fault, why would she still blame you?"

"I think she blamed me for living. If Eddie had been driving, he wouldn't have died, I would have. I always felt it."

"I think you have that all wrong, Shay. She probably thought that if he was driving he could have avoided the accident, like a guy is just naturally a better driver."

"I don't know about that, but she would just shake her head and say, 'Why were you driving, Shay? Why wasn't Eddie driving?' Those were her last words to me. She had been in and out of a coma and I stayed right at her bedside. Then she suddenly opened her eyes and said, 'Why were you driving Shay?' And she was gone."

"Why were you driving?"

"I was driving because Eddie had been drinking. He and his friend had been fishing and drinking beer all day, so when it came time to head back to Charlotte, he tossed me the keys and said, 'Here, you drive.' He was asleep in the front seat and his friend was asleep in the back seat. A truck came barreling at us right on a very narrow bridge and rammed our car into the concrete rails. They never saw it coming. We were almost over the bridge when he barreled on, so the truck driver was charged. It was clear that it was not my fault. I probably should have told my mother the truth, but my mother just could not let go of her pain. Her heartbreak over the loss of her son couldn't be relieved by the reality of the circumstances, so I never added to her pain by telling her that Eddie was too drunk to drive. There seemed to be no other explanation than she wished it had been me instead of Eddie."

"Didn't your Dad intervene in any way?"

"I don't think he paid enough attention to her or to me to even notice. He pretty much withdrew. He was still working and wasn't around much. After he retired he sat in his den all day, and then the Parkinsons started and he didn't feel good enough to care about anything. He was a good man but was never very affectionate."

"So, you suffered in silence all these years, feeling guilty just for being alive?"

"Well, I wasn't debilitated by it. I was able to go on to college and teach, live a normal life. But I always felt like I had to try to make up for it in some way, to always be there for my folks, do the right thing, be the perfect daughter, in some way fill the void in their hearts. And now that they are gone, I sort of feel empty. I have no one. I need to move on, change things up a little, kick up my heels, as Chrissie puts it. It's just so hard to make a decision, to figure it all out. And, like I said before, I have so much to do in the house I dread going home, especially facing Eddie's room. It is left just like it was, like a shrine."

"I still have some unfinished business too, but I'll tell you what. When we get back to North Carolina I will come to Charlotte and help you with Eddie's stuff. You can decide what mementos you want to keep and I will remove the rest for you. Maybe we can help each other with some of these hard decisions. I hate to burden my kids. They mean well, but I feel like I have to be strong for them, not let on that some days are pretty rough."

"It might be easier working with someone who isn't emotionally involved or butting in my business. I feel like all the old neighbors are watching everything I do. You must feel some of that at Palmer Plantation, too, the way they all discuss everyone's business."

"Well, maybe we'll just give them something to watch, spice up their conversation a little. If you come to visit Joan we can get together for a visit too and you can give me your opinion about some things. That sounds like a good way to handle it. I'd offer you a drink to toast our plan, but that might not be such a good idea tonight," he laughed. "Are you going with Babs tomorrow? I think she has some tour planned."

"No, we are planning to take the tender in for an hour or two and walk around a little, just enough to say we put our feet in Croatia. Those extra tours are getting expensive so we are saving for Venice. Maureen will be making our plans as usual. Are you going ashore?"

"I don't know what Mitch is doing. He has a hot date tonight. I was going to spend more time with him, but it looks like he may have found his own solution to his problem. If he isn't going ashore, I'll look for you, maybe bum around with you."

"Good. So Mitch has a lady friend? He is a very attractive man and has a great personality. It is a surprise that nobody has picked him off yet. But Joan will be disappointed to hear that he had a date. I think she has a thing for him, but don't say anything."

"You're kidding," Grant laughed. "Joan has a thing for Mitch? And you are surprised that no one has 'picked him off' yet? Is that how the ladies talk about available guys, like you are picking cherries?"

"Well, you know what I mean, a handsome available man doesn't come on the market that often."

"On the market? Is that what women say, on the market?"

"Sure, it means that a guy might be interested in dating or ready to have a new relationship, or something. Don't guys have some term they use for available women?"

"Sure, I just told you one. The ones they are interested in they refer to as 'hot', you know, ready for a new relationship, right? A hot one, or hottie. You get the idea."

"Yes, Grant, I get the idea, but I don't think most women are looking for that. They are just thinking about dinner or a show, or something. They only want a man for a nice evening out, for companionship, a man to keep company with, that's all."

"Well, I can guarantee you that most guys are not just thinking about dinner, or a show, or *something*, Shay," he laughed. "It may start out that way, but it won't stay that way very long. Guys don't want to be thought of as just an escort, someone to have dinner with, someone to accompany a woman here and there. I promise I won't say anything to Mitch, though. But in case you are thinking about going cherry picking yourself, I could probably be talked into lunch tomorrow. I'll look for you. Now, I better let you go in to your room before I think of *something* to do besides lunch tomorrow."

She could feel the blush spreading across her cheeks. "Good night, Grant."

He put his hands on her shoulders, and then gently stroked her hair, his hand lingering slightly, running the silky thickness through his fingers. "Good night, Shay."

Mitch was sound asleep when he entered the room. The light was blinking on the phone and he picked it up and listened to Jodee's message. He would call her in the morning.

The launches would begin ferrying passengers to shore around 9:30 and the Atheneè would set sail for Venice at 3:00, allowing for only brief excursions to shore. Dubrovnik lies on the eastern shore of the Adriatic and is considered one of the more picturesque cities along the beautiful Dalmation Coast. The city itself sits on Mount Srdj, jutting out into the sea, presenting a majestic view of the stone fortification walls surrounding the old town and the huge round tower that dominates the city, highly recognizable as the most widely used pictorial representation of the city. Joan, Maureen, and Wanda were planning to stroll around the shops near the dock, but Shay had read about the maze of narrow streets in the old town and the two fourteen century convents that stand at opposite ends of the walled off city, and hoped to stroll around there. She was also hoping to find Grant and perhaps stroll with him, really much more interested in the Grant part than in the convent part, but she didn't tell the gals that part. She was hesitating, stalling, hoping he would be on the next tender, but noticing the absence of Grant, seizing upon the opportunity to accompany Shay, the abandoned Charley stepped right in, offering to go with her. Having no ready excuse, Shay accepted his offer and the two set off together.

Grant and Mitch had their usual breakfast together on the Lido deck, catching up on last night's news.

"So what happened, Mitch? I didn't expect you to be asleep when I came in. Didn't you get penciled into the schedule?"

"After you left I got to thinking about it, Grant. You know, thinking that I would just blow her off. If she wants to be with me she'll find out I'm a little hard to get."

"Right. You don't want to be too easy. Did you hear from her?"

"I didn't talk to her. I went out with Ralph and Charley, mostly looking at women. They're both looking too. It was a nice evening. When I got in the message light was blinking, but I didn't answer it. That was probably her."

"Yeah, that was probably her, Mitch."

"What did you do? No one could find you after you didn't come back to finish playing. My bet is that you were with Jodee, right? And Charley was looking for Shay. He couldn't find her either, but we think she probably went back to the room and went to bed. Joan makes excuses for her and told Charley that, anyway. I can't figure that guy out. He doesn't seem to mind it at all that his trip got all screwed up when he got in a fight with that gal he met last year. He just laughs it off. I think he has the hots for Shay, now."

"Maybe he just likes shipboard romances, loves 'em and leaves 'em."

"Maybe so. Nice enough guy, but no one knows anything about him, only that he is from New York, but when you ask him a question he never really answers it. Just kind of strange that way. He has made himself right to home with the Palmer people, that's for sure, real sociable."

"You would think it would be a little awkward, wouldn't you. But the Palmer people are really friendly, so that makes it easier. Are you going ashore with me?"

"Yeah, as long as we're back by 2:00 because I have to be at the hospitality table then. They are still booking things for Venice. Maureen and Babs will help me. Joan offered to help too. She's going on shore for a little while. She's a really nice lady."

"Yeah, she is. I'm surprised she hasn't been picked off by now. An attractive lady like her doesn't come on the market very often, Mitch. Ralph acts pretty interested in her. He's probably planning to make his move soon. I wonder if she is interested in anybody."

"I doubt it. She just hangs around with Maureen and Wanda. She's the one I met way back in Istanbul, the one who walked around the Grand Bazaar with me. She's a nurse, moved from Indiana, lives over there by the park in Palmer. Her daughter lives next door to Shay in Charlotte. She has another daughter in Pennsylvania. Her husband was a doctor. I think she is sixty three. She doesn't go to the singles club. But I don't know too much about her."

"Well, ask her some questions, maybe ask her out for lunch, or something, act a little interested. I'll see you later, Mitch"

"OK, I'll meet you at the gangway at 11:00. We can walk around a little and get the flavor of the place."

Grant headed for the computers. An email had come from Megan and another from Leighanna.

To: Daddy
From: Megan
Hi Daddy,

Back home. We are still so happy about Matt. Did you hear from him? I'm not supposed to tell you his surprise, so I won't. Misty flew home with me. She is still throwing up, but Matt doesn't think it is anything to worry about it. So don't worry, Daddy.

We are all so sorry for you about the trip. Aren't there any lectures or programs you would enjoy? It must be awful being so alone. I wish you weren't going to Venice tomorrow. Why don't you just stay on the boat? When you get home I want you to come shopping with me and pick out a piano. I think the boys will be ready for lessons very soon, and when you come visit, which will be much more often, I hope, you will have something to do.

Hugs and Kisses, Megan

Reply: Nice that you are keeping Matt's surprise from me. I will try not to worry. I went to an exciting lecture about Tectonic Plates—fascinating stuff. At two and four the boys are not ready for lessons but I will help you choose a piano. Heading to bingo now.

Hugs and kisses, Daddy

To: Mommy
From: Leighanna

Well, just what I thought, Bill didn't come over last night!!! So much for good advice. He did send me flowers, though. Real pretty roses. Now what?? He wants to come over tonight, so he probably expects me to show my appreciation for the flowers. What do you think? Tell me what to do, Mommy.

Your desperate daughter, Leighanna

PS: Keeping one of the boys overnight now. Better than his mother picking him up at 3:00 am. SHE IS PAYING, TOO!!! Hoorah!!!

Reply: Dear Desperate Daughter. Nice about the kid. Nice about the flowers. Suggests he is still interested. Fix him a nice home cooked meal, like meat loaf and mashed potatoes and gravy. And bake a pie. DO NOT SLEEP WITH HIM!!

Love, Mommy

He hit send and went to meet Mitch at the gangway.

There were several shops, street vendors, and artists lining the dock area. Mitch and Grant were browsing when Wanda discovered them. "There you are. We were looking for you. Grant, come look at these paintings over here. I've found the perfect one for you." Joan came right up and the four of them strolled to the display of paintings. Wanda was right. They were lovely and Grant selected two water colors and one acrylic to add to his little collection.

"Wanda, you will have to help me get this stuff framed when we get home."

"I'd love to help you, Grant. And don't forget, I am going to help you place that beautiful rug, too."

"I won't forget, Wanda. It's really hard doing those jobs without a woman telling me where to put things."

Wanda and Joan exchanged glances but said nothing, but it sure sounded to both of them like Grant Albright intended to stay put.

"I thought I might find Shay around here too," he said, casually looking around.

"Oh, she and Charley headed to the old town to walk around," Wanda said, in spite of the looks from Joan, who was shaking her head and finally putting her finger to her mouth in a shush signal. Wanda tried to swallow her words, but it was too late. Grant excused himself and turned to Mitch.

"See you later, Buddy. I have some business to take care of." He set off at a pretty good clip. He spotted them right away, strolling down one of the narrow streets lined with shops and flowers. He didn't hesitate a minute. He walked right up to them and gave Shay a pretty good hug, looking her right in the eye.

"So, I have found you. The gals told me where to look. I'm sorry I was late for our date." And turning to Charley, he said, "Thanks a lot for watching over her for me, Charley. Would you care to join us for lunch? We were planning a quiet little lunch away from the others, but you are welcome to join us."

Realizing he was out maneuvered and probably out of his league as well, Charley graciously declined the invitation. "Glad to oblige, Grant. Anytime. Guess I'll go find Ralph and see what he is up to."

Grant had not let go of Shay, and she had not protested as he headed down the street with her. "That was a surprise, Grant. I am so glad you found me. Charley offered to walk with me since it looked like you weren't coming. He is very friendly."

"Friendly, my foot. You need to be more careful who you go off with, Shay. Nobody knows anything about that guy. He seems nice enough, but we had a date for lunch, remember? When we get to Venice I am keeping you right with me so I can keep an eye on him and see if he continues to pester you. He is making a move on you, Shay, and you are supposed to be acting like you are interested in me, remember?"

"Oh, yes. The Jodee thing. I almost forgot. By the way, where is she lately, Grant?"

"She's working. They are keeping her pretty busy, for which I am very grateful. Let's find a nice little place to eat, somewhere by ourselves. I'm beginning to enjoy our quiet times together more and more. We can probably kill another hour before heading back to the ship." He knew he had come on pretty strong, was probably upsetting her, but, damn it, he was pissed, and he didn't really know why.

Hearing the testiness in his voice, the sound of impatience or disapproval of her apparent transgression, Shay sat quietly, grateful for the interruption by the waiter. Grant ordered a bottle of the local wine and then instructed the waiter to pour her half a glass and leave the bottle on the table.

"You know, Shay. You don't really know anything at all about Charley. Doesn't it strike you a little strange that he so easily blended into the Palmer group? It doesn't seem to bother him at all about the big ruckus over his split with what's her name."

"I think her name is Phyllis. And I think he is very bothered by the whole thing. He is trying to be friendly with everyone because he is stuck with the group and doesn't have much choice. He feels like an outsider, like me and Jodee. That's the only reason he hangs around me. He thinks of me as an outsider. The Palmer group, while they are very friendly, are also very cliquish. He no longer feels welcome."

"Bullshit. The Palmer Group has bent over backwards to make you feel welcome, haven't they? You certainly haven't been treated like an outsider."

"No, because I am with Joan. Things would have been different if Joan had rejected me or couldn't stand me. I am very grateful for her friendship, and for yours. Phyllis has other Palmer people to support her. Even Ralph did his part by offering to let Charley share his room, which was very, very nice of him, but it was really more of a gesture to help Phyllis, than Charley. I feel rather sorry for him. I wonder what happened between him and Phyllis. It sure all blew up, didn't it?"

"Reality probably set in. It started out as a shipboard fling, a love boat fantasy, and built up in their minds to be something more than it was. It doesn't surprise me at all that it didn't work out."

"Yes, it was probably too good to be true. And they expected different things, too, and a different ending."

"Women are just foolish romantics, Shay. It surprises me that he ever fell for it in the first place. That was the really stupid part. I can't believe any guy would fall for it."

"Don't you believe in romance, Grant? Don't you think it's ever possible to meet someone on a cruise ship and fall in love with that person?"

"You mean like in that movie we watched? That was just a story, just make believe, Shay. Hollywood. It doesn't happen that way in real life." And then, his anger dissipated, he winked, "Besides, most people don't live anywhere near the Empire State Building. How could that work in real life? That was a dumb place to meet. If it were the real thing, no way would he have left her alone for an entire six months. If you love someone you make plans to see them sooner than that. We better head back now. I have to meet Jodee at two thirty."

"Yes, I wouldn't want you to be late. She might just stroll off with someone else."

He got the dig. "I'm trying to help her, Shay. She'll be waiting for me. Are you going to come to the lounge tonight? We'll look at the calendar and figure out when you want me in Charlotte. I need to go to California, too."

He had returned Jodee's phone call before he went ashore and had listened politely while she told him of the latest developments. Things were going from bad to worse. She was waiting for him in her room.

"So, what's up? Why all the outrage now? I thought you wanted to get under Schwartzman's skin. Wasn't that the whole point?"

"He came to the late show and seemed to be enjoying it, laughing and clapping with the audience. After the performance I went backstage like I usually do. Everyone was so happy, really thrilled with their performance, but he didn't come back. The musical director came in and announced that there would be a cast meeting at ten o'clock this morning and that Miss Jordan was expected to attend too. That really made me mad because of how rotten he is to everyone, but I thought I would go to offer moral support to everybody and hear what he had to say. But as I was leaving the director handed me a note. Here, have a look."

The note said in big letters, "SEE ME TOMORROW AT 1:00 SHARP!!! Itzach Schwartzman."

"So then I didn't know what to do. If he wanted me at the cast meeting why did I have to meet with him again, and since you weren't here, I had to go alone. So I went to the cast meeting this morning and he comes waltzing in, all smiles, like he was enjoying the prospect of slitting throats, but he was real polite. He told everyone that he understood their frustrations with the progress of the new show, and how glad he was that they had added a few things, and he even thanked them."

"Well, that all sounds good, Jodee."

"Wait, just wait. He turns toward me, and right there in front of everybody, he says, 'And I wish to extend my personal appreciation to Miss Jordan for her efforts. But please be reminded that all changes to the script and routines remain for my final approval. I am a patient man, and might I remind you all that I have considerable experience in these matters, but it appears that Miss Jordan has taken it upon herself to relieve you of some of your apprehensions and anxieties about my disapproval of various aspects of the production. Therefore, please be advised that any personal issues you may have with me regarding the performance are to be presented to Miss Jordan, who will in turn, present them to me. I will be meeting with her regularly as we proceed to provide outstanding entertainment on the beautiful Atheneè.' And then the musical director handed out a copy of the little speech so everyone could refer to it. Here, look at this. You can just imagine how embarrassed I was."

Grant looked at the copy of the little speech and began to laugh. "It sounds to me like you won, Jodee. It's not exactly warm and fuzzy, but it shows he is willing to work with you. I don't see what you are so upset about. Did the meeting go well at 1:00?"

Worked up now, sarcastically imitating Schwartzman, Jodee continued. "Well, he was all pleasant and everything and said he really wanted to work with me and everything was real nice. And then he says, just so matter of factly, like I had nothing to say about it, he says, 'I am bringing in a new piano player and I want you to work with him.' I said, well, I didn't think I wanted to work with a new piano player. I want to work with Grant. And you know what he says? He says, 'Well, Jodee, Grant is not the right accompanist for you.'"

"He probably is right Jodee. The new one may be far better than I am."

"We will never know, because I told Mr. Schwartzman, 'No way. I absolutely refuse to sing with any other accompanist. If Grant goes, I go.'"

"Jesus, Jodee. You might want to think about this a little more. There is always a chance that it could work out better for you in the long run. It might lead to something really great. Did he say anything else?"

"He said you were out of the Casablanca Lounge as soon as we get to Venice."

"What did you say then?"

"I said I was out of here in Venice, too. I quit!"

Their conversation was interrupted by a knock on the door. A huge bouquet of roses was being delivered. The card said, "To Jodee. Please join me for dinner at the Captain's table tonight. I will escort you at 7:30 for cocktails in the Captain's private reception room. Izzy Schwartzman"

"Holy Cow! What should I do?"

"For starters, get your hair done. And wear that turquoise bespangled dress you wore the other night. And high heels. Show him what you're made of, Jodee. And don't be too hard on him. Shine up to him. I think he is trying, in his own way, to make amends. Think of the cast Jodee, they are depending on you now. Do it for them."

He headed for his own room. There was a note under the door and he picked it up.

"SEE ME ASAP!! IZZY"

Shay returned to her own room to find Joan in an absolute tizzy. "Can you believe it, Shay? I just can't believe it. Of all the stupid things, this takes the cake. Look. Read this."

It was an email from Chrissie.

To: Mom
From: Chrissie

Guess what. My mystery man from California is back in the picture. I haven't heard from him in days and now he tells me he is coming next week. Next Week!! And he wants me to set aside a few days for him to find a place to live. And he wants a house, four bedrooms, three baths, nice yard, close to the hospital. Who does he think he is fooling? He said he was single!! And then he says he needs to stay in some kind of extended stay hotel while he looks and wants me to find a place for that too. What's with this guy, doesn't he think I have a life??!! I am meeting him at the airport Tuesday night. His flight doesn't get in until 1:30 a.m. He said he was picking up a new car Wednesday so I offered to pick him up at the airport so he wouldn't have to rent a car just for the night. Pretty stupid planning on his part. Sheesh!!

I hate him already, I think, but sure hope he buys something. I haven't sold one thing all month, Mom. Maybe real estate isn't right for me. I'll keep you posted. Hope you two are having a good time. Forget about men. I think we are all better off without them!

Love, Chrissie

"I can't figure her out, Shay. And meeting him alone at the airport in the middle of the night and driving off with him! The worry is just awful. You think you have your kids raised and your life is going to be serene, and then they do stupid things that worry you to death. Sometimes I wonder what I did so wrong to have raised such stupid girls. Chloe doesn't have sense enough to come in out of the rain, and now Chrissie, who I thought had it all together, is just making a fool out of herself over some man she has never met."

"Joan," Shay chuckled. "I don't think it is that bad. Chrissie sounded pretty discouraged about men. I don't think she will do anything stupid. She just wants to sell him a house, that's all."

"Oh, you don't know Chrissie. Even when she was a little girl she had a way of saying one thing and meaning something else. I just know she is going to fall all over him. And it is so dangerous to meet some strange man at the airport in the middle of the night. And why do you think he wants to live near the hospital? It's because he knows where she lives. You live there too, Shay. You know how close you are to the hospital. I tell you, he has been stalking her, has found out everything about her. All of that is available on the internet, you know. For two cents I would call the police. She should sell her own house to him. She needs to get out of that big place. I know she put all that work into it and it is just beautiful, but that was before. That was when she thought she would fill it with babies. This is now. She needs to get out of that neighborhood. It is a family neighborhood, no place for a single woman." Then realizing she may have stepped on Shay's toes, she quickly added, "You know what I mean, Shay, for someone young like Chrissie. She just turned thirty, for Pete's sake. She needs to be where there are young people, men her own age. The single men around there are old widowers or divorced."

"Yes, Joan, I have noticed that too, and I agree with you. My mother used to refer to those men as other women's leftovers. She always said that was what I was going to end up with, some other woman's leftovers."

"That sounds awful. I never meant it that way. I was only thinking about Chrissie's age. What an unkind thing to say. That must have really hurt, Shay."

"It did hurt at the time, Joan, so be careful what words you use when talking to Chrissie. Try to calm down, don't conjure up all kinds of awful things. We'll write back to her and ask a few questions, see what she has to say. You'll be back home next week. Everything will be fine. Chrissie won't do anything stupid. Grant says life is just a big crapshoot, anyway. But you have to let Chrissie roll her own dice, Joan"

"Maybe so, but I still think she needs to get out of real estate. It is too risky."

"She needs to find her own way without others adding unnecessary opinions or hurtful comments. Let's go and answer her email now and try to offer her some encouragement. Who knows, maybe this guy will buy a house. After we send the email we can have dinner and go listen to Grant play."

"How did that go today? We all noticed Grant's expression when he heard that you were off with Charley. He got a really stern look on his face, like he was mad, and headed right off. I guess he caught up with you."

"Yes, I think he was irritated that he had to catch up, but we had a lovely time. You know, I still don't know how to take him. Sometimes he is so attentive, so considerate, acts like he is enjoying being with me, and then he turns around and says something just the opposite."

"Shay, sometimes men don't know how to express themselves. They are clumsy with words. I think he is really fond of you but is guarded. Mitch says Grant needs to get back in the swing of things, you know, just get used to being single again. He was married for a long time, Shay. Mitch said it was really hard on him. He needs time to work through it. It takes time."

"How long was he married?"

"Mitch said almost thirty years."

"Does Mitch say anything else about him? Grant doesn't say much at all, doesn't mention anything about it. Only once, on the trip to Delphi, he said something about missing her, but that he could handle it. I never know what to say about it either."

"I don't think Mitch is too crazy about that Jodee woman. He says really nice things about her, but he told me today he wished Grant would find someone to settle down with and leave show business behind. By 'show business' I think he meant Jodee."

"That's interesting. Grant couldn't wait to get back to the ship because he had a meeting with her. He says he is just trying to help her with things, but he seemed pretty anxious to get back. Do you think he is having sex with her?"

Joan couldn't believe her ears, totally shocked that Shay had asked the question, but very aware that most of the Palmer group were discussing it and speculating, the general consensus being yes. "I don't know. Shay. All that lovey dovey stuff would suggest it. But Mitch says he doesn't think things have gone that far, that it is just show business stuff. And, of course, Wanda doesn't believe it. She defends him all the time. She thinks he hung the moon."

"Did you spend the rest of the time with Mitch?"

"Yes, he just hung around. Ralph was talking to Maureen and Wanda so Mitch and I strolled past the shops. He sure is a lovely man. He kept asking me questions. It was almost funny. I felt like I was being interviewed for a job. He is the sweetest man."

After meeting with Jodee, Grant had checked for email. There was one from Matt and another from Leighanna.

To: Dad
From: Matt

Things pretty hectic here, but all is well. Hope to have BIG news by the time you get back. DO NOT PLAN TO COME TO CALIFORNIA!!! Just tough it out on the ship, Dad. A good time to jog and go to the fitness center – you might want to start looking at women again. It will help pass the time.

More later, Matt

Reply: Can't wait to hear about BIG news. No plans to look for women.

To: Mommy
From: Leighanna

Bill is back!!! He came over last night and was a different man. Played with the kids, asked me about the baby, asked how I was feeling, and if I needed anything. I think things are going to work out. I fixed dinner— meat loaf and mashed potatoes and gravy, and baked a cherry pie.

DO NOT COME TO RENO, MOM!!! DO NOT COME!!! NOW IS NOT A GOOD TIME!!! More later.

Love and Hugs, Leighanna

PS: We ate the pie for breakfast!!

He hit print, folded the paper and put it in his pocket, and headed to Schwartzman's office.

"Glad you're here, Grant. This Jodee thing has really thrown me for a loop. I tried to break the news to her about the new piano player and she blew up. Quit. Right on the spot. Says she won't sing with anyone else but you. And she is leaving in Venice, day after tomorrow. You gotta stop her, Grant."

"No, Izzy. You have to stop her."

"I can't tie her to the mast, for God's sake. I want to talk to her about my new dinner club, make the deal, but now she will only sing with you. What would it take to get you to change your mind, Grant? How much would it take for you to make the deal so she will stay?"

That's a pretty interesting offer, Iz, but you are the one who said I was all wrong for her. You are talking about the job, aren't you?"

"I'm talking about whatever it takes, Grant. Just get the job done, keep her on this ship and play for her, or whatever else she wants from you."

"You still don't get it, do you Izzy? You can't just buy people or seduce them into doing what you want. You have to treat her right, respect her feelings about things. You can't just present your plan and have her jump through your hoop. You don't want me in the picture. You want her. So you are the one who has to do whatever it takes to get the job done."

"Grant, I lost my wife over ten years now. All I know is the business end of things, the pragmatic way to get things done. I have no idea how to entice a woman."

"The flowers are a good start. She really liked them. And the invitation for dinner with the captain, that was a stroke of genius, Iz. She really liked that. She is getting all fixed up for the occasion. You're doing great. Maybe dance with her a little tonight, and ask her for lunch tomorrow or to spend the day in Venice with you. She would really like that. And how about that necklace you had me buy for you? Did you ever give that to her?"

"No, I planned to give it to her when she signed the contract with me, sort of to seal the deal. But so far, no deal."

"That's what I mean, Iz. That is all wrong. That is okay when you are married to a woman, or making up, or something, but when you are courting you just give her the present just because you want to. No strings attached. See the difference? Just go ahead and give it to her and say something sweet like how beautiful she will look in it. You just go ahead and take a chance. It is all just one big crapshoot, Iz, but you have to roll the dice. Just go for it."

"What if she turns me down, Grant?"

"She won't, Iz. She won't."

Venice

Grant had started playing promptly at nine o'clock, selecting a lively rendition of *The Entertainer*, by Scott Joplin, the theme from the movie *The Sting*, and then adding other ragtime favorites before slowing the pace with hits from *Fiddler on the Roof*. He had started playing songs from big Broadway musicals each night and his regulars had asked that his choice be posted outside the lounge each day so they could plan ahead. They had a contest each day to see who could name the most songs from that show. There was a line half way down the hall waiting to get in, but Shay had arrived early enough to get a seat right in his line of vision. She was sitting with the gals. Ralph, Charley, and Mitch were at the next table. He noticed that three waiters were working the room, shuttling back and forth to the bar, and he felt a sense of pride that things were going well. Now, if he could just get things going as well in Jodee's life, he could concentrate on the other aspects of his own. Whatever the hell was happening with Matt didn't sound like a disaster so he wouldn't book a flight to California yet. He caught Shay's eye and winked and mouthed, "Later?" She responded with a little nod and wave, which he acknowledged with a huge smile before glancing away.

Joan was watching her very closely. Shay had spent some extra time on herself tonight. Usually just a quick shower and change of outfit and she was ready. But tonight she had put on three different outfits before deciding on a cute little jacket dress she hadn't worn before. She had fixed her hair two different ways before fastening it at the nape of her neck, a casually elegant look that was good on

255

her. And she added eye shadow, a pretty lavender color that brought out the color of her blue eyes.

At the end of his first set Grant came right over and pulled up a chair.

"So, how are my favorite ladies tonight." he teased. "Out partying, I see."

Wanda spoke right up. "We came to watch you, Grant. And to make sure that no women snatch you away from us. We hear that you are not behaving yourself, so we have come to protect you."

"No need to worry about that, Wanda. No women are bothering with me. It's Mitch you need to protect. Someone needs to show him a good time before he gets picked off by some hussy."

Joan was all ears. She had been watching Mitch closely, too, had even made eye contact with him a time or two, smiling at him like some giddy school girl. She also had paid a little extra attention to herself tonight, wearing a dress for the first time, and she wondered if he had noticed.

"You ladies all good?" Grant asked, pointing to their nearly empty glasses and signaling to the waiter. "A round of refills here, and charge it to my room," and then turning to Shay. "One more for you, then that's it. Tomorrow is Venice and I want you feeling good. I'll see you when I finish," clearly announcing his intentions to them all. "And you all need to know that the ship arrives in Venice around ten tomorrow morning, so be on the starboard side. You don't want to miss anything. It will be spectacular."

When he finished playing for the night, he and Shay walked to their usual chairs on the Promenade deck and talked until well after 1:00 a.m. When he finally returned to his room the phone was blinking, but he didn't bother to listen to the message.

The beautiful Atheneè would make her majestic entrance along the Grand Canal, arguably the most beautiful sail-in on all the seven seas. Venice is spectacular from the water, her beautiful architecture nearly unchanged through the centuries, so often photographed and familiar that even first time visitors feel as if they have been there before. Built entirely on water and surrounded by water, the city is both dependent on and threatened by the very element by which it rose to such power and grandeur, her buildings standing in water for centuries, testament to the skill of the Venetian architects. They would pass by the Doges Palace and the Piazza St. Marco, where the huge dome of St. Mark's Basilica dominates the skyline, along with the famous bell tower, to its left. Gorgeous mansions line the canal, homes of the wealthy merchants of Venice during the days of Venice's dominance of world trade. These mansions served as both warehouses at water level for goods shipped and received via the canals and as fabulous family living quarters on the upper floors. Venetian skill at shipbuilding and the necessity of sailing skills for sheer survival sustained its position both as merchant traders and warriors until new ports around the world made visits to Venice less attractive. The city fell to debauchery and decadence, sustained by the vast wealth accumulated during its heyday, wealth mostly created by the valued commodity of salt, distilled in Venice and shipped worldwide. Edible gold, it was called.

Grant had found a great place to sit and watch the spectacular scene. He and Mitch had enjoyed an early breakfast and had gone ahead to secure a place for Shay and Joan. Grant had pushed Mitch to ask Joan to spend the day with him and Shay, having presented the plan to Shay late the night before. Grant had a map and pointed out the attractions as the Atheneè made her way to her berth at the commercial port, and then the four of them boarded a launch and headed into the city. Grant had cautioned Shay to wear her walking shoes because high tide brought water into the piazza, so she should be prepared. The four spent the entire day sightseeing together, enjoying the splendor of Venice. They spent over an hour visiting the spectacular St. Mark's Basilica, where they saw fabulous works by Michelangelo and the crypt of St. Mark. The Venetians believed that it was important symbolically for them to possess the remains of their chosen Saint, and built the original crypt in the lower level of the Basilica. Because of the repeated flooding through the centuries the crypt was determined to be at risk and was relocated to the main level and placed behind the high altar in 1811, where it remains. Grant pointed out the four bronze horses they had learned about in Istanbul, the ones looted by the Venetians and placed in St Mark's.

They shopped for Murano glass and Grant bought a piece for Shay as a souvenir, and he bought beautiful leather bookmarks, encouraging Mitch to buy some too. He selected a gorgeous tablecloth in a shop that had been in business on the piazza for over three hundred years selling exquisite Venetian lace. And they all helped him pick out two fabulous masks, popular souvenirs almost as synonymous with Venice as the canals themselves and representative of the city's reputation for licentious revelry. He also added several exquisite gold charms to his collection, and for his girls he bought cameos surrounded by marcasite filigree. Joan followed his lead and bought one for Chrissie and one for Chloe and Shay treated herself to a lovely cameo of a young girl, carved from a beautiful gray shell and set on black onyx. Mitch wasn't much of a shopper, but again following Grant's lead, he loaded up on small cameos for all of his girls.

They had lunch at a table right on the piazza, where a string quartet provided music. They visited the many shops surrounding the square, walking side by side, Grant guiding Shay's arm and even holding her hand as they crawled through the narrow, low tunnel in the Doges Palace. They fed the pigeons and took a ride in a gondola. And as they passed under the Bridge of Sighs, they were surprised to hear Jodee call. She was sitting in the back of a gondola that was just passing them, and she wasn't alone. Itzach Schwartzman was comfortably seated next to her. Grant smiled and waved, nodded to Izzy, and put his arm around Shay. It was the best day of Shay's life.

The little group returned to the docked Atheneè with plans to return for a quick after-dark gondola ride before Grant had to report to the Casablanca Lounge. It would be his last night performing there because the new piano guy was arriving tomorrow and would go right to work. Grant would start in the Adventure Lounge at his usual time tomorrow night. He hadn't told anyone except Mitch about the change, hesitant to say anything since he wasn't very excited about the move, and he wasn't entirely confident that Jodee would even decide to stay for the rest of her contract. If she still left tomorrow, there would be no reason for him to leave the Casablanca lounge. The new guy could just go to the Adventure lounge, right? Wrong.

Izzy S. had a contingency plan of his own. If Jodee would not stay on the ship then he would not either. He had booked a seat on the same flight to New York, just in case, and would wrangle a seat right next to her, like he did last time. That way he would have her as a captive audience while he made his pitch. And he would put the new piano player in the Casablanca Lounge and let the cute little *Tits and Ass* girl from the chorus line have a shot at it. He would like to give her a break, and she was all wrong for Grant Albright.

Grant hadn't talked to Jodee today, hadn't heard about the dinner at the Captain's table, and hadn't expected to see her with Izzy, but just in case Izzy struck out, Grant held his trump card in his pocket. As soon as the foursome returned to the ship, he excused himself, arranging to meet them again at the gangway at 7:00, and went directly to Jodee's room.

"Hi, can I come in?"

"Thank goodness you are here, Grant. I've been waiting for you. I guess you got my message. I was hoping you would get it before Mitch got back. I didn't want him to hear it."

"I didn't go back to the room. What was the message?"

"Oh no! I was so upset I just said, 'Call me. I am going to slit my wrists.'"

"My God, Jodee, why would you say something like that? That's not very funny, you know."

"I was so furious with Izzy I didn't know what to do."

"So, what happened that was so terrible?"

"Well, last night was just wonderful. I left you a message telling you all about it. The Captain treated me like I was the queen, or something, and Izzy was so polite and nice, and nothing was really said about me quitting. The Captain just kept complimenting my singing and telling me how he appreciated my turning things around in the Fez."

"Okay, that sounds good."

"After dinner we went up to the Crow's Nest and danced. He is a pretty good dancer, too."

"That's good. So you enjoyed dancing with Izzy."

"I was talking about the Captain, Grant. The Captain kept asking me to dance."

"Oh. What was Izzy doing while you were dancing with the Captain?"

"He was just sitting there. I finally went and asked him to dance! If I was ever going to shine up to him, like you suggested, just for the sake of the cast, I had to take things in my own hands. He is a pretty good dancer too. Finally, he says to me, 'Jodee, I wish you would change your mind about things. Why not spend the day with me in Venice tomorrow and we can talk some more?' So, I said that would be lovely, and I did, and it was wonderful. Just wonderful."

"Alright, so what made you so mad?"

"Right after we saw you on the gondola, he says to me, 'See Jodee, Grant has already replaced you. You will have to spend the rest of your time with me, now. Here you were being so loyal to him and quitting on me, and he is already out with another girl. We can have dinner together again tonight. I have a surprise planned for you.' He said it real nice, but I thought it was his usual smart aleck self, making that crack about you replacing me. I could see it was just Shay you were with, so it didn't mean anything."

"I think he was joking, Jodee. He was flirting with you, teasing. Give him a break! What did you say?"

"I said, 'Why do you think I'm leaving, Izzy? I'm not interested in staying on board with either one of you. And I am not comfortable working for you. I am going to Reno to be with my daughter.' I wanted to knock him right out of the boat, right into that dirty water."

"Look, Jodee. I think you need to rethink the whole business about leaving. Izzy was just teasing. He really wants you to stay and he is right to get a real accompanist for you. He wants you to be successful. He knew it was only Shay, and he knew you knew it was only Shay. For Pete's sake, everyone knows Shay is just a friend from home. He wasn't trying to hurt you. He's was trying to keep you on the ship."

"You know Leighanna needs me, Grant. That's really why I'm leaving. I just let Izzy think it was because of him, but he looked so hurt I felt sorry for him so we are having dinner again tonight. I'll tell him the truth about Leighanna then."

"Speaking of Leighanna, I have another email from her." He handed her the paper and she read.

"Meat loaf? Why in the world did she make meat loaf? If you are going to cook to catch a man, you don't fix meat loaf. You make lamb chops or standing rib. The cherry pie was okay, but I sure wouldn't fix meatloaf. Where did she ever get such a stupid idea?"

"Is that all you can say?" he laughed. "What's wrong with meatloaf? I like meatloaf. I could probably be had for meatloaf and mashed potatoes and gravy, and cherry pie. Sounds like Bill is a pretty level headed guy after all. And now you don't have to go to Reno, Jodee. You can stay on board and finish your contract, see where things lead."

"Thank goodness for that. I thought she was going to call my bluff this time. Usually when I threaten to come she solves her problem right away, but this time I was getting worried that I really would have to go. Threatening to go is my version of tough love. If she doesn't stop me, then I know she really needs help. Now I don't know what to think. What do you think, Grant? Do you think she needs me and isn't saying so? This Bill guy is pretty much off and on. I think I'll see if I can change my ticket for Rome. That's only a few more days, anyway."

"Good idea," Grant laughed. "Crisis temporarily over, anyway. I keep getting mixed messages from my kids, too. Come sing with me tonight. It's my last night in the Casablanca Lounge before they kick me out."

"I wondered when you were going to tell me that you were moving to the Adventure Lounge. It's been a rumor around here for days, now. I knew you weren't leaving the ship," she laughed. "I'll see you tonight, Shug."

Mitch, Joan, and Shay were waiting at the gangway, but it wasn't going to be the intimate little group Grant was planning on. Also waiting were Ralph and Charley and Maureen and Wanda. It was getting harder and harder to plan for any alone time since the close knit Palmer Plantation gang just assumed that every plan was a group plan and all were invited. Grant and Mitch did manage to commandeer a gondola for just the four of them and Grant guided Shay to the back where the gondolier would be serenading them with Italian love songs along the way. At one point Grant casually draped his arm around the back of her seat and fiddled with her hair, which she had pinned up in a casual arrangement that left loose tendrils dangling. Shay was almost giddy with the pleasure of the moment, wanting it to last forever and dreading the inevitable letdown that would follow. They stopped for some caffè before heading back to the Atheneè and she couldn't help but notice how Joan was gazing at Mitch, nodding in agreement with everything he said, hanging on every word, glowing as Mitch showered her with attention in near gallant perfection. Grant had adopted a far more casual manner with Shay, guarded, but pretty assuming in his role as escort, polite, but not as obvious as Mitch, sometimes rather bold, yet restrained, continuing to send mixed messages. Perhaps he did think of her as just a friend from home, safe and comfortable, but with no strings. She would try to keep her own heartstrings tightly wound.

"Would you care for another caffè before we head back?" he asked. "It is guaranteed to keep you awake while I play tonight. Then we can go out when I'm finished and plan for a short shore visit tomorrow before the three o'clock sail-away. I am planning to spend the time with you. OK?"

Mitch didn't follow up with an invitation for Joan and, seeing a fleeting look of expectation and disappointment cross Joan's face, Shay spoke right up. "Perhaps we should not make any specific plans for tomorrow. Let's just play our days by ear from now on. This has been a lovely day, but we don't want to plan for too much of a good thing. We don't want to get tired of each other with so much left to see on the trip," she laughed.

The minute Joan and Shay returned to their room, Joan started right in on her. "Why did you turn down Grant's invitation for tomorrow? For heaven's sake, Shay, he couldn't be more obvious. He was all over you today, like white on rice. Everyone noticed."

"Mitch was plenty attentive to you, too. But I think Grant is a little pushy, not nearly as sweet or considerate as Mitch. I think that's why Mitch didn't suggest anything for tomorrow. He is being polite and trying not to overstay his welcome. Grant just dictates what he wants. I don't know how to take him."

"I don't know how to take Mitch, either, but I can tell you this, if Mitch McConnell ever looked at me the way Grant Albright looks at you, I would absolutely swoon. The difference is that Mitch and I are both older, probably a little cynical, but certainly a little more cautious. And I don't plan to in any way push him. If it is to become something more, it will. If not, that's disappointing, but not the end of the world. But Grant is young, Shay, and so are you. And he is still a little awkward and vulnerable. I think he comes across as dictating because he wants you to think he is confident and self-assured. He is used to being in control of things, that's all. Underneath he is probably a little concerned that you might reject him, like you did tonight."

"Believe me, the last thing in the world I want is to reject him. Do you really think he felt rejected?"

"Yes, I do. He looked hurt. And you did it right in front of his best friend, adding embarrassment to the equation. Have you ever been rejected by a man, Shay? Have you ever had a man you really cared about, reject you?"

"As a matter of fact I have, Joan. And it broke my heart, and it was very embarrassing. That's probably why I have never entered another relationship. I'm afraid of ever giving my heart to another man."

"Tell me about it, Shay. Tell me what happened."

"I was teaching first grade, my third year. I was twenty five. There was this precious little boy in my class and there was a notation on his records that his parents were in an acrimonious divorce, so my heart went out to the little guy. The mother came in to have a conference and she was lovely, said all the right things, just wanted me to know of the situation and to be sensitive if there were any signs of difficulty with the boy. The following week the father came in. He was very handsome and very nice, and said all the right things too. Well, a week later he came again and invited me to go to the zoo with him and the boy because it was his weekend to have him. It sounded innocent enough to me, so I went and we had a wonderful time. And he kept calling me and gradually we had an affair. We were always discreet about our behavior and I fell madly in love with the guy. Then one day a sheriff's deputy arrived at my classroom door and I was served papers. Apparently the ex had hired a private detective and I was named as correspondent in the divorce and also with alienation of affection with both the husband and the child. North Carolina still has that law on the books. I was just blindsided. I thought they were already divorced and didn't even know about alienation laws. She was suing the father for sole custody and planned to take the boy to California. And of course she wanted damages from me. Because those cases are rare, it appeared in the paper. The father immediately dumped me, hung me out to dry. I had to get a lawyer and I was put on administrative leave because my behavior was deemed inappropriate for a teacher. Six months later I was assigned to another school and out ten thousand dollars for the lawyer. The claims were eventually dropped, but I was completely devastated. It was stupid of me to get involved in the first place and I realize that now. I was so happy about my own situation, thinking how we could become a little family and all, that I never thought about how hurtful that could be to the mother. That's when I heard my mother referring to divorced or widowed men as other women's leftovers. She said that's what happens when you mess with leftovers. Of course, it was meant more as a dig to me rather than as an insult to the men. She wanted me to find a guy who was still single, one who had never been married. She harped on it constantly, but the older I got there were fewer and fewer still single men available."

"I hope you aren't thinking that Grant is another woman's leftovers, Shay, because Grant Albright is no one's leftovers. No, he is not still single, as your mother meant it. He has been a loving husband and father. He has provided for his family, been strong for them, and honorable in every way. He knows what is important in life. Mitch says Grant is the finest man he has ever known. Any woman could be proud to be chosen by Grant Albright. He deserves to be loved, Shay."

"I know and I think I might be falling for him, but what if he isn't serious about me? We barely know each other. What if I am just a convenience right now, only a temporary fix? He doesn't even believe in shipboard romances. And what about Jodee? Where does she fit in? And what about his kids? How will they feel? And his wife? He loved her very much, you know. Would I just be her replacement, always being compared to her? I don't think I can deal with that. It is all so daunting, almost overwhelming, and I am so afraid of being hurt again, Joan."

"Shay, love comes when or where you least expect it, but you have to seize it. Like Grant says, life is just one big crapshoot, but you have to roll the dice. Love is a risky business. There are no guarantees. If Grant asks you to wait for him tonight, let him know how you feel, that you appreciate his kindness and his attention. You don't have to throw yourself at him, or do anything ridiculous, but be there for him. Don't expect him to always say just the right thing in just the right way. Remember, this is new for Grant, too, and he probably is wondering what you are thinking. Now, we better spend a little time fixing ourselves up. These two great guys deserve at least that much effort from us."

Grant had been more than a little ticked off about Shay's rebuff and a little hurt too. She had begun to mean far more to him than he had ever intended, but if she wanted to play hard to get, he could play too. When she entered the Casablanca Lounge with Joan, he ignored her.

Mitch was trailing right behind them and held Joan's chair and took the seat next to her and Joan smiled demurely at him. And when Mitch asked Joan what she would like to drink, Joan said, "Choose something for me, Mitch. Something that fits the mood for Venice." And when Mitch asked her to go back into Venice for a short time tomorrow, she said, "Oh, I would love to, Mitch. Wasn't today just wonderful?" And when he suggested that they slip out of the lounge and take a little stroll on the deck when Grant took his break, she said, "Why, that would be perfect, Mitch. Thank you."

Shay took it all in. When Grant didn't even come over to their table during his break, the other two excused themselves and went for their stroll. Jodee had come in to wait for her turn, and seeing the vacant seat next to Shay, slid right in. Jodee looked beautiful in a soft pink silk with crystals across the bodice. The waiter came right over with Jodee's usual drink and when the waiter turned to Shay, she said, "Please, I'll have whatever Jodee is drinking."

"Good choice," Jodee said. "It helps me relax before a performance. Just kind of loosens me up. Grant started me on these. Hasn't he ordered one for you before?"

"No, he hasn't, but I'm hoping it brings me the same benefits it brings you. My nerves are shot."

"So are mine. This trip has been one big fiasco for me. If it weren't for Grant and his help, I probably would have jumped overboard," she laughed. "What's been bothering you? You seem pretty down. Not man trouble, I hope. I'm having man trouble, kid trouble, and career trouble, so maybe I can be of some help to you. I'm really experienced with trouble, Shay. Thank goodness I have Grant to help."

A little unnerved by Jodee's constant reference to Grant and certainly not intending to share her own experiences with her, Shay replied with just a hint of sarcasm. "You appear so poised, so confident, so in control of everything, Jodee. I can't believe you have any problems at all, at least not any problems that Grant can't fix for you."

Sensing that the mention of Grant had caused the tension in the conversation, Jodee replied. "Grant? I hope he isn't part of your problem. He is the solution to my problems. Just tell him what is troubling you. He will help. He told me he was planning to go to Charlotte to help you with your house. He is really a great guy, Shay. He wants to be helpful, that's all. Or if you want me to ask him something for you, I'd be glad to."

Grant had just returned to the room and started playing. Jodee sashayed her way to the piano, planted a kiss on top of his head, and started to sing. An older gentleman dressed in a fine tailored suit slipped into the seat next to Shay, nodded and said, "May I join you?"

Shay nodded politely and turned her attention back to Grant, catching his eye and giving a little wave. He nodded in return and continued playing. Jodee was fabulous tonight, looked gorgeous and sang better than ever. The gentleman applauded enthusiastically at the conclusion of each song and Jodee sidled up to him as she sang *As Long As He Needs Me,* ending with a flirtatious kiss on his forehead and the gentleman took her hand and kissed it. Grant was watching the little scene, grinning from ear to ear. At the conclusion of Jodee's performance, she and the gentleman excused themselves and left together. Shay downed her drink and ordered another.

When Grant finished playing, he walked around the room, shook hands with some of his regulars, signed a few autographs, returned a few hugs from enthusiastic ladies who had become virtual groupies, and headed right for Shay, taking the seat next to her. "Now," he said, "about tomorrow."

"Oh, Grant, I'm so sorry about how I handled that. Of course I would love to go back into Venice with you. Today was just wonderful." And then, emboldened either by sheer desire or the effects of the drink, added, "Shall we plan to go in by ourselves?"

"That's more like it," he said. "Now let's go up to our little secluded spot and enjoy some peace and quiet." It was 1:30 a.m. when he finally said goodnight at her door.

"Thanks for today, Shay," he said.

"Thank you, Grant. It was really lovely."

"It was a rather bittersweet pleasure for me, but being with you made it more sweet than bitter. Vonnie and I had our last trip together here in Venice and I had rather mixed feelings about going ashore today, but my dread turned to delight, and I thank you for that." He leaned into her and gave her a tiny little kiss on the cheek before adding, "Ten thirty? At the gangway?"

"Yes, ten thirty, at the gangway, Grant."

Cat 2

Grant had slept like a rock. Shay not so much. She had tossed and turned, reliving the evening, touching the cheek where the perfect little kiss had been so gently placed, dying to wake Joan and tell her everything. She didn't know that Joan had returned to the room only shortly before she had and was happily relishing the events of her own evening, lying quietly on her bed, pretending to be sleeping, not wanting to share the events with Shay just yet, cautious, restrained, thrilled.

Maureen called at 7:00 a.m. "Good morning," she announced. "I know it is early but you have got to hurry up to the Sports Lounge. There is terrible news on the satellite TV. I'll meet you up there. Groggy, both women quickly dressed and dashed to the Sports Lounge where most of the Palmer people were already gathered. The weather satellite picture was displayed on the giant screen and no explanation was needed for these coastal dwellers. A category 2 hurricane had smacked the Virgin Islands and was skirting the Florida coast with a projected trajectory right for the Carolinas.

"Oh My God!" they said. "Did you put up your shutters?"

"I hope there is no flooding. We dropped our flood insurance."

"We covered the big glass in the back, but nothing else."

The ditsy darling, Nannette Guppie, was wringing her hands, lamenting repeatedly, "What should I do? What should I do?" Her shipboard squeeze was nowhere in sight.

"How much time do we have? Do they know yet where it will hit?"

"They never know until the last minute. My neighbor has my dog. The poor dog will be scared to death. Honey, did you send the dog's tranquilizers with him?"

"My neighbor has a key. I hope she takes my pots in. They will blow right through the sliding doors."

"If the power goes out everything in the freezer will spoil. And without air conditioning the mold will be everywhere."

"I told you we should never have left New Jersey for a place that gets hurricanes."

"I hope the dock master secures my boat. That damned boat is more trouble than it's worth."

"Are they evacuating? Mandatory?"

"Should we try to book a flight? Maybe we can get home before it hits."

"Why bother. You might not be able to get in the neighborhood if they evacuate or reverse all the highway lanes."

This sort of disaster was right up Mitch's alley. If there was one thing that Mitch enjoyed more than golf, it was projects to be organized and directed and he immediately took charge. "Ok, everybody, listen up. I will attempt to post a notice on the hour and keep you all informed on what is happening at Palmer Plantation. The storm might even fizzle out like usual so no need for everyone to hang around all day just waiting for news. I'll stay here and set up a communications command center so we are prepared if things do get worse. Just go ahead and enjoy your day. I'll set up shop right outside here."

Ralph immediately volunteered to help. He would sit at a computer and send individual messages for people, like asking a neighbor to take in a grill, or something. He would contact the captain of first responders and give them the names and addresses of those traveling with the group so they could ask the fire department to check on the property for damage. Charley, who hailed from Long Island, had volunteered to assist him and he wanted a list of those who had working phones and their numbers so they could be contacted.

Grant had joined Shay and Joan, winking at Shay, who realized she hadn't even brushed her teeth or her hair in the rush, and she quickly glanced around at the other women, noticing that some were still in pajamas and robes. Others were wearing mismatched odd combinations that had been grabbed at random as they rushed to the Sports Bar. Mitch had run his fingers through his hair and his shirt wasn't tucked in, but even disheveled he had the presence of someone in control, in charge. As usual, Grant looked like a million dollars. The light blue dress shirt he had worn last night was tucked in his khakis, open at the collar, and his sockless feet were in shiny Bass Weejuns, pure Myrtle Beach. Shay could have hugged him. The only telltale sign of rushing was the stubble of dark growth on his face. She had never seen him unshaven and kept glancing at him, admiring his youthful sexiness and no longer denying the fact that she was so sexually attracted to him. She quickly smoothed her hair back and straightened the shirt she had hastily pulled on over her head, braless.

"Let me check with Mitch and see if he needs any help," Joan said, edging forward.

"Yeah, he would probably be glad to have you help him today, Joan," Grant added. "I guess we can go on with our plans, Shay. I don't think they need any more help right now. I'll give you some time to dress and then pick you up at nine. We can make a pretty good day of it. We sail at three thirty." His eyes had lingered at her chest and impulsively she wrapped her arms around herself. Had he noticed? Boy, had he ever.

He arrived at her door promptly at 9:00. She had showered and washed her hair and let it hang loose to dry while she dressed in a sundress and then quickly changed into a pair of linen slacks and a pretty soft pink top, and slipped on the ugly walking shoes. The water in the canals didn't appear very clean even though the Venetians insisted that it was, but nonetheless she didn't want her feet in it if it flooded into St. Mark's Piazza at high tide. She put a scrunchie in her bag to use after her hair finished drying and was waiting for him, excited and thrilled about spending another day with him after she had almost blown the chance.

"Ready?" he said. "You look nice. I like your hair like that. I hope that you don't mind that I didn't shave this morning. I have to play at a cocktail party at six and then again in the Adventure Lounge at nine. They are moving me there tonight. I'll shave when we get back. I'm glad you wore those shoes again. I meant to remind you. You saw the color of that water. And long pants are good too for climbing in and out of gondolas." And his eyes paused again at her chest, but she didn't wrap her arms around herself this time.

The day was glorious. He couldn't have been more attentive, more fun, relaxed and relieved to be alone with her. "Let's spend most of our time just riding around in a gondola. I'll charter a private one for us. I have a map and a guidebook and the gondolier can point out some of the significant places along the way and he can select a good place to eat, too." He held her arm when they walked, and he put his arm around the back of her seat as they sat in the back of the gondola. She had taken the scrunchie out of her bag and started to put it in her hair.

"Don't," he said. "I like it loose," and he began to stroke her hair, letting it drape around his fingers. "I hope you don't mind me doing that. I hope you don't think I am out of line. It's just that I am fascinated by your hair. I never gave much thought to hair at all, but when Vonnie got sick the first time, which was while we were still in Raleigh, she had chemo. Everyone thinks she got sick after we moved to Palmer, and that was how she wanted it, but the truth was she had been sick two years before. Anyway, she had chemo and all of her hair came out, all of it, everywhere. It just devastated her. The ladies who visited in the hospital demonstrated ways to tie scarves, and we bought her a few wigs, but mostly she wore baseball caps. I tried to cheer her up, told her how cute she looked, how much I loved her with or without hair. Made love to her. Nothing helped. She just hated it. She didn't have long hair, just above her collar and she had never fussed much with it, but it always looked nice, you know, and I just took it for granted. Well, anyway, it grew back and she had radiation and they said she was in remission. She felt good and decided she wanted to move, wanted a new house, new friends, a new life. I didn't really want to move and I wasn't ready to retire, but it seemed to be doing her some good, so I went along with it. Let her build the house like she wanted, didn't put very many restrictions on the money, just happy that she was doing well. The doctors had told me she only had about two years, but she was doing so good that I wanted to believe that she would beat the odds. There is a very fine line between hope and denial, and I had to hope for her, for our kids, for myself. But about six months after we moved, she got sick again and had more chemo. And her hair came out again, and when that happened, it was like she lost hope, like she knew. The hair part was almost worse for her than the cancer."

Shay sat silently, listening, feeling uncomfortable with the fact that her hair brought such sad memories to him, guilty in some way. Was he wishing she were Vonnie? Did he resent her hair? What was he expecting her to say?

He tightened his arm around her shoulder, his eyes glistening. "Thanks for listening, Shay, for just letting me get that said. I don't know why I felt I needed to tell you that, but I love your hair and it makes me feel guilty, even a little disloyal. I can't explain it, but it is important to me that you know that I loved Vonnie very much, but that doesn't mean that I can't appreciate the things that make you so special. I can't deny my love for Vonnie in order to have feelings for someone else, but I am trying to figure it out. I think it is a little like when your kids are born. When the first one is born you love it so much, more than you thought possible. And when the second one is on the way you wonder if you will love it as much, and you do, and it doesn't reduce how much you love the first one. When Vonnie died I vowed I would never love again, never let myself in for such pain again. But meeting you has helped me see that I can. Even if this is just a little shipboard fling and doesn't mean anything, even if we don't meet at the Empire State Building, it will all be worth it, just to know you."

Shay slipped the scrunchie back into her bag and nestled into his arm. "Maybe we should plan to meet somewhere other than the Empire State Building, Grant. Let's think of a place closer to home," she said with a warm lilt to her voice, changing the somber tone of the conversation.

"Good idea. How about the beach? We can get there whenever we want. We won't wait for six months like in that movie, that's for sure. And as I recall, there is a certain little activity that you have yet to experience on the beach," he teased. "I want to be there for that." Just as he finished his sentence a light fluttering object floated down and landed on her lap.

"Look, a feather, Grant. A pretty white one."

"It's probably from one of the pigeons around here." But he took the perfect little white feather and tucked it between the pages of his Venice guidebook.

"Speaking of the beach, I wonder how the storm is doing."

"Do you think your house will be alright, Grant?"

"Yeah, it's built to all current hurricane standards. It's all brick. Maybe a shutter or a shingle or two might go, that's all. But your place in Cherry Grove is older. It has weathered a storm or two in its day. Those old places can really take it. It will be fine. Mitch will figure out a way to get it checked on if the storm makes landfall in that area. We have a few days yet. Are you coming to the lounge tonight? After I finish we can go to our usual quiet place on deck. I need to unwind a little after playing and I like that quiet little place we have staked out because I'm not bothered there by autograph seeking people and those regulars who seem to find me wherever I am. It helps that I'm with you, too. They hesitate to approach then. I can't go anywhere alone without being bothered."

Damn, he sure could break a romantic spell, but covering her disappointment that he hadn't suggested that he enjoyed just being with her, she said brightly, "Yes, it is pleasant there, isn't it?"

Grant headed to the Sports Lounge where Mitch was manning the command center. Storm Central, he called it.

"How's it going, Buddy? Did you two have a good day?"

"Yep, real good. How you doing here? What's the latest on the storm?"

"Not too much change, still projected for the Carolinas but picking up speed."

"Did you have good help all day?"

"Sure did. Joan just left a few minutes ago. We're having dinner together at six and then taking in another show."

"You seem to be enjoying her company, Mitch. Any progress on your list? You better make a move on her before she gets picked off by someone else."

"You'd be surprised at the progress I've made. I'll be catching up with you real soon. But she's a real lady, Grant. I don't know if I can get to the bottom line with her before this trip is over. I'm taking it real slow in that department."

"Why? Don't you think real ladies like sex? She might surprise you. I thought the bottom line was the whole idea, but maybe we shouldn't be aiming for that anyway. You know it's okay with me if we take that off the list."

"I bet you aren't making any progress with Shay, either. You got time for a beer? I've got something to tell you."

"Sure, I've got a few minutes. What's up?"

They went inside the Sports Lounge and each ordered a beer. "There's something you should know about Shay, Grant. Joan told me today. I think it might help you to understand her a little better, you know, in case you are having trouble getting anywhere with her."

"Yeah, she just doesn't let her hair down, does she? I might as well give up on her. I should never have let you talk me out of Jodee just so you could win the bet. We should have counted what happened in Istanbul. Maybe we should stop betting on women. Let's bet on something easier to predict, like where the hurricane will make landfall."

"OK, fifty says the Charleston area. And another fifty says a category 1."

"I'll take that and raise to a cat 2, Outer Banks. This one is moving pretty fast."

"You're on."

"Alright. So tell me about Shay."

Mitch told the whole story about Shay's affair and the charges of alienation, and how heartbroken she had been about it all and how she was afraid to ever get involved with a man again. And about leftovers. "I'm only telling you this so you don't get mixed up in all of that, so you don't get involved only to have her bolt on you. She sort of blew you off yesterday. I don't know how you talked her into going with you again today, but I would be careful if I were you. No point in betting on a lame horse, Grant. You don't need to get too invested in that kind of a situation just to win a bet."

Grant listened, nodding occasionally, mentally reviewing his conversation with Shay earlier, and recalling his own revelation of feelings for her. He took a deep breath. "Look, Mitch, I'm a big boy. I know you are sharing this for my benefit and I appreciate that. It does help to understand why Shay is so cautious, but damn it, it's all just a crapshoot anyway and as far as she is concerned, I'm going to keep rolling those dice. She's going to find I'm not that easy to get rid of. It's only a shipboard thing, anyway. How much do we have on the bottom line now, two big ones or three?"

"I think we're at three to the winner. I didn't know whether to tell you or not, but I'm glad I did, just so you know what you're up against. Joan says Shay is a wonderful person and any man would be blessed to have Shay Porter in his life. Joan says she is pure gold. But it might not be worth losing the bet over her."

Shay had returned to her room and found Joan beside herself with worry. There had been no email from Chrissie.

"I was sure I would hear from her today. My girls will be the death of me yet. And now this big storm is coming. And that California man is coming. I should have gone home before this. Now Mitch is counting on me to stay and help him. He says he is sure Chrissie is alright, but he will have Ralph contact her too, just in case."

"I'm sure you will hear soon. Mr. Mystery Man from California isn't supposed to come until next week, so there is no need to worry now. The storm won't affect Charlotte. I only remember one bad storm hitting Charlotte. That was Hugo. Chrissie will be fine. Did you spend most of the day with Mitch?"

"Yes, all day, in fact. And we are having dinner together again and going to a show. He has Babs and Maureen working the hospitality desk for him while he manages Storm Central. And between you and me I don't think Babs was very happy about the fact that Mitch didn't ask her to work with him, but it was his idea, not mine. Honestly, I think she comes on pretty strong at times and I don't think Mitch likes to be pushed. Did you have a nice time with Grant?"

"Yes, as usual he was charming. He has to play a cocktail party at six and then work the Adventure Lounge at 9:00, so I guess I will order room service and take a nap. These late hours are taking a toll on me and he is getting tired too. They have him working all the time. It would sure be nice to have some down time."

"Well, better make it a short nap because Wanda and Maureen are planning on having dinner with you and then going to the Adventure Lounge afterward. They are acting sillier than school girls about me and Mitch, telling me what to wear, asking me what he said, and if I think he is interested. Can you imagine? Such a fuss over a simple date. It's not like it means anything, you know."

"Of course not, Joan. Just friends, like Grant and me. It doesn't mean anything romantic. How could anyone think that it is a romance? There is nothing romantic about it." Joan had laid out three outfits for Shay to help her pick.

Grant had headed to the computer center to check his email. There was one from Misty.

To: Daddy
From: Misty

I have cried for you all day just thinking about you in Venice all alone. I think this trip was a terrible mistake, Daddy. Matt thinks you should tough it out but I think you should come home just as soon as you get to some place with an airport. Have you heard his big news? I don't know how he will manage it, but you know him. Superman! Megan still thinks we should go back and help, but I haven't been feeling so hot. Mom would have flown right out, and Megan tries to take her place, but I called Matt last night and he does not want us there!! What do you think, Daddy? Should we go anyway? I know Megan worries too much but she might be right this time.

Please try, try, try to have a good time, Daddy. We all feel so bad about your lousy trip and the terrible time you are having and we love you and want you to have fun.

Hugs, Misty.

Reply to: Misty, Matt, Megan

For Christ's sake will one of you please tell me what the hell is going on!!

HAVING A BLAST HERE!!! BOOZE AND WOMEN EVERYWHERE!!!

Hugs, Daddy

It was three thirty and he felt the ship begin to move. Sill time to shower and shave and have a drink before the cocktail party gig he had been assigned to. Damn, this was way more of a job than he had planned on. There was a voice message from Jodee. "Need to talk, Shug. Things happening. The new piano guy is here. Name is Carlos. He is about twelve years old! Call me."

"Shit."

He placed the call. "Hi, what's up?"

"Carlos what's his name came on board this morning and we met in the Casablanca, since that is where he will be. He was real tired from flying overnight from Vegas, but was very pleasant and he spent a few minutes playing the piano and then he called for a tuner. Said the piano was too bright and wanted it voiced."

"What? That piano is perfect. Do you know if they voiced it?"

"I don't think they did because I called Izzy right away and told him and he said he would have them wait for you. I knew you liked it the way it was so Izzy said they could move it to the Adventure Lounge, just swap out with that piano."

"I haven't even touched that other piano, but Carlos probably should try it before they swap them, because the piano in the Casablanca is voiced perfect for you, Jodee."

"Do you think you should talk to Izzy about it? I think he is trying to make everyone happy. But I was thinking that it might work out best if I just sang with you in the Adventure Lounge."

"The whole idea is for you to work with Carlos, not me. But I sure don't want somebody punching holes in the felt trying to voice the piano. Can you meet with me right now? Go right to the Casablanca and I'll meet you there. I'll call Izzy and see if he can meet with us too."

"Should we ask Carlos to meet with us?"

"No."

Izzy was waiting for them, perfectly tailored, his only nod to cruise casual was the thousand dollar pair of Italian loafers on his feet. Jodee had rollers in her hair, early preparation for her first appearance with Carlos tonight. Grant was still dressed from the day but he had untucked his shirt before returning Jodee's call and had not bothered to tuck it back in. His hair was tousled, and the dark stubble on his face gave him a rugged, outdoorsy look.

"Hi, Shug. You look like you pulled an all-nighter. We better call security to escort you when we finish here. Those groupies you have won't be able to keep their hands off of you," she laughed. Izzy noticed Grant's ruggedness as well, thinking it had been very wise to separate Grant and Jodee. No way could his Italian loafers compete with that. Grant went right to the piano and sat down, playing a few runs and chords, listening carefully.

"Did anyone touch the piano, any technician or tuner? Jodee, come here, and he started playing *All The Way*. Jodee began to sing, following him, looking for clues in his expression, glancing at Izzy, pausing, waiting, anxious, and secretly hoping that Grant would insist on staying in the Casablanca Lounge, playing just for her. They were great together. Izzy was listening intently, seeing again the dynamic, seeing that chemistry that was sheer magic, recognizing gold when he saw it and reassessing his plan to replace Grant. Carlos could play the Adventure Lounge and Grant could stay put. Or Grant and Jodee could both work the Adventure and up the drink sales there. And he would up the ante for Grant to move to Vegas. Together they were dynamite, perfect for Izzy's. And he would put aside his impresario hat, dump the Italian loafers, and fight like a man. Damn it, he wanted her. Period. And he wanted her at Izzy's. And he wanted her in his life. And he would tell her tonight.

Watching from the door, unnoticed, was Carlos. He had taken a short nap and then decided to go check on the piano again. But, standing there watching the impromptu performance, guessing that the pianist was Grant, and that the Italian loafers belonged to Schwartzman, he decided to back away, slink away to oblivion, avoiding the failure that was sure to follow, one more disappointment, one more lost opportunity. He should have kept his mouth shut about the piano.

Jodee had finished the song and was standing there waiting for someone to say something, waiting to hear the words she longed for from Grant, and waiting for Schwartzman to bless them, but Schwartzman did no such thing.

"So what's the verdict? The piano sounded pretty good to me. Do you want to move it or do you want to play the other one, Grant? Either way is fine with me. Did you work with Carlos at all, Jodee? Let's get him down here and get everyone on the same page. Hearing his name as he was turning away, Carlos took a big gulp of air and entered the room.

"Carlos Romerez," he said, offering his hand to Izzy. "A real pleasure to meet you, sir. And Grant Albright, I presume? You sounded even better than Jodee said. I can see I have some pretty big shoes to fill."

"Come in. Come in. Glad you showed up, Carlos," Izzy said, grasping his hand. "We were just discussing the piano situation. Since Grant is the senior man, I will let him make the decision. Perhaps if you played again and then played the one upstairs you would feel better about this one. Grant can make a wooden box sound good, but we want you to be comfortable too."

Grant stepped away from the keyboard so Carlos could sit down. "Play whatever you like, Carlos."

Carlos ran his fingers up and down the keyboard a few times and then started to play, slowly at first, trying to read their faces, then upping the tempo as he segued into *Blue Tango.* He was brilliant, obviously beautifully trained and well prepared. His dark good looks and youthful appearance, belying his thirty six years, were the stuff of heartthrobs, sure to attract a following of women of all ages. Best of all, he was a married man with young children, working gigs in Vegas, just praying for a permanent room, a place he could become identified with. He had no idea why he had been summoned by the great Schwartzman, but every player in Vegas knew that if Schwartzman called, you went. When he got the call from Schwartzman to come to the Atheneè for a special audition, he tapped into his savings account, booked a flight, packed his music, and went. Everyone also knew that Schwartzman reimbursed travel expenses. An audition with Itzach Schwartzman was always a blind audition. No one ever knew what they were auditioning for. That was how Schwartzman did things. He thought that he got a better picture of performers when they didn't know what the job was and didn't try to give him what they thought he wanted. He alone knew what he was looking for and would know it when he saw it. Carlos was not expecting to be an accompanist and had prepared a solo repertoire.

When he finished playing, Grant stepped right up "Great, just great, Carlos. I guess you know that Jodee will be singing a couple of sets with you each night and the rest of the time you go solo. Let me know if there is anything I can help you with, like the repertoire, or anything else you need. I think this piano is perfect for Jodee, maybe a little bright for you, but I think you will find it works in this room, especially when it is full of people. She's easy to play for, Carlos. Just take your cues from her. She's a real pro. You two will be great together."

"Thanks, Grant. Are you sure you are OK with the other piano? I'll switch if you want me to."

"No, it doesn't matter, Carlos. No one gives a shit about the piano player anyway. Our job is just to sell booze."

Carlos had a stricken look on his face. After years and years of practice and study and years of trying to put together steady work to make a decent living playing the piano, the reality of Grant's statement really hit hard. Suspecting that he had been a little blunt, Grant added, "Carlos, you are talented way beyond this gig. I didn't mean that you didn't matter. You are here because you do matter, because you are good. It's just that we all have to justify our presence, and the scorecard in these piano bars is based on liquor sales. It's all part of show business. It's why they call it show business and not show play, or show fun. Right, Izzy? But, between you and me, Carlos, this really is fun, so loosen up. There is no pressure, no newspaper review, and damned little money involved. Just let Jodee take the lead. She'll have them eating out of your hand. This could lead to something very special."

"Boy, you had me reeling there for a second, but I get it. I get it that it isn't about how good I am, but about how much the folks enjoy it. I'll give it my best shot, but I'm pretty nervous."

"We all are, Carlos, we all are. Well, I think we are done here for now. Good luck tonight."

"Not so fast, Grant. I'm changing the time slots around a little. I want you to have some flexibility, so be thinking about it. Jodee and Carlos will be leaving with me in Rome, so you can have your choice the rest of the way. Your contract runs to Barcelona and I'm counting on you to keep things running smoothly."

Jodee was standing there speechless. How dare he assume that she was going with him? Grant walked up to her and gave her a little kiss on the cheek. "Hang in there, Baby. Just hang in there." She had no clue what was being planned for her.

Grant checked his watch and excused himself. "Gotta go, Guys," he said. "Some of us have real work to do. I have to play for some big reception now. Nice to meet you, Carlos. See you later, Jodee."

The cocktail party proved to be quite an event. Ethan had told him that the family had personally requested Grant for the affair, and they had provided a list of music to be included. The event required formal attire. Grant had groused about that since tomorrow was another official formal night, but he showered, shaved, and donned his tux, glancing only briefly at the musical requests, and headed to the private room where the event was being held. He had never been in that room, hadn't given any thought to the piano or the requests, chiding himself as he entered for being so grossly over-confident and unprepared, but then it was just a little private party, so it didn't make much difference, did it?

There was an attractive older couple hosting the affair, which was on the occasion of their sixty fifth wedding anniversary. They had hosted this entire cruise for all of their children and in-law kids, grand kids, and even great grand kids, as well as a few special friends and relatives. This reception was the main event. It was catered to the finest detail. Large ice carvings of gondolas adorned the table and an array of hors d'oeuvres looking like exquisite miniature sculptures was being served by tuxedo clad waiters. There were huge floral arrangements placed all around the room and a spectacular cake created as a replica of St. Mark's Basilica was placed on a large round table where it could be admired by all. There was a large board placed off to the side, covered with pictures taken of events, gatherings, children, the usual collection of family memorabilia. The ship's official photographer was creating photos as a permanent record and was checking off a list of names to be sure he snapped everyone there. He even took Grant's picture.

Grant went over the list of musical selections that had been provided, traditional love songs and wedding songs, and then noticed for the first time the note at the bottom of the list, a special request to please wait until after the benediction, and then finish with *The Lord's Prayer*. The usual toasts were made, jokes were delivered with style and class, and favorite family remembrances were shared. The honored couple had requested *Save the Last Dance For Me* as their special song, and Grant watched as the man held his bride of sixty five years in his arms, dancing with a grace unexpected for a man well into his eighties, gazing lovingly into her eyes. It was like a fairy tale, a fantasy party built on dreams and hopes and grace, the perfect family, the perfect life, unaltered by events or time, blessed by the fates. Grant was moved by all of this, overwhelmed, almost overcome with a sense of his own loss, for what was gone and for what was never to be, punctuated by a rare feeling of resentment for the favors granted some and denied others, the unfairness of it all, the randomness of life's gifts. What was it about this family, these people, that was so special that they were so favored, so bestowed with rewards, so spared of life's harshness, its meanness, its unrelenting pounding of tests and trials and tribulations?

Grant's thoughts were interrupted when the patriarch stood to address the gathering. He thanked them all for coming, for sharing this special day with them, and asked them to join him in a prayer of thanks for all their blessings, for their many years together, for the richness and fullness of their lives. When he finished he nodded to Grant, and Grant began to play. He hadn't played *The Lord's Prayer* in a long time, and he offered a little prayer of his own that he could play it with all the reverence and beauty it deserved, especially grateful for Ms. Eula Bartlette's insistence that he master it. His fingers eased across the keyboard, the familiar rendition filling the room as they listened with heads bowed, then humming, and then singing along as beautiful as any choir of angels, from hearts filled with love and gratitude, and responding to the final amen chord with "Amen."

Afterward, the celebrating couple personally thanked him and several other of the guests approached him, offering gratitude and thanks for his giving of his time and for sharing his music with them. One son escorted Grant to the memorabilia board and pointed out pictures of his Dad in Italy during the war, proudly pointing to the light blue ribbon with the white stars, holding the Medal of Honor received by his father for extraordinary valor. "He met Mom in Italy. She was a war bride. They were married in St Mark's Basilica, which is why they wanted this party here. This is a picture of our little brother. He died when he was twelve. That was a hard time for them. This one is of my sister. The baby she is holding was their first grandchild. He died shortly after. This picture is of us kids the Christmas right before Dad got home from Korea. Mom had a lot of lonely years while he served in two wars. This is Mom in her wedding dress, just a plain ordinary everyday dress. They got married in the city clerk's office first, never had any kind of a big party, so Dad wanted her to have this one. This is a picture of our farmhouse. We're from Iowa. The house burned down when I was six, the barn too. They lost everything. Had to start over from scratch. This is a picture of Dad graduating from college. They had three kids by then. He went on the GI Bill."

Grant shook the son's hand, thanked him for allowing him to share in their family celebration, and made a point of returning to the father and thanking him for the privilege to be a part of their celebration and thanking him for his service to the country, acknowledging his receipt of the Medal of Honor. "It's been an honor to play for you and your family, sir."

As he left the reception room he took off his tie and opened his tux jacket and headed straight to the Adventure Lounge. Two piano techs were finishing working on the piano.

"Hi, Mr. Albright. We just voiced her for you. We got it as close to your other one as we could. This baby is a little bigger, but I think you will like her. The space here is lots bigger too and more open. Worked on the action a little too. Feels real good."

"Thanks, guys. I'm sure it will be perfect."

"Mr. Schwartzman said to do whatever you want with it, so just let us know. We didn't touch the other one. We know you like it just the way it is."

Grant glanced around the room, a room that was enough bigger that the personal touch was gone, that ambiance of intimacy that he liked. People were already coming in, his groupies, that gaggle of ladies from Des Moines, and the Palmer Plantation gang, and a whole group from somewhere, wearing name tags. Shay was there with Maureen and Wanda, and Wanda starting clapping loudly when he sat down at the piano, so naturally, everyone else started clapping too. Grant grinned from ear to ear, shaking his head in amazement, and took his seat. He looked over at Shay and winked and then started playing. The strains of *Blue Tango* had been running through his head since hearing Carlos play it so beautifully, so he decided to give it a go. It rang out across the entire room and into the large open area, center ship, and soon folks were standing four deep at the large arches that framed the lounge, and waiters were busy scurrying back and forth with trays of drinks. Liquor sales were up two hundred per cent that night. Afterward Grant and Shay slipped away to their little spot on the deck and he told her about the cocktail party.

"It's funny," he said, "how things aren't always what they look like. Here this family just looked so perfect, like they were chosen by the gods for everything wonderful, and then I heard about them, and it just blew me away, how they had overcome things, some pretty bad stuff. It makes me wonder if anyone is in control of anything, or maybe it's not what cards you're dealt, but how you play the hand, you know, like things are probably more important on the back end instead of on the front end. Even if it is all just a crapshoot, even if you can't stop some stuff from happening, sometimes you can get out of the way, or duck, or land on your feet, or at least get back up. These people were really something."

"I'm glad it turned out so nice for them and that you could play for their party. They must have heard you in the Casablanca Lounge that they knew to request you."

"I don't think so. They asked me where they could hear me again. It was Ethan who gave me the note saying to play for them. I guess I was the only one available. Tomorrow is a day at sea. Let's lay low and enjoy the day together. I'm not scheduled for anything that I know of. Have you made any plans?"

"Not really. Wanda is all wound up about the inn her niece has bought in Vermont and is turning into some kind of retreat and spa, a conference center kind of thing. She wants us to go look at the flowers in the floral department with her and take pictures of arrangements. Her niece and her husband are wanting her to move to Vermont and take over the decorating and then handle special events for them."

"Boy, I wish she could have seen this reception. It was fabulous. I'll see if I can get copies of the pictures for her. Do you think she'll go, move there?"

"I don't know, but she sure is wound up about it. But I would love to have some down time, too. Let's set a time to meet and then I'll have something to work around to go with her too."

"OK, how about we start with breakfast, then sit around the pool. Then walk around the deck, and then have lunch. Then we can sit around the pool some more, maybe take in a movie, take a nap in side by side chaises, then get ready for cocktails. We have to get dressed. It is formal, remember. Then dinner, and then I play. How does that sound?"

"Perfect"

At Sea

Grant usually got up before Mitch, but today Mitch was already dressed and ready to go when Grant began to stir.

"Gotta go," he said. "Gotta check on Louisa. She looked like she was really picking up speed last night."

While most of the country got familiar with the names of major storms when disaster struck some coastal region, those who lived in coastal areas used the names of storms as casually as if they were relatives, some just more obnoxious than others. The powers in charge of such things had dubbed this storm "Louisa" long before the season even started, so the name recognition would become only as powerful as the storm itself, a rather dubious honor. Coastal residents used this name recognition as a point of reference and comparison and names such as Hugo, and Fran, Camille, Andrew, and Katrina held particular significance, not just for dollar amounts equated with the damage, but for the often painful or difficult times that followed, some weathered better than others. Like the great depression of the thirties, the experience and hardships were not easily forgotten, providing memories handed down from one generation to another. While coastal dwellers sounded rather cavalier about storms, they had learned to respect them, and most folks were pretty well informed and reasonably prepared in case a storm should actually live up to its hype. In hurricane parlance, a cat two meant a category two designation of ninety six to one hundred ten mph winds, but did not include the size of the storm or the speed of its trajectory, the storm surge, or the place of landfall. Yet this category designation is usually the most familiar one, ranking storms between

287

one and five, and is the one used to alert the projected landfall area for preparedness. Locals know to prepare for more than wind.

"Let's hope it doesn't grow. I'll keep checking in with you to see how things look. I'm spending the day with Shay."

"That go pretty good yesterday?"

"Pretty good, I think. But I wouldn't bet the farm on it. These shipboard flings usually don't amount to much."

"That's what Joan says too. But, hell, Grant, a fling has got to start somewhere, doesn't it? Too bad Shay doesn't live in Palmer. Joan and I plan to see each other when we get back there. Just keep things simple, you know. No need to rush into something."

"Yeah, no rush, that's for sure, except I still plan to win the bet. We only have three more nights before Joan and Shay leave at Civitavecchia for their Rome visit. If we don't score with them by then we have to start over with new ones. Let me know if you want the room. By the way, I'm making pretty good progress, so you better get your game on."

"Not so fast. How will I know how you're doing in that department? Where do you two disappear to every night? Joan says Shay doesn't get in the room until almost two some nights. How will I know if you're getting any?"

"You'll know. She'll have a huge smile on her face."

"You cocky devil," Mitch laughed, and added, "Go get her, Tiger." Mission accomplished, he thought. Grant was going to be alright. He had his mojo back.

Throughout the day Mitch manned Storm Central with Joan at his side, keeping a close eye and ear on the storm's progress, informing some, reassuring others, and even consoling one. Ms. Nannette Guppie had become a regular at his briefings, wringing her hands in despair about all the what-ifs. She would ask Mitch what if the storm caused the water to rise here in the Adriatic, could it cause their ship to sink? And what if it changed direction, could it come all the way to Italy? And what if they couldn't get back home? That would be the worst part because she would miss her book club meeting and did he think he could contact them and ask them to postpone the meeting until she could get there? Mitch had no patience with simpletons, especially this particular simpleton. He had disliked Nannette from the gitgo and she had cemented his opinion when she posted those pictures of Grant and Jodee for the whole world to see. Since her shipboard squeeze apparently had evaporated into thin air, Mitch had become the target of Nannette's neediness and she stood at the desk most of the day pestering and pelting away at everyone who approached the table. Mitch had treated Joan to a barrage of unkind descriptive expletives uttered under his breath each time Nannette approached them at Storm Central, never even apologizing for his language. Joan had spent a good part of the time muffling laughter and trying to keep Mitch from throttling the annoying woman with his bare hands. Then she had an idea.

"I might have a solution, Mitch," Joan offered.

"I hope so because I can't stand that nincompoop stupid dame another minute," Mitch said, loud enough for several others to hear. "It's a wonder her new boyfriend didn't throw her overboard. He probably threw himself overboard, just to get away from her." When Nanette approached again, five minutes later, Joan smiled sweetly.

"Nannette, dear, I am so glad you came back. Do you think you could help us out? Your suggestion that the water here in the Adriatic might rise and sink us was just brilliant and made us think. Wouldn't it be lovely if you spent the entire day, and tomorrow too, taking your fabulous pictures of everyone on board, passengers, crew, everyone, so that there will be an historical record of everyone enjoying their last day. Just in case, you know. Just think, you would have pictures for surviving family members, and for newspapers, maybe even the Readers Digest. And be sure to make a list, identifying everyone. It might even help with insurance claims. I think there are about three thousand on board, counting everyone. Would you do that for us, dear? This is the perfect time to start with everyone on board today."

Nannette looked stunned at the suggestion, her mouth and eyes wide open, not quite sure if she should feel important or not, but after all, she really did take nice pictures, so of course they would want her to do that. "Oh, I would just love to help out. I just adore helping out. And I would just adore being part of Mitch's team," she exclaimed. "I'll get pictures of everyone, pretty pictures, ones good enough to use for an obituary or to be framed and put on a casket at the viewing. If we all drown will there still be a viewing? I never went to a viewing before where someone drowned. Well, there would still be a service or something so they could put the picture with the flowers. I wonder if we get refunds if we all drown. You know, for the unused days. I think they should do that, don't you, Mitch?"

Before Mitch could answer he felt that familiar poke on his thigh, that under the table poke recognized by husbands around the world, clearly signaling that he was to keep his mouth shut, so he put his head down on the desk, covering it with his arms, and didn't even respond.

Grant met Shay on the Lido deck. She looked real cute in linen slacks and the ruffly shirt she had worn earlier.

"After we finish breakfast would you mind going to the computer center with me? I'm hoping to hear something from my kids."

"I hope you aren't as frazzled about emails from your kids as Joan is about hearing from Chrissie. She is just beside herself. I heard her talking to Mitch when he came to the door this morning and he said he would go check with her. Mitch seems to have a calming affect on her. I hope she hears something today."

"You know her daughter, don't you? What is the problem with her?"

"Yes, she lives next door to me. She is a beautiful girl. Turned thirty last month. She is selling real estate and has taken up corresponding with some guy in California who wants her to find him a house in Charlotte. He is coming next week and wants Chrissie to pick him up at the airport in the middle of the night. Joan is afraid he is an ax murderer or a fiend of some sort. That online stuff scares her to death."

"It is wise to be cautious. It seems a little much to ask of your real estate agent. She should tell the guy to take a hike, or at least a cab. Does she know anything about him?"

"No, just that he wants a house near the hospital. She is to put him up in one of those extended stay hotels until they find him something. Joan is so worried and now she is worried about the storm too. I told her it wouldn't reach Charlotte. I only remember one really hitting Charlotte. That was Hugo."

"I remember that one. We were slammed once in Raleigh, too. Fran did a real job on us. Huge oak trees were down everywhere, roads blocked for weeks, power out. Place looked like a war zone. We'll have to keep an eye on Louisa, but it is rare for storms to pack such a wallop so far inland. Usually it's just a lot of rain."

"That's what I told Joan, but I guess it is hard not to worry where your kids are concerned."

"It is. I've been worried about my son on this whole trip. He was involved in court just after we sailed and I really felt like I should be there. His sisters ended up flying out to L.A. to be with him. I felt helpless being practically on the other side of the world. I've spent this whole trip checking for emails from my kids, waiting to hear something."

"Did it go well for him? Nothing real serious, I hope."

"It was pretty serious. He was involved in a custody suit. Not the usual kind, but more complicated. He was living with a girl and she got pregnant but she didn't want to marry him. Thank God, because she turned out to be a real nut job. Anyway, after the babies, she had twins, she decided she didn't want them and was going to put them up for adoption because it was the humane thing to do. She's a real wacko, one of those do-gooder, save the world types, and she wanted to share the bounty of her womb with some less fortunate couple so she could continue with her humanitarian work. She has a PhD in some crap studying microbes in Uganda, or some hell hole somewhere, and the babies were an inconvenience. My son wanted them and he had signed their birth certificate as their father, but she challenged it, said he wasn't the father, so he had to go get tested just to prove they were his. He has had them from the beginning because she didn't want anything to do with them. They're ten months old already. This has been going on that long, only he didn't tell us. We knew about the babies. I saw them right after they were born and again in June. He just said that Adesio, or whatever the hell her name is, was on some research project. I think she made that name up. It means earth goddess, or some shit like that. It didn't look to me like it was such a good set up but we didn't know about the lawsuit then. I always told him not to knock anybody up he wasn't married to, but kids don't listen. Anyway, my girls went out to be character witnesses because this tough female judge who was assigned to the case wanted him to prove that he could provide a home for them. Turns out the judge wasn't so bad after all and she gave him sole custody, and Adesio signed away all parental rights, but you can never guess what the hell some judge is going to say. It just pisses me off that he had to go through all of that. The whole thing really pisses me off."

"Well, at least he got them. That's a relief. He doesn't have to worry that she will just up and dump them in some Godforsaken place. How in the world did he ever get involved with her in the first place?"

"It was right about the time Vonnie died and I think he was reeling from that. He was close to his mother. And Adesio was very beautiful, very exotic, and he was probably thinking with his, well, you know, not thinking clearly. He looked right past what a fucked up screwball she was."

"It must have been a very stressful time for you, too. It upsets you to even talk about it."

"It was awful and if he had told me everything I wouldn't have signed on for this trip. Sometimes kids try to keep things from you so you don't worry and end up making it worse. It's hard enough being a parent as it is, and now that Vonnie is gone there is only me to help if they need something. You think when your kids get grown, all your worries will end, but sometimes I think the worries are harder. When they are still at home you have some say in things, some control, but as they get older they don't always want your opinion. And Vonnie was sort of a filter, sort of protected me from some stuff, acted as a buffer, because sometimes I was too blunt, or didn't see their point of view. She was better at it. Now all three kids are telling me there is a big surprise coming only they won't tell me what. I think Matt needs help, but he doesn't want any of us out there. If I don't find out something soon, I'm going to go to California as soon as I get back.

"You must wish he lived nearer."

"I do. It would be much easier for all of us. It's tough on him, being a single father and working. I sure hope he is real careful before getting involved with another woman. I hope he has learned his lesson. Women can be a real problem."

"Yes, I'm sure men have to be wary of women, Grant. They are lurking everywhere. But I think he will be very careful, very selective, now that he has his babies to think about."

They headed to the computer center. A bonanza! All three kids had replied.

To: Dad
From: Matt

    For God's sake, Dad, stop worrying! It will spoil my surprise if we tell. The big reveal is coming real soon!
    About the booze and women. Way to go, Dad!!!

                        Love ya, Matt

    Reply: Can't wait for big reveal. Will try not to worry between times, what with the booze and women everywhere. Have a surprise of my own! Love, Dad

---

To: Daddy
From: Megan

    DADDY!!!!!!! For heaven's sake, you are a grandfather!!! Please, please be very, very, careful. Be very suspicious of any woman who shows interest in you. She is probably up to no good. Times have changed since your day, Daddy. And, admit it, you don't know much about women. Matt's big surprise is still on go, but only time will tell if he can pull it off. I want to help him but

293

he doesn't want me, which hurts my feelings. Mommy would have gone.

Don't worry, Daddy, but please, please stay away from the booze and women. How did you do at bingo? Remember how you used to play bingo with us kids, Daddy. Try to have a good time.

Love and Hugs, Megan

Reply: I like women who are up to no good. They are more fun. And it just so happens that I know quite a bit about women. Don't worry so much. Have a surprise of my own, but can't tell!!!

Love, Daddy

To: Daddy
From: Misty

OMG!!!!! OMG!!!!!OMG!!!! I can't believe it. My very own Daddy out boozing it up and carousing with loose women! OMG!!!!OMG!!!!!OMG!!!!!! I called Megan and we laughed ourselves silly. It was hilarious. No way, Daddy. You didn't fool us for one minute. Maybe you should start thinking about women, though. You know, just for dinner, or something. Nothing romantic, or anything, just dinner. Or maybe have a little shipboard fling, figuratively speaking, of course.

"I have a surprise too when you get home Daddy, a really, really big surprise. Am dying to tell you, but it is surprise.

Love and kisses, Misty

Reply: Hold on a minute. So you think the whole idea of Daddy enjoying booze and women is hilarious?????

Women are throwing themselves at me!! And with enough to drink, some of them look pretty good, too. I have to beat them off, figuratively speaking, of course.

Can't wait to hear your surprise. I have a surprise for you too, but can't tell. It would spoil everything!!!

Love and kisses, Daddy

He hit send and just sat there, shaking his head. Shay had been sitting right next to him only casually glancing at the screen, afraid to sneak a look but dying to know what was going on.

"Everything OK?" she asked.

"Yeah, just more joys of parenthood. Still don't know what the big surprise is, so I told them I had a big surprise for them too."

"What? What big surprise do you have?"

"Guess."

They headed to the storm center where Mitch and Joan were busy passing out hurricane tracking maps Mitch had found on the internet, helping people plot Louisa's path. Louisa had skirted the coast of Florida, swamping the place with as much as eight to ten inches of rain and picking up speed as it headed toward South Carolina. Jim Cantore from the Weather Chanel was in Charleston where winds were picking up and the water looked angry, but wasn't breaching beyond the beaches. The consensus was Charleston looked like a good bet. Grant watched the telecast and then looked at the hurricane map and drew his own line.

"What do you think, Buddy. Charleston a good call? She's almost a cat 2."

"Yeah, but it's moving fast. Just a slight veer and it hits the Outer Banks. I think we will be lucky. But if it doesn't veer, Palmer Plantation better look out. Surely they have battened down the hatches by now. Any word on evacuation?"

"Yeah, I'm in touch with the security people down there. The back section has a mandatory but they are keeping the front open, just urging people to go. It seems a little premature for that but they really worry about that bridge back there. I think Myrtle Beach is going to announce a mandatory evacuation at 2:00. They are already heading out in droves. Charleston is going under lock down. Savannah and that whole area is mandatory. They are really getting ready. I don't know about the Georgia Brunswick places. I would think that Jekyll and St Simons, that whole section, would have left too. The road from Hilton Head is one big parking lot."

"People are beginning to pay more attention to these warnings than they used too. But my money is still on the Outer Banks. We'll probably just get wind and rain, no big deal. Do you need any more help here? We ran into that ditzy Guppie woman. She's taking pictures of everyone and bragging about being on Mitch's storm team."

"Joan came up with that idea, something to keep her busy. She is driving everyone crazy. But we're fine here. Lots of other people are stopping by for information, people from Florida and all up and down the coast. Ethan keeps stopping by. They really appreciate what we are doing here. He sent up all kinds of donuts and stuff and said he would deliver lunch too."

Shay stepped up to Joan. "Did you hear from Chrissie? We just came from the computer center and I was thinking about you."

"No, not yet. We'll go again when Mitch takes a break. The rest of today will pretty much just be watch and wait. Mitch is doing a wonderful job here."

Grant turned to Shay. "Ready? I think the next item on our schedule is a walk on the deck." They passed the day checking on the storm, sipping Bloody Marys on the deck, lunching in the bistro, walking the decks again, snoozing in chaises, holding hands, standing at the railing gazing at the beautiful blue waters, Grant's arm around her waist. And a tender kiss when he dropped her off at her room to dress in formal attire for cocktails before dinner. And every single bit of it caught on camera. Click. Click, click.

There was a message waiting for Grant when he returned to his own room. Jodee.

"Hi Shug. Have a good day? Carlos and I rehearsed for over an hour. He plays beautifully, but could you stop by around 6:00? Izzy moved Carlos up to that time slot. He didn't say so, but I think it was so you could come by. We are doing OK together, but there is something missing and we can't put our finger on it. I miss you, Shug."

He called Shay. She was just stepping into the shower. "Can you be ready a little early? I have to stop by the Casablanca to check on Jodee. OK? It shouldn't take long."

"Would you rather just pick me up later, when you are finished?"

"No, Shay. This day belongs to us. We only have a few more days left. I don't want to waste a minute of it. I'll see you at 6:00."

Shay hurried through her shower and slipped on the lovely blue lace gown she had worn for the first formal night. It was the only gown she had, thinking that one was enough and never anticipating the presence of a special man in her life. He had complimented it the first time she wore it, and it was a beautiful dress, but still. She began to work on her hair, experimenting with different styles and finally decided to pin it up with a special crystal clasp she had purchased. It took her four times to get it the way she wanted and then it looked too severe and she practiced loosening it and trying again. Finally, in desperation, she coiled it around her hand before clasping it, but one stubborn section insisted on springing loose. Joan had come in and offered to help.

"I always loved to play with Chrissie's hair when she was little. Here, let me see if I can fix it the way I did Chrissie's hair for her wedding to that jackass," she laughed. "It was just fancy enough, but a section hung down in a casual way that was really flattering."

When she finished, Shay turned to have a look. She barely recognized herself. "You are a genius, Joan. I love it. I look so different, sort of sophisticated, but comfortable, not too fancy."

"Here, let me do your eyebrows. I'll shape them just a little. And you need mascara, too. Do you ever use it?"

"Rarely. Do you think it's too much makeup for me? I only wear makeup for special occasions."

"This is a special occasion. You look beautiful. Grant is going to love it."

"I hope he doesn't remember that I wore this dress before."

"He won't. Men never notice things like that."

He arrived exactly at 6:00, impeccable in his tux. "Wow! You look lovely, more beautiful than ever. I was hoping you would wear that dress again. Wanda helped me pick this orchid especially for it. Do you want me to pin it on for you? I used to be pretty good at this." He removed the corsage pin and slipped his finger under the dress fabric behind the exact spot he wanted to place the orchid. She could feel his fingers against the bare skin of her breast and impulsively drew in a big breath of air.

"Relax. I won't stick you. I have lots of experience." He pinned it perfectly. "There, that should hold. If it falls off, I'll just do it again. Over and over, if that's what it takes." Shay could feel herself flush with excitement and embarrassment and hoped Joan didn't read too much into it, but Joan read it perfectly. Grant Albright was making his move. Big time. And he didn't care who saw it.

When they arrived in the Casablanca Lounge, Jodee was singing and Carlos was playing perfect accompaniment. Izzy was seated to the side and Grant and Shay took seats right in the middle. There were very few people there. When Jodee finished she went right over to Grant, and Izzy turned his chair to join them.

"What do you think, Grant? Something is missing, but we don't know what."

Carlos pulled up a chair and Izzy said, "I can't put my finger on it either, Grant. Obviously, it's not you up there, but there is something different." They talked right across poor Carlos, as if he weren't even there.

"Let me hear something else. Have you tried something sort of torchy? Can you do *Can't Help Lovin' Dat Man of Mine*?"

Jodee and Carlos went back to the piano and they were both perfect but it took Grant only a minute to see it, and he stopped them. "Jodee, turn and face Carlos. Sing it just to him, like he is the only man on the planet. And Carlos, look right at her, watch her chest, watch her breathe, watch her move. She gives little signals she doesn't even realize, but when she starts to sway, you sway. When she inhales, give her time. You just need to get to know each other. Sense her moods, Carlos. You are a husband, you know how to sense a woman's moods. It's the same thing. It's not always how it is written. The way you are doing it now it sounds like you are taking turns, she sings, then you fill in. And Jodee, Carlos is a man, not a mind reader. While he is adjusting, give him a little more. In rehearsal always look at each other. If you get a chance, dance with each other. You can learn a lot about a woman by dancing with her, how she feels the music, how she responds. You don't learn that in music school. Come by the Adventure Lounge tonight and when I see you there I'll play some of our stuff and you two can dance to it. You don't need to practice the music, you need to practice body language. One session and you'll knock it out of the ballpark. And something else, Jodee. When you are singing to the room, step forward so Carlos can see your backside. Go on, move forward and start to sing something. Now Carlos, watch her rear end. She moves her right hip on a phrase when she breathes. Learn the lyrics and say them to yourself as she sings and keep watching her rear end."

Jodee pretended to be shocked. "Why, Mr. Albright! I wasn't aware that you were watching me so closely."

"Miss Jordan, you are unaware of many things," he teased.

Carlos was feeling more and more awkward, like a fool, really, and pretty sure he was being put on. He didn't know Grant well enough to question his advice, so as Jodee began to sing, he kept his eyes on her rear end, which made them both feel foolish, and Jodee began her hoochie coochie moves, hamming it up.

"Good job, Grant," Izzy said. "Can I speak with you privately for a minute?"

They stepped into the bar and Izzy continued. "Were those suggestions on the level? I never heard any of that stuff before, Grant. The dancing sounded like a really great idea. But watching her rear end? Where did you hear that?"

"Hell, Izzy. I made that all up. Jodee was so nervous she just needed something to release the tension. Carlos is really good, probably the best trained musician on this ship. He doesn't need any advice. I was just giving him something to look at while Jodee gets her game back. He'll enjoy the view. Jodee has a pretty cute rear end, Izzy. You have noticed that, haven't you? But she is intimidated by him. Even he can't read someone who is standing there like a board. She didn't have that trouble with me because she knew I didn't know what I was doing. Jodee totally lacks self-confidence, Izzy. She talks a good game and God knows she is a terrific singer, but underneath she is scared to death. She needs a man to lean on. She needs a man for just about everything. And you're the guy who is going to have to help her with everything, Izzy. She is going to need lots of support when you open that highfalutin dinner club. You'll have to spoil her, coddle her, pamper her, whatever it takes. And you better plan on being very generous with Carlos. With his talent and good looks he will get other offers. And something else. He is younger. You are going to be getting younger members, the tech boys and hedge fund guys, younger men. And Carlos knows their music. And their wives are going to be real happy with him too. He will be a great draw so plan to pay him plenty."

"I intend to, Grant. You have been a godsend, making all of this work. Maybe I should take piano lessons. It might change my luck with Jodee. You and Carlos are having all the fun."

"Trust me, Izzy. It's not a piano you need."

When Grant looked back into the Casablanca Lounge he saw Jodee and Carlos, doubled over with laughter.

Grant signaled to Shay and she rose and followed him. "Shall we go? Let's have cocktails in the Fez and dance. They are playing beach music tonight."

"Grant, I haven't danced in years. I probably don't even remember how."

"It will come back. Any girl who grew up spending summers in Myrtle Beach has beach music in her blood. And besides, I want to take my own advice and feel what mood you are in. Helpful information I might need later."

Beach music and shag dancing are synonymous with Myrtle Beach. Of course Shay loved beach music. Of course she was familiar with the Embers, and The Drifters, and The Tams, and The Band of Oz. And, of course, she could shag.

"Did you ever go dancing at the pavilion?" she asked. "I heard The Drifters the first time there. My brother taught me how to shag there. And we used to cruise. Ocean Drive was the best place."

Most of the dancers in the Fez were doing a swing jazz combination. Grant gave her that little nod and winked. "Let's shag. Let's show 'em how it's done. Let's show them how two kids from North Carolina move to an eight count." He started with simple steps and then added steps like Belly Roll and Boogie Walk, and Sugarfoot, upper body straight, feet doing all the movement. And he was right. It did all come back. And when the guys in the duo finished with the beach music they added a beautiful slow arrangement of *Carolina Moon*. Grant pulled Shay into his arms, holding her close, whispering, "I can't wait to get you to the beach." And she knew he wasn't talking about shagging. He was right about something else too. Dancing with a woman did give a guy a lot of information about her mood. He pulled her closer, feeling her body next to his and her hand caressed the back of his neck. Over her shoulder he saw Nannette Guppie and closed his eyes to avoid contact.

Click

Afterward they had a quiet dinner in the exclusive small restaurant and then headed to the Adventure Lounge. The room was packed, but there was an empty easy chair near the piano with a sign propped against the back. Reserved for Miss Shay Porter. Draped over the back was the beautiful lavender pashmina Grant had purchased in Ephesus. "In case you get cold. I noticed it was cold in here last night," he said, nodding and winking that way he had. The Palmer group was seated up front, collectively grinning as two of their members were in the spotlight

Click.

Jodee and Carlos arrived with Izzy around 10:15 but Jodee wasn't planning to sing with him tonight. She looked beautiful in a shimmering gold gown and he noticed it right away. Around her neck was the beautiful gold Greek key necklace Grant had selected in Athens. When he took a short break she approached the piano and he gave her a peck on the cheek.

"Look, Grant. Isn't this exquisite? Izzy gave it to me at dinner," she said, pointing to the necklace. "He said it was to seal the deal, but I have to wait until later tonight to hear about the deal. He said he picked out the necklace in Athens. Doesn't he have exquisite taste?"

"Yes, exquisite taste, Jodee. Exquisite," he replied, somewhat offended by her enthusiasm and envious of the compliment being bestowed on another for his selection, perhaps even jealous of Izzy. Or resentful.

"He gave Carlos an envelope but he didn't show it to me, but from the look on his face and from the way he kept thanking Izzy, I think it was a check. Carlos seemed overwhelmed by it. The two men shook hands, and Izzy said, 'Deal? Then we have a deal, Carlos?' And Carlos just kept saying, 'Yes sir, we have a deal, Mr. Schwartzman. We have a deal.' I don't know what the deal is but they both seemed pretty happy with it."

"So you find out your deal later tonight, but he gave no hint, huh? When you find out later, tell me about it."

"I will, but whatever it is Grant, I think you should be included in the decision. I don't want to make any plans without your approval. You always seem to know what is best for me" She didn't mention that she recognized the box the necklace was in, the one she had seen Grant have wrapped in Athens. She would never mention it, never tell Grant or Izzy that she knew, but she would wear that necklace every day. It would be her signature piece, her constant reminder of their love.

Doomed

The Atheneè had steamed through the night on course for the Bay of Naples, making port at 7:30 a.m., unbothered by talk of storms, unhindered by wind or rising waters, and largely unaware of the pending dread and doom being perpetrated by one particular passenger. Ms. Nannette Guppie had taken it upon herself to inform every human being in her path of the pending and possibly imminent sinking of the ship, appearing everywhere with her camera as she informed the unsuspecting that she was acting in an official position, at the personal request of the Director of Storm Central, as photographer of the potentially drowned passengers. Most cooperated, some laughed, and others shrugged, but some became unglued, complaining loudly. And the problems landed right in the lap of Ethan, the cruise director. Usually these little rumors quickly dissipated, were easily dispensed with, and disregarded, but this particular rumor, like Louisa itself, was gaining intensity.

To add to this wave of misinformation, Ms. Guppie had convinced Charlie, the dumped one, to encourage the Palmer group to supply him with email addresses of kids, neighbors, next of kin, etc, so that they could be notified of any problem, just in case. Once she had that list she would secretly attach the photos she had been snapping. Even if the ship didn't sink the pictures would be appreciated anyway, a thoughtful and wonderful surprise for everyone. Most of the Palmer group had obliged, thinking it might be a good idea to contact the kids or a neighbor if the storm did hit the coast or if they needed to change travel arrangements. Joan had given him Chrissie's address, Mitch had given his son's, and Grant had given Megan's. Shay had added Chrissie's address too. Nannette had spent most of the previous day snapping pictures of everyone and sorting through the many she had taken along the way, pictures at Ephesus, Mykonos, Athens, Venice, in the dining room, the lounges, around the pool. Everywhere. Click. Click.

At 8:00 a.m. Ethan hit the "On" switch that allowed him to broadcast through the entire ship. "Good morning, Ladies and Gentleman and welcome to the port of Naples for our two day visit. Many of you will be visiting Pompeii and others will spend the time exploring Naples. Two excursions will be heading for the Amalfi Coast. As you can see, our beautiful ship Atheneè has arrived safely in port. It has come to my attention that certain passengers have become unduly worried about a looming disaster spread by an uninformed and excitable individual. Please be reminded that the Atheneè has an impeccable safety record and is equipped with every possible technology and safety device known to mankind. If you should hear any further rumor of pending disaster or be confronted by a distressed photographer, please report it to Mr. Mitch McConnell at the Storm Central desk located outside the Sports Bar. Those of you who are concerned about the storm heading toward the southeastern U.S. coast are also advised to visit Storm Central for the latest updates. Enjoy your stay in beautiful Naples."

Mitch was red faced. "I'll kill that bitch."

"What bitch?" asked Grant.

"That Guppie bitch. She started all of this rumor shit about the ship sinking because of a hurricane half way around the world. Now I have to try to calm everyone down. And she is taking obituary pictures of everyone, making us look like ass holes."

"Calm down, Mitch. I saw her last night taking pictures. Everywhere we went she would appear. But obituary? That's a little far-fetched, isn't it? She's harmless."

"She's lethal, that's what she is." The phone rang and Mitch reached for it. "Oh, good morning. Yes, I heard. Now don't be upset, everything will be alright. No, no, don't think that for a minute. It is not your fault. You didn't cause any of this. I should have put an end to it right away. I should have never let you get involved. It was my responsibility. There, there. Don't be upset. Are you dressed? I'll stop by for you in a few minutes. Everything will be fine." he cooed. "I know you are worried about her. We'll have breakfast and then check email. Now powder your nose. No need for tears. I'll be there in a few minutes."

"Who the hell was that? Was that the Guppie woman, full of remorse? You sure didn't sound very pissed with her."

"It was Joan. She's all to pieces because it was her idea for the Guppie woman to take the pictures, just something to get her out of our way. And she is worried about her daughter, too. I gotta go. She needs me." He dashed out the door.

Grant was meeting Shay for breakfast and continued dressing. The phone rang again.

"Hi, and good morning. Did you sleep well? I did too. Yes, it was a lovely evening. Yes, I heard. Has Mitch picked her up? It will all just blow over, just like the storm. Nothing to worry about. No, she shouldn't blame herself. No, I don't think we should stay on board and help them. Yes, it would be nice to help and we can stop any rumors we hear. Shay, I think Mitch would prefer to be alone with Joan. He's not the least bit worried about the rumors. He just wants to comfort Joan. And he doesn't need us around. OK? You ready? I'll be there in a minute."

Babs was taking the group to Pompeii for the day. Since Joan was so upset, Wanda and Charley, who had both been to Pompeii before, had offered to man Storm Central so Mitch could spend his time reassuring passengers that they were in no danger. But Mitch had other plans. He would spend the entire day lounging around the ship comforting Joan. They would check for email, and they would sit poolside sipping Mai Tais, and they would have their rooms to themselves. Grant and Shay were headed to Pompeii, a seven hour trip.

After breakfast and a stroll around the deck, Joan and Mitch headed for the computer center. Joan entered her password and her email opened. There was a note from her daughter Chloe, just the usual how are you stuff, and one from Chrissie, a long one.

Joan could feel herself tense up and Mitch put his arm around her shoulders with a soothing little pat as she began to read.

To: Mom
From: Chrissie

Guess what. HE CAME LAST NIGHT!!! He sent me an email saying his plans had changed and asked me to meet him last night instead. You will not believe!!! I went to the airport and waited and waited and finally his flight came and I kept looking and looking, and finally here comes the most gorgeous guy, but he's not alone. There is a little, (very short) older lady with him. He is carrying a sound asleep baby in each arm. And three flight attendants are following behind with car seats and diaper bags. I'm the last one waiting so he comes right up and says, "Chrissie? Hi. I'm sorry the flight was so late. Thanks for waiting. I wasn't sure if you would." I nearly died.

It took us forty five minutes to get the luggage and the car seats and everything in my car and we drove to the extended stay motel. Got there like at 2:00 a.m. and there was no reservation. Like a crazy woman, I had forgot to change the date when he did. And there were no rooms. I almost died. So I said he should just come to my house for the night, since he had the babies, and all. He didn't explain anything, but accepted and we went to the house. (I am whispering because they are still asleep, the babies.) He is drinking coffee and reading the paper. Did I say he is drop dead gorgeous!!!

Anyway, today we house hunt. Oh, and he picks up his car today, but he can't get it until after 2:00 so he asked if he could borrow my car because he has a meeting at 10:00 and wants me to help Emelda baby sit. The little lady is Emelda. She is his housekeeper.

Then I have to take him to the dealer to pick up his car. Somewhere up town. After that we will get on the computer and make a list of houses he wants to check out. And he needs to shop for baby food and diapers. He seems to have everything under control.

Will keep you posted. Oh, and he only has one week before his moving van gets here so we have to find a move in ready house. Quick!!! Oh, and he needs to buy strollers so he has something to put them in, the babies. He didn't bring his double stroller because it won't fit in a car. He has thought of everything.

Did I tell you he is DDG? (Drop Dead Gorgeous)

Don't plan to come right away, Mom. Now is not a good time! Do not worry! Have fun.

Love, Chrissie

"Oh my God, Mitch. She has lost her mind. She has brought a total stranger into her home. A man and a strange little lady. They are up to no good. They probably plan to take over her life. He is already completely controlling her. He has moved right in. He probably found her real estate stuff on line and has been staking her out, plotting to take everything. I just know he is some kind of con man, or worse."

"Calm down, now. Let's think this through. He has babies with him. That doesn't sound so threatening. He probably just needs her help. I feel sorry for him, traveling alone with two babies. I wonder where the Mrs. is."

"Those babies are just a diversionary tactic, just something to bemuse her while he does his trickery. He's already planning to steal her car. There probably isn't even a new car at all. And if there is a Mrs., she will be arriving next, but she's probably just an accomplice. What do you think I should do? Do you think I should try to get a plane out of Naples as soon as possible and head to Charlotte?"

"Let's give it a little thought, Joan. She probably doesn't have to worry about her car as long as the babies and the little lady are at the house with her. He wouldn't leave without them and he surely didn't come from California just to steal a car. And there has to be a Mrs. somewhere. I would suggest that you just answer real nice like, so not to scare her, but suggest that she needs to be a little cautious about things. And tell her to get the hell out of there as quick as possible, make an escape plan, just walk out of the house, leave everything, and call the police."

It took them an hour to compose the response and by then Joan was totally to pieces so Mitch took her to her room, slipped in, and spent the afternoon comforting her.

In the meantime, Grant and Shay were enjoying the ruins of the doomed Pompeii. The eruption of Vesuvius in 79 AD and the destruction of Pompeii and surrounding towns was one of the most cataclysmic natural disasters in recorded history. First there was the violent eruption that rained down some fifteen feet of pumice material causing roofs to collapse and spreading fire from overturned lanterns, and the first wave of death. Early the next morning there was a violent discharge of hot gases with devastating effects on the population, followed by two more violent discharges, the last being the most horrific, consisting of a thick stream of pyroclastic material. The doomed city lay buried and forgotten for centuries before excavations began in the mid seventeen hundreds. Work continues today with some two thirds of the city uncovered, revealing a vivid picture of life in ancient Roman times, so well preserved as to appear almost frozen in time. Unfortunately those ruins that have been uncovered are now victim to the ravages of the atmosphere and visitors, suggesting that perhaps it would be wise to let the rest remain safely entombed.

Grant held Shay's hand most of the time as they strolled through the ancient streets past well preserved homes and shops, admiring the many artifacts and wall paintings. They were amazed at the detailed replicas of victims as they died in place, created by a unique method of filling the voids left by decomposed remains with plaster.

Babs had made special arrangements for lunch and the group immediately began joking about all of the erotica, which usually comes as a shock to visitors. It appears that the citizens of Pompeii had enjoyed and tolerated an active and diverse sexual aspect of life, evidenced by the uncovering of several brothels and detailed artistic renderings of sexual acts. Guidebooks available in the nearby shops warn the unsuspecting of their sexual content, some focusing on it more than others. Several members of the group had purchased the uncensored versions and were passing them around for others to see, all thoughts of the impending arrival of hurricane Louisa out of their minds.

On board the Atheneè, Wanda and Charley were holding down the fort at Storm Central when the satellite broadcast was interrupted with the news that Hurricane Louisa was projected to make landfall in the vicinity of Myrtle Beach about 11:00 p.m., packing winds around 105 miles an hour, making it a category 2 storm. They hadn't seen Mitch for several hours and repeated calls to his room went unanswered, leaving Charley with the decision to call Babs, who was in Pompeii, and alert her of these latest developments. Babs immediately relayed the information to the Palmer group, who accepted the news with resignation, privately sharing concerns but generally concealing any personal angst. Babs suggested that Charley go ahead and release a statement to all of those on the email lists informing everyone's kids, neighbors, friends, whoever, that they were aware of the situation and would keep in touch. Ralph contacted the Palmer Plantation First Responders and the Fire Chief. And Ms. Nannette Guppie hit send and forwarded over two hundred photos.

When the group returned to the ship most of them headed right for Storm Central to see the satellite report themselves. The storm was kicking up quite a surf and estimates of a storm surge were beginning to be made and live action shots were appearing regularly, usually with some reporter from the weather channel holding on for dear life while he demonstrated the awfulness of the wind and torrential rain. Shots were appearing of flooded parking lots, precariously dangling street lights, and lonesome cars dangerously maneuvering the nearly deserted streets. A few stragglers could be found for an interview, a FEMA preparedness report was reviewed periodically, and for good measure, a local yokel could be found to relate his personal experience, usually with excited embellishment to enhance his allotted three minutes of fame.

Grant looked around for Mitch, who was conspicuously absent, and asked Charley where he was. "Haven't seen him all afternoon. I think he is with Joan."

Wanda turned to Shay. "I'm glad you are here. I'm worried about Joan. She went to check on her email and I haven't seen her since. You know how worried she is about Chrissie and the storm." Shay turned to Grant. "I better go to the room and check on Joan. See you later."

"OK. I'll pick you up at 7:00."

Shay was putting her key card in the door when it opened and there stood Mitch, somewhat disheveled, but grinning from ear to ear. "Hi. Guess I better go check on Louisa."

"Yes, have you heard? It is heading right for Myrtle Beach. They are looking for you at Storm Central."

Joan appeared from behind him, already dressed for the evening. "Hi. Did you have a nice trip to Pompeii?" sounding just so nonchalant about everything. "Mitch and I are headed for early dinner just as soon as Mitch changes. Did I hear you say the storm is heading for Myrtle Beach? We're stopping by Storm Central before we go to the dining room. We left Wanda and Charley there alone all day, didn't we Mitch?"

"Yeah. We'll relieve them after dinner unless they need me right now. It might be a long night if things are beginning to heat up. Is Grant back in the room?"

"Yes, I believe he is."

"Alright, Joan. I'll hurry and change. Do you want me to pick you up, say in fifteen minutes?"

"Great. I'll fill Shay in about Chrissie in the meantime."

Grant had a message from Jodee waiting for him.

"Hi, Shug. Can we talk sometime this evening? I'll be in the Casablanca between six and seven. I will stop by the Adventure later. Had a long talk with Izzy."

He immediately returned her call. He was still on the phone when Mitch entered the room.

"So, did he give you any specifics? Did he have details? Jodee, that doesn't sound like such a good idea to me. Should I talk to him? No, no, I don't think so. It sounds like he is sincere but we should be together when you tell him that. Has Carlos said anything? Yeah, that could be a stumbling block. Jodee, for Pete's sake, let me take care of it. Yes, give me twenty minutes. Me too. I know. I know. We'll straighten everything out. Me too. Bye-bye."

"What was that about? It sounded serious."

"Yeah, it is. How was your day? Everyone was looking for you."

"I spent the day with Joan. She had some scary news from her daughter about that guy who came from California. That's a bad situation"

"Did the guy come already? I thought it was supposed to happen next week."

"It was, but then he showed up in the middle of the night and is staying at Chrissie's house. Seems to have moved right in. Joan is beside herself. I told her to have Chrissie call the police."

"Yeah, good idea. She needs to get out while she can. No telling what kind of weirdo he is. He sure has balls to move right in. She lives right next door to Shay. I'll warn her too so she doesn't arrive home to find some creep in her house."

Joan was filling Shay in. "Here, read this. It is worse than I ever dreamed. Mitch helped me compose a reply. We told her to get out right away and call the police. And Mitch signed the email with me because she won't do whatever I suggest."

Shay read the email. "It might not be sinister at all, Joan. Chrissie would have red flags all over the place if he seemed like a creep. It could all be on the up and up. There are babies involved, and the little lady. Chrissie is just helping him out, just being charitable. And she is sure to sell him a house. By the time you get home he will have moved out."

"Would you have let him in your house?"

"Hell no, but then I am a natural born scaredy-cat. Chrissie is more of a free spirit, more of a risk taker. And she said he was drop dead gorgeous, which probably influenced her decision making."

"You think? That's the only thing she was seeing. Otherwise it makes no sense at all."

The phone rang and Joan answered. "Hi Grant. She's right here."

"Hi, sure, that's OK. No, no problem. I'll wait. No, really, I don't mind, Grant. Yes, I know, I understand. It's no bother at all. No, I will not wait outside his office. I will probably go check my email and hang around Storm Central. No, Grant. We can just see each other later. I'll see you sometime after 9:00. Fine."

Joan was listening closely. "Well, that didn't sound so good. Didn't you have a good day?"

"We had a perfectly wonderful day. Therein lies my problem. He dazzles me all day and then dumps me the minute she calls. I think I have had enough of it."

The phone rang again. "Look," he said. "I will meet you by the hospitality desk at the dining room at 7:30. I promise. I'll walk out of the meeting if we're not through. OK? I'll fill you in then."

"Alright," she laughed. "7:30 then."

"That sounded better." Joan said.

"Yeah. Drop dead gorgeous has a strange effect on the thinking process, doesn't it?"

DDG

Back in Charlotte things were humming along. Chrissie and Emelda had finished giving the babies a bath and were enjoying a cup of coffee while the babies took a nap. Emelda was very efficient with the babies, and very loving, cuddling and cooing as she tended them, and offering little suggestions to Chrissie about things such as diapers and kinds of food they could eat from the table. And she seemed enthralled with Mr. Drop Dead Gorgeous, always nodding and smiling at him, jumping at his beck and call, and keeping a very close eye on Chrissie, never leaving Chrissie alone with the babies, not even for a minute. When DDG returned from his meeting he played on the floor with the babies for a time before asking Chrissie to take him uptown to pick up his car, which turned out to be a brand new Toyota van with all the extras. Then he suggested that they meet back at the house and if the girls were still asleep they could go to the store then. He knew his way around the grocery store better than she did and loaded up on supplies, baby food, diapers, steaks for dinner, and wine.

"Do you have any liquor in the house?" he asked, and when her answer wasn't very reassuring, he asked for directions to the nearest ABC store. And he paid for everything and carried everything in and Emelda began putting it all away. She had taken over the kitchen, shooshing Chrissie out every time Chrissie tried to help.

At five o'clock he poured Chrissie a glass of wine and fixed himself a martini. He helped himself to the barbeque tools and lit the grill, without asking, and grilled the steaks for dinner. Emelda had baked potatoes and fixed a salad and DDG had poured more wine and played with the girls in the backyard, letting them crawl around in the grass. After the girls were down for the night he suggested they go to the baby super store and buy strollers so they could start taking the girls for walks. They never once looked at house listings on the computer. At eleven o'clock that evening DDG opened his computer. Chrissie opened hers, but was really peering over the top, watching him.

"Holy Shit! I can't believe this!" he said, looking closer at the images appearing on his screen. "Holy Shit!"

Chrissie opened her email and immediately opened one from some name she didn't recognize but the subject was Doomed Cruise Ship Atheneè. "Oh My God!!" she exclaimed as she closely examined the pictures that were unfolding in front of her eyes.

"What?" said DDG. "Bad news?"

"Oh My God! That's my mother!"

"Where is your mother? Didn't you say she was traveling?"

"Yes, she is on a cruise ship. Quick, turn on the TV for some news. I think the ship is sinking."

"My Dad is on a cruise ship too," and he stopped mid-sentence and leaned closer to the screen. "Holy Shit! Is your mother on the Atheneè?"

"Yes, I'm getting lots of pictures," and then she stopped, examining closer, and looking over the top of the screen at DDG."

He was looking at her. "Come over here," he said, patting the place next to him. "Look at these. Which one is your mother?"

"There, there!" she said. "That's my mother!"

His cell phone rang and he got up to get it. "Hi. Yes, they are coming in now. He did? Good, that's good news, but, wow, those pictures. No, I'm not upset. I think it's great. Yeah. Which one do you think is the surprise? Me too. She looks more likely, but he could fool us. Yeah, what a hoot. She is? She'll get over it. No, don't mention the pictures to him. Tell her not to let on that she has seen them. We won't say a thing. No, it's nothing. He's just getting his feet wet, that's all. I think it's a good sign. Me too. Thanks for sending them. Love you too. Bye"

"My sister," he said in response to Chrissie's questioning expression. "Her husband called the cruise line and there is no truth to anything about trouble on the ship. It looks to me like everyone is having a great time."

He rejoined her on the sofa as they looked at pictures of couples and of women mugging for the camera, and of Joan and her friends, and Joan with Mitch, and Mitch holding hands with Joan, and Mitch kissing Joan, and of Grant kissing a platinum blonde, and Grant holding hands with her and of Grant by the pool with her and in a tuxedo with the same blonde in a sexy shiny evening dress. And of Grant in a tux seated at a piano, and Grant surrounded by a group of women wearing name tags, and Grant dancing with another blonde, his eyes closed and her hand on the back of his neck. And Grant kissing her and Grant holding her hand, and Grant kissing her again.

Chrissie's eyes about popped out of her head. "That's Shay!" she said. "She lives right next door. She's with my mother. Wow! I can't believe my eyes! Which one is your Dad?"

DDG got up and poured them another glass of wine. "He's the one in the tux. Here's a toast to the folks," he laughed.

"You look just like your Dad, Matt."

"Does your Mom know about me?"

"I told her you were here, but I didn't give very many details. She wrote back that I should call the police."

"Call the police? Why would you do that? You knew I was coming. You didn't, did you?"

"Of course not, Matt. She worries about me, that's all. I'll write to her now and let her know that I am safe and sound. She is afraid of the whole online meeting thing so I downplayed that part. I just told her you were looking for a house. She doesn't know we have been chatting for months and months before you decided to move here."

"Don't mention that you have seen the pictures, either. Your mom will be home soon and she can meet me then. When does she get back? I'll move out this weekend, even if it's just to a hotel. I don't start work until next week. We can do some serious house hunting over the weekend. Did you tell her about the girls? I know

I should have told you about them, Chrissie, but I was afraid you wouldn't want to meet me if you knew I had two babies and a housekeeper. Most women wouldn't have, and I didn't want to lose you before I even got to meet you. I know that was a little deceptive but something told me to take a chance. You really did go out on a limb for me. It was a little risky for me, too. But life is just one big crapshoot, so I took that chance and rolled the dice, and I'm really glad I did."

"The babies threw me for a loop, Matt. I wasn't expecting that. And you haven't done much to convince me that there isn't going to be a Mrs. Albright following soon. Is there?"

"No, Chrissie, there is no Mrs. Albright, and there has not been one. No more surprises. I am an open book from now on. But I still think it is probably better not to tell your mother you have seen these pictures."

"I told her you had babies with you. And a little lady. And how you had figured everything out, that's all. I don't know why she freaked out."

"She freaked out because she thinks I am up to no good, that's why. She doesn't know that I'm not a total stranger. She probably thinks I'm some creep making a move on you. I don't want my Dad to know I'm here either. I was trying to surprise him with this move. And he says he has a surprise too. From these pictures, it's quite a surprise alright."

The late night weather report was coming on the local channel and they turned to watch. Apparently Hurricane Louisa would be making landfall in the vicinity of Myrtle Beach and Charlotte was under watch for heavy rain and strong winds by morning.

"I better go outside and put the grill up closer to the house, and those flower pots should probably be moved too. Any chance of putting my car in your garage in case some limbs fall?"

"Go ahead. Just move some stuff aside and you can pull in next to me. I'll drop my Mom a line and then help you."

To: Mom
From: Chrissie
    Mother!! Please stop worrying!!! I am fine. No
problems. No police! We will find a house tomorrow.
He is sleeping on the couch in the upstairs den. As usual,
I am alone in my king sized bed in the downstairs master
bedroom. Not to worry!!! Storm warnings tonight, just
rain and high wind. He starts to work on new job next
week. I am learning to tell the babies apart. I think they
like me. Lots of houses for sale, don't worry. Storm won't
be bad. He is wonderful! Don't worry.

                                      Love, Chrissie

    It was already raining hard. They lost power at 3:00 a.m.
    Chrissie was wide awake, listening to the roar of the wind and
the torrential downpour outside. It was pitch dark as she tiptoed to
the sliding patio doors in the den to check on the patio furniture. She
was feeling her way around the sofa when she stepped on a squeaky
toy, which scared her out of her wits, causing her to jump and fall
over the ottoman with a thud, knocking down the lamp as she fell.
Hearing the crash, the smashing of glass, Matt grabbed the flashlight
he kept next to him and came flying down the stairs.
    "Chrissie?" he called. "Chrissie, is that you? Where are you?"
    "Over here, in the den. I just killed myself on the ottoman. Be
careful where you walk. I think the lamp broke."
    "Are you alright? Did you hurt yourself? Here, let me help you
up."
    He carefully helped her to her feet and she winched in pain. "I
think I broke my toe. It's killing me."
    "I'll have a look at it. A bad stubbed toe can really hurt." He
picked her up and carried her to her bed. The rain was coming in
sheets and the wind was howling. "I'll go upstairs and check on the

girls and get my phone and then come back down. It still sounds quiet up there." He returned in two minutes flat.

"How does the toe feel now?" he asked.

"Maybe a little better," she said.

"Good. I better stay right here and keep an eye on it. If you need to get up for anything, I'll be right here to help." He slid in beside her.

His phone rang around 4:00 a.m. "Yes, sure. Yeah, you can call on this number. I'm available any time. Fine. If I don't hear sooner, I'll come in at two. Yes, I am happy to. No problem."

"Who was that?" Chrissie asked.

"The hospital. They want me to start work this weekend. The storm will cause lots of problems so all hands have to be ready."

"What do you do at the hospital?"

"I'm an ER doctor, Chrissie. I just joined the practice that runs the emergency room at the hospital. As of this minute, I am on call."

"You didn't tell me you were a doctor."

"I know. Now let's get back to what we were doing."

She nestled back into his arms.

Stormy Weather

After hearing Jodee's disturbing news about her deal with Izzy and then having to upset his plans with Shay, Grant wasn't in the best of moods. He gulped down a martini before stopping by for Jodee and heading to Schwartzman's office. If this was going to be a showdown with Izzy, he needed some reinforcement. Jodee was nearly in tears and Grant steeled himself for the unpleasant task ahead. Izzy was waiting at his open door and they went right in.

"So," Izzy said. "What seems to be the problem? Jodee and I settled on several things this afternoon and she has probably told you most of it. We are in agreement about everything except you, Grant. Did you tell Grant what your terms are, Jodee?"

Jodee stiffened slightly, keeping her composure as she explained that she simply could not accept Izzy's very generous offer if it did not include Grant. "This all sounds so perfect, like I said, Izzy, but it just isn't right to exclude Grant. If it weren't for Grant you would have never heard me sing. Would never even have heard of me. I don't want to hurt Carlos, but it just won't work without Grant. I won't do it without him."

Usually nothing floored Grant, but this pronouncement had taken him completely by surprise. "Jodee, I thought you were just concerned about the terms of your contract. I thought you wanted me to discuss the terms with Izzy. This discussion isn't about me. The contract is about your job at Izzy's new dinner club. Izzy has a business to run and he has made a very generous offer. I haven't seen it in writing yet, but it sounded more than reasonable. Perhaps if we go over it line by line you will feel better about it."

Izzy interjected. "I have offered to let Jodee write in items she wants to include, whatever she wants, but it all seems to hinge on you, Grant. You know I offered you an opportunity to change your mind, and I am willing for you to play for Jodee. She knows that. I have offered you some pretty generous terms and I am prepared to reopen that offer. I have written a number on this scrap of paper, a number that might help you make your decision." He handed the paper to Grant.

Grant read it and put it in his pocket.

"I acknowledge your generosity, Izzy, but I also recall that you didn't think I was right for Jodee, and I agree with that assessment. Jodee, this is a fantastic opportunity for you, a chance to finally catch that rainbow. Don't put me between you and your rainbow. I am not negotiable. I will do whatever I can to help you, whatever you need. I will come to Vegas, but only for visits. I will do whatever I can to help make this work. And Izzy will do whatever you need. Don't throw away your dream, Jodee. I can't be everything that you want from me. I can't give up my life while you make yours."

Tears were streaming down her face and he took her in his arms. "Please, Jodee. Let me go."

She straightened and wiped her tears. She had heard what she needed to hear, the words she had prayed that he wouldn't say, but knew that he would. He had cut her loose, had given her her wings, had blessed her rainbow. But he would not come along.

"Go," she said. "Go to her, Grant. She is waiting."

Shay was a nervous wreck. This business of playing second fiddle to Jodee was weighing heavily on her and yet she couldn't force herself to break from him. What a fool she had been. She needed to refocus, get on with her plans, create a life for herself, stir up some excitement, get out of her rut. She would move, definitely move, to Montana, or maybe to Maine, or to Mongolia, wherever. And she would get her doctorate, or maybe go to law school, or join a commune or a convent, whatever. She would not tell him her plans or say anything stupid, like she would miss him or how much she wanted to meet him at the beach. No way. She would just say goodbye, shake his hand and wish him luck, and then get on with things. She would walk away before he did.

"Hi. Ready? I thought we'd go for a cocktail on deck before dinner."

"Did your meeting go well?"

"Yeah, lost a million dollars, blew a great career opportunity, and hurt someone I'm very fond of. Other than that, it went pretty good. How about you? Anything exciting happen to you while I was gone?"

"Yes. I've been propositioned three times, had two marriage proposals, and planned my future."

"Good. Then we will both enjoy our peace and quiet later," and he wrapped his arm tightly around her. Later she took her usual seat in the lounge while he played.

When Jodee entered the room, she went right to him and engaged him in a brief conversation. He turned back to the keyboard and started playing the familiar introduction and Jodee sidled up beside him and began to sing *Over The Rainbow,* looking lovingly at him, pouring her heart out. At the end he stood and took her in his arms, kissed her, and announced, "Ladies and Gentleman, Miss Jodee Jordan," to a warm round of applause. Then he played several pieces that Jodee and Carlos could dance to and watched as they moved together, close, Carlos moving gracefully, smiling at her. And then Izzy cut in and waltzed her right out of the room. And she was gone. When he finished playing, he politely acknowledged the applause and mouthed thank you, but he didn't pause to visit with any of the guests or sign any autographs, and barely looked at the Palmer Plantation group. He went right to Shay. "Ready? Let's go get some air," and she sensed a slight change in him, a brusqueness, serious, sad.

They took one turn around the promenade deck and then headed to their favorite spot. He had held her hand all the way, but his mood was still somber. They sat without talking, safe in the silence, expectant, braced for whatever was coming. Shay spoke first.

"Is there something bothering you, Grant? Did Jodee bring disturbing news?"

"No, not at all. She had good news, news that I have been waiting to hear. News that will change her life for the better, I am sure. But somehow it feels like I have lost something, like her gain is my loss. I owe a lot to Jodee, Shay. She allowed me into her life, allowed me to feel needed again, to feel without fear. And tonight was a good-bye and we both knew it. If it hadn't been for her I probably wouldn't have let myself fall for you, Shay, not because I wanted her, but because of her, I wanted you." He put his arm around her and drew her close. "You do know that I have fallen for you, don't you? I told you that in the gondola, didn't I?"

"I think you mentioned something like that, something about the Empire State Building. Wait, I remember now, we decided not to meet there. We decided to meet at the beach, I think. I believe there was something you wanted me to experience," she said, trying to lighten the conversation some.

"Well, I will refresh your memory. We decided to meet at the beach and share that certain experience. We just didn't decide on a specific place. You did agree to that, didn't you? You're not backing out on me, are you? I'm not losing you too, am I? He felt a tightness in his chest, exposed, panic, and he pulled her close and kissed her. "I want to meet you at the beach, Shay."

And that little voice inside her whispered, "Trust him."

"Did you really do it on the beach, right there in the sand, like in *From Here to Eternity?*" she teased.

"No, I was just pulling your leg. But I know people who did. Do you think you would like to try it?"

"Maybe after I get to know you a little better. Tell me more about yourself. What things do you like Grant? I want to know everything about you. We need to know each other really well before we meet at the beach to share that experience."

"We know a lot about each other already, Shay. We've spent hours talking together, getting to know each other."

"But I want to know more. I only know you don't like eggplant, or lamb."

"Or brussels sprouts or beets. Not too crazy about guacamole, or hummus, or casseroles. Boy, did I ever get casseroles when Vonnie died. No casseroles."

"That's a pretty long list. Maybe you should tell me what you do like."

"I like lots of things, steak, potatoes, pork chops, fried chicken, turkey and dressing. And gravy. I love gravy, and meatloaf, and ice cream."

"And I know you like to shop."

"Like to shop? What gave you that idea? As a matter of fact, I don't much like shopping at all. Vonnie did all our shopping."

"You bought so many things, I just assumed you liked shopping."

"Vonnie always bought lots of stuff for the kids and for us when we were on trips. I guess I was just doing her part out of habit. I like the stuff though. It's nice to have for memories. I really do like the street art."

"That's funny because you seemed to know so much about the things to buy that everyone else followed your lead in making selections. Alright, what else do you like? I know you like golf and the piano."

"I like the beach and the mountains, and martinis, and, since you are making a list, Miss Porter, you need to add this. I like to be on top."

She was always put a little off balance when he tossed these sexual innuendos her way. She wasn't sure how to take him. Was he just trying to shock her, embarrass her, expose her naiveté? Did he think of her as a virginal old maid, mocking her by making risqué comments at her expense? Or was he feeling her out, anxious for her response, risking rebuke or rejection. And that little voice whispered, "Roll the dice, Shay."

"I'll keep that in mind, Mr. Albright."

He had his arm around her, examining her expression and gave her response a little squeeze.

"OK," he said. "Your turn. Tell me what you like.

"Alright. I like pretty."

"Pretty? Pretty what?"

"Pretty everything. Sunsets, snowfalls, flowers, dishes. I love dishes, and glassware. I always thought, if I ever had a home, a real home with all the trimmings, kids, a husband, a dog, I would fill that home with pretty things. Just a young woman's fantasy, I guess."

"What else besides pretty. What do you like to do?"

"Let's see. I like long walks on the beach, and quiet, romantic candlelit dinners for two. Isn't that what all those singles ads say?"

"Be serious. I want to know what you like to do."

"I am being serious. I like to read. I like concerts and plays. And boat rides. And one other thing you need to know, Mr. Albright. I like to be on the bottom. Of course, I have very little experience with bunk beds, and none on top."

"I shall keep that in mind, Miss Porter. It is always good to have that information ahead of time. No bunk beds."

He leaned over and began kissing her again, like he meant it. There would be no more little pecks. He was going to win the bet fair and square. And he had no intention of waiting until they were at the beach.

Hurricane Louisa was battering the Carolina coast with heavy wind and torrential rain, but it had been downgraded to a tropical storm by the time it made landfall. The Palmer folks were gathered at Storm Central for the latest report before turning in for the night, relaxed, relieved to hear that there was no serious damage and no travel plans would have to be changed. Mitch was reassuring everyone that he was making sure that all property was being checked on, but just in case, he suggested that they contact some of their neighbors themselves. One report said that the power was out, but it was probably already restored and he was pretty sure that all the roads were open. One of the men reported that he had been on line and had heard from his kids and how much they had enjoyed seeing the photos that had been attached, and he wondered if anyone else had seen the pictures.

"What pictures?" they asked.

"The ones Nannette has been taking. She has sent them to everyone on your list, but you won't have them yourself. She only sent them to the people on your contact list."

"She needs to send them to us too. Can she do that?"

"Sure, I'll ask her to do that."

It would be morning before any of them received the pictures, but already several others were getting responses from friends, neighbors, and kids. Mitch cast an anxious glance around the group and spotted Nannette as she was entering the room.

"Nannette," he called. "Can I talk to you for a minute?"

Delighted to be recognized by him and personally requested, she headed right for him.

"Do you have your camera with you?" knowing full well that she never was without it. "I am hearing wonderful comments about your pictures. It was so thoughtful of you to send them out even though we didn't all drown. I'd love to see the photo stream. Let's go in the sports bar here and you can show them to me right now."

"Oh, I just adore pictures, don't you? I would just adore showing them to you." They disappeared behind the door to the bar and Mitch took the camera from her and began to scroll. Joan had followed him in.

"HOLY SHIT!!

He handed the camera to Joan. "Oh My God!" He would spend the rest of the night comforting her.

Grant and Shay hadn't stopped by Storm Central, content to spend the time canoodling on the deck and planning their last day together. "I think we should go to Capri. Should I see if we can get a ferry or launch over there? It's only about an hour from Naples, I think. I haven't heard that Babs is planning on taking the group there and I want to be alone with you, wherever we go."

"Capri would be wonderful. Joan said the group was taking a bus tour down the Amalfi coast, so we should have the isle all to ourselves."

"Alright, The Isle of Capri it is. I'll have Ethan pull some strings and get us a boat over there. It was almost two in the morning when they parted, oblivious to the photo stream that was beginning to hit everyone's email.

Logistics

A note had been slipped under the door and Grant anxiously unfolded it and read. Ethan had come through. They would board a launch for Capri at 10:00.

"OK, Mitch. This is it, the last day before Rome. Should we settle up now or do you want one more chance to catch up? Tonight is the last night. I'll give you the room if you want it."

"What makes you think I haven't already caught up? Things are really heating up in that department. We'll check the score tomorrow morning after they leave."

"Alright, I'll give you one more chance. By the way, were you at Storm Central all night? You didn't get in till after three. Joan had the do not disturb sign on her door when we walked by around midnight so Shay didn't go in. She didn't want to wake her up. We didn't even go up to check on the storm. How's that going. Any news yet?"

"We both lost that bet. Hit Myrtle Beach but was downgraded to a tropical storm. No serious damage anywhere. Everyone is in a tizzy about the pictures, though."

"What pictures?"

"The ones the Guppie woman sent out all over the world. Your kids got copies. You'll be hearing from them."

"They're just pictures of us, right? What is everyone in a tizzy about? The kids will probably enjoy them. Did she send us copies too? I want to see them."

"You will. You will. You'll hear from your kids too, trust me."

"Now that Storm Central is out of business what are you going to do today?"

"We're still hanging around to help people get in touch with neighbors and kids, check on pets, stuff like that. Joan says the group is headed to the Amalfi Coast on a bus, but we might just go in to Naples for a few hours."

"We're headed for a quiet day on Capri."

Grant picked up Shay around 9:30. "Let's go check our email. Mitch says there are pictures of the group."

He entered his password. There was an email for Jodee from Leighanna and he printed it without reading it and then opened an ominous one that said Doomed Cruise Ship Atheneè and started to scroll.

"HOLY SHIT!!!"

Shay was leaning over his arm looking too. "Oh my God, Grant. I hope your kids didn't get these."

"They got 'em. I'll be hearing from them." But there was nothing from the three Albright kids.

"Joan will die if Chrissie got these. Did Mitch say anything? She didn't say anything about pictures. I hope she didn't see them."

"She did. Mitch spent the better part of the night with her. It's a good thing you didn't go in the room to get your sweater when you saw the do not disturb sign. I don't think she was sleeping."

"Really? You don't think anything was going on do you? Maybe they were watching a movie, like we did. I know Joan is nuts about him but I can't believe that things have gone far enough for, you know, *that*."

"I absolutely think things have gone far enough for *that*, as you put it. I don't know that it has, but I know that he would be open for it. And I couldn't be happier for Mitch. He's been lonely, Shay. He puts on a good front but he really is lonely. Joan's girls should be thrilled for her, glad that she has found someone. Mitch is a great guy. They should encourage the relationship. If Chrissie says anything negative about it, set her straight. This isn't just a shipboard fling. They are planning on seeing each other when they get back."

"I think Chrissie will be thrilled for her mother. She worries about Joan being alone. What about your kids, Grant? What will they think about the pictures?"

"They will think I have lost my mind. Misty will cry, and Megan will scold, and Matt will think it is funny, like good old dad is a hoot picking up women, just having himself a fling. And none of them will believe there is anything to it."

"Do you think you have lost your mind, Grant? Do you need to be scolded or cried about? Is it laughable? The pictures aren't that bad, and they show you having a good time with lots of different people. They are right that there was nothing to any of it."

"They're not going to be upset about those things. They're going to cry and scold and laugh because I led them to believe that I was having a lousy time so they have all been feeling sorry for me. And just for the record, they are wrong. There is something to it, Shay. Come on, we have a launch to catch."

The Isle of Capri lies nineteen miles south of Naples and is easily accessible by ferry. It is a popular tourist destination, hosting thousands and thousands of visitors on its tiny four by two mile spit of land. The main attraction is the famous Blue Grotto but Shay and Grant decided not to allot time for that. They also decided not to wait on line for the funnicula ride to the highest point for a spectacular view. Instead, they decided to wander the streets with hundreds and hundreds of others. The main activity seemed to be people watching, searching for a glimpse of a celebrity or member of the hoi polloi and paying exorbitant prices for souvenirs and food. As lovely as it was, realistically, it was just a high end tourist trap, but none of this phased Grant or Shay. They strolled hand in hand, exchanged loving looks, ate at a very pricy cafe, and paid outlandish prices for wooden inlaid music boxes that played *On The Isle of Capri*. The strains of the popular song could be heard all over the island as shop keepers kept the thousands of music boxes wound, providing a cacophonous symphony of the catchy tune that created a rather tiring replay in many a visitor's head for several days afterward. It was a perfect day.

When they returned to the ship, Grant kissed her at her door with plans to pick her up for the captain's farewell dinner. Then he headed for the shopping arcade and entered the jewelry store.

"Hi, Mr. Albright. I've got your package right here, all wrapped and ready to go. Whoever the lucky lady is, she is going to love it." He planned to give it to her at dinner.

Mitch returned to the room while he was dressing. Grant had noticed that Mitch had laid a lot of clothes out on the bed and there were piles of stuff on the chair.

"What's up, Mitch. What are you doing?"

"We need to talk, Grant. Things have changed since this morning. I hope you don't mind, but I'm planning to leave tomorrow. My contract is open ended and you don't need me around for the rest of the trip. It's only eight more days."

"Why? What's up?"

"It's Joan. I don't want her going home alone in case she has some damage to the house. I don't want her to have to cope with it by herself. And she is so upset about this Chrissie thing I plan to drive her to Charlotte just in case she finds a real problem there. I'll get that creep out of Chrissie's house. We talked to Babs about it and she got me a plane ticket but it wasn't on the same flight as Joan's so I just came back from the reservations desk and we changed Joan's ticket too so we are together. I'll rent a car and drive back to Palmer from Raleigh. Then Babs couldn't get me in the same hotel in Rome, so we got a room in another hotel for three days. We decided to go ahead and do Rome while we are there, but not with the Palmer Group. They won't even miss us."

"That's quite a surprise, Mitch. But, sure, it's fine with me. Do you want to settle up now or do we wait till morning?"

"I was thinking about that too, Grant. I think you win hands down. I'll just pay you off now. We have to have our luggage in the hall right after midnight and we leave at 8:00 in the morning. I think I owe you three big ones. We can just write off the little stuff."

"I'm not sure, Mitch. You might be giving me more credit than I deserve. You're right about Shay. She is a hard nut to crack. No points there."

"Then we should count Jodee. You scored first, so she should count. I still owe you three big ones."

"No you don't Mitch. Nothing happened with Jodee. I was just pulling your leg about Istanbul. I was just putting you on. And the rest was all show business. Nothing happened there."

"Are you shitt'n me? Nothing happened?"

"Nope, nothing happened."

"So we're tied then?"

"Yep, put your money away, Mitch. But I still bet you I get lucky before you do. Should we start counting right now? I'll put five on it."

"What's the time limit? How many days do we have?"

"Let's say whoever gets lucky before he gets back to Palmer wins. Honor system. I'll even give you a leg up since I have to start over. I'll let you count Joan. Deal? Five bucks?"

"You're on. Five bucks says I get laid first, right?"

"Yep, but I still intend to win fair and square."

"Double or nothing?"

"Double or nothing."

Grant tucked the little box in his inside pocket and headed to Shay's room. They decided to stop by Babs' table so Grant could say his goodbyes, but to sit by themselves for their last dinner. He waited until coffee was served. "Here," he said. "I have a little something for you."

"How sweet of you, Grant. Can I open it now?"

"Sure, go ahead." She carefully unwrapped and opened the box. "Oh, how lovely! Help me put it on. He reached across the table and put the beautiful little charm bracelet around her wrist. On it were all the charms he had bought along the way. Together they identified each one, those from Istanbul, and from Ephesus, and from Athens, and Venice. There was one unusual one on the end. "What is this one for? It's a pair of flip flops."

"It represents the beach. Just planning ahead," he said with that wink and nod.

"It is beautiful, Grant. Thank you so much."

Later Shay took her usual seat in the Adventure Lounge while he played his final night there. Jodee came in for one last time and sang beautiful renditions of *What I Did For Love,* and *I'll Always Love You.* Then she exchanged a few words with him and he got the folded email out of his pocket and handed it to her. "Here, good news from Leighanna." She kissed him and whispered, "Thank you for everything, Grant. I'll be in touch." He returned her kiss, his embrace lingering.

Mitch was watching. "Nothing, my foot," he thought.

Afterward Grant and Shay headed to their usual place on the deck. Shay had been showing off the charm bracelet to all the Palmer people, just beaming, and they exchanged knowing glances. "I'm glad you like it," he said. "There is plenty of room on there to add more. We should plan another trip."

"That would be wonderful. I hate for this one to end but I really need to get back to the room and pack. Joan is already packed. Our bags have to be out after midnight."

"Did Joan tell you about Mitch?"

"She said he was going home too. That was a surprise, but I didn't hear why."

"Some business he has to take care of."

Shay stood to leave and he held her hand. "Don't go, Shay."

"I must. I haven't even started packing."

"I mean, don't go. Stay. Stay with me for the rest of the trip."

"I have to get back, Grant. And I am already way over budget. And there wouldn't be a reservation for me."

"No, you don't have to get back. And I have already checked with the purser's desk. There is no problem with you moving in with me. You can have Mitch's side. There is plenty of room. It's not till the end of the world. It's just to Barcelona. Please stay with me."

And that little voice said, "Roll the dice, Shay."

"I better go tell Joan. She'll be wondering about me."

"So, was that a yes?"

"Yes, Grant, that was a yes. I'll stay with you."

Early the next morning they stood at the rail waving goodbye to Jodee and Izzy and saw the Palmer Group off. Then they headed to the reservations desk. "We need to change your flight. You can fly back to Raleigh with me. My car is in long term parking there. Then we'll go to Palmer for a few days, maybe longer, and then I will drive you to Charlotte and we'll stay there and get to work on the house. And we need to get a flight to Vegas to check on Jodee, and then go to California and check on Matt. And we need to make reservations at the beach. I know the perfect place. Let's go check our email."

Pay dirt!

To: Dad
From: Matt

Alright, here is my big surprise. I am in Charlotte!! Wanted to wait until you got home and surprise you. I am moving back to NC. Want the girls to grow up here. All is well. We will come see you just as soon as you get back.

Now, what is your surprise?

Love, Matt

Reply: Great news. Why Charlotte? Why not Raleigh—great hospitals there. Or maybe closer to Meg. Charlotte? You don't know anyone there. I'll come visit you when you are settled unless you need help sooner. DON'T COME TO PALMER RIGHT NOW!! IT IS NOT A GOOD TIME!!

Love, Dad

To: Daddy
From: Megan

Can't wait for you to get home. The boys and I are planning to be there right away to help you unpack. We will have a nice long visit. And we can finish cleaning out some stuff. And we can take the boys to the beach. I will stay as long as you need me. I don't want you to come back to an empty house, Daddy. I don't want you to be lonely. We were going to surprise you and all meet your plane but Matt has to work so we will have a big party just as soon as you get home. All of us.

What is your surprise?

Love and hugs, Megan

Reply: PLEASE DO NOT COME RIGHT AWAY!! NOT A GOOD TIME FOR ME! I will not be lonely! Love and hugs, Daddy

---

To: Daddy
From: Misty
Hi, Daddy

Have you heard Matt's news? Isn't that wonderful! We are planning a big reunion with you as soon as you get home. We will all be together again. Won't that be wonderful? We know how lonely you are. We will be right there with you. And I will tell you my surprise and you can tell me yours!!

Love and kisses, Misty

Reply: PLEASE DON'T PLAN REUNION YET!!! NOT A GOOD TIME. MAYBE THANKSGIVING. OK? Yes, we can share surprises. Love, Daddy

---

They took a private car for the forty eight mile drive into Rome, and a short tour of the city, seeing only the highlights and tossing coins in Trevi Fountain to guarantee that they would return. Back on the ship, Shay unpacked her things, using all the spaces vacated by Mitch.

Grant kept out of her way and when it was time to dress for dinner, he said, "Do you want me to leave while you dress? You call the shots." As they headed for the elevator Grant stopped and exchanged a few words with the room steward. When they returned much later, Shay entered the room first.

"Oh! Look Grant. The room steward has made two swans out of the towels. Isn't that darling?" Then she realized what had been arranged. The two beds had been put together to make one. "Grant, there is some mistake. What should we do?"

"I'll think of something," he said, winking. He took her in his arms, kissing her, his hands caressing and exploring, confident, experienced. She felt the zipper on her dress slide down her back and she let the dress fall to the floor and stepped out. He placed it over the chair and returned to her, holding her, kissing her, eager, and then he stopped as quickly as he had started. He gently pushed her away, held her at arm's length, and with that nod and wink of his, said, "I don't have to worry about knocking you up, do I?"

"As flattering as it is that you think that might still be a possibility, no, Grant. You do not have to worry about that."

"Good. The last time I knocked up a girl I wound up with a whole houseful of kids. I sure don't want that to happen again. I already have enough kids for both of us, Shay."

He took her back into his arms and began to finish what he had started. Afterward she lay in the warm strength of his arms with her head on his chest and listened as he talked about the future.

Vermont—Six Months Later

Wanda was in an absolute tizzy, dashing about, checking on every minute detail of the arrangements. She drew in a big breath, made a final mental check of everything and walked into the grand parlor where the festivities would take place. Charley was putting the final touches on some flower boxes he was installing outside on the terrace and she walked to the window where she could watch him, admiring his work. What a Godsend he had been. They had enjoyed each other on the cruise and had continued to correspond. After she moved to Vermont to help with the remodeling and decorating of the Maple Valley Inn and Spa, she had called him with a question about the heating system. Charley had owned a very large maintenance company in Manhattan and he knew everything about everything when it came to such matters and he came right away to help solve the problem, gradually helping with more and more projects until he just moved to Maple Valley and became a part of the staff, seeing the project to completion. The Maple Valley Inn, Spa, and Conference Center had opened to rave reviews and was enjoying tremendous success. Wanda had overseen all of the decorating and continued to supervise the staff who handled all special events. This would be their first wedding. The small altar where the couple would take their vows had been lovingly crafted by Charley and he had attended to a million little details, as eager to make it the perfect occasion as Wanda was.

The staff would arrange chairs for the ceremony itself and remove them afterward for the formal reception. The buffet tables were in the adjoining dining room waiting to be adorned with ice carvings artistically cut to resemble gondolas and the floral pieces were waiting in the cooler to make their appearance at the last hour. The china and candles were already on the tables and five assistants were busy in the kitchen assembling hors d'oeuvres into miniature works of art. Wanda had studied the pictures that Grant had given her of the anniversary party he had played for on the ship and she was hell-bent on replicating them, much to the frustration and consternation of her staff. She intended to make them signature presentations at other major affairs. The pastry chef had created a beautiful cake in the shape of a cruise ship, copying a picture of the Atheneè to get it just right. The guests would be arriving tomorrow.

As was the case with most weddings, the affair would also serve as a reunion of assorted friends and family. Jodee would arrive first. Her flight from Vegas came at an inconvenient time for connections, so Charley had agreed to drive in to the city to get her. The others would be arriving at all hours of the day. A casual welcome reception would be held tomorrow evening at six o'clock for a meet and greet, and the ceremony itself was at eight o'clock, with the reception following. The piano had been placed to the right of the huge stone fireplace, waiting for Grant. Charley came in and gave her a peck on the cheek.

"Alright, Old Girl, I think we are ready. I'll pour us a sherry and we can sit a spell." She kicked off her shoes and sank into the plush softness of a chair, exhausted, excited, satisfied, and happier than she ever imagined she would be again. By this time tomorrow it would all be over.

It dawned a beautiful day, a perfect Vermont spring day, chilly but with bright blue skies, the hills springing to life with budding trees. Maureen and Ralph arrived together. They had formed a partnership of sorts, continuing to recruit members for the singles group, and had just returned from one of Babs' trips, this one to the Caribbean. These trips had really caught on after the first cruise had been dubbed the Love Boat, with many tellings of the romances that had begun or ended on Babs' trips. They usually sold out well in advance. Wanda was overjoyed that they came. In spite of her total happiness at the Inn, she missed her two dearest friends, Maureen and Joan, and she had been ecstatic to hear that they would all be here at the same time. A whole assortment of McConnells were coming, a mix of kids and grandkids. The Albright kids were all coming, grandkids in tow. Joan's daughters, Chrissie and Chloe, would be there, and Shay. Quite a few of them planned to stay over for several days, spending time visiting with siblings they didn't see often and becoming more acquainted with the new members they would be welcoming into their extended family. They would be relaxing in the spa, taking carriage rides around the beautiful grounds, and be pampered by the attentive staff. The bride and groom would be leaving the following morning en route to Hawaii for an extended honeymoon.

Jodee arrived in a gorgeous full length sable coat, wearing a beige cashmere sweater dress. She had lost the few pounds that had been dogging her, and she looked spectacular. Her hair was a little longer, cut in a stylish shape, and around her neck was the beautiful gold and diamond Greek Key necklace selected by Grant. She changed into a turquoise silk for the ceremony and reception. The women were all oohing and aahing over the eight carat pear shaped diamond ring she was sporting on her left ring finger. She hugged everyone, was warm, charming and gracious, but stood out in the crowd, receiving the usual admiring looks from all, comfortable with the attention.

The women were all beautifully dressed in proper wedding attire. Grant's daughters were lovely in dressy cocktail suits and Megan had her two boys there, age five and three, and she and her husband were quietly trying to keep them still. Misty was holding her new baby girl, who was peacefully asleep in her arms. She had named her Catherine LaVon, but she would not be called Vonnie. She would be called Catherine or Cate. Joan had chosen a beautiful pinky cream silk with matching shoes, and had lightened her hair a few shades, highlighting the slight tan she had. Chrissie was six months pregnant and she and Joan had fussed about how tight Chrissie's dress was over her tummy, but Chrissie was so proud of her baby bump that she insisted on walking down the aisle in the dress. Shay had on a beautiful lavender lace, rather low in front, accenting her great figure. She had a wiggly toddler on each side of her. It was decided they were too young to participate, so Shay had volunteered to keep tabs on them prior to the ceremony. When it started, the little lady, Emelda, who traveled everywhere with Matt, would take responsibility for the girls, who were adorable in matching pink velvet.

The men were dressed in suits except for those in the bridal party. Grant, Mitch, and Matt were in tuxedos and Grant took his place at the piano and played softly in the background as the guests took their seats. The reverend Mr. Matthews took his place and Jodee stepped forward to sing her first number, The Hawaiian Wedding song. She stood close behind Grant's right shoulder, glancing lovingly at him as she started, and the chemistry was still there. When she finished, Grant stood and joined Mitch and Matt to the right of the altar and the bridal party started down the aisle. Chloe came first, a vision in pale green, and took her place at the left of the altar. Then Chrissie, prominent baby bump and all, followed, glowing, radiant in her pregnancy. Matt looked lovingly as she made her way down the aisle, turning left and joining Chloe.

Grant stepped aside and played a few bars of Wagner's *Bridal Chorus* and they all stood to welcome the bride. Beaming, the groom stepped forward to meet her and they stood side by side as the reverend Mr. Mathews began. "Dearly beloved, we are gathered here in the name of God to join together this man and this woman in holy matrimony." And he went on to remind them of God's covenant, of the many blessings bestowed upon the families present, of the joys of a lasting union, gently giving recognition to those who were no longer with them by adding that out of despair came hope, out of the ashes sprang new life, and that the shadow of loss did not dim the light of love. He repeated the verses from I Corinthians 13: 4-8, familiar verses about love. And then they took their vows, carefully repeating the words, smiling lovingly at one another. And it was over. Mitchell Edwin McConnell had married Joan Elizabeth Robinson.

Maureen and Wanda were mopping tears of joy, Mitch's five kids stood and applauded, and then they all descended at once, surrounding Joan and Mitch, hugging him, kissing Joan, kissing one another, in one huge display of love and affection.

Matt kissed Joan and hugged Mitch and went directly to Chrissie, taking her into his arms for a huge bear hug. The little lady, Emelda, had emerged with the darling twins and Matt took one in each arm as they circulated through the room, greeting and meeting many of Mitch's family for the first time.

Grant went to Shay's side, took her his arms and kissed her soundly. "Let's congratulate the bride and groom and then find a quiet place where I can make out with you, like on the boat."

"Behave," she joked. "I have responsibilities here, you know. After all, I am a grandmother now. I'll tend to you later, sweetheart."

Shay greeted Joan with kisses, both women overjoyed with the events of the last several months.

First it had been the shocking discovery of Matt living in Chrissie's house, followed by the announcement shortly after that Chrissie was pregnant and she and Matt would be married Thanksgiving Day. Grant had called Wanda and she had gone into high gear and planned a beautiful little ceremony in the chapel at Palmer Plantation. It was perfect timing because the kids were all coming for Thanksgiving anyway, although it had been a little difficult for Shay because she wasn't quite sure of her role in the family and it was the first time they would all be together. The kids were all aware that she was living with their Dad and she wasn't sure how they felt about that. It had been Grant who had insisted that they not spend even one day apart. After many sleepless nights, Shay decided to do Thanksgiving just the way they had always done it, lovingly using the china and special family decorations, and not changing one single thing in the house so it wouldn't look like she was taking over. Joan and Mitch would be there too because Chrissie was Joan's daughter. The wedding was planned for that evening.

After dinner Grant and Matt disappeared to his study for a few minutes for a private conversation. Matt was looking at the pictures on the shelves, gently touching one of his mother, and then picking up the Angel Ariel, who was smiling on the shelf next to the picture. "I see you kept Mom's angel. Do you believe in angels, Dad?"

"I don't know, Matt, but your Mom did. He gently touched the little angel and bent down for a closer look, puzzled. "That's funny. I never noticed this before." Hanging around her neck was a tiny gold and sparkly necklace, an exact replica of the necklace Grant had selected for Jodee in Athens "That's strange. It reminds me of something I've seen somewhere."

"I don't know if I believe in angels either, Dad. Chrissie does. She thinks angels use people to do their work, only the people don't know it. She says angels are all around us. It makes you wonder, though. Something strange happened to me that I can't explain. People always ask me how I found Emelda and I always say I didn't, she found me. It happened right after Adesio left. I was alone with the girls. They were about ten days old and I was overwhelmed. I was trying to arrange for some nurses I knew to baby sit because I had to go back to work. It was really a low point. Both babies were screaming and the doorbell rang. I had Alexis in my arms and Alexandra was crying in her crib, and when I opened the door, there stood this little lady. She introduced herself and said she was from some organization, angel helpers or something, and said she had been sent to this location. 'See,' she said, and showed me a slip of paper with my address on it. I tried to explain that I hadn't ordered anyone, but she breezed right past me. Went right in, picked up Alexandra and cuddled her and then took Alexis from me, and just took over. It was surreal, Dad. It was like everything was happening in slow motion, sort of floating. I was so exhausted that I didn't have the energy to argue or to stop her. I don't know how much time went by, but by the time I regained my senses, she had taken over everything. She took care of the girls, took care of the house, took care of me. I've never told anyone this before. I still don't know much about her. She said she is from Guatemala. She said she wants to stay as long as I need her. She's great. I take care of her and she takes care of us. She might even be an illegal, but I don't want to know. I didn't ask for any papers."

"It's probably not a problem, Matt. I don't think angels need green cards."

"Well, I guess it's time to head to the chapel. Chrissie is a real game changer, a real Godsend. She is the perfect woman, Dad. Boy, my luck sure changed when she entered my life, like a miracle, like it was meant to be. I know it happened pretty quick, but we love each other. That's all that matters, isn't it?"

"It's a good place to start, Matt. Without it you won't get very far. Life is just a crapshoot, but you have to roll the dice. At least with love you increase your odds."

Wanda had decorated the chapel, made all the floral arrangements, and baked a cake shaped like wedding bells, decorated with love birds and flowers. And Mathew Grant Albright married Christina Ann Robinson at precisely seven thirty on that very special Thanksgiving Day.

Later that evening Grant told Shay what a hit she had been, how much the kids loved her. Oh how she wanted to believe that. As they were getting ready for bed, the phone rang and she heard Grant answer it. She could tell from the conversation, it was Jodee. She knew they talked from time to time.

"Yes," he said. "Of course. Yes, that sounds wonderful. Great. Of course, I'll see you then. Me too. I will, I will. I promise. Same to you. Yes, New Year's Eve it is."

Shay's heart had sunk. He would go. Of course he would go to her.

"That was Jodee," he said, happiness in his voice. "She wants us to come to Vegas for New Year's Eve. A huge opening night for something or other. She is putting us up in their building. I accepted, OK? You never told me, have you ever been to Vegas? I'll get plane reservations for us tomorrow."

It was the most fabulous New Year's Eve of Shay's life. When they woke late the next morning, New Year's Day, Grant rolled over and took her in his arms and then, in his usual way of changing course right in the middle of something, he stopped. "I have a great idea. Let's get married."

"Was that a proposal?" she asked. "Should I look at my calendar?"

"Yes, that was a proposal. Was that a yes?"

"Yes, that was a yes. Do you want a long engagement or should we set a date and start planning?"

"Neither. I want to get married today, right here in Vegas. That's how they do things here, get married right away." He reached for the phone and called Jodee and told her his plan. She returned his call in fifteen minutes. She had reserved the perfect little wedding chapel for four o'clock. She and Izzy would meet them there. And Grant Gregory Albright married Shay Marie Porter that very afternoon.

Now here she was sharing in another event, pondering the situation. Her best friend, who was her son-in-law's mother-in-law, had just married her husband's best friend, who would now be father-in-law to the same kids. Wasn't that right? And they were both grandmothers to Grant's grandkids, so now Mitch was their grandfather too, wasn't he?

Grant had kissed Joan and grasped Mitch's hand, wrapping his other arm around his shoulder. "Congratulations, Mitch. I had five bucks riding on this ceremony, bet Joan wouldn't go through with it once she saw that gang of yours."

"Yeah, I kept them hidden as long as I could, Buddy. What does this make us now, brothers or cousins? Your kid is my son-in-law, and my wife is his wife's mother."

"Yeah, and we will both be grandfathers to the same kids. I think that makes us two of the luckiest guys on the planet."

As everyone began to gather in the dining room, Grant motioned to Jodee. "Come and join us, Jodee. It was great that you came. Everyone was glad to see you and share in your success."

"It was a beautiful wedding. I was thrilled when Mitch called and personally asked me to sing. Izzy was sorry he had to miss it because we want to ask you something, Grant. Izzy and I have decided to get married in Bali. He is spending so much time in Macau on his new project that he wondered if you and Shay would come over and stand up with us."

"Of course. We would love to, wouldn't we Shay? Just let us know when."

"It will be soon. You know, Grant. It's funny. I spent all those years wanting success, chasing rainbows, and now that I have it, it doesn't seem so important any more. Izzy wants me with him. He was going to cut back, but when they dangled this billion dollar project in front of him, he couldn't resist. But he needs me there, Grant. He is a good man. We are auditioning singers to stand in for me during the weeks I am gone and Carlos is fabulous. He is practically running Izzy's and Izzy loves him like a son. You always said life is just one big crapshoot, but sometimes it seems like there is more to it than that, like something else is calling the shots. I mean, just look at us, Grant. What were the odds of meeting you in Istanbul? And the odds that Izzy would be on that plane with me. I don't think all of that just happened at random, helter-skelter, or was just the whims of the fates. Right here in this room so much good stuff has happened. Chrissie and Matt, and the twins, and now a new baby on the way. And Leighanna married with a new baby. And Joan and Mitch, and you and Shay, and me and Izzy. None of us planned for this, but here we are like pieces of some giant puzzle, all fitting together. That can't all just be a crapshoot, can it?"

"You're probably right, Jodee. No one can roll a winning streak like we've had. Maybe we're all playing life's game with loaded dice and don't know it."

He gave Jodee a little hug and then turned to Shay. "Shall we join the others for the celebration, Sweetheart? I hear that Wanda has really made things special."

Around ten thirty Grant took his seat at the piano. Mitch had asked him to play because his kids had never heard him and Mitch had bragged about him, saying it was Grant's playing that had started the whole thing. He played quietly, reflectively, familiar love songs. Jodee joined him for a few and they made no attempt to hide the affection they felt for one another. The gold and diamond Greek Key necklace was sparkling around her neck. In the back of the room, Matt was holding Chrissie in his arms, dancing. Megan and her husband had taken seats with some of Mitch's kids, and Misty and her husband were cozy on a loveseat, holding hands. Shay had taken a seat in her usual place, slightly to his right, in his line of vision, where he always wanted her. She was cradling Misty's baby, Catherine LaVon, gently rocking her. Megan's three year old boy had squeezed himself into the chair with Shay, holding his hand where the baby could wrap her tiny fist around his finger, fascinated by her. The five year old had crawled under the piano and was playing with a toy earth mover Grant had bought him.

Joan had requested that he play *Save the Last Dance For Me* as their first dance and he followed with a beautiful arrangement of *An Affair to Remember*, catching Shay's eye, nodding and winking, mouthing, "later?" She smiled knowingly and blew him a kiss, overflowing with love for the man and gratitude for the woman who had first filled his heart with love and had left him intact, and gratitude for Jodee, who had embraced him and set him free to love again.

Grant took a glance around the beautifully decorated room filled with the love of family and friends. Jodee was right, this was no crapshoot. Something else was at work here, and to no one in particular he said, "Thank you."

About the Author

Leslie Stone honed her writing skills during many years of teaching reading and creative writing to gifted students, before turning to the field of professional training and development, writing and presenting programs for corporations and professional organizations. Coupled with a background in counseling and extensive world travel, she draws from a rich tapestry of experience and information as she crafts her novels. Her first travel romance, *River of Pretense*, was published in 2012.

She and her husband live in North Carolina and divide their time between homes in the mountains and on the coast, where they enjoy entertaining their friends and family.

Ms. Stone can be reached at:
Lesliestone4@aol.com
www.lesliestone5.com